Kozłowski

Kozłowski

Jane Rogoyska

www.hhousebooks.com

Hardback ISBN: 978-1-910688-73-1

Cover photograph by Marzena Pogorzaly
Cover design by Ken Dawson
Typeset by Polgarus Studio

Published in the UK

Holland House Books
Holland House
47 Greenham Road
Newbury, Berkshire RG14 7HY
United Kingdom

www.hhousebooks.com

Pamięć nareszcie ma, czego szukała
Memory's finally found what it was after

(Wisława Szymborska, *Memory Finally*)

The *politruks* move amongst the mass of prisoners waiting by the rails, shining torches in their faces, taking down their names and rank. The roll call goes on and on. Kozłowski shivers, his coat soaked through from the driving rain. He has not seen Edek since the ambush. Is he dead? Wounded? He strains to find a familiar figure amongst the thousands of men.

"Feliks! My goodness! How wonderful to see you alive!"

A group of lieutenants cluster around a brown leather suitcase, on top of which a man is seated, asleep, his shoulders covered by an enormous sheepskin rug. The officer named Feliks greets the group with delight, friends lost and now found. They exchange anecdotes about their war with an air of lighthearted unconcern, seemingly oblivious to the misery of their surroundings.

"...encountered him just outside Lublin looking for all the world as if he were setting out on a picnic. '*Mon cher ami*,' he said. 'Why don't you join us? We're heading for my estate. I'm told the cellar is still intact...'"

"That restaurant on Nowy Świat where we met last month, bombed to smithereens..."

"...carrying furs and a silver candelabra. I said to her, 'My dear, are these the most useful things you could think of bringing?'..."

Kozłowski thrusts his hands deep into his pockets, staring at his boots as they gradually sink deeper into the grey mud. A young blond-haired lieutenant glances over at him enviously. His own summer boots are soaked through.

A rumbling noise signals the arrival of a train of empty box-cars. It looms out of the darkness, rattling on endlessly until, finally, it comes to a halt and the prisoners are ordered to get inside. They clamber on board, spreading mud everywhere, an outbreak of false jollity covering the sense of shock that seizes them as they enter the dark carriage.

"I do beg your pardon, are those your legs?"

"They're not tree trunks, that's for sure!"

"After you, I insist!"

Each man seeks a space for himself, forming a line along the wagon's edges, their legs spread out before them. The last to climb in must squeeze themselves into the middle, back braced against back, legs intertwined.

The guard pulls the door across the wagon and bolts it shut, leaving a small gap about four inches wide, flashes of torchlight penetrating an otherwise total blackness.

The train begins to move; the jokes cease; the prisoners gradually fall silent. Kozłowski, squeezed in the far corner of the carriage, his back pressed uncomfortably against the metal wall, checks the luminous dial on his watch. It is 3am on September 26th 1939. It is nearly a week since their capture, not even a month since the beginning of the war. He closes his eyes, squeezing them shut, as if by doing this he might keep the fear that is rising in his throat at bay.

I

The past in the present

dziś z dalekiego kraju
otrzymałem starą kartkę

today I received an old postcard
from a distant country

(Tadeusz Różewicz, *Postcard)*

1. In between

en route to England, 1946

The room on the upper deck of the transport ship is stiflingly hot; the talk, delivered in English by a sharp-faced major, is long. Kozłowski forces himself to concentrate, testing himself to see how much he can understand.

"If you choose to join the Resettlement Corps you will be subject to military regulations for a period of up to two years. In return you will be housed in one of the camps marked on here." The Major points with a little stick to a series of pins dotted over a map of the United Kingdom. "You will receive a small salary commensurate with your rank and length of service, and you will be offered training and lessons in English. The aim is to make your transition to civilian life as swift and effective as possible...."

Beneath his feet, the ship's engines throb steadily. Through the salt-spattered porthole Kozłowski can see only a vast expanse of grey sea. The brilliant blue skies of Italy seem already to exist in another world.

"Are there any questions?"

Someone raises a hand and asks, in Polish, "I would like to know what provisions have been made for our families. Are we able to bring our wives and children over from Poland?"

As the question is translated, dozens of pairs of eyes fix the major with such intensity the Englishman flinches.

"If you are still separated from your family, please be patient: your loved ones will be brought to England as soon as possible. Regarding Polish citizens remaining in Poland, I am afraid the British government has no control over their situation."

A murmur arises from the audience; the major's voice rises accordingly.

"I understand that it is distressing for many of you to hear this, but

5

we have no means of forcing the Polish government to grant exit visas to their own citizens."

The murmur reaches an indignant crescendo at this naming of the 'Polish government', not recognised by those in the room. The major indicates the pile of papers next to him.

"I have forms here for you to fill in which will permit you to begin the process of resettlement..."

A crowd swiftly gathers around him. Kozłowski stands at its edge, waiting until the enthusiasm has died down. There is only one question on everybody's lips: what now? England? Canada? Australia? The USA? Most of the men on board the ship no longer have homes to return to: the eastern border regions are gone; Wilno is no longer a Polish city, nor is Lwów. Rumours have been filtering back from Poland of returning soldiers arrested, AK members shot or thrown in jail, the trial and disappearance of the Moscow Sixteen. The atmosphere fizzles with uncertainty and fear.

Andrzej emerges from the scrum, a sheaf of papers clutched in one hand.

"I've taken their papers just in case, but I'm off to Australia as soon as I can get the forms signed. Why don't you come too, Zbyg? They need doctors, it's sunny all the year round, there's plenty of space, and the women are all Amazons! What more could a man want?"

Andrzej hasn't changed: tanned and slim, he exudes the same air of youthful self-confidence that reminded Kozłowski so much of Edek when they first met. Andrzej pauses, as if divining in Kozłowski's silence some uncertainty.

"You're not thinking of going back, are you?"

"Of course not! I'm just waiting for—"

Andrzej grabs his arm. "Because it would be madness for people like us to go back. You do know that, don't you?"

They dock in Southampton on a drizzly day in late October 1946. *Get used to it*, one of his colleagues in Italy had said, *if you're going to stay in England, you've got to get used to the rain.*

A bus takes them through the city, past rows and rows of identical two-storey houses. There is little sign of the war here: no ruined buildings, no craters, only empty streets and soot-smudged windows. As they leave the town behind Kozłowski presses his face against the window, eager to catch his first glimpse of the famous English countryside. The brilliant, rain-soaked green of the fields does not disappoint, but the air of neatness pervading the peaceful villages through which they pass, with their swinging pub signs and baskets of flowers, unsettles him. For the first time, the reality begins to sink in: is this to be my home? When the bus draws to a halt on the edge of a field and he sees the nissen huts clustered together like barrels, Kozłowski's first feeling is one of panic.

This time, the meeting is for medical personnel. They shiver in the nissen hut in overcoats and scarves, huddled together for warmth. The talk is given by a Polish doctor:

"…thousands of injured soldiers who still need your help. Many speak no English; their wounds will not easily heal. The British government has provided funding for their care – there are medical facilities in all the main resettlement camps, as well as larger hospitals in London, Liverpool, Edinburgh, Glasgow…"

Outside, a single leaf clings to the branch of a skinny tree, lone remnant of the summer. Kozłowski and a group of others spent the morning scouring the wood for fir cones and twigs to burn in a vain attempt to keep their hut warm.

"Equally, you are, of course, at liberty to make your own way in the United Kingdom. I can give you general information about the medical system and the qualifications required. You may be aware that the British government is establishing a National Health Service and there will be a need for medical personnel. The main requirement, of course, is that you speak English."

Dear Dr and Mrs Cochran,
  Well, finally here is the postcard I have promised you. As

you can see I am studying hard to improve my English. I am going to need it now! Since end of the war I was working in the military hospital in Italy, but now Polish II Corps is disbanded and I am in England. I think of you both often and with fond thoughts. Persia is often in my memory.

Best wishes,

Zbyszek Kozłowski

He places the postcard in the strange red pillar box bearing the inscription *GVIR* and turns to walk back along the narrow country lane, glad to be outside and alone. In his pocket is an unopened letter from Elżbieta, postmarked from India. Doubtless it will be full of news of Zosia and Olek, with the usual postscript about his 'odd little friend'. Elżbieta is the most assiduous of correspondents, and yet the least desired. There is only one person whose voice he wishes to hear right now. Until he hears from her, he is merely marking time.

Sparrows flit in and out of the tangled hedgerows, swooping over the bare fields in search of food. From a distance, the nissen huts remind him of pigsties. The demobbed soldiers have already given them a nickname: *beczki śmiechu* – barrels of laughs. Families have started to arrive, a trickle of sunburnt mothers and children disembarking from India and Africa to be greeted by husbands and fathers from whom they parted four, five, six years ago. Kozłowski has seen them, the stiff, awkward men holding hands with a bewildered child who has just been told that this stranger is to be addressed as 'Daddy'. His fellow doctors are already fewer in number: they slip away, some to take up posts in other resettlement camps or army hospitals, others to begin new lives in other lands. Andrzej is gone, "Off to Oz!". Everywhere, it is the young who are most advantaged, the young and those who speak English. He is grateful now, as he has been on so many occasions in the recent past, for Dr Cochran's gift, offered by the kindly doctor and his wife on his last visit to the American Hospital in Meshed. They had kept him pleasantly detained with tea and cakes and gossip then, when he could put it off no longer and he told them that he really had to go,

Dr Cochran handed him the parcel, carefully wrapped by his wife in brown paper. Inside it, an English language textbook and a dictionary.

"I may be wrong, Dr Kozłowski," said Dr Cochran, in his American-accented French, "and perhaps I am overly patriotic, but I believe that English is the language of the future. You're a smart young fellow: this might help you get ahead."

"Send us a postcard, won't you, when it's all over?" Mrs Cochran reached up to embrace him warmly. "In English, mind!"

He had wanted to tell them how grateful he was for their kindness, to explain that his experience in Persia had reminded him, just at the moment when he most needed it, what it meant to be civilised. As usual, he had not found the words. He had murmured his thanks and taken his leave, clutching the brown paper parcel. Those few weeks in Meshed had marked a transition in his life: a hiatus, filled with unexpected meaning, between the closing of one chapter and the opening of the next. An in-between time. Like now, perhaps.

2. Typhus or malaria

Kozłowski's orders are to deliver the convalescing staff officers to the American Mission Hospital for a check-up, after which a decision will be made as to when they will be fit enough to continue their journey to join the rest of the army in Iraq.

"Good morning, sir," he addresses the affable-looking doctor who greets him in the director's office. "I have with me the six officers from the General Staff, as instructed—" He stops.

"I'm sorry, I don't speak Polish," says Dr Cochran, in English.

"I – er – my English is very little."

"Ah - *Français? Deutsch?*"

"*Je préfère parler en français.*"

"Excellent!" continues Dr Cochran genially, in French. "My wife is just getting breakfast. You'll have something to eat, won't you? I'll bet a dollar you're hungry."

A small, plump woman bustles into the room bearing a tray laden with fresh bread, eggs and coffee.

"Please, don't get up—" begins Mrs Cochran, in English, as Kozłowski gets to his feet.

"French, dear—"

"Oh, yes. Sorry. Wait, I have it in Polish, the children have been teaching me. *Proszę nie wstawać.* Is that right?" She pours coffee into a china cup.

"My patients—"

"Don't worry, your men are being taken good care of. You need do nothing except wait here and relax while our doctors examine them."

"Go ahead, please. Help yourself." Dr Cochran indicates the tray of food. Kozłowski realises that he must have been staring at it with an expression of foolish bewilderment.

"I'm so sorry—" he begins again, still unable to bring himself to reach for the beautiful, soft, white bread. He is conscious that they are looking at him not only with kindness, but pity.

"Young man, eat up. There's plenty more where this comes from."

Kozłowski looks around at this pleasant room, with its soft green curtains and the solid oak desk with a vase of yellow flowers standing on it; Dr Cochran in his crisp white coat; Mrs Cochran holding out a coffee cup asking if he would like a lump of sugar in it. He half expects Dr Levittoux to walk into the room and ask him about the patients to be seen on their morning round. The world lurches unexpectedly under his feet. He reaches out to steady himself.

"Please, Dr Kozłowski, why don't you sit down?" Dr Cochran helps Kozłowski to a chair. "Take it easy for a while."

"Thank you." He feels ashamed of his weakness. "Thank you."

"God bless you," murmurs Mrs Cochran, laying her hand on his shoulder.

After breakfast, they offer him a tour of the wards. Dr Cochran explains that most of the children who arrive in Meshed are looked after by Professor Kopeć at the orphanage in the centre of town, but the more serious cases are brought here. A dark-haired boy with a bandaged head lies sleeping, a drip in his arm. Next to him, a girl watches over him. She brightens when she is told that Kozłowski is Polish.

"Look what they've given me, Doctor!" She holds out a tray with a jigsaw puzzle on it. The picture shows Łazienki Park in the autumn, the statue of Chopin in the foreground. "Isn't it splendid?"

There is a buzzing inside his head. The walls seem to shift slightly, the girl's voice becoming muffled.

"Are you quite alright, Doctor?" Dr Cochran's voice seems to arrive suddenly in his head, without passing through his ears.

Kozłowski takes off his glasses, pressing his fingers into the bridge of his nose in an effort to gather his thoughts. What is he doing in this beautiful, white hospital? How did he get here? The American is saying something to him but for some reason he cannot hear it properly. It is hot in here, unbearably hot. He pulls at his collar, trying to loosen it. He is thirsty. His head aches, as if someone is pounding on it with a hammer.

"Do you mind if I take your temperature, Dr Kozłowski?"

They sit him down in a consulting room. On the wall is a picture of a peacock, painted in bright, swirling colours. Kozłowski stares at it hard, waiting for the colours to come into focus, but they refuse to cooperate. Then Dr Cochran is placing a thermometer in his mouth, counting the time passing on his wristwatch. What is the American doing? Can they not see that all he needs is some fresh air? He stands up, mumbling that he just needs to step outside... Then he faints, collapsing heavily onto the spotlessly clean tiled floor.

Time has lost its reliable, linear form. There is dark, there is light; there are voices, water poured from a cup onto his parched lips, cold sheets, damp, sweat. A period of peace, the thirst gradually abating, the heat in his body cooling; then movement, a rolling motion; the ceiling above him unfurling like a flag. Where are they taking him? Again, darkness; silence; then light; a face comes into focus: the kindly nurse appears above him.

"Flowers," she says, pointing to the bedside table where a bunch of white blossoms droop in a tiny blue vase. Who has brought him flowers?

Gradually, the noises around him begin to distil themselves into discrete elements: the chirrup of a bird; laughter; two voices talking, no, three, one low but soft, familiar to him; another deep, masculine, the third higher, light - a child's? A cool cloth wiping his forehead; hands, rough and dry, finding a vein for an injection. Then, dreams, vivid and terrifying.

Before him is a vast expanse of ice. In the distance, a boat. A group of men are jumping from the stern, one by one: Tomasz, Zygmunt, Ralski, Biały, Dr Levittoux – he sees their faces with such beautiful, familiar clarity.

Zbyszek! Hellooo! How wonderful to see you!

Tomasz strides towards him, waving joyfully. *Hellooo!*

Be careful of the ice! he calls. *Can't you see it's beginning to crack?*

Tomasz cannot hear him. He keeps walking, grinning, waving. *Helloooo!*

There is a crack, and a dark round hole appears where Tomasz was. The others keep walking, oblivious to Tomasz's fate.

Don't come any further! The ice will break!

Now Zygmunt comes.

Helloooo!

Then he, too, is gone, sucked into the freezing sea. One by one they disappear, until Kozłowski is hoarse from shouting. He falls to his knees.

Please! He cries. *Please, I beg you, take me instead!*

Finally, after days and nights as uncountable as they are indistinguishable, the fever begins to abate and Kozłowski understands that he is ill. After two years of resistance his body has finally succumbed. Is it typhus or malaria? He checks his body for symptoms: fever, weakness, sickness, all present, but these could apply to either disease; then, hazily, he recalls the buzzing in his ears, the blinding headache, the aching back. It is typhus, he thinks, with relief. Typhus can be cured, so long as you survive the first days. Malaria can only be temporarily dismissed from the body, and can return, years later, without warning.

The voices around him follow a regular pattern. Silent at night, rising gradually in the morning then, when he can hear the chirruping of birds and the distant clatter of dishes, there is a prolonged silence and he understands that he is in a ward with others who, for some reason, leave for a time during the day, returning in the afternoon – or is it the evening? – to sleep.

Until now he has rarely opened his eyes, every attempt hitherto resulting in a blinding pain. Now, he blinks experimentally. The room is in semi-darkness. As the morning sun slowly brightens the sky, a canary in a cage which hangs by the window begins to chirrup; soon

13

other birds outside join its song while the pale blue of the sky deepens to a bright azure. A soft breeze penetrates the sleeping ward, bringing with it the delicious smell of fresh bread. The room grows steadily lighter, revealing the objects around him: a small table, upon which stands a vase of white flowers; beyond this is another bed, from the end of which two bony feet protrude. He explores the end of his bed with his toes, discovering a good few inches of space to spare at the bottom. He tries to haul himself over onto his side but for some reason he has become extremely heavy; his arms appear to have no strength in them. After some manoeuvring, he manages to position himself so that he can get a better view of his lanky neighbour. The man appears to be asleep, and Kozłowski cannot see his face. Slowly, he turns his attention back to those long, bony feet which seem so familiar to him.

The next time he opens his eyes, the light has changed and the sun is shining directly through the windows. Time really is not behaving as it ought. The bed next to him is empty. Did he imagine its occupant? He decides to attempt a more ambitious movement by pushing on the bed with his arms until he reaches a sitting position. Almost as soon as he is upright his head begins to swim, but the sensation soon passes and he is able to lean back against the pillow, find his glasses, and take stock of his surroundings.

The ward contains six beds. The three opposite him are empty but the sheets are rumpled and bear signs of recent occupancy; the bed to his right is empty, the sheets neatly made; to his left the bed is unoccupied but, again, clearly in use, for an open book lies on the pillow. Through the door he can see a nurse talking to someone in the next ward. He hears a child's voice and understands that he is still in the American hospital. His lips are dry. There is a carafe of water and a glass on the table by his bed; he reaches over and takes a sip, feeling the cool water slip down his throat. He sits up a little straighter then, feeling no ill effects, decides to swing his legs down onto the floor. He attempts to stand but his head swims so much he is forced to sit down again. He waits until he feels steady, then tries again. This time, he manages to stay upright, swaying, enjoying the coolness of the tiled floor on his bare feet. At the end of the ward is an open door. Through it is a beautiful courtyard, shaded by trees. Perhaps it is a mirage.

"Well, look at you!" exclaims the nurse, delightedly. Seeing his confused gaze, she switches to French: "*Très bien! Très bien!* You want to go outside? *Dehors?*"

"*Oui. S'il vous plaît.*"

Two trees grow in either corner of the yard, their canopies providing lush shade; climbing plants with dark green leaves and clusters of brilliant pink flowers twine up the hospital wall, and in the centre of the courtyard a fountain gurgles quietly into a shallow stone basin. A red carpet is laid out on the tiles. On it sit three children. They are very still, and very solemn, and very thin. Nearby is a chaise longue and, next to that, a low table and a chair. Kozłowski takes a few hesitant steps into the courtyard and once again spots those feet, hanging over the edge of the chaise longue. Then he sees a head of red hair, streaked with grey, and immediately he knows who it is.

Józef Czapski turns, breaking into a broad grin. "Forgive me for not getting up to greet you but, like you, I find myself somewhat incapacitated."

They find him a wicker armchair and the nurse goes to fetch Dr Cochran to tell him the good news. A tray of tea and toast miraculously appears, with glasses of orange squash and biscuits for the children.

"How long have I been ill?"

Dr Cochran is seated with them under the shade of the large-leafed tree. "Nearly three weeks."

"Three weeks?" So long! "Was it typhus?"

"Yes. We kept you quarantined for a couple of weeks, then we moved you onto the ward."

"When did you show up, Józef? The last time I saw you, I thought I was saying goodbye to you forever."

Czapski explains that, having only just recovered from his double bout of malaria and typhus in Yangi Yul, immediately on arrival in Meshed he succumbed to a bronchial fever.

"What about the officers? I was supposed to be looking after them—"

For the first time since falling ill he remembers the journey which brought him here, the trucks grinding their way over the mountains from Ashkabad, the bored-looking sentries waving them through at the border, the strange feeling of light-headedness he had felt on finally leaving the Soviet Union, as if, for the past three years, a weight had been pressing down upon him which had now been lifted. The odd buzzing in his ears, like tinnitus.

"They're all doing fine and are back at the hotel awaiting orders to continue to Iraq. Once you are fully recovered you will join them. But there's no hurry," adds Dr Cochran. "You need to rest."

Two little girls with long, dark plaits come skipping out of the hospital, carrying between them a large encyclopaedia. Czapski, obviously accustomed to their visits, spreads out his hands, exclaiming, in English, *"Hello, young ladies! What have you got to show me today?"*

"I thought you didn't speak English."

"I don't. That's about the extent of it. These are Dr Cochran's daughters. Aren't they charming? Every day they bring me anything they can find that is connected to Poland."

The two girls, whose rosy cheeks and crisp pinafore dresses speak of good health and plentiful nourishment, place the encyclopaedia before Czapski, opening the book at a page containing pictures of a Polish submarine which Czapski duly admires. The smaller of the two girls then reaches into her pinafore pocket, drawing from it a piece of paper which she carefully unfolds, smoothing it out to reveal a page torn from an American magazine featuring photographs of pre-war Warsaw. As Czapski mimes his admiration of this wonderful reminder of his homeland the little girl grins in delight. Her older sister picks up the paper, holding it out shyly for Kozłowski to admire.

"Warsaw."

"Yes," agrees Kozłowski. *"My city."*

At this piece of information the girls become very excited, pointing at the picture and asking something which Kozłowski suspects is a request for him to show them where he lives. Since the photographs depict the main tourist sights of Warsaw he is not able to oblige so he shrugs and smiles. Mrs Cochran calls the girls inside and they disappear into their father's office, leaving Kozłowski to stare at the bright, colourful photographs of the past.

Kozłowski is discharged the following week, having spent almost four weeks in hospital. Czapski, who is also awaiting transfer to Iraq, is staying at the same hotel. Still weak from his double bout of illness, he spends long hours in his room resting. When Kozłowski asks him what he is doing to pass the time, Czapski replies that he is trying to write an account of their experiences in the Soviet Union.

"It is only since leaving Russia that I have understood that this chapter in my life is finally closed, and only now that I am able to begin to examine it and to try to describe in writing what we have been through. We don't yet know the end to the story of Starobelsk, but I think it's important to try to record in as much detail as possible our experiences while they are still fresh in our minds. Don't you agree? Who knows if it may prove useful in the future."

Kozłowski lies on his bed in his hotel room, reflecting on Czapski's words. Had a single one of their comrades appeared in Totskoye or Buzuluk or any of the places where the Polish army mustered, it would have been easy to accept the theory that many of them had perished in those ice-bound prisons whose romantic names bely their cruelty. It is the totality of the silence that makes their fate unfathomable.

The memory of his recent dream is still vivid. Was this their fate? To disappear without trace into the icy Barents Sea?

The sounds and smells of the street drift in through the open window – the cries of market sellers, the strange honking noise made by the camels, the unfamiliar scent of spices and fruit. Dr Cochran has ordered him not to over-exert himself, but how can it be good for him to lie here, a prey to his imagination and his fears? He needs to be active, busy. Perhaps, whilst he is waiting for his orders, he might offer his services to Professor Kopeć at the orphanage. Surely there is nothing Dr Cochran could object to in such a plan?

Stepping out onto the busy Meshed street for the first time, Kozłowski is almost overwhelmed, at first by the noise, then by the colours: the clothes, the gemstones in baskets outside the shops, the fruit, the spices, the intricate patterns on the carpets laid out for sale. Then, as he grows accustomed to the onslaught on his senses, his heart begins to lighten. There is not only colour here, there is life: raw, wonderful life.

3. Your odd little friend

Meshed, Persia, 1942

"Dr Cochran tells me that you're supposed to be convalescing," says Professor Kopeć, over a glass of tea in his office. "Why don't you enjoy your leisure while you can?"

"It's cool here," pleads Kozłowski, "and calm. Besides, I'd rather be doing something useful than lying idle in my hotel."

"I won't pretend we don't need the help, Dr Kozłowski, but don't overdo it. I don't want Dr Cochran blaming me if you fall ill again."

Kozłowski stands in the doorway to a large dormitory, not wishing to intrude on the work of a jolly nurse who is laying out a tray of tiny glasses, each filled with a dose of medicine. A girl of around twelve years old waits beside her, listening attentively as the nurse explains something to her. The girl - a slight, solemn figure wearing a grey pinafore dress - obediently takes the glasses to the children and waits while they take their medicine.

"I'm very behind with my studies, Dr Kozłowski."

They are seated in the dormitory, the young girl perched on the edge of her narrow bed, Kozłowski on a wooden chair opposite her. Politely, he scans the exercise book which she is holding out to him, open on a page with 'Secondary Education' marked in large, rounded letters.

"So in maths, for example, I should really be at level 5 but in reality I'm closer to a 3." She turns the page to reveal another heading, 'University Education'. "I will specialise in my third year, taking options in paediatrics and trauma, which are my two preferred subjects. Then here," she flips over the page, "is a list of Polish universities, ranked in order of excellence according to what the doctors here have told me, so that I can think about where I would like to study. I should like to go to Lwów, because that's where my family is from, or maybe the Jagiellonian University in Kraków, because Professor Kopeć says it's the best." The girl closes the notebook, smoothing it carefully before placing it in the drawer of the table by her bed. "I'd better get on," she says, glancing at the clock. "It's time for the children's medicine."

"Felicja's mother and younger sister died on the journey from Kazakhstan to Totskoye," explains Professor Kopeć when Kozłowski questions him about the girl. "From exhaustion, by the sounds of it, or starvation. Her father was in the army. We think he was captured but we're not sure if it was by the Soviets or the Germans: she is hazy on the details. Rynkowski was his name." Her need for order, he observes, is perhaps a direct result of the trauma she has endured. "Although, who knows? Perhaps she has always been so precise."

One day, Felicja enters the dormitory wearing a stethoscope around her neck.

"Professor Kopeć said I might borrow it," she says, with pride. "May I listen to your heartbeat?"

Kozłowski leans forward so that she can place the stethoscope on his chest. She listens for a moment, frowning.

"I don't think this stethoscope is very good. I can hear something, but it's awfully faint." She takes the earpieces from her ears. "Unless, Dr Kozłowski, you have a very weak heartbeat."

"There's nothing wrong with my heartbeat, I can assure you. Perhaps you haven't put the stethoscope in the right place."

"I put it exactly where the Professor showed me!"

"May I, Felicja?" He holds out his hand. "Put the stethoscope back in your ears. You see, the heart is situated on the left-hand side of the chest cavity. Rather lower down than the collar bone, about a hand's width, so." He places the metal disk onto his chest. "Now can you hear it?"

"No – Wait! – Yes! – A bit…"

Kozłowski adjusts the position of the stethoscope and Felicja's eyes suddenly light up with excitement.

"Oh, yes, now I hear it! Boom-be-de-boom! It's like a galloping horse!"

Tadeusz Biały whittling out the centre of the stethoscope he made from wood.

Lieutenant Biały, I can confidently state that you are still alive.
Well, that's a relief!

The memory assaults him, seizing him by the throat like an assassin.

"Come and see the new children," says Felicja, with an abrupt change of subject, "a whole crowd of them has just arrived."

The new arrivals consist of a group of around twelve boys and girls of various ages. Two of them, Felicja informs him, have already been removed to the American Hospital.

"They're very sick with dysentery," she says, one professional to another.

Some of the children are sleeping, others sit, gazing listlessly at the bustle going on around them as one nurse takes the children in pairs to wash whilst another whisks off their filthy clothes, shoving them into a large sack to be taken away for disinfection. A boy cries out in fury, tugging at the nurse's hand as she tries to lead him towards the bathroom.

"I don't want to wash! I don't want my hair cut off!"

"My dear," explains Felicja, "you have lice. We have to cut your hair. It will grow back."

That first shower, when they were taken to the public baths in the rain. Tomasz protesting as they tried to shave his hair. An officer being forcibly shorn, like a sheep, with a Russian boy's knee in his back.

On the far side of the room sits a girl. She has her back to the others, her lank hair resting on her shoulders like strands of rope. There is something familiar about her.

Kozłowski walks slowly to the end of the dormitory so that he can observe her without drawing attention to himself. She is looking down at something in her hands – is it a little doll? He cannot see – her grubby fingers playing with it constantly. When she looks up, sensing his gaze, he sees that her eyes are a dull grey. Her jaw is square, just like her father's.

"Zosia? Zosia Kozłowska?"

A vague look of curiosity enters her eyes as she scrutinises him. Somewhere deep inside her tired young soul, perhaps, a tiny flicker of hope stirs. "Uncle Zbyszek?"

"Professor Kopeć," he calls out, "this girl here: she's my brother's daughter."

Kopeć looks up from his work. "Well, that's good news at least. Are you her only relative?"

"No." He sits down next to her. "No, I'm not. Zosia," he speaks very gently, because he can see that she is very weak, "would you like to hear something wonderful?"

Her fingers stop playing. She gives a little shrug, then starts twiddling with the doll's hair again, winding it round and round her finger.

Nearby, Felicja watches them.

"Your mother—" Zosia's fingers stop again. This time Kozłowski can feel an intense concentration in her. "—and your brother Olek are alive and well. Zosia? Do you understand? Mamusia and Olek are fine. I saw them when we were in Tashkent. Your mother is with the Polish army. She's working as a nurse. They're in Persia, in a place called Pahlevi. They went there by sea. I can contact her and tell her that I have found you. She was so sad, thinking that she had lost you. When she left the Soviet Union, do you know what she said to me?"

At last, the girl looks up.

"She said, 'Look out for Zosia for me.'"

When she came to say goodbye to him in Tashkent, Elżbieta had thanked Kozłowski with curious formality for his help. She turned and bent down to scoop up a handful of black soil and slipped it into her pocket, explaining that once they were out of Soviet territory she would throw it overboard.

"But first I will spit on it. I will never return to Russia, Zbyszek. If they try to make me come here again, they will have to bring me in a coffin." Her face softened abruptly, and she grasped his hand. "Look out for Zosia, won't you?"

"And now I've found you."

Professor Kopeć proposes that he send a telegram to the military authorities in Tehran. "If your sister-in-law is attached to the army, they will find her and inform her of her daughter's presence here. Then we will see what can be done to reunite them."

Before he leaves her, bathed and clad in a clean nightdress, tucked into bed, Kozłowski succeeds in convincing Zosia to allow the nurse to wash her doll, on condition that it will immediately be returned to her. The little figure stands sentinel by her bedside, its string hair steadily dripping water onto the table. Zosia stares at the doll as if she fears that, if she looks away, the hope that she has just been given will immediately disintegrate.

"When is my mother coming?" she asks the nurse.

"Soon, my dear," replies the nurse. "Hopefully she will come soon."

Soon, soon. A familiar lullaby.

On his way back to the hotel, Kozłowski passes the great shrine of Imam Reza, its enormous turquoise and golden domes silhouetted against the cloudless sky. A crowd of women, dressed from head to toe in black, follow a tour guide who leads them across the broad piazza towards the shrine complex, an umbrella held aloft above her head. The woman is explaining something to them in a language Kozłowski takes to be Arabic rather than Persian. She is dressed in western style, her black hair twisted in an elegant chignon, her feet clad in patent leather court shoes. The linguist Szumigalski's single visit to England left him with a lingering memory, not of ancient palaces or towns, but of the lush green of the grass in the rain and a young guide dressed in a yellow cardigan, a string of pearls around her neck. Młynarski said he never stopped talking about her. In English, of course.

4. Soon

Meshed, Persia, 1942

Each day, Zosia asks if her mother is going to come for her. Each day, the nurse responds, "Soon", until Zosia begins to realise that, once again, she has been duped: there is no hope; her mother is not going to come. Daily she weakens, refusing food and drink, turning her face away from the little doll to face the wall.

"Please, Professor, there must be some way of hurrying things up!" Kozłowski paces anxiously in Professor Kopeć's office. "She'll die."

"I know." Kopeć's voice is sharp. "But what can I do? There are thousands of children in a similar situation. I've done all I can."

Kozłowski sits by her bedside, trying to coax her to eat, describing in minute detail everything he can remember that his sister-in-law told him about their journey. "She went to buy some food, didn't she? She took Olek with her and she left you on the train. What happened then, Zosia?"

"An old man helped me. He gave me his food and stayed with me until we reached a station where he said he had to get off. He gave me money and some bread, and he told me to get off the train when it reached Yangi Yul, but I made a mistake and got off too soon. Then I got lost. I tried to find the army camp but I couldn't. I slept outdoors and I ate all the bread. I was very hungry. I went back to the station and asked a lady how to get to Yangi Yul. She told me to take the train that was standing at the platform and she offered to buy my ticket for me, so I gave her the money but she never came back. I slept at the station. The next day another train came, so I got on board and I hid. A kind lady let me climb into the luggage rack and she covered me with a blanket when the man came for the tickets. When I got to Yangi Yul everybody had already left. I think I fainted. They took me to a hospital and put me on a train with some children who didn't have parents, we took a truck over some mountains and they brought us here."

"Zosia, please believe that your mother will come. Eat something, just a little. She will be very sad if she arrives and you are ill."

He can make no headway with her. She continues to refuse food just as she continues to disbelieve all assurances that her mother will come to fetch her. She has embraced despair with the same determination that Felicja has embraced a future which leaves no room for uncertainty.

They are seated in the courtyard outside, two glasses of fruit juice on a table before them. The afternoon heat is intense and most of the children are indoors, asleep. Kozłowski's shirt sticks to his back; his feet, encased in British army boots, are swollen and sore. Felicja, apparently untroubled by the heat, picks up a date, contemplating it curiously before biting into it.

"What is saffron?"

Kozłowski has become accustomed to the abrupt leaps of thought which characterise Felicja's conversation. "It's a kind of plant that looks like an orange thread. They put it in food and use it to dye clothes: it makes a vivid yellow colour."

She nods thoughtfully, spitting the date stone into her hand. "If I plant this, will a date tree grow?"

"Possibly."

"It's nice that you've found your niece. Nobody talks about my father anymore. Does that mean that he's dead?"

"It means that they don't know where he is, so they don't know if he's dead or not. I hope very much for your sake that he is alive."

"I hope very much that Mama is alive but I know she isn't."

"That's different."

"Why?"

"Because you know for sure that she's dead."

She takes another date and starts nibbling around its edge.

"What is your father like, Felicja?"

Felicja thinks carefully. "He was always in a bad mood when he came home from work. But I liked it in the holidays. Sometimes he would lift me up and carry me around on his back. I was little then, of course."

"What did he do?"

"Now you're talking about him as if he is dead."

"I'm sorry. I meant, what did he do before the war."

"That's clever. I like that answer. He was a lawyer."

"How old were you when the war broke out?"

"Nine. I'm twelve now. Where did you study medicine?"

"At the University of Wilno."

"Is it a good university?"

"Very."

"Is it a good place to study medicine?"

"I think so."

"Better than Lwów?"

"I don't know. I think they are both very good."

"Do you have a specialism?"

"Not yet."

"Why not?"

"Because the war broke out before I could decide."

"If you could have a specialism, what would it be?"

He reaches up involuntarily to touch his glasses. "Eyes. I've always thought I'd like to specialise in eyes."

Felicja nods. Wiping her hands on her skirt, she gets up. "I need to write something down. Excuse me."

"Has there been any news from Pahlevi?" asks the nurse.

"Not yet. Apparently a telegram has been sent but God only knows how difficult it is to find someone out there."

"If she goes on refusing to eat she's going to die."

Kozłowski looks at the thin, still girl. "Perhaps Felicja could try."

She stands awkwardly by the bed. Then, ignoring Zosia, Felicja picks up the doll and says something to it. At first, Zosia shows no interest but then she rolls over and watches as the doll answers back. She smiles.

When he returns to the orphanage that evening Kozłowski finds Felicja curled up next to Zosia. She smiles up at him sleepily.

"I persuaded her to drink some tea with sugar."

"Oh, well done! You clever girl! I knew that if anyone could do it, it was you."

"She's like Alicja."

"Who's Alicja?"

"She was my best friend back home. Zosia likes all the same things."

"She told you what she likes?"

"She told the doll. That's the secret. She talks to the doll."

"How very clever of you to work that out. How did you know?"

"Because dolls understand things that grown-ups don't."

"Ah. I see. Well, I must remember that. You really are going to be a wonderful doctor, Felicja."

"I know."

They dine in an Armenian restaurant close to the hotel, Kozłowski, Czapski and two of the remaining convalescent officers, the subject of their conversation their imminent departure for Iraq. Movement orders have now arrived, with Czapski due to leave in four days' time, while the date of Kozłowski's departure – a week hence - is dictated by the needs of the two officers whom he will accompany. After dinner, they stroll along the tree-lined boulevard, back to the hotel. There is a slight breeze now in the evenings, a sign that summer is almost at an end. At the hotel, the receptionist calls Kozłowski over, handing him a telegram from Tehran. It is from Elżbieta:

"ON MY WAY. ARRIVE MESHED SEPTEMBER 14TH."

5. I will not cry

During the next few days the pace of Kozłowski's life accelerates as Elżbieta arrives and Czapski's departure, as well as his own, approaches. He accompanies his sister-in-law to the reception centre, Elżbieta bombarding him with questions all the way while Olek sits next to her on the leather seat, observing his uncle in silence with his huge, solemn eyes.

When they arrive at the orphanage, Elżbieta pulls her shoulders back like a soldier about to go into battle.

"I will not cry in front of her."

Of course, as soon as she sees her daughter, so thin, so frail, so very weak, she cannot help herself: she takes Zosia in her arms and sobs. Zosia does not cry; instead, she looks at her mother in wonderment, as if she thinks Elżbieta is a mirage which might at any moment evaporate.

The other children in the dormitory stop what they are doing, turning to gaze at this family reunion.

It is soon settled: with two children to look after, there is no question of Elżbieta travelling to Iraq. Professor Kopeć suggests a neat solution, proposing that Elżbieta apply to serve as a nurse at the orphanage in India. As soon as Zosia is strong enough, Elżbieta and the two children will accompany the next convoy out of Persia.

On Czapski's last night they are joined at dinner by Elżbieta, whose long and graphic account of the journey to Pahlevi dominates the conversation.

"You should have seen the chaos. The disease! Crowds of people squashed together on those dreadful boats. You have it easy here, living in a hotel. The fortunate few, that's what you are. Goodness knows, Zbyszek, you've landed on your feet. The rest of us chasing a few crumbs of bread. I will never forget the journey on that boat. A mother

and her child actually died right next to me, think of that! Poor Olek!"
She speaks without pause, the words gushing from her in an
unstoppable torrent. Kozłowski glances around self-consciously to see
if the others share his distaste for this unembarrassed litany of woes.
Czapski and the others, however, are listening with interest, murmuring
words of sympathy. It is I who am at fault, he thinks: I see self-pity
where they see only her suffering. I have lost my compassion.

Elżbieta is now relating in minute detail the precise circumstances of
her loss of, search for and reunion with her daughter. "Had it not been
for the kindness of that man!" she exclaims. "If we only knew his name!
It is proof, is it not, that charity is not completely absent from this
terrible world in which we live?… Her face when she saw me! My poor
girl!" As she thanks God and fate for restoring her beloved daughter to
her, she turns to Kozłowski. "We should be grateful, Zbyszek, that your
illness kept you here. Imagine if you had not been unwell! You would
have travelled on to Iraq with the rest of the army, quite unaware of my
poor Zosia's presence. And you have been so kind to her!" She grasps
his hand fondly, and he feels a stab of guilt at the thoughts which have
just been running through his head. "You see," she addresses the guests
gathered around the table, "I believe that there is such a thing as fate,
God places us like pawns upon his great chessboard and we have no
choice but to follow the path set before us."

At the end of the evening, Czapski accompanies Kozłowski upstairs,
confessing that he is too preoccupied with the morning's journey to
sleep.

"I've a not entirely disgusting bottle of wine in my room," he adds,
with a dry smile. "I'd be more than happy to share it with you if you'd
care to keep me company."

They spend the rest of the night talking, the main topic of their
conversation Czapski's work of the past weeks.

"What is your view, Józef, after all this time? What do you think
happened to them?"

Czapski weighs his words carefully. "I am convinced that they were
sent to a camp in the very far north or east of the Soviet Union, whether

to Kolyma or Franz Josef Land I have no idea. In view of the nature of these camps, I think it likely that many of them perished there, from the cold, from sickness, injury, or exhaustion. But I remain hopeful that at least some may eventually reappear."

"Of course, there is another possibility."

"Which is?"

"Which is that the Bolsheviks decided it was not in their interest to release them."

"You mean they may have deliberately ignored the amnesty? Yes, I have thought of that. But what about the 'big mistake'? Why would they say they had made a mistake if they were keeping them hidden from us deliberately?"

Somehow, the conversation has ended up with the same question to which they always return, spurred by a shared sense of bewilderment or perhaps shame. Why is it that we were taken to Griazovets and not to wherever it is our friends have gone? Why are we here today, in Persia, and not with our comrades in the north? Why us and not them? Is Elżbieta right, Kozłowski asks himself, and it is all a matter of fate, of some great, divine plan? Was I meant to be here and they were not? The thought fills him with self-disgust.

"Do you think the staff knew?"

"They must have known, Zbyszek, don't you think?"

He remembers Vasilevna crying after Dr Levittoux's departure.

Our dear, good Dr Levittoux has gone!

By the time their conversation finally ends the sun has risen and the hotel staff are stirring downstairs. They stand together at the window, watching the shopkeepers as they lay out their wares for the day, dozens of metallic bowls filled with varicoloured stones which glitter in the morning sunlight. In the distance, the huge, pink sun rises from behind the mountains.

A week later, Kozłowski too must leave Meshed. When he arrives at the reception centre to say goodbye to Elżbieta she is in a meeting with Professor Kopeć, so he goes in search of Felicja, finding her seated on the ground in the courtyard, a human skull placed before her, her notebook open on her knees.

"What's that?"

Felicja holds out the notebook, in which she has painstakingly drawn a picture of the skull, complete with annotations. "Professor Kopeć lent it to me. It's an anatomical model."

He compliments her on the accuracy of her drawing. "I had a friend once," he says, sitting down cross-legged next to her. "His name was Tadeusz. He found a skull in the earth and drew it, just as you have done."

"Was he a pathologist? I am very interested in pathology." She pronounces the word as if she has only recently added it to her vocabulary.

"No, he was an illustrator."

"Whose skull was it?"

"I've no idea. I'm leaving, Felicja. I have to join the army in Iraq."

She nods, intent on correcting something in her drawing.

"Professor Kopeć tells me that you're going with my niece and nephew on the next transport to India."

She nods again.

"Keep an eye on them for me, will you? Make sure Zosia gets well. I know there will be doctors there but I don't think any of them will be nearly as efficient as you."

She looks up, smiling, and holds out the back pages of her book, where, under the heading 'Zosia', she has drawn a graph, with dates marked on the horizontal axis and weight in kilograms on the vertical axis. "I've made a special chart to show her progress."

"I knew I could count on you. Well, goodbye, Felicja. I hope we meet again some day." Awkwardly, he places his hand on her head.

She does not reply. When he looks back at her, she is still absorbed in her drawing, head bent over the page, a young girl carefully following a straight line with a ruler.

6. You poor chump

Southampton, England, 1946

In the freezing Nissen hut an English lesson is underway, led by a young Oxford graduate who, for some reason, seems convinced that the best way to equip his students for their new life in Britain is to familiarise them with the works of P G Wodehouse.

"Hullo! I say, you haven't brought your racket, you poor chump."

On the table lies a pile of pamphlets, advice for the new arrivals from a Pole who spent the war in England:

If an Englishman is kind enough to invite you into his home, you must thank him for the invitation, but try not to take too frequent advantage of it. If you do refuse, do not on any account do so rudely. Say that, regretfully, you are unable to come. Use the word 'sorry' or 'very sorry', 'so sorry', or even 'awfully sorry'. Words cost nothing, and it shows that you really do regret that you cannot oblige. You will hear this word about a hundred times every day. People use it when they bump into someone or tread on someone's toe.

There was a lecture like this, once. The red-faced *politruk* Kaganer dispensing Soviet wisdom to a room full of filthy prisoners who had come inside to escape the rain. Then, winter was turning to spring. Now, the ground is hardening as autumn gives way to an unexpectedly icy December. Kozłowski's most pressing need is not for English lessons but a warm winter coat. For three weeks he has waited, gazing out of the steamed-up window at the leafless trees, half-listening to the lessons and the talks, his mind wandering aimlessly between the past and the future. In the evenings, he does not participate in the endless discussions about where to go and what to do. Nottingham, Sheffield, London, Wales: where are the jobs to be found? When others ask him about his plans he replies only: "I'm waiting to hear from my girl."

When the longed-for telegram finally arrives, he packs his army rucksack with indecent haste, taking the first available ticket for the first available train and hurrying off without a backward glance at the field of barrel-like huts. I'm not staying here, thanks all the same, I've had my fill of camps. I'm just passing through on my way to London, where Hanka has just arrived.

7. Hanka in the desert

Quizil Ribat, Iraq, 1943

A row of tents disappearing into infinity. The dry heat of the desert. Sand everywhere, in kit bags, in socks, between one's teeth. Unfamiliar creatures causing panic in the tents at night: scorpions, black-widow spiders, snakes. Army routine: drill, exercise, lectures, mess, sleep. British uniforms, Polish command, names filled with nostalgia for regions already lost: 3rd Carpathian, 5th Wilno, 6th Lwów. Józef Czapski's newspaper *The White Eagle* bringing culture to the men, concerts to distract them, theatre performances to make them laugh. For Kozłowski, a hospital in a white tent and the continuing battle with malaria and dysentery. Time off spent resting, exhausted by the heat, which drains his energy and makes his tropical uniform stick to his skin. By day, patients have a bucket of water by their bed to cool them; at night, the heat is sucked out of the atmosphere and they lie with their teeth chattering.

Kozłowski gazes down at the lines of beds in the tented dormitory. An epidemic of malaria has seized the camp and the field hospital is full. Most of the patients are asleep; some shift restlessly. The canvas walls of the hospital billow, tugging against the guy ropes, a frantic pinging coming from the flagpole outside. The lamp above his desk sways in the gusts of wind which penetrate the interior of the tent, releasing a smell of paraffin which stings his nostrils. He peers through the flaps at the clouds racing across the sky, revealing - in glimpses that last barely a couple of seconds - a huge, copper-coloured moon.

He has brought a book to keep him company, but he has no desire to read. Among the papers tucked inside the cover is a postcard from his mother. Dated November 1942, it has taken several weeks to reach him, via the Red Cross. As usual, since there is little of genuine interest that she is able to communicate, she has limited herself to observations about the weather (cold: the first snow lies on the ground already), her health (as good as can be expected) and that of his father (ditto), the welfare of Gosia, who continues working in Kraków (*She sends me only cheerful news. It makes me wonder if everything is alright*). Her joy at the receipt of a postcard from India, including greetings written by dearest Olek and Zosia themselves, and her urgent desire to discover the fate of Staś. At the end of the letter, a few words are added in a hasty post scriptum: has he heard anything more on the subject of Starobelsk? If he has any news at all, however trivial, she begs him to pass it on for the sake of Mrs Levittoux, whom she meets on occasion in the queue for bread, and who is close to despair. *It is the silence that torments her, poor soul.* She concludes with greetings from his father and an expression of gratitude that at least one of her sons is alive and well. *Medicine has clearly saved your life, as well as all the lives which you are doubtless saving in the course of your work. Stay well, my dearest son! With all a mother's love.*

Kozłowski considers these last words. Not for the first time, he asks himself whether it was his profession which led to his selection in the group of prisoners who escaped the mysterious fate of their comrades. But, if he was chosen because, as a doctor, he was considered less of a threat to the Soviets, then what of Levittoux? Kołodziejski? Grüner? Wolfram? Men of infinitely more experience than he. Some were professional military doctors, granted, but not all. What about the vet, Łabędź? What harm could he have represented to anyone, a man whose only sin was to place a splint on the leg of an injured mongrel? He thinks back to that single interrogation, to the urbane officer from Moscow who spoke so convincingly of his interest in medicine and tricked him into saying things which – twisted in the mouth of the Russian – sounded so different from the way he had intended them.

Major Lis always spoke of Colonel Berling, at the Villa of Bliss, exhorting them to consider "the bigger picture". What is it that he is failing to see?

Lying unopened within the covers of his book is another letter, arrived today, which he has not yet had time to open. It is from Elżbieta, from India.

Dearest Zbyszek,

Greetings to you from Balachadi! Well, you will be pleased to know that we survived the journey through Afghanistan. Thank God the drivers were issued with arms in Meshed! There are tribesmen on the border who will attack the convoys, given half a chance. When I first saw those tall brown men with their enormous turbans and their rifles, I nearly fainted! Then the leader of the convoy explained that the turbaned men were Sikhs who could be utterly relied upon to protect us. And they did, most courageously. We were not attacked, thank Heaven, but I saw some very nasty-looking men on horseback who followed us for several miles before they eventually gave up. I suppose they realised they had no hope of success. What they would want with a convoy of half-starving children I do not know! I will spare you the details of the journey. Suffice to say that it was long and hard. When we arrived we were greeted by an Indian princess. Just imagine! A princess! The driver told me that it was the princess who offered to take in so many orphaned children. I can only say that I am eternally grateful to them. The warmth of our reception! The kindness of the local people and the Poles here (there is quite a little community here already, with teachers, nurses, and even a priest) – neat little dormitories with fresh white sheets, classrooms, a bell to call us to chapel on Sunday, there is even a scout troop! The priest here is a very kind man who came here with the first convoy back in March. The weather is extremely hot and humid here and the dust gets into everything. I find it at the bottom of my bag and in my pockets. I have been working at the little clinic here. It is the usual set of problems, as you can imagine: dysentery, of course, and malnutrition, as well as malaria – we have mosquito nets but there are still many cases. We are managing it with the kind help of those around us. I expect you are wanting to know how the children are faring. Well, I am happy to tell you that you would not recognise Olek: he grows stronger by the day and mischievous with it! He cheeks his teachers and the other day pulled the tail of a cow (which got him into terrible trouble, as cows here are considered sacred; he would have done better to pull the tail of an elephant. Yes! We have seen these exotic creatures! Here they are considered as essential to labour as horses are to us). Zosia is still thin but she has begun to recover her spirits; she studies hard, trying to catch up on what she has missed, and joins in with the scouting activities. She's a good girl. I am also studying: yes! I am learning English and, although I am a poor, slow student I am beginning make progress. Would you like a cup of tea? *There is a very kind Scottish engineer who helps us with every kind of problem we encounter, whether it is fixing the water pipes or the holes in the tin roof. For the moment we converse in a mixture of Polish, English and sign language (mainly the latter) but I am improving every day. I must go now, dear Zbyszek: I have been writing this during my break and must get back on duty. I hope that conditions in Iraq are better than they were in Tashkent (surely they must be, now that you are under British command?). I pray for your safety and your health. Try not to exhaust yourself and become ill again.*

Your loving sister-in-law,

Elżbieta

Oh, and PS, your odd little friend Felicja asks to be remembered to you. She and Zosia are quite devoted to one another, although Felicja spends so much time with her head in a book I wonder she has time for anything else.

Kozłowski folds up the letter and slips it between the covers of his book. How cheerful and kind his sister-in-law has become. She writes with an affection she would never have bestowed upon him in person. It is the relief speaking, perhaps, the sheer joy of being away from the war.

A patient suddenly sits bolt upright, shouting: "*Mamo!*"

Grateful for the interruption, Kozłowski gets up to attend to him.

Later, it starts to rain, a few drops at first, then in torrents, beating down on the canvas in a furious tattoo. Winter has arrived, not a season of snow and freezing cold as it is in Russia, but one of monsoons and tempests which threaten to rip the tents apart.

He stumbles into bed at four and falls into a deep sleep. By the time he wakes up, the wind has dropped and the rain has ceased. When he leaves his tent to go to the mess for breakfast, he halts in astonishment at the sight before him: overnight, the desert has bloomed; tiny red flowers are dotted everywhere.

There is a sign where the camp meets the desert: Quizil-Ribat to Warsaw, 2,950 km.

One evening, Czapski comes in search of Kozłowski, informing him with an unaccustomed air of excitement that there is someone he will be glad to meet. Kozłowski follows his friend obediently but without excitement; he knows better than to hope.

As soon as he sees her he knows who she is: she wears the British tropical uniform of blouse and skirt, her fair hair knotted back under the AWS hat. On most of the girls the uniform looks shapeless and unflattering, but she is as slim and tall as a reed.

"Zbyszek, I'd like you to meet Tomasz's sister, Hanna Chęcińska. She's teaching the *junacy* in our little school here."

"So you're Hanka." He grins at her stupidly. "How wonderful!"

Love finally touches him. It seizes him, lifts him and deposits him in blissful bemusement on a remote golden strand, far from his familiar world. Hanka does not speak of Tomasz's absence. Instead, she fills the silence with laughter and merriment, as if she can illuminate the darkness by the sheer force of her being.

"I feel as if I already know you, Gosia spoke of you so often. It was such a comfort to her, being able to imagine you and Tomasz together in that dreadful place. In fact, she and I used to have a joke—" Hanka breaks off with a mischievous smile. "That's for another time. You look like her, you know. Gosia."

Now she is explaining how she and Gosia became friends when they were students in Kraków, remarking how clever Gosia is, how lucky she was to get that job at the chemical institute – "Very prestigious for someone so young, don't you think? But I suppose it's not news to you: she is your sister, after all. Have you heard from her recently?" – but all the time she is speaking he is not really listening but gazing at her, enchanted. When she laughs his pulse quickens; he feels giddy with sudden, absurd joy.

They meet often: Kozłowski, Czapski, Bronisław Młynarski and Hanka, talking late into the night, the three men captivated by this beautiful, vivid echo of their friend. Although, as a rule, they rarely discuss Starobelsk with others, Hanka's curiosity, her determinedly light-hearted questions and comments—

"Of course, Tomasz's lectures *would* be all about his Great European Plan. He and our brother Jan used to argue constantly about it. I could recite the details of it by heart even today. Did *anyone* agree with him?"

"He beat you all at chess, you say? I can only imagine that you must be very poor players because I used to trounce him regularly!"

—her teasing, fond remarks answer a need in them to talk of what they saw and did during those seven months, drawing them out so effectively that their experience returns to them as it was lived, untroubled by the shadow which now hangs over its memory.

"Do you remember the time the mobile shop turned up with that consignment of fabric from goodness knows where?" Młynarski leans back in the canvas chair, a glass of whisky in his hand. "Dreadful, garish stuff in awful colours! And Olgierd said to the woman— 'Which do you think will make the most elegant undergarments, Madame, the flowers, or the pineapples?'"

"And you bought a pair of ladies galoshes! I remember the first time you put them on, Bronek! Even Kopyekin laughed!"

"What was the name of that dog, the one who carried messages?"

"Little Foch! Ah, yes, dear Foch! And Łabędź's dog Linek, remember him? Such a fine moustache. Remember when he broke his leg?"

Młynarski breaks off, tears welling unexpectedly in his eyes. Mortified, he hurries from the tent, leaving the others to sit in awkward silence until Hanka saves them, raising her glass in a toast.

"Here's to Linek and Foch, hirsute but happy!"

When Młynarski returns, freshly composed, to excuse himself as a sentimental fool, the conversation has moved on.

Kozłowski and Hanka linger outside her tent, whispering and giggling like teenagers. He wants to tell her what Tomasz said to him as they left the clinic that day. Instead, he kisses her, again and again then draws back, looking into her eyes as if he will find in them the answer to his unspoken question.

"You look just like Tomasz sometimes, you know," he says. "Especially when you laugh."

There is a lake near the army headquarters at Quizil-Ribat. On rare days off, Kozłowski takes Hanka out on a boat, rowing into the centre of the lake and letting the boat drift while they lie on their backs, side by side, gazing up at the peacock-blue sky while the sun warms their skin. They speak of the *junacy* and the *ochotniczki*, the schoolboys and girls who practise military drills and march in the desert between classes, and of Hanka's attempts to instil in her class of teenage boys an understanding of Polish grammar when all they want to do is go to war and fight. She tells him about Kraków under German occupation, how Jews were herded into ghettoes, how a hundred professors from the Jagiellonian University were murdered.

"That was in 1939. What it must be like now I can only imagine."

"Why did you go back to Lwów? It must have been a dangerous journey. Tomasz was very concerned about you." He does not add that her brother made himself so ill he almost died.

"My father was unwell, my mother was all alone. It seemed wrong to stay in Kraków when I could be of help to them."

"How on earth did you manage to get there?"

"It was fairly easy to get from Kraków to Warsaw. It was Gosia's boss who got the papers for me. Once I reached Warsaw I went to my brother Jan's house but his wife told me he'd joined the AK and was living in another part of town under an assumed name. Imagine that – they can't even meet! I managed to get a message to him and he asked his friends in the AK to help with papers, but it took weeks. It was a relief to get home finally, even with Lwów under Soviet occupation."

One day he ventures to ask her what happened in April 1940, when she and her parents were taken from their home at night and deported to Kazakhstan. Her account is brief and limited to the facts: her father's health was weak and he did not survive the journey; her mother became ill during the winter of 1940 and died early in 1941. After the amnesty, Hanka made her way south alone, finally catching up with the army at Krasnovodsk, where she joined the Women's Auxiliary Service, crossing with the bulk of the army to Pahlevi. When he tries to persuade her to speak further of her experiences, Hanka replies that there is nothing she cares to remember from that time.

"Unlike you and your friends from Starobelsk."

"That sounds almost like an accusation."

"Not at all. I'm glad you were happy there. That Tomasz was happy."

"We weren't *happy*. How could anyone be happy under such circumstances?"

"When the three of you speak about it it sounds as if you were."

"Młynarski makes everything sound amusing."

"Were you *un*happy, then?"

How can he explain it to her? That in their shared suffering they formed a bond stronger than—

"—what? Stronger than your love for me?"

"Of course not! That's not possible."

One day, by chance, he encounters Major Lis outside the field hospital, striding towards him with his distinctive rolling gait. Smartly dressed in

British desert uniform, Lis is in his element now, preparing his men for battle.

"Although there aren't enough officers, of course, not decent ones at any rate." Sheer force of habit makes him drop his voice. "And we all know why. Oh, they've sent us officers from London, but they're a hopeless bunch, arrogant and stuck in the past. The sooner they train up the cadets the better, as far as I'm concerned. I'd rather have a bright nineteen-year-old under my command than one of those old fossils from London." He changes the subject abruptly. "Guess who I saw the other day? Berling. Can you believe it, he actually smiled at me and said hello, as if we'd bumped into each other at a cocktail party! General Anders may have forgiven him but I can tell you I do not find it so easy." A jeep pulls up beside them; Lis glances at his watch. "I have to go, Dr Kozłowski. Duty calls." He jumps into the jeep and disappears in a cloud of sand.

The same day, he comes across Julia in the hospital mess. She tells him that Edek made it back into Poland without being caught, but once he reached Warsaw the Nazis found him and threw him into prison.

"When they discovered that he was a doctor they let him work in the prison hospital, so I reckon he got off lightly. Typical of Edek, don't you think?"

She looks up at him, shading her eyes from the sun. There is something in her gaze – expectation, or is it hope? – that makes him want to hurry away. He makes an excuse about being late for his shift and retreats into the tent.

"See you around," she calls after him.

8. The forest

Quizil Ribat, Iraq, 1943

They crowd into Czapski's office, desperate for more detailed news. Czapski, seated behind his desk, is helpless to answer the barrage of questions.

"Do they know about this at home?"

Yes, Czapski replies, everyone in Poland is aware of the discovery.

"And what do they think? Have the AK been in touch with London?"

Czapski hesitates. "It is apparent that, in those parts of Poland which are under Nazi occupation, people are inclined to believe the Soviet version of events. Given the reports of Nazi brutality that have reached us here," he adds, as the cries of protest threaten to disrupt the meeting completely, "it is easy to understand why this might be the case."

"And London?" persists the questioner. "What does London say?"

"I think they, too, are uncertain whom to believe." This time, he cannot quell the uproar. Czapski raises his voice above the storm of protestations. "General Anders has given me permission to share with you the fact that he has personally sent a telegram to the Polish Minister of Defence in London with a detailed account of the efforts made by him – and by me – to find the men who were missing from the three camps of Kozelsk, Starobelsk and Ostashkov. In this communication, he has made it quite clear that in his opinion there can be no doubt who is responsible for this terrible crime."

Two weeks ago, on April 13th, an announcement was made by German radio concerning a place named Katyń Forest, near Smolensk in Russia, an area that has been occupied, since late 1941, by the Germans.

"I have very little information so far," continues Czapski, but I can read aloud to you the text of the German communiqué, if you would like to hear it:

"A report has reached us from Smolensk to the effect that the local inhabitants have mentioned to the German authorities the existence of a place where mass executions had been carried out by the Bolsheviks and where 10,000 Polish officers had been murdered by the GPU (NKVD). The German authorities accordingly went to a place called Kasogory (or Kozy Gory - Goat's Hill), a Soviet health resort situated 12km west of Smolensk where a terrible discovery was made. A ditch was found, 28m long and 16m wide, in which the bodies of 3,000 Polish officers were piled up in 12 layers. They were fully dressed in military uniforms, some bound, and all had pistol shot wounds in the back of their heads. There will be no difficulty in identifying the bodies as, owing to the nature of the ground, they are in a state of mummification and the Russians had left on their bodies their personal documents. It has been stated today that General Smorawiński from Lublin has been found amongst other murdered officers. Previously these officers were in a camp at Kozelsk near Orel, and in February and March 1940 were brought in cattle freight cars to Smolensk. Thence they were taken in lorries to Kosogory and were murdered there by the Bolsheviks. The search for further pits is in progress. New layers may be found under those already discovered. It is estimated that the total number of officers killed amounts to 10,000, which would correspond to the entire cadre of Polish officers taken prisoner by the Russians."

Czapski adds that Radio Berlin announced in a further bulletin that medical commissions from neutral countries had arrived on the spot to investigate the crime and are proceeding with the exhumation of the bodies.

"It appears that a second communiqué was issued by the Soviet information bureau on April 15th."

The text of the Soviet communiqué he also reads aloud in quiet, measured tones.

"In the past two or three days Goebbels's slanderers have been spreading vile fabrications alleging that the Soviet authorities carried out a mass shooting of Polish officers in the spring of 1940 in the Smolensk area. In launching this monstrous invention the German-

Fascist scoundrels did not hesitate to spread the most unscrupulous and base lies in their attempts to cover up crimes which, as has now become evident, were perpetrated by themselves.

"The German-Fascist report on the subject leaves no doubt as to the tragic fate of the former Polish prisoners of war who in 1941 were engaged in construction work in areas west of the Smolensk region and who fell into the hands of German fascist hangmen in the summer of 1941, after the withdrawal of the Soviet troops from the Smolensk area.

"Beyond doubt Goebbels' slanderers are now trying with lies and calumnies to cover up the bloody crimes of the Hitlerite gangsters. In their clumsily concocted fabrication about the numerous graves which the Germans allegedly discovered near Smolensk, the Hitlerite liars mentioned the village of Gniezdova. But, like the swindlers they are, they remain silent about the fact that it was near the village of Gniezdova that the archaeological excavations of the historic 'Gniezdova burial place' were made."

Amidst the energetic cursing of Soviet lies many of those present sit in silence, overwhelmed by grief.

Some days later, a smaller crowd assembles in Czapski's office, a handful of former prisoners from the three camps, along with relatives of the missing men. Czapski does his best to relay the more detailed information now in his possession, informing them that a team of Polish Red Cross officials has been sent to investigate, as well as an international commission organised by the Germans, although the Soviets are refusing permission for the formal International Red Cross investigation requested by the Polish government-in-exile. Confirmation has arrived from London that the bodies of General Smorawiński and General Bohatyrewicz have been conclusively identified amongst the dead.

"I have been asked to clarify one vital point to you." Czapski looks up from his papers. "It seems that when the Nazis made their initial announcement it was with a view to creating the maximum propaganda impact. They are doubtless aware of the number of our officers who are missing and rounded up the numbers accordingly. However, the facts on this matter are now completely clear: the number of bodies has been confirmed to be less than half the original stated and correlates almost exactly with the number of prisoners missing from Kozelsk camp, that is, around 4,000 men. Given the relative proximity of Katyń to Kozelsk, it makes sense that the bodies discovered there belong to inmates of that camp. This terrible discovery leaves unanswered, of course, the question as to the whereabouts of our comrades from the camps of Starobelsk and Ostashkov," continues Czapski. "But it leaves little room for hope, I'm afraid."

Those few unhappy survivors of Kozelsk drift outside slowly, followed by relatives of the murdered men, some clinging to one another, others alone.

Młynarski and Kozłowski linger by the door. As if by tacit agreement, they wait for everyone else to leave.

Młynarski speaks first: "Do you think there's any chance the others might have been treated differently, Józef?"

Czapski does not answer.

They all know of the startling similarities between the three camps. They were all emptied at the same time, with the same procedures, the same rituals and promises.

You are leaving, said Kirshin, *for a place where I would like to go myself.*

"I have some pictures." Czapski draws from a large brown envelope a sheaf of photographs. "I did not have the heart to share them more widely."

The first shows a group of delegates gathered around a large trench, at the bottom of which lie dozens of bodies squashed together like sardines, all wearing Polish army uniform. In the second picture, the bodies are seen more closely. Amongst the men gathered around the grave Kozłowski recognises the head of the Polish Red Cross, Skarżyński. A priest stands a few paces away from the others, his face averted from the grave. The third photograph shows two men, one in German uniform, the other wearing medical robes, conducting a post-mortem on a body. A group of civilians is gathered around them, observing their work; one of the civilians has a notebook; another a camera. At the edge of the group stand several German officers.

"Their hands are tied with rope," Młynarski scrutinises one of the photographs carefully. "Do we know how they were killed?"

"They were shot in the base of the skull." Czapski indicates a trajectory that passes from the back of the head to a point just above the eyebrow. "A single shot. It's a classic Cheka method."

Dr Dadej, dressed in rags, points to a small, round hole on the left-hand side of the base of a skull. Kozłowski can almost smell the damp scent of the snow, the cold penetrating his nostrils, Dadej holding the skull up in silence, his eyes obscured behind filthy glasses. At the time, it was Dadej's hands which he noticed: the dirt under his fingernails. How could a doctor allow himself to fall so far? The sense of shame which kept him from naming Dadej to Tadeusz Biały as they walked back to the barracks...

"There is one more picture. Of General Bohatyrewicz. I'm afraid it's rather gruesome."

There is a uniform, complete with the insignia of a general: gold braid, and a row of medals, a four-cornered hat, a greatcoat, a belt, and leather boots. There is a skull and there are bones, and what is left of the flesh and muscle is black and sunken. The hair is still thick; a moustache rests upon bared teeth. A small round hole is visible above the right brow.

Before Kozłowski, more vivid than ever, are the memories of those final days before they left Starobelsk. His last sight of Tomasz Chęciński: that absurd hat crammed on his head, the shabby coat, his head turning back towards them as he marched towards the gate, a smile as brilliant as the spring sunshine on his face. The words scratched into the ceiling of the railway carriages at Kharkov: "They have brought us to Kharkov, they are getting out and bringing cars..."

The silence that surrounds his comrades from Starobelsk has changed, no longer an absence but a sinister presence: a threat, a black raven, a hooded executioner. His friends have not simply disappeared, they have fallen into a place of darkness where there is no oxygen, no colour, no light. No life.

Hanka comes to see him one afternoon in May when he is on duty. She has been busy the last few weeks, she explains. The cadets are preparing for exams, so she has not had any time off.

"I'm sorry," she says. "I know how busy you are."

He looks at her carefully, as a doctor examines a patient: there are dark shadows under her eyes; her fingernails, he notices, are bitten to the quick.

There is nowhere private where they can talk: outside, the heat weighs heavy as a boulder; inside, the ward is filled with patients.

"I'm due to finish soon. Can you wait?"

She nods.

"See you in the mess?"

They sit at the end of a long table, trying somehow to keep separate from the hundreds of others who are seated near them, talking and laughing.

"So what do you think, Zbyszek?" she says, eventually. "Was my brother shot in the head and thrown into a ditch, like those unfortunate men from Kozelsk?"

"Just because they've found the men from one camp, it doesn't necessarily follow that all the prisoners were treated in the same way—" Even to himself he sounds unconvincing.

"Do you still think it's possible that Tomasz drowned on the way to Kolyma?"

"It's as plausible an explanation as any other."

"But you don't believe he could be alive."

"It is my conviction," replies Kozłowski, in a low, emphatic voice, "that until such a time as their bodies are discovered there will always remain a possibility – however faint and improbable it may be - that they are still alive."

She contemplates him with something close to disgust. "Your *conviction*? Goodness, the way you express yourself, Zbyszek. Really."

She taps a cigarette from a packet and lights it, not meeting his gaze. Her hands, he notices, are trembling.

"You know," she says, suddenly, "during those early months of the war, when we learned that you and Tomasz had been captured together, Gosia and I used to tell each other a story: when it was all over and you both returned to Poland, Gosia would introduce you to me. She was convinced that we would hit it off. She even used to joke about us all getting married. Why are you looking at me like that?" She bursts out laughing. "It was just a joke, Zbyszek! Goodness, you take everything so seriously!" She pours wine into her glass and drinks it down in one gulp, avoiding his gaze. "It was just a silly joke to cheer ourselves up," she repeats, softly.

9. A happy little place

Palestine, 1944

When, in January 1944, the Polish II Corps is finally transferred from Palestine to Italy, there is little time to say goodbye. On the day before his departure Kozłowski has the afternoon off, so he climbs onto a crowded bus and makes his way to the little building on the outskirts of Jerusalem which serves as a school for the *junacy*.

Through the open window he catches a glimpse of a row of tousle-haired heads facing the front of the class. Snub noses, freckled cheeks; one boy staring idly at the ceiling, another – only his hand is visible - twiddling his pencil in his ear.

"...an example of the vocative being 'Dear Leszek!' or 'Ewa, come here!', 'O Caesar!'... Jurek, give that back! No, Jurek, that's not a vocative, I'm telling you to give Grzegorz his book back..."

Laughter. Kozłowski lights a cigarette and closes his eyes, enjoying the warmth of the sun on his face. He remains like this for several minutes, oblivious to the scraping of chairs and banging of desks that signify the end of the lesson.

"You look contented as a cat."

He opens his eyes to find Hanka standing in front of him. "Nice place for a school."

"Isn't it? I've fallen on my feet. I get to sit out the rest of the war in a beautiful, warm country, safe from danger, doing a job I love."

"Now you put it like that, I'm envious."

They stroll along the pleasant, tree-lined street towards a small park where mothers sit on benches while their babies sleep. Children play on swings, their chatter drifting towards them.

"It's funny," he says, "I never dreamed of travelling the way some people do. Leaving Wilno for Warsaw was enough for me. And yet, I've been halfway across the globe. When this war is over I want to find myself a little patch of earth somewhere, a city apartment or a house in the country, I don't mind which, but I want to stay in one place and put down roots, like a tree."

It hovers between them, the meaning behind his words, as it has on so many occasions during their conversations over the past few months. This is what I want after the war, he is saying but not saying: do you want that too?

"When I was a child," she replies, "I had a map of the world pinned to the wall of my bedroom and I made little flags which I stuck in all the countries I planned to visit when I was older."

"Where did you dream of going?"

"Oh, crazy places: the Antarctic, Africa, Australia – my choices were dictated solely by the wildlife living there. I'd read somewhere that certain animals are being endangered by man's desire to hunt, and I decided that when I grew up I would travel to these countries to protect innocent tigers and elephants from evil men with rifles. As you can see, protecting innocent children from the evils of poor grammar is the nearest I got to fulfilling that particular ambition."

He laughs, gazing at her tenderly. "You're so like Tomasz – I know, I know – you don't like me to say it, but it's true. Your idealistic passion, your need to be of service—"

"We are less alike than you think." Her voice is terse. "The biggest difference being that I am alive and he is dead."

He is too shocked to speak.

"I'm sorry, Zbyszek—"

"No, it's my fault." Flushing, he hurries to cut her off. "Shall we sit down somewhere?"

"I need to get back. The break is only fifteen minutes."

On the way to the school he tries to take her hand, as he would normally do, but she affects not to see it, reaching up to adjust the strap on her bag. He feels foolish, as if Hanka were a stranger whom he has mistakenly greeted as an old friend.

"I had another card from Elżbieta."

Hanka seems relieved at the change of subject. "How is she getting on?"

"They seem happy. They've set up an entire Polish village on the land of an Indian prince – a school, a chapel, shops, everything they need."

"Has she found some friends?"

"She speaks a lot about a Scottish engineer who helps them with various things – I can't remember his name, McLaren or Macdonald or something. A Presbyterian."

"Her English is good, then?"

"I've no idea."

She studies him carefully. "Would you mind if she developed a – a friendship with another man? I mean, after your brother's death—"

"Goodness! It had never occurred to me. Do you think so?"

"You said she spoke a lot about him—"

He considers the matter. It is true: Elżbieta's letters are full of the helpfulness of Donald or Harold or whatever it is he is called. "I hadn't given it any thought, but if it came to it, no, of course I wouldn't mind. Let her make a new life for herself if she can. She has every right to do so. We all do, don't you think?"

She looks down at her hands. "Of course we do."

In the school yard, a young cat twines itself around Hanka's legs.

"You're our little bit of wildlife, aren't you, puss?"

The cat flops onto its side and stretches out, purring, as Hanka strokes its stomach.

The boys are already waiting. Through the half-open door Kozłowski glimpses elbows resting on desks, feet shuffling restlessly on the floor, crumpled bits of paper being thrown across the classroom.

"You'd better go before they start misbehaving."

He waits, looking at the curve of her back as she continues stroking the cat. Eventually, she stands up, fixing him with her clear, light gaze.

"So it's off to war with you. I'm glad that I don't have to worry too much about you being killed. Although I suppose they bomb medical stations too."

"That's a cheering thought."

She raises her hand to touch his cheek. "Keep safe, Dr Kozłowski."

He kisses her once on the cheek then, again, softly, on the lips. "Write to me."

"I will."

"Ooh, look! Miss has a boyfriend!"

A skinny boy with blond hair that has been shaved to his skull stands at the door, grinning. There is a scraping of chairs as his classmates get up and soon he is joined by a crowd of curious faces peering out to witness the entertaining spectacle of their teacher embracing a thin young army officer with wire-framed glasses and curly dark hair.

"Ooh Miss! Do you love him, Miss?"

With a quick squeeze of her hand, he walks away.

"Does she love you back, Lieutenant?" calls another boy after him. "Are you going to marry her?"

"Mind your own business and go back to class."

"Back to your seats, please, boys."

"Is he going to Italy, Miss?" asks the blond boy.

"Yes."

"I wish I was going too. I'd like to fight the Germans."

"You'll get your chance soon enough. Meanwhile, you need to learn something so that when you've finished shooting Germans you have a job to go to."

"I'll look after you while your boyfriend's gone."

"That's enough now!"

It is a happy little place, the cadet school in Palestine.

10. Victory, at last

They arrive in Italy in the winter and go into battle in spring. The delicate white blossom that normally covers the trees at this time of the year has not had a chance to grow: the bombs that ravaged the monastery of Monte Cassino have ripped off their branches, leaving only stumps, a forest of amputated limbs. It looks, thinks Kozłowski, surveying the field of battle from the medical station just behind the lines, like the set for a particularly gloomy opera.

As doctor to the 16th Battalion of the 6th Lwowski Light Artillery, Kozłowski spends his days in a field dressing station patching together the torn bodies of his men (since he has been assigned to the battalion, he thinks of them as his). Stretchers are carried down a narrow track from the ridges above him, bringing patient after patient from dawn until late into the night. The casualty rate is high, the injuries often fatal; wave after wave of soldiers go up and few return. It ought to be grim, yet it is not: there is a sense of shared purpose among these men who have come from every corner of the world, from America and New Zealand, France and Poland. There is a powerful belief among them that they are the stronger side, that they will, eventually, prevail. With the trials of battle comes the joy of brotherhood and comradeship. He tries to describe it to Hanka in a letter but he cannot. On paper, it sounds macabre to find oneself filled with the joy of living when faced with so much death.

The second week in May marks the first wave of intensive attacks on the monastery. On the night of May 16th 1944, the 16th Battalion attacks enemy positions and takes the northern section of what is known as Phantom Ridge. Despite heavy German counter-attacks, the terrain is held. That night they go up the hill, the elation that comes with victory pushing them onwards.

It is not yet midday. Kozłowski sits with his back against the brick wall of the farmhouse, snatching a meal while he can: a slice of white bread and an enamel cup filled with sweet black coffee. Beyond him, in the distance, columns of smoke rise from the hill; at its top, in silhouette, is the ruined majesty of the monastery, flanked by the jagged trees. The sky is the palest blue, tiny wisps of cloud floating across it like feathers. He scarcely registers the constant booming of the mortars, nor the rat-a-tat of machine guns. Then, unexpectedly, the gunfire ceases and, for a few brief moments, there is silence. Above him, a skylark begins to sing, its voice perfect and clear, as if it has been waiting only for this moment. On the ground next to him, ants crawl in single file, oblivious to the warring giants above them, each carrying a minute crumb of Kozłowski's bread over the mountains of dried mud, curdled by thousands of boots, which surround the dressing station. A short distance away, untouched by the endless comings and goings of the stretcher bearers, a patch of grass grows lustily, and wild flowers blossom among the green blades, tiny blooms in delicate pinks, yellows and whites. He thinks of Edward Ralski and his rapture at the arrival of spring, sees him crouching at the base of the poplar tree, his delicate fingers touching the tiny green shoots which had braved the chilly March air, looking up at Czapski, eyes shining.

A bumble bee passes from one flower to another, making the long stems bend with its weight. How do bees fare in battle? Are they untroubled by the bullets as they fly across the battlefield in search of pollen? Or does a passing missile sometimes catch their tiny bodies and bring them down, to lie helplessly in the mud, their little black legs cycling endlessly? He smiles: his thoughts are becoming absurd. The call comes from inside: "Incoming wounded, doctor!" It is time to get back to work.

Dearest Zbyszek,

It is not even six months since the army left and yet it seems like years. I read about the progress of the war when I can find a newspaper; sometimes, if I'm lucky, I am able to listen to the

BBC. Mrs Pilatowa has made friends with the British cultural attaché and we are invited, from time to time, to take tea at his club. It is a most peculiar place, filled with British officials in long shorts who are too old or too decrepit to take part in the war, reading their copies of The Times *or snoozing in armchairs.*

Meanwhile, my cadets continue as mischievous and troublesome as ever. They ask me daily if I have news of my 'boyfriend in Italy' and nag me to tell them all about your exploits. When I told them that you are a doctor they were most disappointed: not enough shooting or killing for their taste! Enclosed is a small memento of Palestine. With all my best wishes for your safety and good health. Say hello to Major Czapski if you see him.

Hanka

Between the folded sheet of paper is a pressed orange blossom. It has left a small, damp imprint on the page. He raises it to his nose and sniffs it carefully: the tiniest remnant of its scent lingers, like a ghost.

In May 1945 the Polish II Corps march, victorious, through newly-liberated Bologna. With a group of his comrades Kozłowski goes to a bar and drinks until he passes out. When, some days later, news comes of the end of the war in Europe, he leans back in his chair and thinks, for the first time since 1939: what next?

11. Filling the silence

London, 1946

"You don't think it's something you might have mentioned to me before now?"

His anger makes her nervous, so that she, in turn, reacts angrily. "I never promised you anything, Zbyszek."

"Didn't you? Well, silly me, I thought you didn't need to."

Hanka is silent, staring down at her hands which are twisting themselves around a small linen handkerchief. Round and round, until it is taut, like a rope.

She is renting a room in Hampstead in the house of an elderly Polish professor, the uncle of a friend of hers. Kozłowski, meanwhile, has found digs near Gloucester Road which he is sharing with three other demobbed army medics. There is no privacy to be had in either case, so they have arranged to meet outside, on Hampstead Heath. It is a weekday, and the wild expanse of parkland is almost empty.

They stand side by side on Parliament Hill, looking down at the vast city sprawling beneath them. Kozłowski wants to be exhilarated by this sweeping view of London, the dome of St Paul's just visible in the distance amidst the devastation of the City; he wants them to be standing here full of hope for the future, planning the next stage of their life together. Instead, he looks at her tall, slim profile and wonders why he has understood her so little. She asks him for a cigarette and as he cups his hand around hers to light it he feels the warmth of her skin although she shivers, pulling her raincoat tight around her body.

"All the time I was in Palestine, and then Egypt, I tried to put the future from my mind. Then, at a certain moment, I realised that I no longer had an excuse not to think ahead: the war was over; I had a choice between going home or staying abroad. I knew that for you there is no possibility of returning to Poland—"

"I never said—"

"We both know you would be mad to go back, Zbyszek."

She continues, speaking hurriedly as if she is afraid of being interrupted. She tells him that she has examined carefully the arguments on either side of the debate: her own suffering at the hands of the Soviets; the death of her parents and the fate of her brother; the permanent loss of her family's home in Lwów; the probability that she will be regarded with suspicion by the authorities and the certainty that the promised elections in January will deliver a government controlled by Moscow. On the other side of the balance is her family: her eldest brother, Jan, in Warsaw, his health weakened after two years in Pawiak prison, the loss of his wife meaning that he will struggle to support his two young children. She lays out the same arguments that have preoccupied his mind for months, but she marshals them in favour of a different conclusion.

"I'm not stupid. I have no illusions about what I am going back to. But if I stay here, or if I go to Canada or Australia or wherever they will have me, I will always be an exile. Please," she takes his hand, "I don't blame anyone for not going back. I understand, truly I do. But I have a brother in Warsaw who needs my help, and a niece and a nephew – two children without a mother. They're all that remain of my family. I also have a longing – the most intense longing, Zbyszek, I can scarcely describe it to you – for my home."

She looks almost old, sitting on the park bench with her shoulders slumped.

"But what if home is no longer what you hope it will be? What if home, too, is an exile?"

"Stalin won't live forever. I had a letter from a friend and he says that he's excited about rebuilding our country. He says there's a real thirst to move on, to put the past aside and build a better future."

Kozłowski has seen letters like this, urging soldiers to return to the motherland, typewritten missives written, no doubt, by the NKVD or its newly-minted Polish equivalent.

"You sound just like Tomasz. Always looking for the idealistic argument."

"That's just it, don't you see? It's always about Tomasz! It's suffocating me!" Seeing the look of shock on his face she softens, taking his hand. "He's gone, Zbyszek, and there is nothing you can do to bring him back. You and I cannot fulfil their dreams for them, however much we would like to. Our love is just an echo, a cheap mirror-image of the real thing. A proxy love."

"I – I don't know what you mean—" He is suddenly close to tears. "What do you mean?"

She is silent, contemplating him with weary regret.

"But I love you, Hanka. If you asked me to return to Poland with you, I would do it happily, whatever the risks."

She smiles now, raising her hand to touch his cheek, as she always does. "No. It won't do."

But don't you see? he wants to say. I have waited for you. I have put off all of my decisions until you came. I thought that it would not matter where I was, because you would be there with me and I would not have to face the future alone. Now you are telling me that the memory of my friend is getting in the way of my love for you, that you and I are just stand-ins for Tomasz and Gosia, as if I don't see you for who you really are, or somehow do not let you breathe. But it's not true, Hanka. I love you not because you remind me of Tomasz but because of who you are.

All of these things he would like to say but he does not, because he knows that she is right. And he knows that the fact that he cannot say it is what she does not love about him: his inability to speak of what he feels is, to her, as grave a sin as ignorance.

He sees now that Hanka's easy, joyful correspondence, alive with observations about the world around her—

Did you know that, under the Romans...?

I discovered only recently that in medieval times...

There was a strange, blue-feathered bird in the garden the other day...

—had not been a signal of their shared understanding, but of her reluctance to discuss a shared future. He had simply filled her silence with his own desires.

They part at Victoria station, where she boards a train to Paris, thence to Berlin and Warsaw. Despite her bright promises of future visits, holidays in England and trips home to Poland for him, they both know that they will not meet again. He watches the train move slowly off, the steam rising into the sooty London sky until, swallowed by the clouds of smoke, it disappears from view.

12. Sea legs!

en route for Canada, 1946

Dearest Zbyszek,

I am so sorry we missed each other in London. We were there for such a short time, and it seems you arrived a few days after me. I was looking forward to introducing you to Edward, and the children were longing to see their Uncle Zbyszek. You would not recognise them – two tall children, brown as berries! Well, Zosia is nearly an adult now, so pretty and cheerful, you would not believe she's the same girl who almost died in Meshed. Well, well, our grand family reunion will just have to wait. Once we are settled you must come and visit. Or perhaps you are thinking of settling in Canada yourself? So many Poles are heading this way. Edward's brother will put us up to start with, but hopefully we will soon find a place of our own and then we can think about guests. I am writing to you, by the way, from the boat. We have been aboard for nearly five days now and already I feel completely at home – I have found my 'sea legs', as they say! Well, dear Zbyszek, I will close now because they are calling us to supper. It has been a long war and there is still a great deal of sadness in my heart when I think about what we have left behind: my beautiful little Magda, and dearest Ignacy, of course. I comfort myself that they are together in heaven, may the Virgin Mary protect them! I wish you all the best for your future and look forward to seeing you again soon.

Your loving (former) sister-in-law,

Elżbieta

PS Your odd little friend, Felicja, is to go to the United States. Imagine that! She has relatives there, apparently, who are willing to take her in.

13. The lucky few

London, 1946

A blast of warm, wet air greets Kozłowski as he enters the dark basement of the Polish Air Force Club in Earl's Court. He pushes his way to the bar, past the crowd of men drinking warm ale in pints, conversing in loud voices about their wartime exploits in the skies above Europe.

"There I was, almost out of fuel, and Jerry comes at me – da-da-da-da-da! My wing is hit. I'm losing height. I'm going to have to bale out unless I can get her up a little. I push down the throttle, lift up her nose and suddenly I'm above him. I've got a clear line of sight on the little bastard. I can even see the fellow's teeth! I swing her round, take the controls and – bosh! He's hit! Suddenly he's in a spin, heading straight for the Channel. I push her on just a little bit further; the old bird is in a bad way now and I'm losing height. The white cliffs are up ahead. If I go any lower I'm done for. But then – thank Heavens! – I see a nice flat field in front of me so I set her down amidst the cows and I am back in good old Blighty!..."

They are lucky, he reflects, these lucky few: their war was fought entirely on the winning side, from high up in the air. It was a war of daring exploits from which great yarns are still being spun, thrilling stories to enthral impressionable young women. And yet, even the pilots are not immune to the subtle change that has come about since the end of the war. Some people do not understand why so many Poles remain in Britain.

"Why don't you go home?" they ask. "The war is over now. You're taking our jobs."

He takes his beer to a table and sits down to wait for Młynarski, who is in London for a few days, en route for New York. A young boy with a shock of blond hair and an unmistakeably Slavic face makes his way to the table next to him, two pints of beer balanced carefully in his hands. He is wearing baggy trousers and a broad-shouldered jacket in a style which Kozłowski has never seen before. The boy dumps the beers on the table and sits down next to his friend, who wears a Fedora pushed back from his forehead. The boys are talking about cards, girls, bars, and jazz, their language peppered with American slang which Kozłowski does not understand. Neither boy can be older than eighteen, yet they possess an air of sophistication which seems to belong to another era, a future to which they evidently belong and Kozłowski – he realises – does not. Another boy joins the pair, squeezing past Kozłowski with a "You don't mind, do you?" He shifts slightly, taking small sips of the warm, bitter ale which he has not yet learned to love, and glances at his watch, hoping that Młynarski will arrive soon. He feels out of place in this crowded bar full of Poles who seem so at home.

Finally, there he is, tanned and elegant in a dark woollen overcoat, apologising good-naturedly as he dodges left and right in an effort not to spill people's drinks, before popping like a lemon pip from the scrum.

"Sorry I'm late. It's snowing out there, can you believe it?" Młynarski shakes a dusting of snow from his overcoat, hanging it carefully over the back of a chair which he borrows from the boys at the next table. "How wonderful to see you, Zbyszek! It's been so long." Ignoring Kozłowski's half-drunk pint of beer, Młynarski produces a bottle of vodka from one pocket and two shot glasses from the other. "What? What are you smiling at?"

"I was remembering the first time I saw you at the railway line in Jarmolice. You, Feliks, Zygmunt and Olgierd. You all seemed so terribly sophisticated. I was envious as hell." He laughs. "Nothing has changed!"

The first hour is spent catching up on old news: Młynarski's illness in Cairo, his service in Italy, the long journey to London en route to New York, where his sisters await him. As he listens, Kozłowski realises that the prospect of life abroad holds no fear for his friend and that it is with no sense of trepidation that Młynarski is about to embark on the long Atlantic crossing; rather, it is with a feeling of intense relief at leaving Europe behind to return to a country where the war has been lived at a distance. When Kozłowski, in turn, tells him of Hanka's decision to return to Poland, Młynarski listens sympathetically. With an instinctive understanding of the misery that is threatening to engulf his friend, he gallantly keeps Kozłowski company while he drinks too much and, at the end of the evening, escorts him back to his lodgings. The snow has stopped momentarily and the sparse traffic throws up a slushy spray which falls into the gutters. Rare passers-by hurry along, heads down, hands deep in their pockets. They walk along Harrington Gardens to Ashburn Place, Młynarski steering his unsteady friend across Gloucester Road.

"You don't have to accompany me, you know. I'm quite capable of walking home by myself."

"I'm sure you are, but since I'm off to New York tomorrow I'll enjoy your company while I can, if you don't mind."

"Everybody's leaving. You're going to America, Czapski's in Paris…"

"Now, now! You're getting maudlin. Come on, let's get you home before you freeze to death."

"I don't have a home!"

"Goodness, Zbyszek, no wonder you rarely drink! Come now, exile is a grand Polish tradition. You'll soon find some friends and then you can make your own little Poland right here in London."

"I can't think of anything worse."

Młynarski laughs. "Maybe. But you will get used to it and you will find friends – whether Polish or English hardly matters. As soon as you start working you'll find your feet again, Zbyszek. Once you have a job it will all flow from there. You'll see."

Kozłowski is dimly conscious of the simple kindness of his friend. He pats Młynarski clumsily on the shoulder and nods to show that he understands what is meant, even if he is not yet ready to act on it.

As they say goodbye, Kozłowski has the sense that he is letting go of the last familiar person in his life. He wants to cling to Młynarski and beg him not to leave him here alone, in this strange country. Yet, as they embrace, it is Młynarski who has tears in his eyes.

"Look at me! Where's my stiff upper lip, eh? You see why I'm much better suited to life with those brash Americans whilst you, my friend, have just the right measure of reserve to do well in England. You'll find yourself a nice little house in a quiet suburban street and it will probably be twenty years before you and your neighbours ever work up the courage to say good morning to each other."

"Just because I don't wear my heart on my sleeve doesn't mean I don't have feelings!"

Młynarski shakes him fondly by the shoulders. "I'm joking, you silly chump."

Kozłowski sits down abruptly on the doorstep, his head aching.

"Why are we here and not them, Bronek? I can't bear it."

"How about you find your door key," replies Młynarski, lightly, after a pause, "and we'll get you inside?"

Kozłowski feels his way along the corridor in the dark, fumbling clumsily with his key for several minutes before he finally manages to insert it into the lock. No late-night guests, no noise, no smoking, no alcohol, no drunkenness, the landlady had said. He stumbles inside, tripping over a pair of boots which have been left carelessly by the door.

The blackout blinds have not yet been taken down and the room is impenetrably dark, but his two roommates do not stir as he crashes about. His head aches: the effects of the alcohol have now worn off, leaving him with a raging thirst and a sense of dull exhaustion. He stretches out on his bed without undressing and closes his eyes.

"Come on, then," calls someone impatiently. *"Tell us what you can see."*

14. Oh, Gosia!

London, 1946

The official who receives Kozłowski at the offices of the government-in-exile in South Kensington contemplates him with a curious mixture of pity and envy.

"Perhaps you might consider giving us a deposition, Dr Kozłowski, about your time in Starobelsk?"

"I'm sure Major Czapski has said everything that could possibly be said about it."

"Still, we would be grateful if you would consider it. I will fetch your letter directly."

The letter is from his mother, written in the autumn of 1945, and sent via a friend who managed to leave Poland in the chaos following the end of the war and who, passing through London on his way to the United States, left the missive in the care of the military authorities, where it has awaited him ever since. It is the first correspondence he has received from his mother in over two years. He reads it there and then, seated in a leather armchair in the deserted lobby.

Gosia came to Warsaw in early 1944. She was not well. She had clearly not been eating and she seemed depressed. She took a leave of absence from the chemical institute and kind Dr Robel managed to get her a pass to take the train to Warsaw. She wanted to be at home, she said. Such a joy it was to have one of our children back under our roof! I fed her and looked after her, and by the summer she was almost restored to health; she was going to go back to Kraków but for some reason the Germans stopped their work at the Institute so she stayed on with us. I was glad at first, but then – why did she do it? – Oh, Zbyszek, why didn't I stop her? – she joined the Uprising …

His mother interrupts herself, her grief for the fate not just of her daughter but of her city expressed in a series of incoherent half-sentences which tumble over each other in her desire to convey – for the first time since the beginning of the war – exactly what she feels:

…the destruction wrought on our city – burning the buildings as they retreated – Józefów thankfully too far, remains untouched – Gosia trying to help, she never took up arms, tending to the wounded men – they took them out and shot them like dogs – boys some of them, just boys – you remember the Wiśniewski twins? Killed, both of them – just boys… Your father's health, worse than ever – the final blow, dear Gosia, little Gosia, my darling girl – Not even a gun that killed her but an infection. She became ill and there was no medicine to treat her. They brought her back here and I looked after her myself, but it was too late. She died of sepsis in September 1944. She kept talking about Tomasz. Was that her young man? What happened to him, Zbyszek? Do you know?

"Dr Kozłowski?"

Abruptly recalled to the present, Kozłowski looks up to find the official leaning over him. The reception area is busy now as people arrive for a meeting.

"Dr Kozłowski," begins the official, discreetly, "I wonder if we might impose upon you? One of our administrators here, Mrs Pożarska, asked if you would do her the kindness of visiting her in her office. It will only take a minute …"

Kozłowski folds up the letter, glancing only at the final line.

Dearest Zbyszek. Stay in England. We love you. Try to find Staś.

He follows the official because he is too dazed to refuse, up the thickly-carpeted stairs to an office on the first floor.

The walls are cluttered with paintings depicting scenes from Polish history; above a leather-topped desk hangs a portrait of General Sikorski. Mrs Pożarska is seated on the edge of a polished mahogany chair, her ankles neatly crossed, in an attitude of nervous expectation. She wears a cardigan draped over her shoulders, a thin gold necklace with a single pearl around her neck. On her left hand is a signet ring.

"Thank you for taking the time to see me, Dr Kozłowski." Her eyes are small and bird-like, almost black in colour. She hesitates before continuing, her voice high-pitched. "Dr Kozłowski, when you were in Starobelsk did you by any chance know a man named Olgierd Szpakowski?"

"Olgierd? Yes, he was in the same block as me."

She blinks rapidly, as if she had not, after all, been expecting this reply. "He is – was – my brother."

A vague memory stirs, of Olgierd mentioning that his sister worked as an administrator for the government-in-exile.

"I would be grateful, Dr Kozłowski, for any information concerning my brother that you are able to recall. How did he cope, for example, with your – ah – situation?"

"Olgierd?" he almost laughs. "Olgierd coped extremely well with our situation, Mrs Pożarska, better than any of us. He always seemed to know precisely what was needed. He was very generous, too. He shared everything he had."

Her little black eyes bore into him, waiting for him to tell her more. He hesitates, searching in his memories for something he can say to her. He cannot mention the arguments, nor his own distaste for Olgierd's political views. *Look at you, with your Red newspapers and your lectures! Why don't you go and move in with Commissar Kirshin while you're at it?*

"I remember, Mrs Pożarska, that he had a sheepskin rug which he had somehow managed to drag all the way from Poland."

"A rug?"

So you think Stalin had the right idea invading Poland, is that it?"

"Yes."

She shakes her head, as if trying to evade a wasp. "He never had a rug that I knew of. Tell me, Dr Kozłowski, what is your opinion concerning the perpetrators of the Katyń massacre? Do you think it was the Nazis who did it, as the judges of Nuremberg would have us believe? Or was it the Bolsheviks?"

"There is no doubt in my mind that it was the NKVD who murdered those men."

She nods with a kind of savage pleasure. "Some people here understood. Ambassador O'Malley, he spoke the truth. He realised that it couldn't have been the Germans, because of the trees."

It occurs to him that the woman is mad. "I'm sorry, I don't understand. The trees?"

"The trees they planted on top of the graves at Katyń. It was obvious that they were over two years old, which means the Germans could never have done it. Anyone with eyes could see it, but *they* were only concerned with keeping Stalin happy. One might as well try to placate a rattlesnake." The words are spoken with a bitter hatred. "It still amazes me to think how men like Churchill and Roosevelt could have been so taken in by him! Now – *now* they're beginning to see the truth. Now that they have given away half of Europe to him, they see who he really is. And yet still they say 'Let's see how the elections go'!"

He wants desperately to get away from this stuffy room, with its decaying antiques and ancient portraits, from this atmosphere of furious patriotism. He wants to think about Gosia, and his mother, and Hanka, although he does not want to think about any of these things.

"And my brother, Dr Kozłowski? All those poor men from Starobelsk? The NKVD murdered them, too, didn't they?"

As he hurries down the stairs to emerge, finally, into the fresh air, a memory accosts him, a stranger intent on violence: his first night in the desecrated church, he and Tomasz Chęciński squeezing themselves into place, side by side, amongst the thousands of men stacked up in rows like farm animals. A conversation.

"Dr Kozłowski, I was wondering –"

"Please, call me Zbyszek – It seems idiotic to be so formal, under the circumstances."

Chęciński smiles in relief. "I'm Tomasz." He hesitates. "I know Kozłowski is a fairly common name but - I don't suppose you have a sister, do you?"

"A sister? Yes, I do. She's in Kraków. She's just finished university."

"Her name isn't Gosia, is it, by any chance?"

"Yes. My sister's name is Gosia."

Oh, Gosia!

He walks fast, past the tube station and the little gaggle of Poles hanging outside the new Polish café on Thurloe Street. He wants to get away from it all, from the memories of the past, the endless chatter amongst exiles about what might have been, what should have been, what Churchill said and what Churchill did, the legitimate government and the puppet government, rights, dues, insults, national pride... Staś, Hanka, Tomasz, Gosia, Ignacy, his mother's grief... the whole damned lot of them, weighing him down as if they would drown him!

On and on he walks, heedless of the direction he is taking, oblivious to the red mansion blocks and white stuccoed houses, to the busy square lined with shops and the broad street with army barracks on one side and grand hospital buildings set in parkland on the other, on and on, until, eventually, the street gives way to a wide expanse of dirty sky and there looms before him an enormous power station with four tall chimneys pouring out white smoke. He crosses the bridge and follows the river bank, past wharves lined with cranes, flat barges laden with steel and sacks of coal. On he goes, through the gritty, busy, scarred landscape, until, unexpectedly, the Houses of Parliament materialise on the opposite bank. He stops, finally, to lean against the river wall, looking down at the mighty, murky River Thames. It flows past, majestically indifferent to the turmoil within him. What was it his landlady said the other day? "It's all water under the bridge." She was referring to the war, and the loss of her husband. "We have to get on with our lives, don't we?"

He doesn't have to stay in England, he reasons. He could go to Canada, where Elżbieta and her new husband are beginning their new life; or Australia, like Andrzej, or America, like Bronek. New, open countries, unencumbered by the past. Doctors are everywhere in short supply and, thanks to Dr Cochran, his ability to speak English means that he can take his pick. For the first time since 1939 he is free to decide where he will go and what he will do. Except, of course, that in reality it is not a choice at all, because the real choice would be to turn back the clock and resume his pre-war existence. To walk into the Hospital of the Holy Spirit in Warsaw on a summer's morning and go directly to the office of Dr Levittoux to discuss, over coffee, the patients to be seen that morning, before setting out on his rounds. To undo history and wind back time, that would be the thing.

Things are what they are, though, and, being so, the only choice is to go on. And if he is to go on then why not let it be in this vast, indifferent city? Different from Warsaw, of course, little, lovely Warsaw, ruined now, shattered, flattened, and dark. Not as grand or romantic as Paris, where Czapski feels so at home, nor brash and modern, like New York. It is grey, mild, wet most of the time, but it will do.

It is all water under the bridge, she said. Life must go on. She had continued, chattering tediously about keeping a stiff upper lip, got to look to the future, those of us lucky enough to survive, etc. Cliché after cliché in the service of a vague but overwhelming desire to push away the darkness of the last few years. The problem being that those lucky enough to have survived must climb over fields of corpses in order to arrive at their future: that is the price of coming through.

We, the living.

He sees it, now, with utter clarity, that everything he has experienced since September 1939 is no longer relevant, either to himself or to anyone else. The past is gone. His comrades from Starobelsk will never be seen again, his brother and sister are dead, and those friends, like

Czapski and Młynarski, who shared so much with him, have moved on to make new lives in new countries, far away from Poland. And Hanka? Hanka, too, it transpired, wanted to start afresh, free from the burden of his memories.

As a wintry drizzle begins to fall, threatening to extinguish his cigarette, Kozłowski comes to a decision to place the past out of reach. He will face resolutely forward, ignoring the shadows that queue patiently behind him, four thousand Eurydices waiting for the moment when he will turn back, urging him not to turn back. He will take himself far from those areas where Poles gather; he will find a job not in a Polish hospital but an English one; he will speak not in Polish but in English. And he will never fool himself into believing that he will one day return home.

II
Unanswered questions

1. Dr Margaret Maclaren

Kozłowski has been walking all morning in an effort to distract himself before the interview at University College Hospital, rehearsing in his head the phrases he has prepared:

Extensive experience in general surgery whilst serving in the British 8th Army...
Shattered bones, trauma to ligaments and musculature, amputations...
My mentor, Dr Levittoux, a very distinguished orthopaedic surgeon...

Six months have passed since his arrival in England. The promised elections took place in Poland in January, delivering a Communist government controlled by Moscow and effecting the final, irrevocable separation from his former life. It is April 1947, and today Dr Kozłowski has his first job interview.

He is crossing Southampton Row when his head begins to spin, causing people to tut in irritation as they crash into him. Being English, of course, they do not berate him, they simply purse their lips and think disapproving thoughts. He spots a bench in a pleasant-looking square on the other side of the road and steps out into the traffic, almost knocking a man off his bicycle. This one swears. He shakes his fist and says: "Oy! Look where you're going!" and something incomprehensible which sounds like "stupid bugger", then there is a red bus to avoid and a large car driving towards him before, finally, he reaches the bench. He sinks onto it gratefully and leans forward, trying to redirect the blood to his brain as a wave of nausea overwhelms him.

"I say, are you alright?"

She is tall, with large feet clad in flat shoes and wiry hair escaping from a tightly-curled bun. She wears a dark navy coat and carries a leather satchel. Her face, he notices, is covered in freckles. She is smiling at him, concerned.

"You look rather unwell, if you don't mind my saying."

He stands up, then sits down again abruptly as his head swims.

"You'd probably feel better if you put your head between your knees." She gestures. "Your knees."

He wants to tell her that he is fine and that she should not trouble herself, but he does not have the strength to speak so he waits, patiently, until the buzzing in his head begins to abate.

"Forgive me if this is a ridiculous suggestion, but have you eaten today? I'm sorry," the woman continues quickly, "I'm sure you're far too sensible to go without food. It's just that it happens to me sometimes if I don't eat, that's all."

As she says this Kozłowski realises he has eaten nothing since the previous day. Besides the need to preserve his meagre funds, he has a fear of entering shops or cafés in case he makes a mistake in English and orders the wrong thing. As a consequence, breakfast is often his only meal of the day. This morning he was too nervous even for that.

"No," he replies. "It is not ridiculous at all. Your diagnosis is absolutely correct."

She breaks into a delighted smile. "How did you know I'm a doctor?"

"I didn't – I—"

"Oh. Gosh! I'm sorry. You said—"

"Please, don't apologise. I probably said it because I am a doctor myself."

"You are? How wonderful! I've just qualified. Today. This very moment. Look." She rummages in her satchel and brings out an envelope from which she draws, with extreme care, a certificate from the University of London. Margaret Maclaren, it declares, has been admitted by the University College Medical School of the University of London to the degree of MbChB, Bachelor of Medicine. "It's taken years, of course, because of the war. I've done half my training on the job: I probably know more than I would ever have known if I'd done it in peacetime, but the piece of paper – it has taken forever. Then they posted it to the wrong address and it was sent back. But here it is. Finally, I have the right to call myself Doctor Maclaren. Oh, I can't wait to tell my father! He's a doctor, you see. He will simply burst with pride—" She stops herself. "I'm so sorry. There you are faint with hunger and here I am wittering on. Would you care for a banana?" She rummages inside her satchel again and brings out a small, slightly bruised yellow fruit. "I'd never seen one of these until a few weeks ago. I'm still not sure if I like the taste. Please, take it. It'll make you feel so much better."

He eats the banana, chewing it deliberately in small mouthfuls. She watches him attentively until it is all gone.

"Thank you. I'm better now." He glances anxiously at his watch. "I must go – I need to—"

She shoots up as if she has been electrocuted. "Of course."

"No – ah – Miss! – ah - Doctor – !"

She turns back again, beaming. "Oh, I will never get bored of hearing that!"

He finds himself grinning back: her enthusiasm is infectious. "Perhaps I can repay you for the banana ..."

"Oh, really, there's no need!"

"For your kindness, then. A coffee. Or a cup of tea. I believe that is more popular amongst the English."

"Ah, well, I wouldn't know. I'm not English; I'm Scottish. A very important difference. But yes, we like tea too."

The following day they meet in the Lyons Corner House on Piccadilly where, over a single cup of coffee, they talk for several hours. He tells her that he is thirty-four years old, unmarried, originally from Wilno, latterly from Warsaw, that he was a doctor in the Polish army and spent much of the war in Soviet captivity before joining Anders' Army and serving in Italy. She tells him that she is twenty nine, that she was engaged to a naval officer who was killed in 1942, that she spent the war in London working in Great Ormond Street Hospital and that she trained as a paediatrician. At the end of the evening, they arrange to meet the following day, and then again, the day after that, when they celebrate the job offer he has received from University College Hospital.

Thus it is that Kozłowski's war finally ends and his normal life resumes, or rather, it begins, for it is not the same life as before the war; it is different in almost every respect. Margaret brings an abundance of energy and joy to everything she does. Her vigour, her unquenchable enthusiasm, her love of the society of others, are all qualities that Kozłowski himself does not possess. As he comes to know her better, he wonders what it is that she sees in his company: he has no ready supply of amusing anecdotes, like Młynarski; he lacks the kind of fluency in English that will make conversation flow easily; he knows little of British culture. The only thing that he is able to speak about with passion and knowledge is medicine. Yet, she does not appear to find him dull. Rather, she seems to derive enormous pleasure in the discussion of professional matters, and she looks upon his ignorance of all things British as a challenge which must be met with her customary energy, whisking him off around galleries and museums, visiting shops where she makes him converse with the shopkeepers to help him overcome his fear of saying the wrong thing. A steady, watchful fellow. Yes, that's me.

I said wonderful, too!

"You'll need some boots. There's a pair here I can lend you, if they're the right size."

Dr Donald Maclaren, his pipe gripped between his teeth, holds out a pair of sturdy walking boots. "They belonged to Margaret's brother. Try them. Go on."

"They're too big, Donald," says Enid. "He'll never be able to walk in those."

"They're fine—" Kozłowski hops on one foot whilst Margaret, already shod, watches the scene from the stairs with an air of benign amusement.

"It's nothing a pair of thick socks won't solve. Margaret, run and fetch some of Andrew's socks, will you?"

"Really, sir, ah – Doctor Maclaren – it's fine. I don't want to make trouble. I can stay here."

"Don't be daft, young man. You can't not come for a walk after lunch."

Margaret returns with a thick pair of socks and they set off, out of the house and straight into the hills.

"I'm so embarrassed," whispers Kozłowski. "You should have told me I will need boots."

"Don't be silly, Zbyszek. Where would you find a pair of walking boots anyway?"

"Do you think it's alright?"

"What?"

"The lunch. Everything." He has been worrying all the way up to Scotland if he is going to measure up.

She squeezes his arm. "Don't worry. You've passed the test. He likes you."

"How do you know?"

It starts to rain, a light, soft rain which, Kozłowski learns, is called 'drizzle'. In Scotland, Donald informs him, one might describe such a day as 'dreach'.

"A bit of rain won't do us any harm, will it, eh, Enid?"

"Only it does make my hair curl," replies Enid mildly.

As they walk uphill they fall silent, the only sound to accompany them the steady crunch of their boots on the stony path. Without meaning to, Kozłowski draws ahead as Donald halts to fill his pipe and Enid and Margaret, discussing arrangements for the wedding, unconsciously slow their pace.

"Small and simple, that's all we want, Mum. No fuss…"

Tall pines rise on either side of the path, towering above cushions of brilliant-green moss, testament to a climate that is consistently damp. There is a smell of earth and, deep within the forest, a dark, primeval silence.

"Shh!" Donald holds up his pipe, head cocked as a crack of branches is followed by a flurry of wings, a startled bird taking flight. "Look!" he whispers, pointing to a dark spot between two trees; his breath is warm and smells of whisky. "Just there, to your left."

For a fleeting moment, Kozłowski catches sight of a pair of liquid black eyes and a long muzzle before the deer turns, melting silently into the darkness.

"*Jeleń*. I don't know the English word for it."

"Deer," says Margaret.

"Dear? Like 'Dear Sir'?"

"No!" she replies, laughing. "With a double 'e'."

They talk for a few moments about the vagaries of English spelling, which leads to a discussion of Polish names.

"Yes!" exclaims Enid, relieved, as if she has been waiting for the opportunity to voice her confusion on this subject. "Margaret tells me your name is actually Zbigniew – Have I said that correctly? – And that when you are married she will be Kozłowska and not Kozłowski."

Kozłowski explains the small matter of adjectival agreement, and the Polish habit of reducing every name to its diminutive.

"For example, in Polish, Margaret is Małgorzata, which then gets shortened to Małgosia, then Gosia. You can go on endlessly."

"Wasn't your sister called Gosia? So she's really Małgorzata – Margaret – like me."

They fall silent, listening to the crack of branches echoing deep within the forest.

"Ah! If I could only persuade my patients to take a walk in the woods after lunch they would live ten years longer."

"Then you'd be out of a job, dear."

Kozłowski, standing a few paces ahead of the others, gazes back at the wiry red hair of his future wife, a vivid echo of Enid's greying, frizzy locks. Her freckled skin is clear, shining from the exertion, her eyes bright with happiness and humour as she watches her mother attempt to push her curls back beneath her hat. Gosia and his mother often used to joke together, brushing each other's hair in front of the mirror in his parents' bedroom and trying out different, increasingly ridiculous, hairstyles before collapsing onto the bed, helpless with laughter. It was their little refuge, he once heard his mother say to his father when he asked her sternly what on earth could be so funny, from the dominance of men in their family.

The silence of the forest encompasses them. Above him, water drips steadily from one leaf to another. When a single drop slides to the edge of a leaf to land, squarely, on the tip of his nose he exclaims in surprise, raising his finger to wipe the rain from his skin. Margaret laughs. His glasses are flecked with raindrops.

"You should really treat yourself to a new pair of specs," she says, as they resume their walk.

He raises his hand to touch the metal arm with the tiny piece of twisted wire which holds it to the hinge.

"I suppose I should."

After dinner, Kozłowski steps outside to smoke a cigarette. There are no stars tonight. The low clouds hang heavily above him, making the night air mild and warm. The door opens and closes behind him and Donald Maclaren appears, holding up his pipe by way of explanation.

"Enid hates the smell."

Donald falls silent, scratching his beard meditatively. Kozłowski braces himself. Instinctively, he knows that his future father-in-law has come outside to question him.

"Well, well. So Margaret tells me you've decided to specialize in eyes."

"Yes. I will study for the extra exams whilst I am working in general surgery at the University College Hospital."

"You'll apply to Moorfields?"

"I expect so."

"I'm not sure I'd have the gumption to slice into an eyeball, and I'm not squeamish."

They laugh, although Kozłowski does not know what gumption is, and agrees that it might require a certain steel.

"At least you won't be called out at night too often, not like me. In all my working life, I don't suppose I've had two weekends together when I've not been called to a child's bedside, or an old folk's bed."

"I had not thought of that, but I can see it is an unexpected bonus."

"You'll have had a fair amount of experience with surgery, I expect. Pretty gruesome it can be, too. I remember the First War. Of course, then it was all about gas." Donald pauses. "I suppose you've no family to count on."

"Not here, no."

"And I'm guessing you don't own more than what you're stood up in."

Kozłowski flushes. "I will work hard for her. For Margaret."

Donald pats him on the shoulder. "There's no shame in it, Zbyszek. You're young and there is plenty of time to make your way in life. I lost my son in this war. I'd rather have lost every penny I own. You know she'll want to keep on working. She'll not give it up."

"I will not try to stop her."

Donald pats Kozłowski on the shoulder again, relieved now that he has discharged his duty. "Well, well, my lad. You'll do."

They marry in a Presbyterian church in Edinburgh, the bride wearing her mother's wedding dress, the groom in a borrowed suit and a brand-new pair of spectacles. When the priest reads out Zbyszek's full name, mangling it and making it strange, the bridesmaid, Margaret's cousin, gets the giggles, which sets Margaret off, so that, when he places the plain gold band on her finger, the look she gives him is alight with laughter.

After the wedding, they move into a little rented flat in Bloomsbury, to be close to their work – she in Great Ormond Street, he at the University College Hospital. Then, later, when Margaret becomes pregnant with their first child, Tom, they buy a small house in a quiet part of suburban London named Grove Park, in Chiswick. There is a railway station conveniently situated nearby, allowing Kozłowski to commute into work, and it is close to a park, and to the river. When they first step into the dank hallway of the little semi-detached house on Staveley Road they exchange a complicit grin of excitement. The estate agent tells them to take their time viewing the empty property, pointing out that it needs only a little TLC before revealing itself as the ideal residence for a young couple starting a family, and at a knock-down price into the bargain. The young man steps outside to smoke, and Margaret immediately runs upstairs, dashing from room to room, setting out her plans for each in turn.

"This will be the baby's room; this will be our bedroom; the bathroom is disgusting – The bathroom is disgusting, Zbyszek!" she repeats, calling down to him. "It's got some kind of black mould growing up the walls—"

He says nothing, standing at the kitchen door and gazing out at the overgrown garden, where two apple trees are just beginning to bud. He remembers his parents' house in Warsaw, the balcony overlooking the garden with its wild profusion of plants which his mother always insisted were all the more beautiful for being unkempt; the cherry and apple trees which supplied them with fresh fruit and a chain of pies, cakes and pastries which, by the winter months, had taxed even his mother's ingenuity.

"Are you any good with a garden spade?" Margaret comes to join him, slipping her hand in his. She laughs. "I realise I've no idea if you're practical or not."

It was his father who always did the digging, under his mother's exacting instructions.

"To the left, Artur. No, the *left*! That's it. Drop it in. Wonderful! We'll have apples from that in no time."

"What do you think, Zbyszek? I'm already thinking of it as our home."

"Home," he repeats. Then, "You are my home, Margaret," which makes her cry and then apologise at once for being silly.

"I don't know what's come over me," she exclaims, wiping the tears from her cheeks. "It must be the pregnancy hormones."

After the birth of their second child, Kate, Margaret hears that the local GP is looking to expand his practice so she joins him, working part-time, three days a week. Kozłowski, meanwhile, is offered a job as a specialist registrar at Moorfields Eye Hospital. Here, he finds congenial colleagues with whom he can discuss work without ever having to refer to a world outside of their hospital. For four years, Kozłowski never once returns to Earl's Court or South Kensington; he does not read the Polish press. A thick curtain now separates East from West, so there are no letters from his mother, and he writes none. It is easy not to talk about the past because nobody asks him about it. In truth, nobody wants to know. The young are busy building their future: mending, decorating, making good, making new, working, saving, all with the energy of those who know how lucky they are to have survived. The past has stepped aside in favour of love, hope, and new life.

In 1950, a light-blue envelope arrives from the Red Cross in Switzerland informing him that his brother Stanisław Kozłowski died in a labour camp in Magadan in 1948. No detailed information concerning the cause of death is given, the only available records showing that he was captured by the Soviets near the Rumanian border in September 1939. The same information, the letter informs him, has been forwarded by the Red Cross to his mother in Poland. Kozłowski places the letter in the grey folder in the bottom drawer of his desk where he keeps the remnants of his former life: his Polish passport, old letters from Hanka, Gosia and his mother, and a few fading scraps of paper containing lecture notes and other mementoes from Starobelsk.

In March 1952, when his daughter Kate is two weeks old, Kozłowski receives a letter from the offices of the Polish government-in-exile informing him of the existence of a committee, formed by seven members of the US House of Representatives and led by a Democrat congressman, Ray Madden, the aim of which is to right the wrongs of Nuremberg and form a decisive judgement as to who is really guilty of the Katyń Massacre. The committee, the letter informs him, will be visiting Europe during the months of April and May with the intention of holding closed sessions over a period of several weeks. They will take evidence from surviving witnesses of the three camps, as well as from others involved directly or indirectly in the affair. Congressman Madden has managed to obtain access not only to all of the key Polish figures connected to the matter but also to some of the German and US personnel involved. No Russians, of course, will participate. There will be several sittings in the USA, where many of the witnesses now live, as well as sessions in London and Frankfurt. Would he, the letter asks, as one of the 78 survivors of Starobelsk camp, be willing to give evidence to the Committee at its London sitting?

Kozłowski's initial reaction is to throw the letter in the bin. He does not want to speak about Starobelsk, not now, not ever; not yet. What point can there be in stirring up these memories again? And anyway, what can such a commission hope to achieve? It makes no difference knowing or not knowing who is responsible for Katyń, nothing is going to change. His second reaction is to fish the paper out of the bin, place it in his briefcase and take it to work. Here, he examines it again. He is not familiar with the American politicians involved but the list of Polish participants cited includes names so distinguished, as well as those of Józef Czapski and Bronisław Młynarski, that he eventually concludes that he has no right to refuse. If Czapski and Młynarski have agreed to give testimony then so, he reasons, must I.

For several nights before the hearings he is unable to sleep. What will they ask him? What details will they wish to know? What if it were to be discovered in Poland that he has spoken out? Would his family suffer as a consequence? He tries to reassure himself, telling himself that if, at the final moment, he cannot go through with it, all he has to do is not show up.

"Whatever is the matter, Zbyszek?" Margaret, woken by his restlessness, switches on the light. "You've been tossing and turning half the night. And yesterday too."

"It's nothing," he replies. Which is, in a way, quite true: he has said nothing about the committee hearings; therefore, it is nothing. "I must have eaten too much at dinner."

"You ate like a bird. You left half of it on your plate."

2. The commission

The door to the room on the second floor of the Kensington Palace Hotel is closed, a note hanging on the handle saying "Session in Progress. Do not Disturb". Two sheets of paper have been taped over the small glass panes at the top of the door. Along the corridor are a handful of chairs, on one of which a thickset young man with brylcreemed hair is seated, scribbling in a reporter's notebook. Kozłowski waits in the stuffy corridor, unsure where he is supposed to go or what he is supposed to do. The door opens and an official slips out, offering a brief glimpse of a panel of suited men seated at a long table, each with a glass of water, a notepad and pen. The room is thick with smoke. The Committee's attention is directed towards a figure in a dark grey suit who stands before them. He wears a large paper bag over his head, with holes in it for his eyes and mouth; he gesticulates animatedly, the brown bag moving from side to side as he addresses his audience. A stenographer sits at the end of the table, typing rapidly, head bent in concentration.

As the door swings shut one of the taped papers is dislodged, leaving a small gap through which Kozłowski stares, mesmerised by the paper bag. The man with the brylcreemed hair peers over his shoulder through the triangle of glass. He is standing so close Kozłowski can feel his breath on his neck.

"Why does he—?"

"The bag, you mean? He was on the train when they took the prisoners out of the wagons. He was taken off at the last minute."

Kozłowski turns again to look through the pane of glass. So that is Stanisław Swianiewicz, the economist who was the last man to see his fellow prisoners from Kozelsk alive.

"He has family in Poland. They have to keep his testimony anonymous. Do you know him?"

The young man – he must be a journalist – watches Kozłowski

attentively. His open expression reveals nothing except a relaxed good humour. His Polish is unaccented.

"Who do you write for?"

"Just a local rag. I've been sitting here all day. My bum hurts." He laughs. "They won't let anyone in except the witnesses. So, you know him, then, do you?" The journalist nods again towards the faceless figure.

"Not really, no."

"Got a few ideas about who it might be, though, I bet. I can tell. I've got a nose for that kind of thing. Don't worry, I'm not going to print it. I'm not stupid. I wouldn't put it past the Russkis to try something, even here."

Kozłowski feels suddenly as if he is back in Starobelsk and one of the NKVD interrogators is trying to trick him into telling him something. There is the same casual friendliness, the strenuous attempt at seeming not to be too interested in the one piece of information that he is intent upon extracting. The young man seems amiable enough, but if such precautions are considered necessary to protect the safety of Swianiewicz's family, Kozłowski does not want to be the one to cause him harm, however innocently.

"You're mistaken, I'm afraid. I have no idea who he is."

"Are you giving testimony?" continues the journalist, unabashed, glancing down at the grey folder in Kozłowski's hands which he has brought along with him, just in case.

Kozłowski does not reply. From inside the room comes a scraping of chairs as the session comes to an end.

"Just curious, then, are you? They won't let just anyone in there, you know. You have to have some connection with it all."

To Kozłowski's relief the door opens, letting out a wave of stuffy air as an official, leading the witness by the arm, emerges from the room, followed by the commission members. They disappear down the corridor towards the other end of the building.

"Sorry, got to get some more gen." The journalist hurries off after them.

Kozłowski has been directed to a meeting room, where refreshments have been laid out for those who are due to testify. There is no sign of the commission members, nor of Swianiewicz. Perhaps they take their tea in a separate room. Kozłowski stands by the window, not wishing to draw attention to himself amidst this gathering of the great and the good of exiled Poles, amongst whom he recognises General Anders, Lt General Bohusz-Szyszko, Lt General Bór-Komorowski, and former ambassador Stanisław Kot. Outside, Swianiewicz is being helped into a car, the bag still over his head, like a hostage.

There is a low hum of conversation amongst the little group of men, some of whom wear rows of medals pinned to their civilian jackets. Amongst them is an elderly man whom Kozłowski recognises with a jolt as General Wołkowicki.

"It rains a lot in Wales, I can assure you," Wołkowicki says, his medals clanking as he pours himself some tea, "but I can't complain. The home is pleasantly situated. The locals are charming and hospitable. We are well looked after. Coming down on the train yesterday, I was reminded how much I dislike cities, and London particularly – it's a smoky, dirty place. No, I recommend Wales." He looks around at the assembled company. "You should all come and live in Wales."

Across the room Kozłowski notices another familiar figure, also alone, dressed in a baggy suit and a felt hat, a battered leather briefcase clasped awkwardly in one hand as he grasps a teacup in the other. It is the physicist, Tadeusz Felsztyn, last seen in Griazovets. Felsztyn raises a hand in greeting, but he does not approach. An usher enters and calls Felsztyn over. Moments later, the usher returns with an apologetic smile.

"I'm terribly sorry, Dr Kozłowski, but we are running a little late today and we won't be needing you for another couple of hours. You can wait here, if you like, or come back later."

~

Kozłowski lies on his back, gazing lazily at the pale blue sky. The water is fresh and cool; his face, exposed above the water, feels pleasantly warm in the sunshine. He flaps his arms gently to keep himself afloat, sending little ripples out towards the shore. On the river bank he can hear Czapski talking about Proust, an informal lecture delivered in perfect French to an audience of six or seven prisoners who are lounging in various poses on the grass, some in their shirtsleeves, some bare-chested. He is reminded of those days at university when, in the summer months, he would look out enviously from the dissection laboratory to the gardens, where one of the professors of literature was in the habit of conducting his lectures. His students would lie with their hands behind their heads, listening to the words of their teacher, a Buddha imparting enlightenment under a banyan tree, a grey-haired professor under a pine.

From time to time someone chips in—

"*Mais, Czapski, vous ne proposez sûrement pas que...*" or "*Je ne suis pas tout à fait d'accord avec vous...*"

Kozłowski smiles: it does not seem possible to gather together a group of Polish prisoners without at least one of them disagreeing with the argument put forth by another.

He climbs out of the water and dries himself in the sun, fragments of thoughts drifting in and out of focus, the lazy discourse of an idle mind: somewhere in the distance comes the faint, regular hammering of a woodpecker. What joy Edward Ralski would have found in the summer's abundant growth! There are so many plants in Griazovets; there are burdocks which seem to grow even as one looks at them, to a height as tall as a man.

Now Czapski and the others are discussing the similarities between the camps: at Kozelsk, they gave lectures and talks just as they did at Starobelsk, professional men impelled by the same need to retain a semblance of the rituals of their former lives. They too worked on improving their surroundings, although they surely cannot have had a leader as skilled nor as doggedly enthusiastic as Major Zaleski. Even the latrine ditches were given the same nickname. Interrogations were conducted in the same way and to the same apparent purpose.

"It's clear enough that there was a plan involving all three," says Captain Ginsbert. "Ostashkov, Starobelsk and Kozelsk were all emptied at the same time and in the same manner: groups of men were taken from the camp in the direction of home."

"*Damoj*," murmurs Młynarski, reflectively.

"So can't you tell us where they've gone?" an officer from Kozelsk asked the guard, squinting at him in the bright sunshine. "There's only three or four hundred men here. There were thousands more of us."

"They've gone to Germany. You will follow them soon."

This leads inevitably to a discussion: if there is a plan behind the actions of the NKVD, then what are their intentions regarding the men being held at Griazovets?

The sun disappears behind a cloud and Kozłowski feels suddenly cold. He pulls on his shirt, searching in his top pocket for his spectacles. Czapski is seated, hunched over a sheaf of flimsy notes, trying to decipher a mess of tiny pencil scribbles which scramble their way across a cigarette paper.

"What is that?"

"One of Piwowar's poems. Remember?" he laughs. "At least his handwriting is more legible than Tomasz's." Czapski brings out a slim notebook inside which, carefully folded, is a wad of paper, covered with scrawling writing. "It looks for all the world as if a spider had dipped its legs in a bottle of ink and run across the pages."

A burst of laughter from the other side of the stream draws their attention. A group of officers cluster around a powerful figure who is addressing them animatedly. Major Domoń arrived in Griazovets at the end of June on a transport of half a dozen men brought from the Lubyanka prison in Moscow. Pallid, weak, his body marked with scars and bruises, he spent the first few days at Griazovets alone, sleeping. Of the fate of his companions who were taken with him from Starobelsk after the events of November 11th, Domoń knows nothing. When

Młynarski asked him if he had heard anything about Feliks Daszyński, Domoń replied that he had been kept alone in a cell in Moscow and had seen nothing of any other prisoners. When questioned about his treatment at the Lubyanka, he answered merely that violence can strengthen a man's resolve.

After a few weeks in Griazovets, Domoń has regained his strength and, with it, his thirst for conspiracy, swiftly establishing himself at the centre of a group of ultra-patriotic officers, at the head of which is the highest-ranking officer in the camp, General Wołkowicki. These men devote their time to a programme of lectures aimed at strengthening nationalist feelings amongst the prisoners.

"How is it," muses Młynarski, watching the little group of officers as they greet the white-haired general with a smart salute, "that they allow Wołkowicki to get away with it? I heard that at Kozelsk he openly provoked the camp authorities on numerous occasions, but they never punished him."

"It's because of Tsushima, isn't it?" replies Ginsbert. "It doesn't matter what the real man says, his fictional version will always trump the reality."

"They must really love that book to be prepared to forgive some of the things he says," remarks Młynarski with distaste. "I don't like his views."

They have been at Griazovets for two months now, whiling away the idle days in the sun. Far away, the war continues, oblivious to the presence of a few hundred Polish soldiers marooned on Soviet soil. News of Nazi victories in western Europe reaches them in its habitually deformed state through the blaring megaphones, only now, when the prisoners attempt to mine the information for a kernel of truth, they are less able than ever to find hidden signs of incipient allied victory. And so, in the relatively comfortable conditions of the camp, the unity of the men which had previously been held together by shared hardships and their united hope in the swift conclusion of the war, begins to fracture. The group of communist sympathisers who remained discreet in the bigger camps now openly express their support for the Soviets, whilst those who cling to their patriotic ideals have become more fervent in their beliefs, more dogged in the expression of them. As the prospect of an allied defeat looms ever closer arguments that have been simmering for months finally erupt.

Yet, even the most fervent patriots propound their ideas with the grandiosity of soap-box preachers, calling out into the wilderness knowing – in their hearts – that their words are heard by noone, their call to arms in vain. Father Kantak invokes the example of the great Danish King, Canute, who set his throne by the sea shore and commanded the incoming tide to halt.

"Yet the water rose and covered his feet and legs without respect to his royal person. And the king leapt backwards, saying: 'Let all men know how empty and worthless is the power of kings, for there is none worthy of the name, but He whom heaven, earth, and sea obey by eternal laws.'"

By this lesson, the priest seeks to encourage the prisoners to accept their fate.

3. Major Lis

There is a little Polish café on the corner of Thurloe Street which ordinarily Kozłowski would avoid, but he is hungry and it is raining now, so he pushes open the door and steps into the warm, pink interior. Almost immediately, he regrets it. Seated alone in a corner, an empty coffee cup on the table before him, is Major Lis.

"Doctor Kozłowski!"

The expression in Lis's eyes is so desperate that Kozłowski does not have the heart to ignore him. He threads his way through the tables. Besides Lis, there are two middle-aged ladies gossiping and another solitary diner, an elderly man with the rigid posture of a professional soldier, slowly sipping a bowl of *barszcz*. At the far end of the room, three men in suits are at the end of a long lunch.

Lis's grasp is keen as they shake hands. "May I offer you something? I was just about to order another coffee."

The waitress appears with a menu, staring idly out of the window as she waits for them to decide. A group of schoolboys dressed in mustard jumpers and rust-coloured breeches walk past in pairs, shepherded good-humouredly by their teacher; one sleeve of his tweed jacket is pinned to his chest.

"I'll have coffee and the poppy-seed cake, please."

"Just another coffee for me," says Lis. "Thank you."

Without a word, the waitress takes the menu and disappears again.

"How are you, Major Lis?"

Lis toys distractedly with a dog-eared postcard, flipping it over and over in his hand.

"As well as can be expected."

Kozłowski waits as the waitress brings their drinks and a plate with a large slice of cake on it.

"*Smacznego*," she murmurs, before drifting off again.

Kozłowski takes a mouthful of the poppy-seed cake, a brief, blissful reminder of home.

"Are you sure I can't tempt you?"

~

The little room that serves as a library is silent and stuffy, empty save for Major Lis. The librarian, busy reshelving books, glances over her shoulder at Kozłowski as he sits down at one of the tables, shaking the rain from his coat.

"I'm closing in half an hour," she says, in Russian.

Kozłowski draws an unfinished letter out of his pocket and feels for his pencil, rereading the first lines he has written.

"My dearest mother and father, The summer months passed so quickly I scarcely noticed that autumn was already upon us when we were told that we might, at last, write home. We are comfortable here in our new camp, too comfortable, almost—" He breaks off, as an image of Tomasz Chęciński presents itself, seated on his bunk, asking with agonised frustration whether it would not be preferable to be beaten, as inmates of the Lubyanka are, or made to labour till their backs break, like the prisoners in Siberian labour camps. "Conditions are much improved in every way, and as we are few in number there is a great deal less overcrowding in the camp. My health is good and I have been keeping myself busy: we have an allotment where we grow vegetables and a well-stocked library that provides mental stimulation, as do the many lectures given by the other prisoners here. My main mission at the moment is to improve my command of foreign languages..."

He breaks off, dissatisfied. It is hard to call to mind everything that has happened in the six months since they were last permitted to write. So much has changed, and yet nothing has changed. He wants to tell his mother about the long hours he has been spending in this tiny library since the end of summer, to convey to her the miracle of learning which has preserved him from boredom and saved him from despair. He wants to tell her about Czapski's lectures on Proust and Cézanne, and about the chef Antoni, whose need for occupation has pushed him towards some kind of mental breakdown. Instead, his letter reads like a piece of Soviet propaganda.

Major Lis is gazing out of the window at the pouring rain, an expression of profound melancholy on his usually reserved face. Every time Kozłowski visits the library Lis is there, seated in the same spot by the window. He has devoured everything he can lay his hands on, regardless of its content: books on dialectical materialism or the history of agriculture, on mathematics and of poetry. He is indiscriminating, it seems, in his hunger for knowledge. The sense of awkward formality which Kozłowski has always felt in his presence has not receded. They are billeted together in a room on the first floor of a two-storey house along with, from Starobelsk, Młynarski and Czapski and, from Kozelsk, a physicist named Felsztyn, a banker from Lwów named Moszyński who wakes everybody up to say prayers on Sunday mornings, and a medical student named Andrzej whose ebullient personality reminds Kozłowski of Edek. On the ground floor lives another group of seven, including Captain Ginsbert and the pianist Grzybowski. Of the prisoners from Starobelsk, only 78 have appeared in Griazovets; from Kozelsk there are around 200; from Ostashkov 100, making a total in the camp of just under 400 men.

Lis is often silent during the conversations that take place in the idle evenings. His eyes follow everything attentively, his fingers absent-mindedly following the raised ridge along his leg where the scar of his wound lies hidden, and although he sometimes nods, or smiles, or utters a sudden, nervous laugh at one of Młynarski's anecdotes, he rarely speaks. Today, it seems that Lis, too, is attempting to compose a letter. Whatever it is he wishes to say he is not finding easy for he keeps breaking off to stare out of the window, until, finally, he returns his attention to the sheet of paper before him and begins to write swiftly, the scratching of the pencil lead the only sound in the room.

"This is him."

The librarian's gaze is dispassionate, like that of a scientist inspecting a specimen. If Major Lis is her most frequent visitor she gives no sign of recognising him. The prisoners make extensive use of the library; men come in and out of the little room all day; many of them linger, especially now that the weather is getting colder. Perhaps they all look the same to her.

"Pack your things," says the guard. "You're leaving."

"Leaving?" Lis hastily folds his letter. "Where? Is everyone going?"

"Don't ask questions. Go and pack your things."

With a terrified glance at Kozłowski, Lis hurries from the room.

"Did they say where they are taking you?" Captain Moszyński, in his vest, is sewing a button onto his shirt.

"If I knew I'd happily tell you."

Moszyński stops what he is doing to watch Lis agitatedly stuffing his few possessions into a kit bag while the guard waits in the corridor outside.

"Well, who else has been called? Ouch!" Moszyński pricks his finger with the needle.

"I have no idea," snaps Lis. "They don't tend to inform us in advance, or hadn't you noticed?"

Czapski has materialised, his thin frame hunched in the doorway. "Bukojemski, Berling and Tyszyński are going. There are a couple more but I didn't see who they are."

"Reds, all of them!" mutters Moszyński.

"I am not a bloody Red!"

Czapski puts a hand on his shoulder. "Everybody knows that, Lis."

Before he leaves, Lis scribbles an address on an envelope which he hands to Kozłowski.

"Post this for me, will you, Dr Kozłowski, please? Just in case I don't get the chance."

The words hang in the air.

"Of course."

They wait beside a truck at the camp gates, a group of seven men: Gorczyński, Künstler, Tyszyński, Berling, Bukojemski, Morawski, and

Lis, who stands a few metres apart from the others, as if he does not wish to be associated with this 'chosen' group. General Wołkowicki, accompanied by Major Domoń, beckons Lis over, indicating that he wishes to speak with him privately.

"General, I have no idea why they have chosen me ..."

The three men step out of earshot and Kozłowski can only observe from a distance the urgent conversation, during which Wołkowicki and Domoń appear to be issuing Lis with instructions. He is not the only observer: Lt Colonel Berling is watching the three men with an ironic smile, as if amused by their precautions.

Vasilevsky orders the driver of the truck to start the engine.

"Keep your eyes and ears open, yes?" General Wołkowicki grasps Lis by the arm as they draw near again. "And don't sign anything, do you understand? Do not put your signature to any document, whatever they do to you."

Lis's eyes widen. "Do you think they will beat us?"

Major Domoń glances at the guards, who are loading the officers' bags onto the back of the truck. "Look, they're treating you like honoured guests. It's a good sign, Lis. Believe me."

They shake hands. The seven men are ordered onto the back of the truck. The camp gates open. As the truck lurches off into the forest, the last thing Kozłowski sees is Lis's panic-stricken face peering out over the tailgate.

My beloved ones: Days, weeks, and years pass, yet it is only the beginning of the chaos of the old world; the destruction of war is now added to the sufferings of the world, and the flames begin slowly to envelop both hemispheres. War, destruction, hunger, and misery among nations are already old phenomena in the small sector of the globe on which we live. We must, however, persevere and await our fate, mindful of our national posts and of the inexhaustible values of the spirit of our nation...

He feels guilty for reading the letter. He knows he should simply have placed it in the envelope that Lis left for him, yet he longs to know something of the inner life of his inscrutable roommate. He was not expecting this sense of doom, however, this almost biblical manner of expression.

> *I cannot describe to you how I yearn for you all; great poets, like our Adam Mickiewicz, have expressed it in words. Often in my dreams I am together with you.*

At the bottom of the page are the words added by Lis in the library as he was about to leave: *In haste, I will write again soon. All my love, my dearest, dearest ones.*

Embarrassed by this glimpse into the soul of a man confronted with the possibility that his departure from the camp might signal a sinister fate, Kozłowski hurriedly stuffs the letter into the envelope. As he does so, a thin sheet of paper detaches itself from within its folds. It is another letter, dated January 1940, addressed in neat, childish handwriting to Lis at Starobelsk.

> *… I have finished the third class, but in general we have difficulties with learning. I think you know why. Wiesiek polished his shoes so that they may last and look new for a long time…*

It is signed Oleńka.

~

"I assume you're here for the hearings."

The card stops moving. Lis lays it flat in front of him. It is creased, as if he has been carrying it a long while in his pocket. On the front of it is a faded picture of the castle at Malbork.

"Yes. Although I already gave them a statement. Twice, in fact: first in 1945, then again in 1948."

Kozłowski waits for him to say more. Lis has aged: his hair is grey, his skin sagging; he wears an old brown overcoat which is too big for him.

"This is the last card I had from my wife, in 1947."

"They're still in Poland then, your family?"

Lis nods. He holds out the card. "Read it."

"Really, I don't think I—"

"Please."

Reluctantly, Kozłowski takes the worn card, dated March 1947.

My dearest Józef,

You will be relieved to hear that we are all in good health and living with my mother. Oleńka passed her Matura with flying colours. We are all so proud of her. Unfortunately, she was not accepted to study at the University as she wanted. Temporarily she is working in a factory but we are hoping she can apply again next year. Wiesiek is coming up to his final exams now. We are trying to convince him of the wisdom of not discussing certain things with others, but you know what boys are like. He will not listen to his mother.

At the end, another line has been added, in darker ink:

We are all anxious to rebuild our country and move forward into the future. For this reason we think it best if you no longer try to contact us.

Your loving wife, Irena

"What am I to understand by that, Dr Kozłowski? You tell me if you can fathom it because I cannot!"

As his voice rises, the middle-aged ladies turn to stare, eyebrows raised, before resuming their whispered conversation. Without waiting for Kozłowski's reply, Lis grabs the card, jabbing a finger at the first lines.

"The beginning is clear: my daughter was rejected from university because of me. I know for a fact that anyone applying for a job or a place at university has to fill in a form and on that form is a section where you have to give information about your parents. If you are in any way connected with the government-in-exile, with political parties inimical to the communists, with the Polish II Corps, the AK, you name it – for God's sake, Kozłowski, you know what they're like! They have a list as long as your arm of individuals and organisations they disapprove of. Men with a direct involvement are arrested, or worse." He lowers his voice to a whisper. "You know what happened to General Okulicki and the others. Off to Moscow they went and they were never been seen again." He glances around the café, as if he thinks there might be NKVD spies observing them. "Their relatives are barred access to the decent jobs and universities. That is clearly what has happened to my Oleńka..." He swallows. "The bit about my boy I can only imagine means that he has been refusing to toe the line in some way... But this, Kozłowski. What does this mean? Have they got to her? Has she been hurt, or threatened in some way?" His finger, pointing at the line of dark-blue ink, is shaking.

"Perhaps she was simply trying to warn you not to write because it would get them into trouble."

Lis lays his fingers on the table, spreading them out in front of him like a pianist.

"I dream of that cursed villa every night. The Villa of Bliss." In a low voice, he confesses his dream, as if Kozłowski, as a doctor, might be in possession of a cure. "Merkulov arrives at my house in a big black car. He holds open the door and invites me to get in. I want to refuse but then I see, inside, the terrified faces of my wife and children, so I do as he says, but when they close the door my family are no longer there. The driver turns around and says, 'Where to, Comrade Merkulov?', to which Merkulov replies, 'Why, to the Kremlin, of course. Comrade Stalin is having a birthday party and Major Lis here is the guest of honour.'" He pauses. "And Berling said that he was not a communist. I remember Captain Łopianowski screaming at him: 'You had better shoot me now, because I will never sign your treacherous document'."

Kozłowski wonders if Lis is losing his reason.

~

Major Lis hovers in the doorway, as if uncertain of the reception he will receive from his former roommates. He had returned to Griazovets in July, eight months after he was taken, shortly after the astonishing news of the Nazi invasion of the Soviet Union had reached the camp. After a few weeks in a separate building, kept apart from the rest of the prisoners, the returnees have been permitted to reenter the main camp. Rumours have been passing around concerning the activities of the select group to which Lis so unwillingly belonged – that they were kept in luxury and fed caviar and vodka by Merkulov and Beria themselves, and were plotting the incorporation of Poland into the USSR as its seventeenth republic. The villa outside Moscow where they stayed has swiftly acquired a nickname: the 'Villa of Bliss'.

"You were in this villa all that time?" persists Andrzej. "It can't have been too bad, can it? It sounds comfortable, a villa. And you look well on it."

Lis sighs heavily. It is true that he is no longer as gaunt as he was when they last saw him. An air of unhappiness clings to him, however, like old sweat.

"They didn't torture you, did they?"

"They treated us very nicely, I can tell you that. We lacked nothing."

"So what did they want from you?"

Lis falls silent, seemingly oblivious to his small but attentive audience, as though reliving what took place. He seats himself stiffly on the edge of his bunk, his hands tightly clasped.

"Blast Berling! Always going on and on about how we had to see the 'bigger picture'. I said they were being played for fools. Poland wiped off the map! He grabbed me by the throat and called me a fascist swine."

101

~

"Where are you living?" asks Kozłowski, hoping to tempt Lis into less gloomy thoughts.

"Foxley camp, in Herefordshire. I am director of archives there. My English isn't good enough to get another job."

"Do you like it?"

Lis gathers up his things, gesturing to the waitress to bring them the bill.

"We should go."

Outside, the rain has stopped. The sun comes out and, for a fleeting moment, the street gleams silver.

"It's good to see you, Kozłowski. I can't face company most of the time. Sometimes, I think it would have been better to have shared the fate of our comrades."

4. A witness

To his surprise, Kozłowski finds that his hands are shaking as he is invited to take the witness stand.

Chairman Madden: Please state your name for the record.

Mr. G: I will state my name, but not for publication, because I have relatives in Poland.

Chairman Madden: I might state, for the record, that this witness, for the reason that he has relatives in Poland, wishes that his name be not recorded. However, for the record, I can state that the members of the committee have the name and address of the witness about to testify and he will be referred to in the record as Mr. G, in accordance with his suggestion. Before you make your statement, it is our wish that you be advised that you will run the risk of actions in the courts by anyone who considers he has suffered injury. At the same time, I wish to make it quite clear that the Government of the United States and the House of Representatives do not assume any responsibility in your behalf with respect to libel or slander proceedings which may arise as a result of your testimony.

Mr. G: Yes, I understand that.

Mr. Dondero: Do you agree to that?

Mr. G: Yes.

Chairman Madden: Do you swear by Almighty God that you will, according to the best of your knowledge, tell the truth, the whole truth, and nothing but the truth, so help you God?

Mr. G: I do.

Mr. Machrowicz: When did you arrive at Starobelsk camp?

Mr. G: It was the 30th September 1939.

Mr. Machrowicz: How long did you remain there?

Mr. G: I remained until the end of April - the 25th or 26th April 1940. Seven months.

Mr. Machrowicz: What happened on the 26th April 1940?

April is drawing to a close. The sun shines. Spring opens its green heart. The transports become less frequent.

Kozłowski wanders through the empty camp, spending long hours in the sunshine, trying to work out the basis on which he and others have been excluded but, just as there is no discernible pattern in the names that are called to leave, there is no one type of officer who has been rejected. Of his friends, only Czapski, Młynarski and a handful of doctors remain.

He walks on past the Siegfried Line, where some of the remaining prisoners have been ordered to fill in the latrines, past the kitchen where camp officials dish up bread and sour soup, right to the edge of the tall, white wall and the barbed wire, as if from there he might be able to see beyond the camp to the place where his fellow prisoners have been taken.

One morning, at the end of April, his name is finally called.

His hands are shaking as he packs his few remaining items of linen, his army coat, Biały's portrait and the little sheaf of notes taken from camp lectures. At the gate, he searches for a familiar face amongst the crowd of men who are due to leave but there is noone he knows, only Lieutenant Szczypiorski, his pitted face pink in the sunshine as he converses happily with his friends. The isolation of the journey to Starobelsk returns to Kozłowski powerfully. Once again, it seems that he is about to embark upon a long journey without the comfort of companionship. Then he spots Czapski and Młynarski, waiting nearby, their cheerful smiles barely concealing the anxiety he knows they must be feeling at being left behind, and he is grateful simply to be on his way out of the prison gates at last. He falls into step beside a major in his early forties whom he vaguely recognises but cannot name. The man walks with an odd rolling gait, one leg dragging behind the other. The major turns; he has an intelligent, agile face; his small grey eyes are shining with anticipation.

"Home," he says, pronouncing the word with the air of a starving man who has been promised food. "How I have dreamed of this moment."

Home. The end of their isolation, marooned on this vast continent from which there is no escape.

Before leaving the camp, the prisoners are issued with bread and salted herrings. Their identity papers are checked, after which they are taken in pairs outside the gate.

The train that awaits them at Starobelsk station is not the open cattle wagon in which they arrived but a *stolypinka* – a prison wagon – consisting of long line of carriages with blanked-out windows, each carriage containing a series of small compartments with four benches on either side and a cage-like door that is bolted from the outside. Into one of these compartments Kozłowski is pushed, along with seven other men. The doors are bolted, guards are posted in the corridor outside. Kozłowski pulls down the top bench and clambers onto it, while the major takes the bench opposite him and two young lieutenants claim the middle benches, immediately falling fast asleep. The remaining four officers, seated on the bottom row, converse in low voices. Kozłowski realises with a shock that they are speaking in Russian.

For a day the train sits at the station without moving, the men clamouring for water as the sun rises and bakes them like sardines in a barrel. Then, with a lurch, they are off. After seven months in captivity, they are finally on the move. Despite himself, Kozłowski begins to feel the sense of anticipation that accompanies a journey. *Damoj!* Will the camps be under German control? Will he be able to communicate more regularly with his parents and receive parcels from them? Perhaps he will be permitted to work in the camp hospital or even – dare he imagine it? – leave the camp to work in a hospital outside.

At the very top of the whitewashed windows is a narrow gap through which Kozłowski and the major take it in turns to keep watch, noting the names of the places they pass, the sun serving them as compass.

They reach Kharkov that evening, where they are given herring to eat and tiny cups of water which fail to slake their thirst. As night falls, the guard switches on the lights, the yellow bulbs casting a garish glow over the crowded compartments. No information concerning their destination or the length of their delay is vouchsafed, and the prisoners know better than to ask. Remembering the frequent and arbitrary stops on the journey to Starobelsk, Kozłowski prepares to sleep. He twists his body in an effort to get comfortable, and, as he does so, his attention is caught by black marks scratched into the paint on the ceiling, faint outlines of words, written in Polish:

"They have brought us to Kharkov, they are getting out and bringing cars…"

Here is a surname, there dates and initials, a trail of breadcrumbs left for those who follow afterwards. Opposite him the major, too, is studying the ceiling. The scratched comments pose a question: if our fellow prisoners were taken from Kharkov by car, why are we being kept here? Will cars come for us in the morning? Or are we being taken elsewhere?

Mr. Machrowicz: What do you mean by "inscriptions" - where were they?

Mr. G: They were scratched on the ceiling of the railway compartment, above the top bunk.

Mr. Machrowicz: The inscriptions were in Polish?

Mr. G: Yes.

Mr. Machrowicz: Were they dated?

Mr. G: I don't remember exactly, but there were dates from the preceding weeks in April, when the camp was being emptied.

Mr. Machrowicz: Were they signed?

Mr. G: Just first names, but I can't remember them.

Mr. Machrowicz: What happened to you after that?

Mr. G: After that we were taken to Pavlishchev Bór, and then to Griazovets.

The jokes give way to miserable silence as the train begins to head north towards Moscow instead of west towards Poland. When, on passing Tula, the train changes direction once again, spirits rise a little. At least Siberia can be discounted, even if the promised journey towards Poland has been revealed as yet another Soviet mirage.

Damoj. Another lie to add to the thousands of lies they have been told since their capture. Yet, Kozłowski feels no anger, only a sense of empty indifference. Let them take me where they will; I no longer care.

The little group seated on the lower bunks hold themselves apart from the others, conversing ostentatiously in Russian. Their relaxed demeanour suggests that they have already been told where the train is heading. There is a young ensign among them, no more than twenty years old. As he catches Kozłowski's eye he smiles encouragingly. "Join us," the smile says. Kozłowski's hastily averts his gaze. The ensign frowns, resuming his conversation in loud, carefully-enunciated Russian.

For some time now the major has been observing Kozłowski closely. There is something in his gaze – a certain reserve, or is it an air of calculation? – which makes Kozłowski wonder if the man is some kind of informer, or spy. Now, he addresses Kozłowski directly for the first time:

"You're one of the doctors, aren't you? I'm afraid I don't know your name, but I do recall that you looked after me once, on the train after we were captured, when I was shot in the leg."

"Of course! I remember you now. I've been wondering why you look familiar."

"I should have thanked you before now. Lis." He holds out his hand across the compartment. "Major Józef Lis."

The two men converse in Polish, exchanging reminiscences of their time in Starobelsk, and the two young lieutenants on the benches below join in. From time to time, Lis pronounces with particular emphasis the name of some officer or other of whose patriotic stance he wishes to signal his approval. The two young lieutenants, seizing his intent, mention various acts of heroism performed during the September campaign by officers known to them in Starobelsk. Thus, without ever stating it explicitly, one half of the occupants of the compartment conveys directly to the other half their chosen political stance. Kozłowski, always reticent, says little, becoming eloquent only when discussing the iniquities of Dr Yegorov and the virtues of Dr Levittoux.

On the evening of the third day of the journey, just after passing the town of Kaluga, the train turns abruptly south, finally coming to a halt at midnight at a small station named Babynino. Here the officers remain all night, locked inside their compartments until, finally, in the early hours of the morning, a detachment of NKVD officers arrives to let them out. They are ordered off the train and herded once again onto a line of waiting trucks. They set off across flat, barren countryside which not even Ralski could have found beautiful. Squashed between the young ensign and Major Lis, his body lurching up and down painfully as the wheel axles bounce over the uneven ground, Kozłowski eventually drifts off to sleep.

He is woken by an unfamiliar sense of stillness, opening his eyes to discover that the trucks have come to a halt in a clearing in a forest of tall conifers. Before them, bathed in dappled morning sunlight, stands a long, low building, next to which is a cowshed and several barns, encircled by a high wall topped with barbed wire.

This is the transit camp of Yukhnov, also known as Pavlishchev Bór.

> **Mr. Flood:** You were in Pavlishchev Bór just a few weeks, is that correct, before you were transferred to Griazovets?
>
> **Mr. G:** Yes.
>
> **Mr. Flood:** And how long did you stay in Griazovets?
>
> **Mr. G:** Just over a year. From June 1940 to August 1941.
>
> **Mr. Machrowicz:** During all this time, did anyone suspect that there was anything amiss concerning your fellow prisoners from Starobelsk camp?

Mr. G: No. Not at all. We thought that they were in other camps, just like us. Only sometimes there were letters from home asking about them.

Mr. Machrowicz: Letters?

Warsaw, December 1940

My dearest,

How happy I am to know that you are safe and well. You can imagine my anxiety at such a prolonged silence from you: eight months with no news! I need not explain the state we have been in, what with the silence from Elżbieta and the continued absence of news from Staś. Only Gosia is able to communicate regularly. She has been begging me for news of you, and particularly asks after that nice young man she brought to visit here, Tomasz Chęciński. (Has she said anything to you about him, Zbyszek? I cannot help noticing that she seems more interested in hearing from him than she is in hearing from her own brothers! Well, who can blame her? He's a handsome young fellow, and your father liked him, which is a miracle in itself). If he is with you, could you pass on her message? She says she has heard nothing since March, and of course she's worried, although now that we have heard from you she has every reason to expect a letter from him. Meanwhile, with us there is little change: we have had a bumper crop of fruit from the garden this year, which I have been preserving as if my life depended upon it. Food is short – nothing to worry yourself about, of course; we get by well enough – but it is not an exaggeration to say that this year nothing will be going to waste. I have used up every single jar in the house. Stay well, my son. We are thinking of you always.

Your loving mother

Mr. Flood: You left Griazovets in August 1941, after the amnesty, is that correct?

Mr. G: Yes. After the Germans invaded the Soviet Union we were set free. General Anders came and we went to join the Polish army in Totskoye.

5. Nasi!

They are squeezed into a compartment with hard wooden seats, eight of them, still in the same uniforms they were wearing when they were captured almost two years previously: Kozłowski, Czapski, Młynarski, the pianist Grzybowski, the student Andrzej, and three others. The benches are narrow, the corridors crowded, yet there is a festive air among the passengers: there are no guards watching over them, no ration of salted herring to make their throats burn with thirst, and they have each been given a pocketful of roubles with which to buy provisions on the journey.

Kozłowski gazes out of the grimy window at the flat landscape, thinking over the past two years of his life. He barely hears the conversation of his companions, nor registers the sound of Polish soldiers singing in the corridor, their heads poked out of the windows to enjoy the rush of warm air, like dogs in a speeding car. He is remembering the journey east from Warsaw to Lublin as the Germans bombed their way across Poland, the high-pitched cheerfulness of the crowds crammed into the train, their most precious belongings clutched in their arms, snatched from their homes as they fled: feather bedding, wedding cutlery, family pictures, children's shoes. Olgierd Szpakowski, whose enormous suitcase accompanied him all the way to Starobelsk, that ridiculous sheepskin rug, Olgierd's pride and joy.

Where his memories of Starobelsk are carved with a clarity that never fades, the year spent in Griazovets has passed in a blur of routine and relative ease. In all these months he has given little thought to his friends, sinking instead into a pleasant torpor which began with the brilliant sunshine of one summer and ended with that of the next. Now, as the promise of being an active agent in his own life begins to work upon him, his mind turns to those comrades who have not been seen since April of the preceding year. Wherever they are being held, they will surely soon be released and they will all be reunited, soldiers once more in a Polish army. He turns to Czapski:

"How happy Tomasz will be to fight again!"

The train slows and Andrzej leaps up in excitement. "I'm starving! Do you think we'll be able to get something to eat?" He wrestles with the catch until, finally, he manages to get the window open, thrusting his head outside.

The others rise from their seats to join him, each man eager to catch the first glimpse of the first station on the journey south. Before anyone can respond to his question, they are silenced by the sight slowly materialising before them: a dark, amorphous mass that envelopes every inch of the platform, a grey mirage. Gradually, the mass comes into focus, revealing itself to be hundreds of people clustered together waiting: men, women, children, some clutching bags and suitcases, others dressed in rags.

"Look! My God, Look!" An old man raises a skinny finger to point at the uniformed men leaning out of the windows. "Our soldiers. *Nasi!*"

"Jesus and Mary," mutters Andrzej as the crowd of human scarecrows surges forward, "they're Poles."

They stream onto the train, ragged skeletons in tattered *fufajkis* and quilted coats, everyone talking at once. They have come from Archangel, from the Kola peninsula, from Vorkuta, from every corner of the Soviet Union. They are all heading south-west, they say, to join the Polish army.

Everywhere the same story is told of civilians deported from their homes in Soviet-occupied Poland in the spring and summer of 1940, sent to survive as best they could in labour camps in Siberia or *kolkhoze* in Kazakhstan. At every station there are more of them, tens of thousands of starving, sickly people. The train grows more and more crowded, and the battle for space grows fiercer. Their compartment for eight swells to include ten permanent residents – the eight Polish officers plus a young boy from Grodno and a Russian woman who is on her way to visit her grandchildren – as well as several extras who take it in turns to enjoy a seat on a strict rota system.

The landscape begins to change, the empty fields replaced by lush green meadows and thick forests, fields of sunflowers brilliant against black soil, sprawling villages with thatched houses, large Orthodox churches. The fruits and vegetables on offer at the railway stations where they stop grow ever more tantalising: watermelons, apples, tomatoes, cucumbers, peppers, bilberries.

Andrzej returns from a sortie to a station platform with two punnets of ripe bilberries and a spindly cucumber which he proceeds to divide up with meticulous fairness.

"Take it slowly," advises Kozłowski. "We've not eaten fruit for a very long time."

Of course, they all ignore him. Even Andrzej, who should have known better, mocks Kozłowski as he carefully counts out five bilberries, chewing them slowly, preserving the rest in his handkerchief.

"What's the point in trying to save them?" Andrzej munches greedily, the purple juice staining the corners of his mouth. "They'll only get squashed."

They stuff down as much fruit as they can lay their hands on and guzzle the fresh, warm milk that is for sale at every station. Who can blame them? For two years they have been deprived of every kind of fresh food. Now, peasants with tanned skin and almond-shaped eyes look on smilingly as customer after customer marches up to them and, with an air of childish excitement, points at their basket of fruit and buys the lot.

In the corridor, soldiers of the Red Army mingle with the Poles, offering to share their cigarettes and their home-brewed vodka.

Andrzej's eyes are closed, hands clasped over his stomach, his face a tight grimace of pain. Opposite him, Kozłowski dozes restlessly; the atmosphere of the train is close and fetid, and his mind is working furiously to absorb the jumble of information which has assailed him since leaving Griazovets: snippets of news regarding the progress of the war, tales of Polish pilots defending London, of a Polish division that fought in France. Is his brother Staś among them? Or is he to be found amongst these half-starved ghosts who greet them so pitifully at every station?

It takes a week to reach Totskoye. When they finally arrive, the officers jump from the train onto the hot, dark earth and march several kilometres in the gathering dusk, a trail of hundreds of civilians straggling behind them. Finally, they arrive at a Red Army camp consisting of a few rows of tents and a handful of small wooden huts.

Mr. Machrowicz: Mr G, are you able to say when it first become apparent to you that the officers from Starobelsk and the other camps were missing?

Mr. G: It is hard to say. You must bear in mind that there were thousands of people arriving every day from all over the Soviet Union. Czapski was put in charge of registering the new arrivals. It was he who coordinated everything, but it was almost impossible to know for sure where anybody was.

6. Franz Josef Land, Kolyma

"How in heaven's name are we going to remember them all?" Młynarski stares bleakly at the pile of papers before him. "It's over four thousand names. And that's only Starobelsk. There's another four thousand from Kozelsk and six thousand from Ostashkov." He groans. "I took such care over that list. I managed to preserve it throughout the whole of that wretched winter, then they took it from me when we left the camp."

It is November, two months since their arrival in Totskoye. The temperature outside has dropped to minus 40 degrees Celsius. Inside, it is scarcely warmer. Kozłowski, Czapski and Młynarski are seated in a small wooden hut that bears the grand name of 'Assistance Bureau', where Józef Czapski, aided by Młynarski and two other officers formerly from Kozelsk, have been assigned the task of assembling and recording the information brought in by the new arrivals who continue to arrive daily at the army camp.

They have created a new file, arranged alphabetically, where they enter the names of all the prisoners from the three camps who have yet to make an appearance. Every evening after work one of the team sets off out to find the four hundred men who were imprisoned in Griazovets, now scattered throughout the camp at Totskoye, asking them to name as many of their missing comrades as they can. Today, it is Kozłowski's turn to sit with Młynarski, noting down every name he can recall.

"From our barracks, let me see: Chęciński, Ralski, Kwarciński, Hoffman, Szpakowski, Otwinowski, Jelonek, Szczypiorski – he's here, though, isn't he? Then there's Tadeusz Biały, he was next door..."

Czapski enters the hut, carrying a large map of the Soviet Union which he spreads out on the table.

"This might help us. I want to start by indicating the location of the camps where our people have been imprisoned, and then mark the areas from which the deported families have come. It will help us to build up a picture of where precisely all the camps are; then perhaps we can see if any news is coming from a particular area."

Czapski is soon engrossed, marking little crosses to indicate areas where Poles have been imprisoned or deported. Looking at the map, Kozłowski is overwhelmed by the sheer vastness of the USSR: so many of the places are so inconceivably remote, so much farther again than the distance they have already travelled, it is astonishing that any of the former detainees – half-starved and with no money – have made it to Totskoye alive. Czapski locates Moscow, then, moving his finger to the left, finds Smolensk, then Kozelsk, which he marks in green; to the north, near Tver, he marks Ostashkov in red; over a thousand miles to its south, in eastern Ukraine, he marks Starobelsk in black.

He looks up, his clear, kind gaze taking in Kozłowski's disheartened air. "I'm sure we will find them, Zbyszek. I have heard a rumour – a credible rumour – that there are Polish officers in the Arctic regions of Franz Josef Land, and also in Kolyma. Several hundred Polish prisoners were apparently working there in the mines and on the construction of airfields. The area is so remote, it is only possible to leave it in the summer. So, you see, it is far too soon to give up hope. I'm going to Buzuluk soon to present my report to army headquarters; they will be able to send on our lists of names to the Soviet authorities, so we'll soon be in a position to learn more."

"I don't even know where Franz Josef Land is."

"Here." Czapski indicates a cluster of islands at the very top of the map, a vast white land mass marooned between the Barents Sea and the Arctic Ocean. Kozłowski tries to picture their friends in that inhospitable part of the earth. How long would the journey have taken, in April 1940? And what could conditions there be like when even here, in the south, winter temperatures are so severe? They might as well be on the moon.

"And Kolyma?"

Czapski points to a region in the far east of the USSR, bounded by

116

the Arctic Ocean and the East Siberian Sea in the north and the Sea of Okhotsk to the south.

"Once you reach the eastern coast," he says, "the next country is Japan."

In the makeshift medical centre, men queue up before Kozłowski in the little cubicle, their concave chests revealing ribs that stick out like wooden handles, their teeth loose from lack of vitamins, barely able to lift a book, let alone a weapon.

"How old are you?"

"Thirty-five."

The man in front of him grins hopefully; his sparse hair is combed back over his skull; wrinkles fan out from the corners of his eyes; two of his front teeth are missing.

"It's the weather, Doctor, and the work. In Kolyma they made us build the roads in minus thirty. It ages you."

"Kolyma?" Kozłowski studies his patient curiously. "You were in Kolyma?"

When Czapski returns from staff headquarters at Buzuluk, he describes to his friends an impossibly distant, civilised world, a place where he was able to listen to the BBC in Polish and hear Big Ben striking noon in London.

"I handed my report directly to the chief of staff, who gave me some more ideas of the places where we are most likely to find our comrades. I've marked them on the map. I also spoke to Colonel Okulicki and he immediately transmitted the information I had given him and ordered me to draw up a detailed report stating everything I knew about the men at the three camps. I dictated it all to a sympathetic typist—"

"Was she pretty?"

"Do you know, Bronek, I didn't notice."

"How could you not notice, Józef? Don't tell me: your mind was on your job. Of course it was. Do go on."

Czapski, with the faintest smile, continues his account. "The report went on and on. I simply couldn't stop. Everything came back to me so vividly, it was as if I were there again. When evening came, I was still dictating. The poor secretary— !"

"The pretty one—"

"Then the lights failed, and we had to wait for an hour and a half before they came on again. An hour and a half of leisure! I sat there conversing with the young ladies—"

"Oh, Lord, there was more than one!"

"They offered me chocolates. Real chocolates, from London. I would have brought some back for you if I'd thought they would survive the journey."

"I am trying to imagine which I desire more, flirtatious conversation with an attractive young lady, or chocolate, but it's no good. I can't possibly choose. When can we move to Buzuluk, Józef?"

"Sooner than you think. Most of the army is due to be transferred there in the next few weeks. There's one more thing of importance I discovered: I spoke to a major there who gave me some information which I believe sets us on the right track."

The major, Czapski explains, told him that transports, loaded with Poles, had been seen leaving Nakhodka from April 1940 onwards. The date coincides with the dates on which the camps at Starobelsk, Kozelsk and Ostashkov were liquidated.

"I am genuinely optimistic that the mystery surrounding our comrades will soon be solved. Tomorrow, I will be able to tell our 'clients'" – this is how Czapski refers to those who seek information from the assistance bureau – "that General Anders and Ambassador Kot have put in an urgent claim for the return of all the men whose names are on our lists, and that there is every hope that those who are still alive will be sent back to us before the summer is out."

The days and nights merge. Kozłowski's billet in Buzuluk, in a tiny flat with a widow who addresses not a single word to him in all the weeks he spends there, is so cold the ice on the windows is thicker than the panes of glass. He brings her food, sometimes, little tidbits which he has managed to obtain from the mess, leaving them out on the table at night. Always, in the morning, the gift remains untouched. Eventually, since these things are rare and needed by others, he takes the food back. Finally, he stops trying to thank her when she serves him breakfast but eats in awkward silence, pretending to read. Sometimes, as he sets out early for the hospital, he sees her standing at the window, watching him. He never can decide if her reluctance to speak is due to a dislike of the Poles whose presence so dominates the town, or to fear.

Christmas comes and goes, his third in the USSR, his first of the war as a free man. The medical staff decorate the tents, patients are given an extra ration of food, then staff sit down to a feast of beetroot soup, pies and vegetables. Kozłowski does not stay late. He is due at work early the following morning and, for some reason he cannot quite identify, he feels no desire to join in the merry conversations between the doctors and nurses.

Passing staff headquarters, he meets Czapski, also on his way home. They exchange Christmas greetings, then continue to walk briskly for while in silence – it is so cold that to stand still is to invite death. Czapski tells him that he is preparing to make a trip.

"To Chkalov and Moscow. Unless I talk directly to the men at the top, I fear that we will never get any answers about our missing men."

Mr. Machrowicz: Mr. G, as you say, you were aware of the efforts being made to find the missing men. Did you ever, at that time—

At this moment, the door opens and an usher hurries in with an apologetic air. He whispers something to Mr Machrowicz, who rises from his chair.

Mr. Machrowicz: Gentlemen, a matter has arisen which requires me to request a short break in proceedings. If there are no objections, we will reconvene here in fifteen minutes.

The committee rises and files from the room, and Kozłowski is ushered back down the corridor to an empty room, where he is offered a hot drink and asked to wait.

He tries to keep his focus on the commission's last question so that he will be ready to answer it as soon as the session is resumed, but, suddenly released from his role as witness, he is overcome by a wave of exhaustion. He takes off his glasses and presses his fingers into the bridge of his nose. What was the man about to ask? "Did you ever, at that time— ?" He can guess how the question will go on: "Did you ever, at that time, think that they were dead?" No, of course we didn't. Why should we suspect such a thing? No, the erosion of our hope was a gradual thing. Like a chalk cliff battered by the sea, little by little it wore away.

He is glad of the break, for in the chronology of his memory something intrudes which does not belong to the story of Starobelsk, something infinitely closer to home. He remembers with shame his reaction when he first saw her.

7. Elżbieta

Młynarski waits patiently by the door, trying not to glance down at the greenish pulp that oozes from the wound. Three months have passed since Czapski left Buzuluk. In his absence, the army has been transferred south to Turkestan and Kozłowski is now working at the staff hospital at army headquarters in Yangi Yul, near Tashkent. Preparations for the evacuation of the army to Persia, due to begin in April, are in full swing. Outside, trucks weave slowly amongst the crowds.

"What is it?" Kozłowski carefully tweezers fragments of wood from the oozing flesh. The young man sits stoically, enduring the pain without a mumur. He broke his leg on the journey south and made himself a splint from a piece of wood. Fragments of the splint have worked their way beneath his skin and the lower part of his leg is now a gangrenous mess.

As Młynarski remains silent, Kozłowski glances up. "What's going on, Bronek?"

The first thought to cross his mind, as Młynarski leads him towards a row of white tents where crowds of civilians push forward eagerly, begging for news – *When can we leave? Will we be able to join the convoy to Pahlevi?* – is that he is being taken to see one of their comrades from Starobelsk. Who is it, Bronek? Is it Zygmunt? Olgierd? It couldn't be Tomasz, could it? When, instead, Młynarski ushers him into a tent and, with an air of triumph, halts in front of an emaciated young woman and her child, Kozłowski's first reaction is one of disappointment.

Her dress hangs loose; her pale blond hair, tied back with a tattered ribbon, is grimy; her cheeks, once pink and round, are hollow; dark shadows underscore dull blue eyes. In her arms she holds a child whose mouth hangs open, crying for food. In the past few months Kozłowski has seen hundreds of half-starved children and their mothers arrive in

121

the camp, he has seen some of them recover and others die. Always he has regarded them with the strictly dispassionate eye of a professional. Here, though, is his own family, for here is his sister-in-law Elżbieta. The starving little boy, he realises with barely-concealed horror, is his nephew Olek.

"Look, Olek, it's Uncle Zbyszek."

The boy raises his eyes and gazes at Kozłowski expressionlessly. He puts his fingers into his mouth and begins to suck them.

"Don't, darling." Elżbieta takes his hand and pulls it gently from his mouth. "They're dirty. You'll be ill."

The boy utters a feeble mew, like a kitten, and pushes his hand back towards his lips.

"Let's get you to the medical centre, shall we?" says Kozłowski, briskly. "Will he let me carry him?" He holds out his arms to take the boy but Olek clings obstinately to his mother. "Come, Elżbieta. We'll find you some clothes and food."

She asks no questions concerning himself, or Gosia, or Staś, and he asks her nothing about Zosia and Magda, whose absence fills him with dread. Instead, he takes them directly to the clinic, where he uses every ounce of the goodwill he has stored up over the months of his service here to beg for some food and a bed for the child. The nurse looks at Olek with great pity.

"I can't, Dr Kozłowski. You know how it is. He has to wait his turn."

"I can help," says Elżbieta. "I trained as a nurse. As soon as I can get washed and find some clothes, I can work. I'll sign up. I'll do anything. Please. Just let him stay."

The affair is soon settled. Olek is given a tiny bed in the crowded ward; he is bathed and his head shaved. As soon as Elżbieta has been issued with clean clothes, Kozłowski takes her at once to register with the women's auxiliary service. When he sees her again some days later she is wearing a too-large uniform which she has tied with a belt, a thick quilted jacket over the top. He finds her sitting next to Olek, who is asleep.

"Have you eaten? I'm about to go to the mess."

She replies that she has.

"And the boy?" He cannot say his name. It is as if he cannot reconcile the grey, half-starved little creature curled up on the bed with the chubby three-year-old he had known before the war; as if, by not naming him, he can keep his distress at a distance.

"He's had some water, and a few crumbs of bread. It's a start," she adds, briskly.

Later, when he returns from lunch, they sit together by the bed, conversing in low voices so as not to disturb the sleeping child.

"I expect you want to know what happened to the others."

Of course he does, although he doesn't. Elżbieta does not look at him as she speaks but focuses her attention on the thin blanket which covers Olek, smoothing it, again and again, as if she were stroking an animal.

"Magda is dead."

Magda, little Magdalena, popping cherries into his mouth, giggling as she darts away from his pretended anger. I'm going to catch you and eat you up! Six years old when he last saw her. Only eight – or nine? – when she died.

"She caught a fever during the summer. They put us on a farm in Kazakhstan and worked us there like donkeys. There was no doctor, no medicine to save her. We left her there, buried beneath some stones in the corner of the field."

His niece Magda, so mischievous, so cheeky! He imagines the little death: the corpse of the sunburnt girl, lying in a barren field like those he saw from the train.

"And Zosia?"

Elżbieta places the heels of her hands on her eyes and grinds them slowly in a gesture of profound weariness.

"I don't know where she is. We became separated: the train was sitting in the station; they told us it wasn't due to leave for three hours. I had a few Kopećks, so I went to see if I could buy some food. I was carrying Olek with me, and Zosia was on the train, guarding our places.

I found an old woman who had some bread to sell. I was bargaining with her but while we were talking the train started moving. I ran back, but it was too late."

"Did Zosia know where you were heading?"

"Perhaps. I keep telling myself that all the Poles are heading in the same direction, so she has every chance of getting here. But then I think: a young girl on her own, with no money and no one to look after her…" She breaks off, leaning over Olek to hide her distress.

Kozłowski watches her, trying to make sense of what she had just told him. "And Ignacy? My mother told me that he died in the first week of the war."

"It was a stupid death, really." Elżbieta's voice now is matter-of-fact. "He was on a train heading towards Lublin, trying to find his regiment. The train was bombed by the Germans. It was as simple as that. He never even got a chance to fight. I'm sorry," she offers him a thin smile, "I've asked you nothing about yourself or the rest of the family."

"There'll be plenty of opportunities for us to talk. Have you registered Zosia as missing?"

"Not yet. I've not had a chance."

The assistance bureau has expanded its staff to include several women, one of whom listens carefully as Elżbieta describes her daughter.

"She's tall for her age, with long plaits down to here," she indicates her shoulders, "grey eyes, freckles on her cheeks and arms… She was on the platform… If you could ask your friends. If any of them have seen her…"

They promise that they will but, as Kozłowski shepherds Elżbieta from the hut, he knows that as soon as they are gone the women will glance at each other wearily, already certain of the fruitlessness of her request. There are thousands of families just like yours, you see, madam, many of them here in Yangi Yul, all seeking information about their husbands, brothers, daughters, mothers, sons. We, too, have done the same. We have begged these officers here to make sure that, every time they meet a soldier from a camp, they ask him: "Did you meet Lieutenant so-and-so, or Captain such-and-such, whilst you were in such-and-such a place?" But it is impossible. We would be here all day with a list of so many names, don't you see? Think of all the families who have been separated. They number tens of thousands. All asking: *Do you know...? Have you seen...? Have you heard...?*

"I can see they have a lot to do," says Elżbieta, once they are outside. "It must be hard for them."

One of the women pokes her head out of the door, calling after them. "Dr Kozłowski? Major Czapski is back. He arrived last night. I thought you'd like to know."

Elżbieta looks around vaguely. "I must go and see if Olek needs me."

When Kozłowski first met Elżbieta he had been struck by her firm sense of purpose: younger than Ignacy by a year, she had trained as a nurse but gave up her job soon after their marriage in order to bring up the three children who arrived at regular, well-planned intervals. The young family had moved into a house that had once belonged to Elżbieta's grandparents and, bit by bit, with a determination that was as steadfast as it was unyielding, Elżbieta had built up their nest with as little expenditure from their savings as could be managed, strengthening it and fortifying it to withstand the vagaries of fortune. She had not reckoned on a war that would not only take away her Ignacy but her home, flinging her and her children far from everything that had once been familiar and dear. Where once she had been confident, almost complacent, now she has the air of one who is permanently bewildered by events too vast for her comprehension. She asks the same questions, over and over again.

"Do you think Zosia is alright?"

"Perhaps someone found her..."

"Could she have been sent to Buzuluk...?"

As he watches her hurrying off – a pinched, grey, humbled figure – Kozłowski feels guilty for never having really cared for her.

"Those are the specific words he used?" Czapski writes something down, carefully, on a scrap of paper.

Berling nods. "Those were his precise words."

Kozłowski has just arrived at the assistance bureau, where, to his surprise, he finds Colonel Berling and Colonel Gorczyński standing before Czapski's desk.

"Thank you, gentlemen, for your help. I will tell General Anders at once."

Once Berling and Gorczyński have gone, Czapski remains lost for a while in reflection, gazing pensively at the piece of paper in his hand. The room is warm. The afternoon sun penetrates the dirty windows, illuminating motes of dust which hang, like tiny stars, suspended above the shelves of bulging files.

"What did Berling want?"

"He'd heard about my search for the missing officers and wanted to tell me something Merkulov said to them while they were in Moscow. '*My zdzelali bolshoi oshibku.*' 'We made a big mistake.' I'm sorry, Zbyszek. I have to go and see General Anders now. I'd like to tell you about Moscow and about this—" Czapski holds up the piece of paper. "Perhaps tomorrow, when I've had a chance to speak to the General? Bronek will be here."

"They're ready for you now, Dr Kozłowski."

The usher waits patiently by the door while Kozłowski puts on his glasses, takes the folder from the chair next to him, and stands up briskly.

He follows the usher back down the thickly-carpeted corridor, past the journalist, who is still waiting by the door, scribbling in his notebook. The young man glances up sharply as Kozłowski passes by, a look of intense curiosity on his shiny face. Kozłowski can feel the eyes following him all the way back into the room.

[Testimony resumes after a short break]

Mr. Machrowicz: Mr. G, I was asking if, during the time you were still in the USSR, you ever suspected that the missing officers might be dead?

Mr. G: It became increasingly hard not to conclude that something very terrible had happened to them, yes. But there was no proof.

8. Moscow

"My report runs to almost fifty pages" Czapski indicates, on his desk, a thick folder bulging with papers, "but if you wish to save yourself the trouble of reading it and would like to know what I have found out in the past three months, it can be summed up in two words: precisely nothing."

"Come, Józef, it's unlike you to lose heart." Młynarski draws up two chairs, indicating to Kozłowski that they should sit down. "Why don't you tell us about your trip? I'm sure it can't be as bad as all that."

It begins at the station at Kuybyshev, with Czapski stepping across the sleeping bodies of hundreds of civilians who had been waiting for days just to purchase a ticket. The train was already at the station, due, he was told, to leave any minute. For three days he waited, spending the days at the Embassy and the nights seated beside the radio operator, reading French novels borrowed from the Ambassador's library.

"On the third morning, I received a message from the British Military Mission kindly offering to place their carriage at my disposal. Major Campbell, whom I had previously encountered at Ambassador Kot's residence, picked up my bag and led me to the far end of the train. Entering that first-class sleeper was like stepping back in time…"

Czapski describes a two-berth compartment upholstered in turquoise velvet, with mahogany fittings, a private bathroom and ornate mirrors in which Czapski saw, for the first time in two years, his own reflection.

"I must have looked horrified because Campbell very tactfully slipped away, returning later with some tea and asking me if there was anything else I needed. It was all I could do not to throw my arms around the poor fellow's shoulders and weep!"

The journey to Moscow, he says, followed the same pattern as every other train journey they had undertaken since their capture in September 1939, stopping and starting apparently at random, standing for hours on end in stations or in the open countryside. He passed the time playing chess with the British airmen who were travelling with him, acquiring a handful of words in English on the way: *yes, no, please, thank you, of course, old chap, I say.* Major Campbell was the only one amongst them who spoke French.

"I shared the sleeping compartment with a sergeant who insisted on showing me photographs of his family. 'Wales,' he kept saying. 'Wales, do you know it?' In the evening, Major Campbell – bless him for his kindness! – appeared with a pair of flannel pyjamas which he insisted on lending me."

The sergeant, he recalls, made his own kasza for breakfast by crumbling biscuits into a tin of condensed milk.

Czapski speaks for over an hour, relating his fruitless attempts to gain information from General Raichman, the days spent waiting in the Lubyanka to see him, the endless visits to endless offices, down thickly-carpeted corridors and through wardrobes into the secret inner sanctums of the NKVD, each time to be greeted with the same air of polite mystification. It culminated in a final, obfuscating telephone call during which Raichman suggested he go back to Kuybyshev and make his request of Comrade Vyshinsky, something he had already done a dozen times.

"After weeks of waiting I knew no more than I had done before I set out from Buzuluk. There was no other door in Moscow upon which I could knock in the hope of gaining further information. There was nothing I could do except admit defeat.

"I spent my few remaining days in Moscow making preparations for my journey and waiting for a reservation for the train. The officials at the NKVD were most attentive: they sent me off to the Intourist store to collect several bottles of good wine, white bread, sausages and jam. A seat was reserved for me and that was that.

"When I returned to Kuybychev, the army had been transferred to Turkestan. I made my way here and submitted my report to General Anders. It was here that I learned of the conversation that was held between Colonel Berling and his fellow officers at the Lubyanka prison in the autumn of 1940. They had heard about my search for the missing prisoners and came to see me to offer me this information. I immediately went to General Anders and told him what I had heard."

"'We made a big mistake'? Is that it?"

"Yes."

"What did General Anders say?"

Czapski hesitates. "He listened very attentively to my account then, at the end of it, he said: 'I do not wish to discourage you from pursuing your investigations, but neither am I willing to hide from you what I believe to be the truth.' He was silent for a while then, eventually, he said: 'I think of them all as comrades and friends whom we have lost in action.'"

Czapski stares pensively out of the window at the old orchard which surrounds the building. The trees are already in blossom. Spring has warmed their roots and soon they will bring forth leaves, then fruit. Birds swoop low, dipping their wings in the water which gurgles softly down the irrigation channels as they are opened to water the trees. It is almost dusk.

"It was not until I arrived here in Yangi Yul that I finally admitted to myself that I was beaten," continues Czapski. "And yet, I continue to register the missing and the lost; I take depositions, place everything neatly in files, mark little crosses on my map and find myself staring at names which until recently were unknown to me: Kolyma, Nova Zemlya, Franz Josef Land... asking myself if it is still possible that our comrades will one day reappear."

"It's not yet summer, Józef," says Młynarski. "There's still a possibility that they will be found."

Czapski nods. He places the folders in his drawer then leads his friends out of the office, locking the door behind him. "When we were in the icy cold of the Steppe I dreamed of the south, but now that we are here I feel only exhaustion."

They descend the stairs and walk out into the orchard, where a group of men parade up and down under the trees. A breeze blows the white blossom into the air; it drifts down slowly to settle on the grass, like snow.

They reach the edge of the orchard and stand for a moment watching the huge, red sun sink gradually below the horizon, leaving the sky a deep blue, a thin line of yellow just visible before, eventually, it darkens, and night falls.

Mr. Flood: Did you ever see any of the prisoners who were with you at Starobelsk again? To this date, have you seen them since?

Mr. G: No, sir.

Mr. Flood: Do you know of anybody who ever did?

Mr. G: No. I know of no one who did.

9. Memories rising

That evening, when Kozłowski returns home, Margaret pulls his dinner from the oven.

"You're late back."

"I had some work to do."

"You normally call if you're going to be late."

"I forgot. I'm sorry."

"Tommy was so funny at bedtime. He kept saying 'Baby! Baby!', wanting to cuddle Kate."

Kozłowski drops his knife and fork with a clatter and pushes back his chair.

"I'm sorry, Margaret. I have a splitting headache. If you don't mind I think I will go straight to bed."

However hard he tries to keep the memories from rising, he cannot control his dreams.

He is standing by a window, looking out at something - he does not know what - when, sensing the presence of another person, he turns to find a middle-aged woman waiting in the doorway. He does not recognise her, for he has never met her, and yet he knows exactly who she is.

"Mrs Levittoux?"

They sit down, one at either end of a long, polished mahogany table.

"You wish me to tell you about your husband?"

She glances over her shoulder as if she is frightened they might be overheard, then gives a quick nod.

"Mrs Levittoux, you will be comforted to know that he was able to do a lot of good in the camp, helping patients in the clinic. He was in good health for all of our time in Starobelsk, and his strength of character was an example to us all—"

She interrupts him, grasping his hand impatiently. "Tell me, where do you think they have them? Are they keeping them in one of the prisons? Or were they sent to a labour camp?"

"I – I'm sorry, Mrs Levittoux, I don't follow—"

"I worry so much, you see, about his health. After so many years. They mistreat them terribly, I've heard - there's barely enough food to eat. I do worry so…"

He is horrified. "Mrs Levittoux, I think it is almost certain that your husband, as well as all the other men from Starobelsk, is dead."

"No. No. You're quite mistaken. There was no body, you see. No proof at all—"

"But what about Katyń? -"

"Ah, that's quite a different case. Don't you see? If the men of Starobelsk were dead they would have been found by now. The Red Cross, they're very good at following these things up… Look at the case of your brother - your mother found out, didn't she, eventually?" Mrs Levittoux continues speaking, the words chasing each other frantically. "And after all, you're here, aren't you? That's proof that not all men were automatically treated the same. He was a doctor, like you. What danger could he possibly have posed to the Soviets? You must see, it doesn't make sense. Besides, I would know it if he were dead. I would feel it. I would feel it!" She repeats the words with unshakeable conviction.

For a few moments when he wakes he cannot orientate himself: where is he? And when is he? Then he feels the reassuring warmth of his Margaret's sleeping body and remembers that he is at home and that home is in England, not Poland.

Zbyszek?

Gosia stands in the doorway. She is wearing a light summer dress, her hair cut short in a bob as it was before the war.

Zbyszek, where is Tomasz?

III
Starobelsk

Drzewa nie przenoszą się
z miejsca na miejsce
w poszukiwaniu pokarmu
nie mogą uciec
przed piłą toporem

Trees don't move
from place to place
in search of nourishment
they can't escape
the saw
and the axe

(Tadeusz Różewicz, *Tree-felling*)

1. A train journey

"What can you see?"

Zygmunt presses his face against the narrow gap at the side of the wagon, left open to allow the men to relieve themselves.

"Fields," he says, drawing back. "Just fields."

"Is that the best you can do? It's not very entertaining."

The man who has the privilege of standing by the door also has the obligation to describe what he sees outside so that the others, seated crammed in near darkness, can picture it.

"What am I supposed to say? The landscape hasn't changed for the past two days. It's just miles and miles of stubble."

He picks his way back to his place, stepping over the other men's legs, but he is tall and keeps losing his footing.

"Watch where you put your boots, you dirty great oaf!"

"I can't help it." Finally, he regains his place next to Olgierd, who is seated with his back braced against the wall of the carriage, a large sheepskin rug spread over his knees.

"That was lamentable, Zygmunt."

He squeezes himself into the tiny space, threading his legs under those of the man seated opposite him. "I'm a forester, Olgierd. What do I know about fields? I just went to take a leak."

"Some people appreciate a flat landscape," remarks Feliks, seated on Zygmunt's other side. "Most of central Poland is flat as a pancake, after all."

"Flat, Feliks, maybe, but not naked. For me a landscape without trees is like a – a –"

"A girl with no breasts?"

Zygmunt flushes. "No – like a –" he hesitates, the words eluding him, "a lack, as if something vital were missing..."

Feliks slaps Zygmunt on the shoulder. "I know what you mean. Damned wrong, that's how it looks to you."

Zygmunt nods, mollified. "Yes."

Kozłowski sits in silence, observing the group of friends from his position in the corner of the carriage where he is crushed, his back rammed against the wall, his right shoulder painfully compressed by the heavy mass of his neighbour's body. He envies the men their ability to stretch out their legs. He envies them their companionship, too. Over the past days, in the chaos following the invasion and the army's retreat, he has wandered amongst the crowds of defeated men without encountering a single soul of his acquaintance. Even Edek has disappeared.

The man leaning so heavily on his shoulder is a captain who has said nothing since the beginning of the journey but sits with his head in his hands, staring at the floor. Kozłowski is grateful for the man's silence amidst the never-ending arguments between the optimists and the pessimists who spend their time sketching out different versions of the fate that awaits them, the too-loud jokes, the endless dissection of what went wrong with the military campaign.

"If we had turned right towards Stryj instead of left towards Kałusz, we could have been in Rumania by now and on our way to France."

Right and not left. This way and not that. Kozłowski shifts uncomfortably, a buzz of exhaustion burning his brain. Seated opposite him, his long legs butted against Kozłowski's, is the blond lieutenant whom Kozłowski first noticed when they were waiting for the train. The man has said little since the journey began but listens avidly to the conversations around him, smiling from time to time, or shaking his head, as if he is participating inwardly in the discussions. Occasionally, when a particularly contentious opinion is voiced, he catches Kozłowski's eye; there is humour in his bright brown eyes, as if he knows, somehow, that Kozłowski must agree with him that the speaker is a prize idiot.

"He should have been court martialled." The voice belongs to a major seated somewhere in the middle of the wagon. He is referring to the colonel who led them on their blind march across eastern Poland.

"What use would that have been?" replies his companion. "You might as well court martial a sea wall for giving way in the face of a gigantic wave."

Another discussion grows out of the first, this between a pair of cavalry officers, one convinced that their journey across the Ukrainian steppe is the prelude to a short stay in a prisoner-of-war camp, to be followed by their swift release to neutral territory where they will be set free to continue to fight; the other – a self-proclaimed realist – predicts Siberia as their goal and a labour camp their future home.

"Gentlemen, gentlemen!" A colonel weighs into the growing dispute. "Let's not waste time arguing amongst ourselves. The fact remains that we are prisoners of war—"

"Well, are we? We were captured by the Red Army, that's for sure, but who's in charge now?"

"The NKVD, of course! Didn't you notice? It happened at the border."

"It was before that, surely?"

Kozłowski tries to recall the last time he saw the young conscript soldiers who first captured them in the valley at Dolna Kałuska. It must have been just after they crossed the border into the Soviet Union: he had woken from an uneasy sleep to find that the brutish, terrified young boys had been replaced by *politruks* in red-rimmed caps who mingled with the prisoners, calmly answering the barrage of questions put to them about food and letters home and packages and army pay, reassuring the prisoners in singsong voices that anything they required would be provided to them, because there was plenty of everything in the Soviet Union.

There is a sudden commotion nearby, and a torch briefly illuminates the broad, friendly face of a man leaning over a prone body.

"What is it, Bronek?"

"He's collapsed."

"Who?"

"I don't know. He was sitting next to me."

"Is he breathing?" asks Feliks.

"Yes. I think he's just passed out."

Olgierd takes the sheepskin rug from his knees. "Here. Try putting this under him."

As Bronek and Feliks lift the man's head, Kozłowski catches a glimpse of a face: pale, eyes closed, the skin clammy, lips half open.

He leans forward. "I'm a doctor. If we swap places I can take a look at him."

Bronek thanks Kozłowski profusely as he clambers across Zygmunt's, then Olgierd's and Feliks' legs, forcing his way into the tiny space next to the sick man.

The major's trousers are torn and stained with blood. Bronek holds the torch, watching anxiously as Kozłowski presses his fingers into the soft indentation between bone and tendon on the sick man's wrist. The skin is dry and hot to the touch, the pulse racing. Kozłowski carefully tears back the blood-stained fabric, unsticking it carefully from the skin to reveal a deep, suppurating gash above the knee.

"Do you have any idea when this happened?"

"No. He was standing next to me when we were waiting for the train. I don't know him."

The major's eyes are closed, his stillness interrupted by short, violent bursts of shivering.

"If I had some water I could at least clean the wound."

Olgierd reaches over, holding out a water bottle. "Take it. I can fill it up at the next stop."

Kozłowski tips water over the wound and the major utters a scream of pain, his eyes opening to fix Kozłowski with a furious stare.

"It's all right," murmurs Kozłowski. "I'm fixing you up." He casts around for something to bind the wound. "I don't suppose any of you has a clean piece of linen? They took my bandages at the border."

"I could tear off a bit of my shirt," offers Feliks. "Although to be quite honest it might make things worse."

"Will this do?" The blond lieutenant reaches over, holding out a handkerchief. "It's reasonably clean."

Kozłowski hesitates, conscious, in their present situation, of the practical value of all personal belongings, however small.

"Please," insists the man, "take it. It's little enough."

Kozłowski winds the handkerchief around the Major's thigh. There are two initials embroidered on its edge, TC. There is something intimate about this little shred of linen, the kind of gift your mother gives you, or an aunt. He glances up to find the young officer watching him curiously. He must be about the same age as Kozłowski: twenty six, perhaps; twenty seven at most.

"Thank you, Lieutenant—"

"Chęciński. Tomasz Chęciński."

"Kozłowski. Thank you."

As they shake hands over the man's head, Kozłowski notices an odd expression in Chęciński's eyes, a question of some sort. Chęciński says nothing, however, settling back into his place and closing his eyes.

"It can't be long now," says Bronek. "There's bound to be some sort of medical care when we get there."

"When we get where?" grumbles Olgierd. "Nobody knows where the hell we're heading. It could be weeks before we reach our destination."

The discussion stirs once more amongst the exhausted men, like snow whipped up by a storm. Where are we heading? When will we get there? Ever since their capture Kozłowski has tried his best to cling on to a sense of time passing, checking his watch every few hours to note the sequence of days and nights. He knows that they were captured on September 19th; that it was a week before they reached the Soviet border; that on September 26th they boarded the train, and that this was four days and nights ago. Now, as the journey shows no sign of an end, a feeling of lethargy overcomes him, and indifference, and despair. What does it matter how long he has been travelling in this stinking coffin? He longs only for the past, to be back in his old, familiar life, the life he relinquished – was it only a month ago? He searches for a memory that will bring him comfort and finds before him an image of Edek, hands outstretched, with that sly grin on his face, half apology, half challenge. He had turned up at the hospital without notice, as usual, come to visit his girl before his papers came. They were off to Kamieńczyk for the weekend, he said: Agata, Edek and her very sweet friend.

"Help me out, won't you, old fellow? Come with us and keep her company."

They squeezed into Edek's three-seater Aero, the two girls in the passenger seat, Kozłowski rammed in the back, the picnic basket and towels piled on his knees and a record player beside him which Agata insisted they bring. Edek put his foot down and they sped along the empty road, the girls shrieking with laughter while on Kozłowski's arms the imprint of the wicker basket grew steadily deeper.

They bathed in the river and dried themselves in the sun, Edek and Agata lying side by side while Kozłowski gazed up at the cloudless sky and the girl, a nurse from the Ujazdowskie Hospital – what was her name? – leafed through Edek's records. She sat on the river bank, dipping her toes in the water and giggling as he splashed her. In the evenings they danced, the music drifting through the darkness.

To ostatnia niedziela
Dzisiaj się rozstaniemy
Dzisiaj się rozejdziemy
Na wieczny czas...

Julia, that was it. She was pretty, with fair hair worn short, tucked behind her ears, a cardigan draped over her shoulders against the evening cold. He kissed her as they sat side by side on the grass in the dark.

When his call-up papers finally arrived at the end of August he had hurried off into Warsaw to collect his new greatcoat and cap. A strange atmosphere prevailed in the city: on the one hand, preparations for war – news broadcasts instructing citizens to tape up their windows and hide under the table in the event of a gas attack, soldiers marching down Krakowskie Przedmieście, armoured cars racing to and fro; on the other, a population going about its business as if nothing had changed, a summer heat so intense everyone slept with the windows open, Łazienki Park filled with courting couples, children chasing squirrels, the ice cream sellers handing out paper cones, the sound of jazz.

Nic o tobie nie wiem, skąd przywiał ciebie wiatr
Nie znam twoich zalet, ani nie znam twoich wad
Jedną rzecz jedyną, o tobie tylko wiem
Że coś zrobiłaś z sercem mem...

The tailor Rosenbaum measuring him up for his greatcoat, chattering about this and that. Warsaw life, going on just as it always had.

Then he was off. Through the garden gate and off into the future, turning one last time to wave at his parents, his father standing with his arm around his mother's shoulder. Was that really only a month ago? It seems already to belong to a different era.

2. The Steppe

A streak of light penetrates the wagon at dawn, and with daylight comes renewed hope: conversations resume, loud bursts of laughter greet the efforts of the jokers whose self-appointed role is to distract their companions from their situation. The desire to urinate which Kozłowski has been suppressing for almost two days now will no longer be denied. He propels himself from his sitting place, his hands coming to rest on heads, necks, shoulders, his feet trampling on soft flesh as he stumbles over his neighbours' muddy boots. *I'm so sorry... I do beg your pardon...* When he reaches the little gap in the door he unfastens his flies and breathes a deep sigh of relief as, finally, the urgency of nature is answered. Afterwards, he remains there, breathing in the sweet, cold air, the faint scent of the soil tantalising beyond the stench of urine. Squashed inside the carriage, hemmed in by human warmth, he had not realised until now how far the temperature has dropped as they have travelled east. The landscape before him is so vast, so utterly featureless it seems almost two dimensional; there is nothing to give a sense of distance, or scale. As far as his eye can see the ground is covered in pale-yellow grass which undulates in a motion so peculiar it makes him dizzy. The sky is a uniform grey, like a child's drawing, with no shades of blue or white to break up its monotony, no sign of the sun save for a hazy disc to the far right of his field of vision. He imagines what it would be like to stand in the middle of that sea of feathers, how a man might become lost for lack of landmarks by which to navigate, as in a desert.

"Come on, then," calls someone impatiently, "tell us what you can see."

Kozłowski turns helplessly. "There's nothing to say…"

"May I?" A young, dark-haired lieutenant who has been waiting patiently behind him gestures towards the door.

"Be my guest."

"Well?" A weary voice comes from the back of the carriage. "Surely there must be something someone can say about this dreary landscape. Anything to help us pass the time."

The lieutenant turns, and as he does so a thin shaft of sunlight illuminates a pair of startlingly bright blue eyes which, even from the back of the carriage where he has regained his place, Kozłowski can see are shining with excitement. The man's face is as smooth as a child's, his features boyishly handsome. Framed against the doorway, with the sliver of yellowy-grey landscape behind him, he has the air of a heroic prince from a fairy tale.

"Gentlemen, this landscape which appears so featureless to you is in fact the famous Ukrainian steppe."

"Speak up, man! We can't hear you at the back."

The lieutenant nods, clearing his throat. "All my life I have wanted to visit the steppe and here it is, right in front of me. If only the train would stop."

"If it's so exciting, why don't you tell us something about it?"

"Yes, come on, Ralski. And speak up!"

Lieutenant Ralski nods again, smiling to himself as if he has been given first choice of a platter of sweets. "What can I say?" He casts a blind glance around the carriage. "The grass which you see out there is known as feather grass, or '*kovyl*'. Its Latin name is '*stipa pennata*'. It is the most common variety of grass native to this region. One of the most unusual characteristics of feather grass is the way it propagates itself. Like many plants which thrive in a harsh environment, it has developed a wonderfully inventive method of spreading its seeds: in late spring it grows long, silver-grey spikelets which resemble feathers - hence its name. When the wind blows, the spikelets create the appearance of waves for which the steppe is famous. When they are ready, they detach from the plant and are carried by the wind. In this way, the seeds are spread far and wide. But, although they look innocent enough, these little spikelets can be fatal to sheep if they pierce their skin." Ralski continues, the words now flowing from him effortlessly. "Another magnificently clever plant which grows in this region is the Russian thistle, '*salsola kali*'. This one spreads its seeds by forming a gigantic ball which breaks from the main stem of the plant and is borne off on the wind. These balls can travel for hundreds of kilometres, scattering seeds as they go. In America they call it tumbleweed. I've only seen it in films. It's thought they brought it to the United States from Russia or Ukraine in the nineteenth century..."

Ralski goes on to describe the flora of the steppe: he speaks of wild tulips and meadow sage, of veronica and campion, of tiny anemones which carpet the steppe in summer; he speaks of bromegrass, bluegrass, couch grass; of sea cabbage and sea pink, mosses and shrubs; of blackthorn, broom and almond.

Kozłowski, like every other officer in the carriage, is enraptured by Ralski's words, fascinated by a subject he never believed could be interesting. Zygmunt, the great proponent of the forest, leans forward to catch the botanist's description of the settlers who arrived from Russia and Germany in the eighteenth century and cleared the native grasses in order to plant rye, wheat and barley. As Ralski explains how over-grazing led to the disappearance of wild flowers and herbs, how yields declined and weeds grew, the farmers in the carriage nod their heads sagely. When he recounts how the settlers cut down the trees that once thrived in damp areas of the steppe, leading to years of drought and failing crops, Zygmunt addresses Olgierd with an air of triumph:

"I knew a landscape could not naturally be so empty!" Even the steppe, you see, he says, needs trees.

Ralski's impromptu lecture is greeted by a round of applause, causing him to flush and murmur that he had no intention of taking up quite so much time. He picks his way back to his place, a wave of conversation rising in his wake.

A professor of linguistics from Warsaw recalls reading somewhere that, before the area was called 'steppe', it was known simply as '*pole*'...

"... meaning field, or course. Or '*dikoe pole*', wild field, the word '*pole*' deriving from the same root as the Polish word for field, which, of course, as everyone knows, is the origin of the word Poland, the country said to have been named for the vast flat fields which occupy its centre ..."

A lecturer in Russian literature recollects that Chekhov once wrote a short story called *The Steppe*, although he cannot recall ever having read it.

"Gogol was born in Poltava province. That's steppe country, isn't it?..."

"*Wpłynąłem na suchego przestwór Oceanu...*"

Lieutenant Ralski's words have set off a chain of thoughts in his listeners, little sparks which ignite into eager conversations that brighten the darkness and fill the long, dull hours of the journey, allowing the prisoners – for a brief moment – to forget where they are.

"Are you familiar with the work of Ivan Shishkin? Now, there's an artist who knows how to capture a landscape..."

"Personally, I have always believed that the aggressive pursuit of crop yield will lead, in the end, to failure..."

"Have you ever been to America? The Great Plains, now that is a sight to rival this for emptiness..."

"Give me a mountain landscape any day," declares Lieutenant

Chęciński. "There's a wonderful little village near Zakopane. No tourists, but the purest snow, ideal for skiing…"

"Ah, the Tatras! So many happy memories…"

As darkness falls again on the fifth night of their journey, Kozłowski sleeps fitfully, the images conjured by Ralski's words insinuating themselves into his unconscious mind where they mingle with memories of the landscapes of his home.

A sheep lies prone on the operating table at Wilno University, a spikelet of feather grass emerging from its flank. Kozłowski's old university professor, dressed in a white surgical gown, is about to perform a demonstration by removing the stem of grass from the unfortunate creature's flesh. With a flourish, the professor raises his scalpel and leans down to press the blade into the patch of pale, shaved skin.

But what about the gas? The sheep is fully conscious. As the scalpel pierces the skin, Kozłowski tries again to say it: *What about the gas?* The sheep raises its head and utters a piercing scream.

He wakes to find the train slowing, the brakes screeching as metal grinds against metal, before, finally, it shudders to a halt. There is a long exhalation of steam, like a sigh. Kozłowski peers at the luminous dial of his watch: it is just after three o'clock in the afternoon. Most of the men are still asleep. The others sit in the darkness, indifferent to yet another stop on their journey. The officer nearest the door peers out through the little gap.

"We're at a station of some sort. I can't see much. A few buildings, some trees." He describes a grey platform and, behind it, on the wall, a rusting sign, the name of which he cannot make out.

The train remains motionless, creaking and hissing as metal cools and pressure falls. Beyond this is the pleasant silence of a rural railway station.

A bang on the side of the wagon sends the lookout tumbling off balance. Prisoners wake, stirring anxiously.

"What is it? What's going on?"

Then, another sharp bang.

"Everybody out!"

All along the train, the guards are pounding on the wagons with their rifle butts. At these unfamiliar sounds Kozłowski's neighbour wakes and begins whimpering.

"What now?"

There is a loud scraping sound as the bolt is drawn back, then the wagon door is flung open. Bright sunlight penetrates the darkness, revealing eighty men sitting pressed against each other like cattle. Kozłowski feels a searing pain and covers his face whilst his eyes adjust to the brightness.

The captain screams: "My eyes! My eyes!" On and on, until Kozłowski wishes he would shut up. Bronek attempts to stand, but loses his balance and topples onto Feliks, while the sick man, momentarily unsupported, slumps onto Kozłowski's legs, pinning them to the floor.

A guard with cheeks like ripe apples appears at the door.

"Get out."

He reaches into the wagon and yanks the lookout by the collar, sending him tumbling onto the platform.

One by one, the prisoners clamber down while Kozłowski waits patiently at the back of the wagon. His legs are in agony but at least the captain has gone, pushing his way through the others in a hysterical bid to escape, screaming about his eyes, his eyes.

The sick man begins to shiver uncontrollably, his body convulsing in spasms.

"Please!" Kozłowski calls to the guard. "Please, this man needs help!"

Lieutenant Chęciński, now on the platform, tries to climb back inside but the guard prods him with his rifle.

"Move along!"

"But there's a sick man in there – there are others left inside—"

"Yes, they will come too. You must move along now to make space."

Zygmunt and Feliks take an arm each, finally releasing Kozłowski's legs, and drag the major to the edge of the wagon where they hand him down to their friends, jumping down after him. Suddenly terrified that he will be left behind, Kozłowski tries to stand but his right leg is numb then, as the blood begins to circulate again, an agonising pain spreads from his thigh to his toes. He hops to the edge of the wagon and waits there until the pain recedes.

The station is as the lookout described: grey, nondescript, with a block of shabby buildings and a bank of thin trees growing behind them. On the wall is a lopsided sign bearing the station's name, written in Russian: Starobelsk.

Beneath him, on the platform, are hundreds of filthy, grey men. Most wear army uniform, a handful are from the air force. The majority are in battle dress, though some wear summer uniform with lightweight boots and flimsy day packs, as if they were heading out for a picnic. They eye one other with an air of shame, each man avoiding his neighbour's gaze as if fearful that he might see the reflection of his own disgust. This is what it looks like, a defeated army: pinched, diminished, pale.

Up at the head of the train, a guard shouts instructions.

"Form a column, rows of four! March!"

The column of prisoners beneath him begins to shuffle forward and Kozłowski loses sight of his companions.

"Please, let me get down," he addresses the guard in Russian. "Those are my—"

"Shut up!" The guard swings round and shoves his rifle butt into Kozłowski's stomach.

Those are my – what? – he wonders, as he struggles to recover his breath. I cannot call them friends for I hardly know them.

"Now. Get down now."

Kozłowski scrambles down as quickly as he can and joins the huge, shuffling crowd. Slowly but inexorably he is borne forward, away from the train and towards a road which he cannot yet see.

3. Edek

The queue snakes its way around the back of three half-ruined buildings to where the bluff major of the previous night, Zaleski, presides over an improvised canteen. Perched on bricks are several large cauldrons from which he and three other senior officers briskly dole out kasza to the waiting men. Speculating that it might take him until lunchtime to get his breakfast, Kozłowski joins the end of the queue behind an officer who, when he turns around to glance at the new arrival, reveals a white priest's collar tucked behind his tunic. Nearby, a loudspeaker fixed atop a tall post delivers a bulletin in Russian so rapid he can barely follow it.

"... *our brave young soldiers made their way across the defeated land, stepping over the prostrate bodies of the big-bellied capitalists who laid down their arms and fled, leaving their womenfolk and children undefended.*"

"How dare they?"

"It's slander!"

"What? What are they saying?" Those who do not speak Russian look around anxiously. "Is it bad news?"

A series of pips signals the hour.

"*...It has now been confirmed that the capital of the land formerly known as Poland, Warsaw, has been destroyed by the valiant German army. After a short aerial campaign, the city has surrendered.*"

A grey-haired major drops to his knees. "My family! My pretty little ones!"

"This would never have happened if our commanders had conducted an effective military campaign," remarks a captain.

The major gets to his feet. "What do you mean, sir?"

Ahead, a fight breaks out between two officers as one accuses another of pushing in. The argument grows increasingly heated until one of the men, red-faced and furious, yanks the epaulettes from the other's shoulders. Major Zaleski bellows at them to pull themselves together, but they continue to brawl. One of them knocks Kozłowski's rucksack from his shoulder, causing him to spin and almost fall.

"Oh no…" the priest has a look of confusion, almost of hurt, on his country parson's face. "How can they? The shame!"

Kozłowski reaches down to pick up the rucksack and a buzzing sensation fills his head; his vision grows dark, spots of light flash before his eyes; his mouth grows dry.

"Oh dear," he hears. "Oh dear, oh dear…"

Then, blackness.

Someone is calling his name, as if from a very great distance.

"Zbyszek! Hey, Zbyszek! Wakey wakey! There you are! I thought you'd fallen off the face of the earth!" Edek is standing over him, grinning delightedly. "Whoops-a-daisy!" He takes a firm hold of Kozłowski's right arm while the priest, glad of useful employment, takes the other. "Steady on, old fellow. Let's get you sitting down."

They steer him towards a low wall. A young private, eating his breakfast, jumps up to make room for him.

"You stay here, old man. I'll go and get you some breakfast."

Kozłowski wants to tell Edek that there is no point, that the queue is too long, he'll be waiting all morning, but the words do not come fast enough and soon his friend is gone, disappearing into the crowd as suddenly and mysteriously as he appeared. The priest, remembering his own kasza, hurries after him.

Kozłowski waits until the buzzing sensation in his head begins to abate. It is pleasant, for a moment, to cede control, to trust, childishly, to the power of another human being to restore things to their proper order. Now that Edek has reappeared, the panic that has been rising in his throat all morning begins to recede and he is able to survey the chaotic scene before him with something approaching equanimity. Among the swarms of men are countless others who are, like him, alone, exhausted, trying somehow to understand what is required of them in these strange and hostile surroundings. The thought calms him. He takes off his glasses and closes his eyes, pressing his fingers into the bridge of his nose.

He woke this morning, after a restless night spent on the floor of the crowded church building which they call the Circus, to find that Tomasz Chęciński had disappeared. He waited for a while, watching in horrified fascination as a man, carrying a small pail over his shoulder, shimmied up the poles on the edge of the scaffold to reach one of the top bunks. His boots clanged against the metal, sending clumps of mud falling onto the men below, who cursed him as he passed. Everywhere around Kozłowski the prisoners were occupied with the ordinary business of getting up, as if he had landed inside a giant ants' nest where every creature knows its purpose, except him. He waited until he could bear it no longer, then he got up and picked his way towards the door.

He told himself that Tomasz had probably gone to find breakfast. Perhaps he had met some friends. Yet he could not shake off the sense of abandonment on finding himself once more alone. They had bumped into one another last night, after Major Zaleski had made his speech urging the new arrivals to sleep where they could with a view to finding a more permanent berth the following morning. Together they had followed the trail of men into the smaller of the two church buildings, pushing their way inside to be confronted by a scene that he will never forget: rows and rows of wooden bunks stacked one on top of the other on a huge scaffold; on these hundreds of men slept, squashed together, legs dangling over the edges. Hundreds more lay on the muddy floor, squeezed together like pilchards. The stench was overwhelming. They found a space by the wall and slid down onto the floor, side by side. It was then that they had agreed to call each other by their first names, and Tomasz had asked him about Gosia.

"I know Kozłowski is a fairly common name but - I don't suppose you have a sister, do you?"

"A sister? Yes, I do. She's in Kraków. She's just finished university."

"Her name isn't Gosia, is it, by any chance?"

"Yes. My sister's name is Gosia."

"I knew it!" exclaimed Tomasz, reaching over to grasp Kozłowski's hand. "I cannot tell you how pleased I am to have met you!" He leaned back against the wall and closed his eyes, the smile lingering. Then, sensing that Kozłowski was still watching him, he opened one eye again, as if winking. "You look just like her, you know."

"Here you are." Edek reappears carrying a bowl, a group of young NCOs hovering behind him. "Cold kasza. Not quite what you'd hoped for, I'm sure, but it's more or less edible."

Kozłowski spoons the congealed mass into his mouth, admiring, as always, his friend's extraordinary ability to acquire an instant understanding of any given situation. Edek watches him with an air of patient amusement, then, as soon as Kozłowski has chewed the last lump of kasza, he takes the bowl from him.

"Now, my friend, what do you say to taking that same train we came in right back out of here?" Without waiting for a reply, Edek leans forward, conspiratorial. "See these fellows here?" He indicates the NCOs. "They say they're sending the privates and NCOs back home to Poland. For my money it's our best chance of escape. He says," Edek gestures towards a corporal who seems to be the leader of the group, "that we should get out of this place as quickly as possible, before they start registering us." His eyes sparkle with the anticipation of adventure. "What about it, Zbyszek? Will you come too?"

It occurs to Kozłowski that Edek has lost his mind. Even supposing he were to get past the Soviets at the first stage, what then? Wilno is occupied by the Russians, and who knows what will be possible in the German-occupied zone, where he has no family or friends?

"Have you considered the risks, Edek? If you're captured things will be a lot worse than this."

Edek casts an appraising glance around the camp. "I'd rather take my chances on the run than sit and rot in here, thanks all the same." The corporal approaches, carrying a heavy civilian coat which Edek pulls on. "I take it you're not coming, then?"

Kozłowski remembers the five days spent cooped up in darkness on the train, and the week-long march which preceded it. The prospect of making the journey again, in reverse, so soon, fills him with dread.

"Well, good luck, old man. I'll send you a postcard."

Kozłowski squeezes his eyes shut. When he opens them again the crowd in front of him has shifted to reveal, a few metres away, the tall figure of Tomasz Chęciński, surrounded by a group of young NCOs, laughing as he tries on a thick winter coat. An awful sense of betrayal possesses Kozłowski. Impulsively, he strides over to them.

"There you are!" Tomasz turns, smiling. "I've been looking all over for you. What do you think—"

Kozłowski interrupts, addressing him furiously. "So this is how you show your loyalty to your country, is it, sir? This is the conduct of a Polish officer?"

The guards are placing little markers in the ground, on each of which is the name of a vovoidship in Poland. The enlisted men and NCOs, their voices loud and confident, line up behind these talismanic symbols of home. The officers hover nearby, gazing at the familiar names with longing: Lublin, Kielce, Tarnopol, Kraków. It looks like a little graveyard of Poland.

The enlisted men are busily bartering away their mess cans, cigarettes, blankets and coats to the officers who, in exchange, entrust them with messages to take home.

"Remember, it's ulica Akacjowa 8, m4; Rynkowski is the name."

"Tell them I'm fine and send all my love to the little ones. Got that?"

"She's not to worry. Here's my medallion. Give it to her, will you? It will keep her safe."

Kozłowski can bear it no longer. "Shame on you, Lieutenant Chęciński! Shame on you!"

He hurries away, trying not to see the expression of hurt and confusion on Tomasz's face as he stands foolishly, like a man who has been stood up at a dance. Driven by an angry despair he neither understands nor can resist, Kozłowski pushes against the tide of men converging on the central square, desiring only to get as far away from them as possible.

He will not turn and watch as the guards draw back the long bolt on the gate. He does not wish to hear the sound of a thousand pairs of boots shuffling into line, or the voices of the young men who, their spirits high with hope, call out greetings to the officers lining the edges of their path.

"Good luck, gentlemen! We won't forget you!"

"Don't worry! It'll be your turn soon!"

In civilian life, these young men would have been expected to look up to the prisoners they leave behind. They would have treated them with respect, doffing their caps and calling them 'Sir'. These are the men who work in the fields of country estates; they are game keepers, labourers, drivers, mechanics – all of them marching back to their wives, their mothers and their sisters, back to Poland, or what is left of it.

And yet, he cannot resist it: Kozłowski stops – just for a moment – to watch as they surge through the gates. There is Edek, chatting away with his companions as if he has always belonged among them. His bearing is confident, his gestures rough and ready. No doubt his accent, too, has subtly changed. Only as they pass the guards at the threshold of the camp gate do his eyes dart sideways.

Of Tomasz there is no sign.

Kozłowski skirts the main buildings where crowds of prisoners linger, avoiding the round church where he spent the night, from which an endless stream of men issues. On he goes, heedless of the direction he is taking, conscious only of the desire to take himself as far away as possible from the scene taking place behind him. Everything that was once fixed and immutable in his life has disappeared: his country, his family, his friends, his profession. Edek is gone and Tomasz too, most likely, a man who – just for a short while – was a friend amongst a mass of strangers. The only certainties to which he can lay claim are that he is incarcerated in a filthy monastery in the middle of the Soviet Union, that he ate cold kasza for breakfast, and that there is no point in his life when he has ever felt such despair as now.

4. *Grass*

At the farthest edge of the camp birch trees shiver in the autumn breeze. The grass here has not been reduced to mud by the prisoners' boots; the air is cool and fresh, free of the stench of unwashed bodies and dirty clothes. Kozłowski leans back against the thick, white wall which encircles the monastery and closes his eyes.

He remains in this position for what seems like hours but is only minutes; time enough for his breath to return to normal and for the calm quiet of nature to enter his soul. He opens his eyes. Scattered on the ground are piles of curled leaves, their veins brittle, their once-green bodies brown and broken. A crow walks, stately as a priest, pecking at the ground until it locates the object of its interest. A brief tug of war ensues, but the earth is hard here and the worm does not surrender itself easily. Eventually, the crow's determination is rewarded and it flies off, its prize dangling from its mouth. Kozłowski watches as the bird rises clumsily into the sky, black wings flapping. Then he notices that he is not alone: there is another man here, leaning over one of the stones which protrude at odd angles from the ground. Sensing Kozłowski's gaze, the man glances up, fixing him with his startlingly blue eyes.

"Look, there is writing here." Lieutenant Ralski points to the front of the moss-covered stone, where Cyrillic letters have been carved into its surface. "There's a date—" On the lower part of the stone three numbers are just visible, the last obscured by moss. Ralski peels off the little green tuft and places it carefully in the centre of his hand, stroking its velvet surface before turning it over to reveal a dry, black belly like a beetle's. "*Bryophyta*. Did you know that there are over a thousand different varieties of moss, each one requiring a unique combination of light, humidity, shelter, substrate? Tear it away from its native habitat and it will not survive long." He balances the moss on the top of the gravestone. "I found bullet marks on the wall back there."

Kozłowski watches as Ralski's long fingers feel their way across a series of pockmarks in the white plaster.

"Do you think this is where they shot the nuns?"

"Perhaps." Ralski contemplates the bumpy ground. "The graveyard is much older, of course."

Kozłowski is grateful that Ralski does not speak of the crowds gathered in the centre of the camp, nor of the departure of the enlisted men. They are both aware that there is a reason they are here and not there.

"I saw a priest earlier," he says. "In the breakfast queue."

"Yes, I've seen several: Father Alexandrowicz, Rabbi Steinberg, Father Potocki. Perhaps they will allow us to organise services. It would raise morale, don't you think?"

Kozłowski says nothing, thinking of the officers fighting over breakfast.

"Where are you from, Lieutenant Ralski?"

"Poznań. My wife is there. And my daughter Magdalena, my little Magdunia. She's only five." Ralski fixes Kozłowski with an anxious stare. "I've had no news of them since the war began."

They stand for a while in silence, looking back towards the huge, locked church with its crippled spire and the mass of men swarming around it.

"You're a botanist?"

"Yes. A specialist in grass."

Kozłowski suddenly has the urge to laugh. "Grass?"

"It's much more interesting than you might think."

They walk on until Ralski halts, his attention caught by something up ahead. Kozłowski follows his gaze to see a man standing outside a low, fenced-off building at the very edge of the camp. Although he is not dressed in NKVD uniform, something about his demeanour suggests authority, an air of importance despite his casual appearance. He wears a heavy leather jacket; his fair-haired head is uncovered. He is observing them, his hands clasped behind his back.

"Who is that?"

"I don't know. I don't know anything about this place." Kozłowski is suddenly nervous, as if their presence here is against a rule which nobody has yet explained to him. "Look, Ralski, I'd better go. I need to think about finding somewhere else to sleep. I don't fancy another night in that awful church. Perhaps there'll be some free places now the enlisted men have gone."

Ralski's gaze remains on the enigmatic figure. The man has turned away from them now and is conferring with one of the guards.

"Good idea," he says, mildly. He glances up at the pale sky. "I think I'll stay outside a little longer."

Kozłowski skirts the locked building, avoiding the smaller church where he spent the night. The man in the leather jacket is now moving unhurriedly among the prisoners. From time to time he stops, bending his head to listen to the anxious questions which assail him. *When may we contact our families? Will we receive our army pay? Will they issue us with clean clothes?...* Each time, after he moves on, he takes from his pocket a little notebook in which he scribbles, glancing back at the prisoners. The guards, Kozłowski notices, salute him with particular fervour when he passes by. He feels a prickling sensation on his neck, as if he is being observed, yet, when he turns to look back, the man has moved on.

Finally, Kozłowski discovers a series of low barracks which, although in a poor state of repair, appear at least to be watertight. Inside, two doors lead off a narrow corridor, the first of which stands open. He enters cautiously.

"Hello?"

Before him is a long room with rows of bunk beds constructed on wooden frames. The bunks – of which there are at least a hundred – have been built in such a way that they almost entirely obscure the two tall windows. A single light bulb dangles from the ceiling, giving out a greenish glow. Many of the bunks appear to have been recently vacated, presumably by the enlisted men.

"Is anybody here?"

Someone shifts. On one of the top bunks lies an airman, his blue serge greatcoat laid over him like a blanket.

"I'm sorry to disturb you. I was wondering if any of these bunks are free."

The man rolls over to contemplate Kozłowski with dull blue eyes. On one side of his face is an enormous burn, livid and fresh.

"I'm looking for somewhere to sleep. I just arrived yesterday."

The airman gazes at Kozłowski with indifference, then rolls over to resume his contemplation of the ceiling.

Kozłowski shrugs. "I'll take this one, then."

He chooses a top bunk nearest the door, clambering up onto the straw pallet. He tests the comfort of the mattress, wondering whether, like the airman, he might rest a while.

The bunkroom is silent. From outside come the sounds of ordinary daily activity: men shouting to one another, the echoing ring of metal upon metal, a lone bird singing. Now what? He has received no orders; he has no idea who is in command of the camp. The authorities have so far shown no interest in the new arrivals. It seems, rather, that they are more preoccupied with taking men out. He would like to sleep, but as soon as he closes his eyes questions rise up, urgent and unanswerable: are his parents safe? And what of his brothers – Staś, in the air force, stationed near Lwów, Ignacy in the infantry in Wilno? And Gosia, alone in Kraków, the city now under Nazi occupation...

He sits up, banging his head on the ceiling, and scrambles from the bunk. He needs to be outside, active, busy. Anything so as not to have to think.

At the makeshift canteen the queue has dispersed. A portly officer stirs a cauldron of *kasza* with a long wooden baton. He is entirely bald save for two tufts of hair which sprout above his ears.

"What's the situation with food?"

"Three meals a day, if you count tea as a meal. This is lunch." The man grins, indicating the *kasza*. "You get a ration of bread with that for the day. Save it, that's my advice. There's nothing but tea in the evening. *Czajok*. Maybe it'll be a bit easier once the enlisted men have left."

"How long have they been sending them out?"

"Eight, nine days? There are more to go, but it's emptying out." The cook hitches his beltless trousers up over his stomach. "Mind you, there are new men arriving all the time. Trying to cater is not an easy task, let me tell you. But, as I say, there might be a bit more food to go around. Got to look on the bright side, eh?" He pulls the stick out of the *kasza* then plunges it back in again, stirring it vigorously with both hands.

"Do we run our own kitchen, then?"

"Everything, my boy. Everything!"

At this moment a powerfully-built major emerges from the kitchen. "You look like a strong fellow. Chop some wood, will you? We need all the help we can get." The officer, who introduces himself as Major Miller, shows Kozłowski a pile of logs and hands him an ancient wooden axe. "When you've finished there's plenty more inside."

The logs are damp and slippery, and the axe is blunt, but the physical exertion relieves Kozłowski. As his stroke settles into a regular rhythm, he finds his head empty of the anxious thoughts that have been plaguing him. When, some hours later, Tomasz Chęciński comes in search of him, he finds Kozłowski seated on a log drinking sweetened tea which the cheerful cook, Antoni, has given him.

"You decided not to go, then." Kozłowski avoids looking directly at Tomasz, staring instead at the dark brown tea in the enamel mug.

"I don't understand."

"I thought you were going to escape."

Tomasz's mouth drops open in astonishment. "I bumped into the game keeper from my uncle's estate. He insisted on giving me this." He points to the thick winter coat which he is now wearing. "You thought I was going to leave? Is that why you were so angry?"

Kozłowski keeps his eyes fixed on the tea.

"I can't say it didn't cross my mind, Zbyszek, if I'm honest, but it seemed disloyal, somehow, to try to sneak away when everyone else remained behind. Another group's arrived, by the way," he continues, brightly. "They opened the gates and there, right at the front, was Józef Czapski. You must meet him: he's the kindest and gentlest of men, and a great artist. I got to know him a little just after we were captured but we were separated before we reached the border. Poor Czapski looked so exhausted and lost – you remember how we felt, yesterday, when we arrived? – and yet he greeted me as warmly as if we had known each other all our lives. At that moment, all my doubts disappeared: my place is here with my comrades, whatever fate the Bolsheviks have in store for us." He laughs at his own earnestness. "I suppose it sounds ridiculous."

Kozłowski wants to apologise, to explain to Tomasz the feelings of terror and abandonment that have been growing in him all morning, but the words will not come. He forces himself to look up, dreading the contempt he will surely see in Tomasz's gaze, finding instead only friendly concern.

"I'm so sorry, Tomasz, I had no right—"

"Don't be an idiot." Tomasz pauses, a smile hovering on his lips. "You called me 'sir'... I thought you were going to challenge me to a duel!"

When Major Miller emerges from the canteen building some minutes later to find the two young lieutenants laughing helplessly, he mumbles "Glad to see someone's enjoying themselves," before turning on his heel to re-emerge, moments later, carrying another blunt axe, which he hands to Tomasz. "Your friend will tell you what's required."

5. Hello, hello

They are as calm and good-humoured as they were on the train, poking fun at Olgierd, whose sheepskin and leather suitcase full of belongings provide an endless source of jokes.

"We're going to give Olgierd a medal for having carried this lot all the way from Poland, aren't we, lads?" Feliks gestures towards the enormous brown suitcase. "The *virtuti transportari.*"

In they come, one after the other, introducing themselves in turn: Olgierd Szpakowski, Feliks Daszyński, Zygmunt Kwarciński and Bronisław Młynarski, at your service.

Hello, hello. Delighted to make your acquaintance.

Following them, a lawyer, Andrzej Prosiński – miraculously neat, his black beard trimmed, gold spectacles perched on his nose – *Fancy seeing you here!* – who arrives together with an arresting-looking lieutenant in his mid-thirties – *Fred, at last!* – introduced by Feliks as Fryderyk Hoffman from Warsaw, "gifted playwright, fine journalist, rigorous editor and occasional actor", to which Hoffman responds with an ironic bow.

Following them, alone, is a young second lieutenant with cheeks pitted with acne scars who introduces himself nervously as Szczypiorski before diving onto his bunk, then the country priest whom Kozłowski encountered in the breakfast queue. Behind him comes Edward Ralski. He stands in the doorway, contemplating his new home with the air of a guest who has been transferred unexpectedly from a student dormitory to a luxury hotel. As he places his hand on the straw pallet with undisguised joy, it strikes Kozłowski how quickly their expectations have adapted to their circumstances.

A cavalry lieutenant and his coterie of friends who form the core of those residents previously in occupation contemplate the new arrivals with barely-disguised hostility. Amidst the continuing introductions –

Jelonek, at your service.

Adamski, so pleased to meet you!

– they conspicuously fail to offer their names, retreating to a corner where they converse amongst themselves.

"Well, well," declares Feliks Daszyński, "we shall all be very cosy in here, I dare say. I should give you fair warning that there will be many jokes in poor taste, but we're not a bad bunch." This he addresses to the stiff young cavalry lieutenant, of whom he already seems to have the measure. He swings his bag onto a bunk near the wall, whereupon Olgierd engages him in a debate as to whether it is better to sleep near the door or at the farthest end of the room.

"My dear Olgierd, it's cold and draughty by the door."

"Ah, but what about when you need to answer a call of nature? Not so clever then, Felo, eh?"

Soon, the group consisting of Feliks, Olgierd, Zygmunt, Młynarski, Prosiński and Hoffman have settled themselves on adjoining bunks next to Kozłowski and Tomasz. Somehow, within only minutes, it seems to Kozłowski, Tomasz has become not just a part of this group but its very centre, although he is younger than them by several years.

"I never thanked you for what you did for that major," Młynarski folds his army coat to form a pillow which he places on the top bunk, opposite Kozłowski.

"What happened to him?"

"I don't know. They took him off us and said that he would be taken care of in the clinic."

"There's a clinic here?"

A burst of laughter interrupts them, and Feliks calls Młynarski over to adjudicate in a dispute.

"You've known me a long time, Bronek. Take a look at this—" He holds up a photograph, which Kozłowski cannot see. "Now tell these tasteless tatlers that *this* is what true style looks like."

"You're wearing tennis shorts, for heaven's sake!" exclaims Olgierd, grabbing the photograph and examining it with a grin. "You can hardly call that style!"

Later, the artist Józef Czapski appears, his lean frame hunched in the doorway, to be immediately surrounded by a crowd of friends. Kozłowski observes him with curiosity, this well-known artist of whom Tomasz speaks so highly. Tall and extremely thin, with reddish hair streaked with grey, he breaks off frequently to cough into an ancient handkerchief. Although he can only be in his mid-forties, there is a quiet reserve about him which makes him seem much older than his friends.

"Have you come to join us?" asks Młynarski. "Don't tell me you've been in the Circus all this time?"

Czapski casts an envious glance around the room. "I've been wondering what special sin I've committed to end up in one of Dante's circles of Hell."

"My poor Józef. I can't think of anyone less suited to a sojourn in that madhouse than you. Can't you just slip in here and we'll pretend you're a lieutenant? Surely they won't know the difference?"

Czapski laughs. "It's a tempting thought, but I have received my orders: I'm to report to barracks number twelve with a group of other captains—"

He breaks off in surprise as the haughty young cavalry lieutenant, noticing Czapski for the first time, jumps up from his bunk with an exclamation of surprise and executes a low bow, clicking his heels in the German fashion.

"Count Hutten-Czapski," he murmurs. "Such an honour."

The lieutenant does not appear to notice Czapski's evident embarrassment at being greeted in this manner but explains in a drawling voice that he had the good fortune to be introduced to Czapski by his father at a reception at the Royal Palace in Warsaw. He offers his surname by way of introduction, an honour he has so far failed to bestow upon any of the other prisoners: "Otwinowski, at your service."

Czapski asks politely after the young man's father who, Otwinowski informs him, escaped Poland and is now – he presumes – safe in France.

Behind Otwinowski, and unseen, Feliks Daszyński and Fryderyk Hoffman enact a comic mime involving much elaborate bowing and exaggerated courtly gestures, sending a ripple of stifled laughter amongst their friends.

Czapski does not linger but hurries away, anxious not to be caught outside after dark.

"Are we allowed to visit other buildings?" Tomasz asks Otwinowski. "Does anyone know?"

He waits but Otwinowski, now seated and busy polishing his boots with a small linen handkerchief, ignores his question. Tomasz's lip curls at the man's rudeness. He is about to address him but Zygmunt, catching his eye, shakes his head.

The men lie on their bunks, the questions going back and forth like shuttlecocks.

"So who was it who issued the order for each rank to be billeted together?"

"Major Zaleski. He's the Polish officer in command."

"Yes, but who gives him the orders? Who's actually in charge here?"

"It's Berezhkov. He's the commandant, at any rate."

"There'll be a commissar in charge of political matters." Szczypiorski speaks for the first time. "That's how it works in the Soviet Union. At least, I think that's how it works." He ducks back under his bunk.

"That's Kirshin. The one who goes around in a leather jacket. You have to be careful what you say to that man. He takes it all in and writes it down in a notebook."

"But why? What's so interesting about what we say?"

"I tell you, you can't trust the Bolsheviks."

"Why are they keeping the officers here and sending the enlisted men home?"

"What kind of a camp is this anyway? Are we prisoners of war or not? I mean, does anybody know why we're in the hands of the NKVD and not the Red Army?"

Gradually, the questions cease; the men fall silent. Kozłowski twists around on the straw mattress, trying to get comfortable. Before he drifts into unconsciousness, he notices that Edward Ralski is praying, and that Fryderyk Hoffman is scribbling something in a notebook.

Kozłowski is jolted from his sleep by a sharp itch around the nape of his neck. At first, it seems the itch is in his dream, then he realises that it has not ceased on waking. He feels his skin and finds, on his neck, a small, black thing. He brings it to his eyes and nearly cries out: it is a louse. Frantically, he examines his shirt, his underlinen, his uniform.

The little creatures are crawling all over him. The man in the bunk below him wakes. The feeble light given off by the single bulb is sufficient to show him what Kozłowski is doing.

"Hey, look what this fellow's brought in with him! Get out of here, you dirty pig!"

Others wake, leaning out of their bunks to see what is going on.

"Get him out of here," continues the man. "Go on, get out, you dirty bastard!"

"I'm not dirty! I'm a doctor. If I have lice, it's because I've been shut up in a train for days, unable to wash. And besides, in these conditions, if I have them, so do you."

"I disagree," declares Otwinowski. "I certainly haven't got lice. I say we get the scoundrel out of here."

"We've all got them," declares Tomasz. "Anyone who says he doesn't is lying."

"Um, what does a louse look like, exactly?" asks Szczypiorski. "I'm not saying I've got them. I'm just wondering…"

"It's too dark to look for them now. Tomorrow we should tell the camp authorities that there are lice and ask for a bath and soap."

Somebody laughs. "We should be so lucky. We've been here for two weeks without being able to wash."

"There's still plenty we can do to keep them at bay. I can show you in the morning, if you like." Kozłowski waits, hoping that the men will not eject him from the barracks. Nobody replies.

He lies awake, trying not to give in to the horror he feels at the filthiness of his body, and the little insects burrowing into his skin. Tomorrow, he will go to the camp clinic and ask about obtaining soap; he will show his bunkmates how to check the seams of their clothes; he will shake out his mattress and hang it up outside. He will not let the dirt and chaos overcome him.

6. *A petition*

Fenced off with barbed wire, patrolled by guards, the excellent condition of the camp offices is in stark contrast to the rest of the buildings. To their right is a low house, the windows of which are blanked out with lime.

The guard does not return Dr Levittoux's salute but stares sullenly at him.

"What do you want? You're not supposed to be in this part of the camp."

"I wish to see Captain Berezhkov."

"He's busy."

"Then I will wait."

The guard shifts uncertainly. "You're not supposed to go in there."

Very patiently, Dr Levittoux explains his mission: he comes as the representative of nearly 300 medical personnel in the camp, many of whom are among the top specialists in Poland. They have written a letter which he wishes to submit to the commandant of the camp; no, he continues, he will not hand it to the guard, he will give it to Commandant Berezhkov and no one else. Kozłowski listens to Levittoux's smooth, fluent Russian. Many of the older men who were born into a Poland still partitioned received their education in Moscow or St Petersburg and are as at home speaking Russian as they are Polish. Kozłowski's own Russian is serviceable, adequate but without depth. He wishes now that he had made more effort with the language at school. Eventually, as it becomes clear that Dr Levittoux is not going to go away, the guard agrees to ask the commandant if he will receive the prisoners.

Kozłowski had encountered Dr Levittoux outside the small clinic which Kozłowski had finally located after several days spent wandering hopelessly amongst the crowds of departing soldiers and newly-arrived officers. Dr Levittoux hailed his young colleague with the same cordiality with which he would have greeted him if they had bumped into one another in the corridor of the Hospital of the Holy Spirit, immediately inviting Kozłowski to accompany him to a meeting of medical staff which had been arranged in the majors' block. On the way there, between answering Kozłowski's many eager questions – *How many doctors are there here, sir?* ("I've no idea. Upwards of three hundred is my guess.") and *Will it be possible to obtain soap? The men are crawling with lice.* ("No. Not yet, at least.") and *Have you come across a major with a wounded leg?* ("There are so many patients in the clinic right now I haven't had a chance to see them all.") – Dr Levittoux explained the object of the meeting, asking his colleague to stand guard at the door in case anyone should come in. After the meeting was over, the doctors, pharmacists, orderlies and dentists slowly dispersed, conversing in low voices. Kozłowski lingered by the barracks door, watching Levittoux as he collated the sheets of paper.

"If you are willing, Zbyszek, you may do me a further favour."

"Of course. I'd be delighted."

"Come with me to the camp offices. I confess I have no desire to enter those buildings alone."

Berezhkov looks up from his work without returning the salute of either man. "Well, what is it? Be quick, it's late." His finger taps insistently on the desk. He is stocky, with bristling hair cut short *à la* Stalin.

Major Levittoux explains that the purpose of his visit is twofold. As he offers a brief outline of the purpose and content of the letter, Kozłowski wonders what the second reason might be.

"As you will see, Commandant, the letter is signed by many of the medical staff who are presently imprisoned in the camp. We respectfully request that our concerns be addressed by the highest possible authority."

"The highest possible authority," snaps Berezhkov. "You are speaking to the highest possible authority right now. What is this?" He picks up the papers, flicking through them.

Levittoux patiently reiterates the doctors' request, at the end of which Berezhkov stares at him blankly.

"You are asking to leave the camp?" He almost snorts with laughter, glancing down at the letter, with the long list of signatures – professor of this, director of that, head of the other; major, captain, lieutenant. At this moment, the door opens and Commissar Kirshin slips into the room. He is no longer wearing the leather jacket but is dressed in NKVD uniform, his shirt unbuttoned at the collar.

"Forgive me for interrupting. I heard that you had visitors."

With a pleasant smile at the two Poles, Kirshin positions himself discreetly behind Berezhkov's desk, an act which appears to unsettle Berezhkov, who shifts in his chair and clears his throat before loudly restating Major Levittoux's own words.

"So, let us be clear, you are saying that you are here as the representative of the medical staff in this camp and that as such you," he holds up the sheets of paper, "are requesting that you be transferred from the camp in accordance with the Geneva Convention in order either to be returned to your homes or released to work in hospitals."

"That is correct."

"And you wish me to refer this to the highest possible authority."

"At your discretion, of course, Commandant," replies Levittoux, without even glancing at Kirshin.

"Naturally," Kirshin's soft voice carries from the back of the room. "Your request will be considered in all seriousness. You will receive a reply in due course."

"Thank you."

"You said there was a second matter." Berezhkov leans forward, as if eager to regain control over the meeting. "Well, spit it out."

"It concerns camp hygiene, Commandant."

"Hygiene?"

"To be more precise, the risk of the spread of epidemics, specifically typhus." Dr Levittoux draws from his pocket a small piece of paper, from which he reads. "We already have seven cases of typhus and three of amoebic dysentery. Unless the men are permitted to bathe and clean their clothes, these diseases will spread and, as you know," he looks up at Berezkhov and Kirshin, his gaze mild and open, "diseases are no respecters of national boundaries. An epidemic of typhus fever or dysentery will swiftly spread beyond the prisoners."

Berezhkov stands up. "May I remind you that you are prisoners in this camp and it is we who decide what facilities will be permitted to you. It is not up to you to dictate terms. We have our own very well-qualified doctors who will alert us to the necessity – if there is indeed such a need – of any changes in our hygiene policy. Medical examinations will begin shortly, once registration is complete." He lights a cardboard-tipped cigarette, blowing the smoke heavily from his lips. "You may go."

"Do you think they will do anything?"

Levittoux and Kozłowski hurry across the central square towards the barracks. It is dark now, and with the darkness has come a damp, penetrating cold.

"About the letter? Who knows? They may just tear it into pieces as soon as we are out of the door. They may consider it seriously. As to the hygiene situation, if they are not listening now they will soon have to once men start falling ill. I've not yet met their doctor. I'll be interested to see what he is like." Levittoux smiles. "I confess that *Homo Sovieticus* is a closed book to me: I have no idea how to read these new men." He places a friendly hand on Kozłowski's shoulder. "Goodnight, Zbyszek, and thank you. It's very different from our days at the Hospital of the Holy Spirit, is it not?"

Kozłowski walks slowly towards the edge of the camp, attracted by a strange centrifugal pull to mark out the boundary of his prison, like a beetle following a wall in the blind hope that at some point, miraculously, the solid barrier will break and offer a route to freedom. He seeks silence, but in vain: the speakers in front of the church blare out day and night an unstoppable stream of invective against the 'former Polish army' and the land of overweight capitalist landlords for whose sins the Polish proletariat are now paying in blood. Berezhkov spoke of registration, and of medical examinations. Clearly, there is a plan for the prisoners which – in the chaos of arrivals and departures -

has yet to become apparent to them. What then? What is our purpose here? Something ahead of him catches his eye: two men, their heads bowed in deep discussion, one speaking, the other – older, with grey hair and a beard – listening intently. One of them is Edward Ralski.

"Hey, you!" A guard strides towards the men. "What are you doing out here? Inside, now!"

Kozłowski sees the second man hastily make a gesture of benediction over Ralski's head and he recognises the old priest, Father Alexandrowicz. The two men separate and hurry towards their barracks. Any thoughts of staying out longer have dissipated: the guard has spotted Kozłowski now and is approaching, waving his arms angrily.

"Don't you know you're supposed to be inside, you stupid Pole?"

Kozłowski raises a hand as if to say – I understand, no need to tell me twice – and returns to his block.

7. Yes, indeedy

"Come on, my good fellows, forward march. Yes, that's it, hold out the pail – no, closer – That's it! We don't want to spill a single drop of the precious nectar, eh?" Chef Antoni keeps up his hearty commentary all morning as he swings his ladle into the cauldron and brings it out with a slurp. His words are banal and the jokes well-worn, but they keep the men standing in line from reflecting too much on their cold feet or their hungry stomachs.

"Silly old fool," they murmur, with half a smile, "doesn't he ever shut up?"

Feliks Daszyński has formed a habit of whiling away the wait for breakfast by engaging in an energetic exercise regime.

"Have you noticed..." he squats down with bended knees then springs up, flinging his arms out sideways, a cigarette dangling from his lips, "that there is no one here above the rank of Major? And yet I distinctly recall seeing several colonels with us when we arrived at Starobelsk, and at least two generals: General Billewicz was with us when they loaded us on the train and General Sikorski was there when we were captured. Where are those men now?"

"Prosiński told me there were several senior officers brought in with his group," says Kozłowski, "but they were separated from the others on arrival."

Feliks resumes his exercises, this time executing a series of star jumps. "Maybe they're keeping them somewhere else?"

"You look ridiculous, Felo," says Młynarski. "You know that, don't you? Like a mad stork."

"I don't care. I'd rather be ridiculous than cold." Feliks breaks into a sprint, sending mud spraying up the back of his calves.

"Move along now, gentlemen, please! Bowls at the ready!"

In the queue behind them, a haggard-looking major is conversing in loud, American-accented English with a young boy who can be no more than fourteen or fifteen years of age.

"Goodness," whispers Młynarski, "he doesn't seem worried about being overheard."

Kozłowski looks over to where the guards are standing, apparently oblivious to the major's knowing or unconscious act of subversion. Noting their curious glances in his direction, the old man introduces himself, expressing his delight when Młynarski confesses that, having lived for many years in the United States, he, too, is a fluent speaker of the English language.

"Although," Młynarski adds hastily, in Polish, "I don't think I'd risk speaking English unless I were sure of not being overheard."

The Major, immediately seizing his meaning, shoots a glance in the direction of the guards.

"Sh!" he whispers, raising his finger theatrically to his lips. "Mum's the word! How wonderful, though," he adds, unable to restrain his enthusiasm, clutching the arm of the young boy next to him with an air of delight. "A fellow Anglophile!"

There is no need to ask Major Skarżyński how it is that such a young boy has ended up in Starobelsk, for he immediately begins to tell Młynarski, the words tumbling over one another in his desire to recount his story to a sympathetic listener.

"I see how astonished you are, Lieutenant. Yes. You can easily imagine, sir, the torment I am suffering to have my son with me here. *Yes, indeedy.* And when I think of the state his poor dear mother must be in!"

"Have you spoken to Berezhkov?"

"I go to the camp authorities daily. Daily. My boy is an American citizen, you see. We lived in the States for many years. He was born there. Yes. I, alas, lost my rights when I returned to Poland. But he, he is the *real deal*, as they say." The Major's face twists into a grimace; he tugs nervously on his moustache.

"But surely they cannot wish to keep him here. He's just a boy—"

"Only fifteen! But, alas, so far, my pleas have fallen on deaf ears. I am petitioning them to contact the American Ambassador in Moscow, but I've heard nothing yet, although—" Skarżyński leans in conspiratorially. "I have it on good authority," he utters these words with particular emphasis, "*good authority*, that the Americans have taken over representation of Poland's interests internationally…"

Later, as they crouch around the pail of cold kasza, Młynarski repeats this to Feliks Daszyński, who listens with intense interest.

"Surely you don't take it seriously, Felo? The man is clearly beside himself with worry about his son and it has clouded his wits."

"Why not? It makes perfect sense that America should step in to protect Poland's interests. Who else could do it?"

"But America's not even involved in the war—"

"Exactly! That puts her in a stronger position to exert diplomatic pressure on Russia over issues of humanitarian concern…"

"Felo, it's nonsense!" Młynarski glances uneasily at Kozłowski. "Surely you realise that?"

Tomasz enters the bunkroom, sending droplets of rain showering over the floor. "It's vile out there!" He stamps his boots to dislodge the mud. "Guess what?" He sits down heavily on Zygmunt's bunk, taking the bowl which Kozłowski is holding out to him. His cheeks are damp, his eyes shining with excitement. "There's a visitor arriving today."

"Who?"

"I've no idea, but he's coming from Moscow."

"You see?" Feliks turns to Młynarski in triumph.

The gates to the camp swing open and a black car drives in, splattering mud in its wake. It pulls up outside the offices, where a welcoming committee has gathered on the steps: Kirshin and Berezhkov stand at the front, next to an immensely tall man wearing the uniform of an NKVD captain whom Kozłowski has never seen before. His gut protrudes like a barrel over a pair of skinny legs which look scarcely strong enough to support his weight and he has an air of lazy importance, surveying with tiny, piggy eyes the shivering Poles who have gathered under the dripping eaves to wait and watch. Behind the senior officers stand their deputies: Petrov, gaunt and long-nosed, pulling at a cigarette, and Stepanov, smooth-shaven and powdered, immaculately dressed in a smart blue coat. As a guard runs to open the back door of the car, the men on the steps stiffen and salute. Kozłowski catches a glimpse of a heavy coat and a cap, then the man disappears into the building.

Immediately, the camp is abuzz with questions concerning the identity of the mysterious visitor. Is he from the NKVD? The Red Cross? The Red Army? The Soviet government?

When, a short while later, the man emerges from the camp offices and begins a tour of the ruined buildings, followed at a respectful distance by Commissar Kirshin, curiosity grows. He is not in uniform but wears a long civilian overcoat, his trousers tucked into shiny galoshes. An American-style baseball cap covers his hair, the visor pulled down low over his forehead, shading his eyes.

"He's important, that's for sure," declares Zygmunt, observing Kirshin, who appears to be explaining something to the man with great eagerness. "Look at the way Kirshin is bowing and scraping. I've a mind to ask him some questions. It's about time someone gave us an explanation for the way we're being treated here."

At this moment, Major Miller comes hurrying towards them. "Major Zaleski says you should be wary of talking to that man. He is a senior NKVD officer from Moscow. If you do speak to him, be careful what you say. And remember," Miller moves on to the next group, "Kirshin is taking everything in."

Despite the warning, the temptation is too great: as soon as the visitor draws near he is surrounded by a jostling crowd of prisoners who bombard him with questions.

"Sir." A plump captain steps forward, pulling his ragged overcoat around him with an air of injured dignity. "Since you are obviously a man of some influence, could you please tell us whether Polish Army officers are regarded by the Soviet authorities as prisoners of war and, if they are, whether we will enjoy the rights to which we are entitled under international law?"

The man from Moscow smiles blandly. When he speaks, his voice is soft and high-pitched.

"Yes, of course. You are a Soviet prisoner of war and you will enjoy all the rights which are due to you...."

"In that case," Tomasz joins the crowd, peering over their heads. "May we write to our families?"

"Of course you may. Very soon you will be able to write."

"But we have no paper, no pens."

"Of course, we will provide you with writing paper, pencils, pens and so forth.... You will get other items too. There will be a special shop here soon that will sell many useful articles... You will have films, a radio, newspapers and books..."

"What about our pay?" asks Olgierd. "As POWs we are entitled to receive at least part of our pay."

"Of course you will receive your pay... Yes, of course you will be able to assign part of that money to your families... Parcels from your families and the Red Cross will be permitted... Of course... Soon..."

"Soon, soon. A fine lullaby."

The old man's grey beard is matted, his dark civilian coat covered in a thick layer of dirt, and he appears to have lost his belt, for the coat is tied around his waist with a length of string. Kozłowski has never seen him before; he wonders, briefly, how a civilian has ended up in a camp full of army officers.

"You don't believe him?"

"Do you?"

Kozłowski considers the question, watching the eager gaggle of men as they follow the stranger around the camp. The Polish High Command were assured that the Soviet Union had no aggressive intentions towards their army, only to be attacked and taken prisoner. Since their capture, the officers have been told nothing either about their status or the Soviet authorities' intentions for them. What possible reason can there therefore be to believe their promises? And yet, the soothing words uttered by the stranger from Moscow insinuate themselves into Kozłowski's mind: he wants to hope, and the prospect of receiving mail from home, and parcels of food and linen, and money with which to purchase those little necessities such as needles and threads, or shoelaces, which would make camp life so much easier to bear, makes him hungry for the promised bounty to arrive. He finds himself telling the man that, after all, this is not a Siberian labour camp; they are officers, prisoners of war. Speaking for himself, he wants only to be able to send a letter back home…

The little man looks up at Kozłowski with a pitying smile. "Soon, soon," he croons.

Outside the camp offices Major Skarżyński waits anxiously, his cap carefully positioned to cover his straggling hair, a piece of paper clutched in his hand. The boy stands behind him, a slim echo of his father. As the visitor from Moscow finally approaches, Skarżyński straightens. At this moment, a gangling figure steps out from under the eaves.

Feliks Daszyński is considerably taller than the Russian. He peers down at him, ignoring the rain dripping down his neck.

"Is it true," he begins in Polish, "that the United States, through its ambassador in Moscow, is to take over the interests of the Polish Embassy and extend its protection over Polish prisoners of war in the USSR? Would you, in that case, permit us to draw up a petition to the American Ambassador asking that we be freed immediately and be allowed to be returned to a neutral or allied country in order to fight the Germans again?"

There is a stunned silence as the prisoners absorb the extraordinary temerity of the question. Commissar Kirshin, meanwhile, stares at Feliks with an expression of mingled wonderment and horror, as if trying to decide whether he is more shocked by the idiocy of the question or afraid that the visitor will blame him for the fact that the prisoner feels bold enough to pose it.

Zygmunt hastily steps in to translate. As the meaning of the question becomes clear to him, the visitor's face darkens with fury.

"Where did you hear such rubbish?" He hisses, before breaking off, glancing around self-consciously at the shocked faces of those who have witnessed his reaction. He continues, in his smooth, level voice: "Of course you may write a petition. The camp commanders will do everything in their power to ensure it reaches the proper authorities..."

The visit is over. Major Skarżyński only has time to thrust his petition into the unwilling hands of the visitor as, flanked protectively by Kirshin and Stepanov, he hurries back inside. The words which the old man has been rehearsing all morning remain unsaid.

8. A photograph

"Everybody out into the yard!"

While one group of guards frisks the prisoners outside, another group ransacks the barracks, grabbing anything they can find - documents, money, personal possessions - and carrying them to the camp offices.

Kozłowski performs a rapid assessment of the whereabouts of his personal possessions. He has little money, and nothing of value either on his person or in his rucksack. In his greatcoat pocket, however, is his civilian passport. He had almost forgotten about it until now, since at no point in the weeks since his capture has anyone even asked his name. He feels in his pocket. The passport is there, stiff and small. Should he destroy it, or try to hide it? But where? Men fumble in their pockets for wallets, diaries, rings, banknotes, glancing around surreptiously in search of a suitable hiding place, although nearby are only trees, holes in the ground, planks of wood. Since nobody has the slightest idea what the guards are looking for, every object of personal significance is at stake.

Ralski draws two small photographs from his wallet. "What shall I do with these?"

"In your sleeve," hisses Zygmunt.

"What?"

Zygmunt indicates his jacket cuff. "Make a little split in the lining, put them up there. Not the wallet. It's too thick."

With an air of bewilderment, his hands shaking, Ralski tears the lining of his coat cuff and hastily stuffs the photographs up as far as possible.

"You. Line up." A guard points to the first three rows of prisoners. "Follow me."

A line of *politruks* sit at long boards perched on wooden trestles, on top of which piles of papers, documents and photographs lie scattered.

"Place all your military and civilian documents, notebooks, photographs and money here." Petrov indicates the table.

Tomasz is first in line. Reaching into his soaking-wet coat, he brings out a few loose papers and his military identity card. Petrov gathers them up, glancing through them.

"This is it?" He studies Tomasz with the air of a suspicious customs official.

"Yes."

Petrov nods. Tomasz evidently thinks he is being instructed to leave, for he turns. Instead, he is grabbed from behind, his coat yanked from his shoulders. The guards run their hands over his body, turning his pockets inside out. His lack of personal possessions appears to have aroused Petrov's suspicions, for he orders the guards to search Tomasz thoroughly, instructing them to check the lining of his coat as well as the soles of his boots. They tear open his boots, finding nothing, then rip from the lining of his coat a single, small photograph.

"Please, don't take it!" Tomasz lunges at the guard, receiving a sharp blow to his back with a rifle butt which sends him tumbling to the ground.

Petrov scrutinises the photograph impassively.

"Please." Tomasz gets to his feet, his voice trembling. His socks sink into the mud. "Of what possible use can it be to you?"

Without a word, Petrov tosses the photograph onto the pile, making a note in a register.

"Get dressed!"

A young *politruk* with dark, curly hair watches carefully as the guard places Edward Ralski's passport, some Polish money, a calendar and a small tin box on the table before him.

"What is this?" The *politruk,* Mitrov, opens the box and peers inside.

"Just a few specimen grass seeds I've collected. I'm a botanist."

Mitrov stares at Ralski blankly. "Grass."

Ralski nods.

"You wish to keep this?"

"If you will permit me."

"Grass."

"That's right."

Mitrov twists round to show the box to Commissar Kirshin, who leans down, poking his finger experimentally inside the little box, then whispers something to the *politruk.*

"You are lucky that Commissar Kirshin is such a generous man," declares Mitrov to Ralski in a loud voice. "You may keep your specimens. Search him."

Kozłowski watches as the guards take off Ralski's coat and feel their way along its lining, patting the sleeves and turning it inside out. They do not rip the coat as they did Tomasz's, nor do they slit open his boots. Ralski is evidently considered less inclined to subversion than his younger friend. Although this assessment is entirely correct, it hardly requires a trained intelligence officer to form it: whereas Ralski, in his early thirties, has an air of calm rationality about him, Tomasz exudes a kind of suppressed energy, as if he is lacking only the opportunity to rebel.

"You're a doctor?" Mitrov studies Kozłowski's passport. His curly hair peeps from beneath his cap just as Kozłowski's is wont to do.

"Yes."

Mitrov nods, then snaps the passport shut, handing it to the guard to place in a green envelope.

"Do you have anything else?"

Kozłowski pulls his pockets inside out. He has the impression that Mitrov has already lost interest in him.

At the other end of the table a moustachioed captain stands before Stepanov. With a theatrical flourish he holds up his military papers and tears them to shreds, the little pieces fluttering down onto the table.

"You fool!" hisses Stepanov, his cheeks reddening under the layer of white powder. "You think we don't have other means of finding out who you are?"

The captain stands rigid, staring straight ahead.

"Get this man out of here!" yells Stepanov. "And make sure he has nothing more on him."

"You may go now." Mitrov holds out a slip of paper. "This is the number under which your documents will be kept."

I am of no interest to them, thinks Kozłowski, almost with disappointment. The tiny scrap of paper bears a pencilled number and a round stamp: *NKVD — Starobelsk*. He has the absurd feeling that he has just been issued a book from a library.

"May I ask for the return of my documents once you have finished with them?"

Mitrov glances at Kirshin.

"Of course," replies Kirshin. "You may ask."

"Here, hold your hands out."

Kozłowski presses the pump up and down until a stream of icy water issues forth onto Tomasz's outstretched hands.

"What about my coat? Do you think I should try to clean it?"

"It's probably better to let the mud dry off first."

"Fat chance of that." Anger lingers on Tomasz's face as he scrubs at his hands. His boots gape at the toe; his socks are covered with mud.

"I'm sorry they took away your photograph, Tomasz."

Tomasz shrugs, embarrassed, but says nothing.

They walk back to the barracks in silence, where Tomasz is greeted with an outpouring of sympathy: Zygmunt offers him an old newspaper to stuff his boots, while the pink-cheeked priest makes him a present of a pair of socks. As Tomasz, in tears, thanks his comrades for their generosity, Kozłowski wonders, briefly, whose image it was that was so precious to his friend.

9. Come with me

Kozłowski wakes at midnight, unsure what has disturbed his sleep: he is not aware of emerging from a dream, nor are the lice, at this moment, bothering him more than usual. He is about to go back to sleep when he realises that he can hear voices in the corridor, arguing softly in Russian:

"And I'm telling you, you idiot, that he must be here somewhere! I've been in all the other places, so he must be here, right? A tall, thin man with a beard, dressed in a green tunic."

"Tall and thin with a beard and a green tunic, are you joking? That could be any one of them! It's like looking for a needle in a haystack!"

Lifting himself on his elbow, Kozłowski can just see through the narrow strip of window that runs along the top of the bunkroom wall.

"What is it?" The bunk shakes as Zygmunt clambers up beside him.

"I don't know."

Together they press as close to the window as they dare.

"It's Kopyekin," whispers Zygmunt.

In the corridor below the camp messenger, Kopyekin, is talking to the night guard. Seen from behind, Kopyekin resembles a monkey, the back of his flat head covered in wispy hair, his ears sticking out like jug handles.

"His name is Daszyński."

"Well, why didn't you say you had a name?"

"So come on, then. Let's go and look for him."

Across the room, men are waking. Zygmunt drops silently from the bunk and steps across the piles of filthy boots to reach the bunk where Feliks Daszyński is sleeping.

"Felo!" Zygmut shakes him by the shoulder. "Felo, wake up."

Zygmunt just has time to slip back to his bunk as the guard, accompanied by Kopyekin, enters the room, shining his torch into the pale, unshaven faces of the men.

"Daszyński, Feliks," declares Kopyekin in his rasping voice. "Which one is he? *Nu*, come now. We know he's in here."

Kopyekin scuttles from bed to bed, pulling down the covers as if the more he sees of a man, the more the man might reveal himself as Daszyński. The prisoners wait in silence until, finally, Kopyekin finds him.

"Come along now, get dressed and come with me," he mutters.

Feliks takes his time, laughing and joking as he pulls on his socks and boots. "I don't understand a word this numbskull is saying to me. D'you think he wants my autograph?" At the door, he turns to address his friends. "Don't get too excited. If I don't come back you can share out my belongings among yourselves."

Zygmunt, yawning as if half asleep, follows them out on the pretence of needing to urinate. Nobody speaks: nobody wishes to give expression to their fear. *Get dressed and come with me,* said Kopyekin.

The minutes stretch.

As soon as Zygmunt's footsteps are heard in the corridor, Młynarski jumps from his bunk. "Well?"

"You know that small building on the edge of the camp? The one that's fenced off with barbed wire? They took him there."

"That's the special section," says Prosiński.

"Special section? What's that?"

"I've no idea. I heard one of the guards call it that."

"It's Lebedyev's domain." Lieutenant Otwinowski, for once, speaks without the air of studied contempt with which he normally addresses his fellow prisoners. "The fat giant. I don't know what they do there."

All night they lie awake, waiting for Feliks Daszyński to return. *Get dressed and come with me.* Kopyekin's words linger in Kozłowski's mind, like an incantation. Finally, as the first glimmer of dawn begins to show in the sky, the door to the bunkroom opens. Seemingly oblivious to the hundred pairs of eyes observing him, Feliks picks his way across the piles of muddy boots, climbs onto his bunk and turns to face the wall.

When morning comes, his friends gather round him.

"So tell us about it, Felo," says Młynarski. "What happened, eh? Did they give you a grilling?"

"There's nothing to say." Feliks pulls on his boots without meeting his friend's eyes. "I went and came back, that's all."

When Kozłowski reminds Feliks, as he does every morning, to check the seams of his clothes for lice, Feliks snaps at him with unaccustomed ill humour.

"Leave me alone, can't you? Who cares if we've got lice?"

He walks out of the room and is not seen again for the rest of the day.

10. So many colleagues

The consulting room is tiny and oppressively warm. Seated at the desk is a woman of indeterminate age. Her features are refined but her skin is colourless, her grey eyes obscured by heavy-framed spectacles. She wears a white coat, her dark hair pinned back neatly. In front of her is a sheet of paper on which she has written Kozłowski's name, and the date and place of his birth.

"Profession?" She addresses him in Polish, with a slight Russian accent.

"Doctor of medicine."

A smile brightens the grey face. "You are? How wonderful! So many colleagues. I mean," she stammers, looking down again, "that it is a pleasure for me to meet other professionals, although the circumstances..." She shuffles the papers around. Kozłowski notices that her fingernails are bitten to the quick. "Do you have a specialism?"

Kozłowski wants to confess to her that this is a subject which was exercising him greatly just before the war: he had been debating whether to follow his mentor Dr Levittoux into orthopaedics or pursue a long-standing interest in opthalmology. He says only: "General medicine."

"I will take your pulse, your temperature and your blood pressure. Do you have any particular medical problems?"

"No."

Her hands on his wrist are cool and dry. He glances sideways at her as she watches the second hand ticking round the clock. "You speak good Polish."

She makes a note in the file. "My grandfather was Polish. May I listen to your heart?"

He unbuttons his shirt, shamefully conscious of his filthy body, the red marks where the lice have bitten him. "They have not allowed us to bathe..."

She places the stethoscope on his chest, the cold metal sending a shiver across his skin.

"Breathe in. And out."

Her hair smells of shampoo, a clean, fresh scent that makes him long to stand under a hot shower until the memory of this camp, with all its dirt and filth, has been washed away.

She places the stethoscope on his back, and the metal shocks his skin again.

"They should really invent a stethoscope made of something other than metal."

She laughs. "How true! I often feel it is such an inhuman thing. All the instruments of our profession, if you think about it, are made of metal, and cold—"

The door opens abruptly and a square-faced young man wearing steel-rimmed glasses sticks his head into the room.

"What is all this laughter, Dr Vasilevna? Get down to work instead of wasting time with these Poles."

"Yes, Dr Yegorov."

The door slams shut. Dr Vasilevna hurriedly concludes the examination.

"You seem fit and well." She makes a final note. "Send in the next patient on your way out." Her face has taken on an expression of cold indifference.

Kozłowski follows the path that marks the perimeter of the camp. Why had he felt the absurd desire to confide to Dr Vasilevna his thoughts about his career?

A large black crow, perched on a tree root, pecks at the frozen ground. Nearby, crouched over a gravestone sketching the ungainly creature on a shred of paper, is Tadeusz Biały. The crow pulls fruitlessly at an unseen object until, startled by Kozłowski's approach, it flies off.

"Sorry. I didn't mean to scare it. Hullo, Tadek."

"It's alright. It's getting too cold anyway." Biały stands and stretches, greeting his old schoolfriend with a shy grin. "Hullo, Zbyszek. I was wondering when I'd bump into someone I know."

"May I see it?"

Biały holds out the drawing. His fingers are bright red, marked with chilblains. The sketch, roughly drawn, nevertheless captures vividly the crow's determined struggle. Kozłowski is reminded of Biały's schoolbooks, always covered with little drawings – of animals, birds, caricatures of the teachers' faces, each instantly recognisable, more than once the cause of a stern ticking-off.

"I wonder what it was that so fascinated him."

Crouching down to scrape away the earth Biały finds, a few inches beneath the surface of the snow, a large lump of solidified bread. Many of the prisoners throw away their bread because it is so damp and mouldy, inedible even for the desperate. Biały removes the crust, tossing it towards a nearby tree trunk in the hope that the crow will return. In doing so, he reveals something else. It pokes from the ground, a smooth, dirty white something.

Together they jab away at the frozen earth, Biały using the end of his pencil, Kozłowski a dead branch. Finally, a crack appears in the soil and Biały's pencil dives unexpectedly into a small depression, breaking in two.

"Dammit!"

He pulls away the clod of earth to reveal, beneath it, a human skull. He lifts the skull out of the earth and laughs: the broken half of his pencil is lodged between the skull's teeth, protruding from its mouth like a cigarette.

It is only now that Kozłowski notices the man seated underneath the large poplar tree that dominates the centre of the former graveyard. Dressed in tattered rags, a scarf wrapped around his neck, the man is observing them through a pair of filthy, wire-framed spectacles. He climbs to his feet and approaches them. Without a word, he takes the skull from Biały and inspects it with a professional air, moving his fingers slowly over its surface until he finds what he is looking for. With a grunt of satisfaction he nods and points to a small, round hole on the left-hand side of the base of the skull then, turning it around, he indicates a semi-circular chip on the upper ridge of the right eye socket. He raises his eyebrows, before handing the skull back to Biały and resuming his position on the ground.

"You shouldn't sit there, sir," exclaims Kozłowski. "It's far too cold."

The man stares at Kozłowski with profound indifference. He grabs the discarded lump of bread and shoves it into his mouth. His fingernails are caked with dirt.

On the way back to the barracks, neither Biały nor Kozłowski speak of the man. Although Kozłowski recognised him, for some reason he does not wish to tell Biały who he is. It is as if, in witnessing the man's despair, they have surprised him in an act of shocking intimacy.

Before the war, Dr Kazimierz Dadej was the director of a sanatorium for children in Zakopane, a man famous for his energetic dedication to the health of his patients. Czapski pointed him out to Kozłowski once, for they are both billeted in the dismal block of sickly captains known by prisoners as The Morgue. Kozłowski cannot fathom what determines who amongst the prisoners will remain strong and who will give in to despair. Czapski said their squalid living conditions were at the root of Dr Dadej's depression: to a man as scrupulous as he, the dirt rendered everything unbearable. Kozłowski fingers his collar, where raised welts mark the point of irritation where the lice bite and he must scratch.

By the main square, they encounter a group of young officers who immediately fall upon the skull, vying to tell the funniest joke in the silliest accent.

"You former Polish officers of the former Polish army," says their leader in a thick Russian accent, sucking noisily on an imaginary cigarette, "you think that imperialist old effigy Great Britain is going to come to your aid? Think again!"

His friends roar with laughter at the instantly recognisable imitation of Kirshin's deputy, Petrov.

Kozłowski watches the little group as they walk off, slapping their comrade on his back. They wear their coats over their shoulders, their caps at a rakish angle on their heads. The sight of such officers striding down Krakowskie Przedmieście in Warsaw was a familiar one before the war: the flirtatious glances cast at pretty girls, the bursts of laughter at a shared joke; so young, so full of confidence, their leather boots gleaming. As they make their way along one of the wooden walkways that cross the camp, Berezhkov appears, heading directly towards them. They salute him as one, a beautiful, synchronised movement which, as always, Berezhkov ignores. The young captain comes face to face with the camp commandant: one of them will have to step off the walkway in order to let the other pass. His companions, absorbed in their conversation, automatically step down onto the snow, heading off towards the Circus. The captain, however, appears to be deliberating. He pauses, pulls back his shoulders and, looking directly into Berezhkov's eyes, holds his ground. The confrontation lasts barely a second: Berezhkov tuts in irritation then, with a brief, contemptuous glance at the proud young man in the tattered cap whose stance is that of a gentleman offering his services for a duel, steps off the walkway and continues on his way. Kozłowski is puzzled by this concession: the Soviets have been keen to humiliate the Polish officers at every opportunity, taking meticulous care to remove all recognition of rank or status, so that even the guards refer to them only as '*Ty*' – the over-familiar 'You'. The young captain glances over at Kozłowski, and there is in his triumphant smile a hint of a sneer. Kozłowski feels somehow ashamed. Slowly, carefully, he makes his way back to the barracks, his feet sliding on the icy planks.

11. *Go right!*

They sit in companionable silence in Biały's bunkroom, Kozłowski whittling a piece of wood whilst Biały sketches the skull with his broken pencil stub.

"What's that supposed to be, then?" Biały glances curiously at the wooden cylinder with a curved bell-like shape at either end which

Kozłowski is fashioning.

"A stethoscope. Only I can't seem to get through the stem. I'm scared of snapping it."

"Give it here."

Kozłowski hands Biały the blunted scalpel purloined from the clinic, and watches as his friend begins to scrape the wood in tiny, circular motions.

Behind Biały is the table on which he has placed the skull. It faces him, its hollow eyes dark and empty; next to it is the pile of rough newspaper which Biały uses as a sketchpad. Winter sunlight filters through the dirty window and falls in a thin shaft onto the table, over the skull, spilling onto the right side of Biały's body, illuminating the dirty green uniform with the lieutenant's insignia on its shoulder. It renders his pale skin white, revealing in minute detail every hair on his chin, where his thin beard grows patchily, and catching the corner of his bright hazel eyes with their fringe of long lashes which the girls at school always envied.

"How old is your daughter now, Tadek?"

"She's two. There, done it! Why don't you give it a try? I'll be your guinea pig." Biały unbuttons his shirt while Kozłowski places one end of the instrument on his chest, pressing his ear against the other. "Tell me if it's still ticking—"

Kozłowski listens intently. After a few seconds, he declares: "Lieutenant Biały, I can confidently state that you are still alive."

"Well, that's a relief, I must say!"

Kozłowski feels childishly pleased with his new instrument. It serves no practical purpose, giving as it does a reading of a heartbeat fainter than that which can be obtained by pressing a naked ear against a man's chest. Nevertheless, it delights him. He sets it carefully on the sill by the dusty window, wondering if he will ever have cause to use it.

"I saw your brother, by the way, Zbyszek. In Lwów."

"Which one?"

"Staś. He was in civilian clothes and had somehow got hold of a motorbike. He was going to try to make it to Rumania, then join up with the air force again in France. He looked very well. He said to send you his regards if I was to meet you."

When Kozłowski returns to his own bunkroom later he finds an argument in full swing. Olgierd Szpakowski, his ruddy cheeks a brighter red than usual, is loudly setting out his vision of a Poland ruled by and for ethnic Poles. Kozłowski likes the gruff lieutenant, who shares his supply of unusual luxuries with everyone without discrimination, but when he hears him mouthing the crude, nationalistic slogans of the Endecja a sense of weariness overcomes him: these arguments have been rehearsed, in one form or another, since the first days of independence.

"In order to be strong, citizens of the Polish Republic must be united by a common language and common beliefs. That means they should speak Polish and they should worship in the Catholic Church...."

Feliks Daszyński, meanwhile, is setting out his own competing vision of the future based, he declares, "on all that was best about Piłsudski", without the baggage of the Sanacja; on the principles embodied by his father Ignacy, who maintained a true vision of social democracy. "Strength doesn't come from the exclusion of minority groups, telling Poles of Ukrainian or Jewish or German origin that they have no right to be Polish. Strength comes from diversity..."

Some have taken sides whilst others try in vain to sleep. Lieutenant Szczypiorski, seated on the edge of his bunk, listens with interest, his head cocked to one side, like a sparrow. Fryderyk Hoffman looks up from his notebook from time to time, his expression inscrutable.

"Poland will be infinitely stronger and more unified if it is ruled by and for one national group," declares Olgierd, "instead of endlessly trying to placate minorities who all want something different..."

"But, Olgierd, look at Germany! Surely, the future of Poland must reside in a concept of nationhood that is not based on a narrow definition of ethnicity!"

Before a further furore can follow this remark, Tomasz bursts into the bunkroom, bringing with him a gust of freezing air.

"Have you seen this?" He throws a piece of paper onto the nearest bunk.

Registration of the prisoners has begun, and questionnaires have been handed out, requiring each officer to provide the names of his parents, his mother's maiden name, information concerning his military duties, the locality and date of his capture by the Red Army, the job he did in civilian life, and his political affiliations. For those whose families live in the zone of Soviet occupation, like Tomasz, the questions are a source of anger and acute anxiety; they have no way of knowing what the consequences to their families might be of information revealed by them to the Soviet authorities.

"I am not going to answer their damned questions!" mutters Tomasz, crumpling up the paper and throwing it to the floor. "Let them beat me if they want to. I won't do it!"

He stamps the mud from his boots and sits down to begin the lengthy process of taking the wads of newspaper from their toes, folding them over the end of his bunk to dry overnight. Ralski bends down to pick up the paper, smoothing it out, and placing it on Tomasz's bunk.

"To those of you tempted to conceal or fabricate information," said Major Zaleski, "please remember that the NKVD are now in possession of your documents. They can check every detail of your statements."

Staś rides his motorbike through a forest, pursued by German soldiers. He reaches a fork in the path and skids to a halt, unsure which route to take. Kozłowski knows that at the end of the left-hand fork a band of Russian soldiers lies waiting in ambush, whilst the right-hand fork leads to freedom. *Go right!* He opens his mouth and tries to form the words, but no sound emerges. Staś takes a coin from his pocket and holds it in his open palm.

"Heads I go right; tails left."

He flips the coin up into the air – *Heads*, urges Kozłowski. *Heads, heads, heads!* The coin descends slowly, flipping over and over through the air to land, finally, on the forest floor. Tails. With a shrug, Staś picks up the coin, shoves it into his pocket, pulls down his goggles and slips the motorbike into gear. Kozłowski is screaming now, a long, silent cry. *Go right!*

He wakes to find the back of his head drenched in sweat, his neck itching painfully as the salt penetrates the broken skin where the lice have bitten him. For a second or two he does not realise where he is nor how long he has been asleep. The room is quiet; most of the men are asleep, although he can hear low voices conversing in Russian. He rolls over and peers down through the dusty window: in the corridor Kopyekin stands with the night guard scrutinising a piece of paper. Entering the room, Kopyekin calls out:

"Szpakowski, Olgierd."

Without a word, Olgierd rolls from his bunk.

"Come along now," says Kopyekin. "Get dressed and come with me."

Every prisoner now understands the significance of these words: they mean interrogation, although none of them yet knows what that really means since Feliks has refused steadfastly to talk about it, ignoring all questions on the subject, as if it had never happened.

Olgierd straightens his tunic, pulls his shoulders back, and accompanies Kopyekin from the room.

12. Just a forest

"The camp authorities have requested that five hundred physically fit men be made available to work moving the logs that are required to repair the barracks. I understand—" Major Zaleski waved his hand for silence as a roar of protest rose in the crowded church, continuing in his firm, ringing voice. "I understand that it is not customary for prisoners of war to be required to work in this way—"

"Officers," shouted one man. "Officers."

"Yes, I am well aware of your rank, thank you. However, we are also all aware that the Soviet Union is not a signatory to the Geneva convention, nor are we in the hands of the army. I think you will all agree that to labour with a view to improving our living conditions must be infinitely preferable to breaking rocks or mining for gold, as could so easily have been our fate." He said this emphatically, his bulldog face reddening as the more vocal of those protesting expressed their disapproval. "Our choices, gentlemen, are extremely limited. I suggest that we make the best of our situation here and set to our task with all the skill and professionalism which we can muster. Let us show these Bolsheviks what we Poles are capable of, eh?"

A great cheer went up and, as the crowd began to disperse, there was much talk of Polish pride and Polish skills. Zaleski called for volunteers with experience of engineering, planning, building, carpentry, medicine, sanitation and cooking. Kozłowski was duly elected medical representative of blocks number 16 and 17, whilst Zygmunt volunteered to lead the group charged with moving timber, which most of the men in their block, young and eager to be active, have decided to join.

"This is ruining my uniform," Lieutenant Otwinowski presses his shoulder against a filthy log covered in moss and soil. He lets go momentarily to glance down at his tunic, and the log starts to roll forward.

"Hold it!" yells Zygmunt. "Hold it up, we're not ready yet!"

Otwinowski stumbles backwards, crashing into Kozłowski, knocking his glasses to the ground.

"Careful what you're doing!" exclaims Tomasz. "The man needs his glasses!"

Otwinowski ignores him, pressing against the log to prevent it falling farther.

"It's alright." Kozłowski picks up the spectacles to see, with a sinking heart, that one arm has snapped off. He slips it into his pocket and balances the spectacles on his nose.

"You could apologise, Otwinowski," insists Tomasz, once the log has been levered into place.

Otwinowski barely glances at him. "It was an accident."

"There's no need to be so rude—"

"Really, Tomasz, it's fine—"

Tomasz's jaw is tight with anger, his fists clenched. Feliks catches his eye and winks, curling his fists like a boxer and indicating that Tomasz should punch the obnoxious lieutenant on the nose. This has the desired effect: Tomasz bursts out laughing and rejoins his friends. They shift closer to him, joking and patting him on the back as they work, signalling Otwinowski's exclusion.

Gradually, a rhythm is established. The logs roll off the wagon, to be reloaded onto trucks and taken to the sawmill, after which they will be brought back to the camp as planks for use in the construction of the barracks.

For lunch, the men are given sour soup with tiny fragments of meat in it. This increase in rations, minimal as it is, coupled with the tonic effect of being outdoors, improves their mood still further. Olgierd sits apart from the rest of the group, restless and irritable. Casting around in search of an argument, his gaze alights on Fryderyk Hoffman, who is, as usual, absorbed in making notes in his diary. Olgierd glares at him for a while then, eliciting no response, declares:

"Your father's German, isn't he, Hoffman?"

"That's right."

"So you could declare yourself Volksdeutsche. I mean, why wouldn't he, if he could get out of here?" Olgierd addresses this to no one in particular, indicating Hoffman with a jerk of his head. "He could go to Berezhkov and say 'I'm German' and they'd let him out tomorrow."

"If you're trying to provoke me, Szpakowski," murmurs Hoffman without looking up, "you are doing a very good job."

"What's the point, Olgierd?" Zygmunt, who hates arguments, places a hand on Olgierd's shoulder. "It won't make you feel any better."

"Well, it's true, isn't it? He's half German." Olgierd glances at Hoffman then adds, deliberately, "And he's Jewish."

The iron-grey sky lightens with a strange intensity, then the first flakes of snow begin to fall, drifting softly down to land on the men's shoulders and their bent backs. Their hands, already cold, grow red as they try to grasp the enormous, ice-coated logs. All day the snow continues falling, carpeting the ground with a thick layer of white.

On their return to the camp, the prisoners are exhausted but strangely content. The landscape around them has been transformed: a woolly silence envelopes the sparse woodlands which flank the path, the tall conifers bending gracefully under the weight of the freshly-fallen snow. Only Zygmunt seems possessed of a restless energy, striding along with his shoulders thrown back, like a horse released from its stable.

"Ah, smell that!" He takes a deep breath of the cold, pine-scented air. And—

"Look at that, will you?" pointing to a patch of virgin snow marked only by the narrow footprints of an animal. He casts around for someone to share his enthusiasm. Feliks bursts out laughing.

"Goodness, Zygmunt, you look like my old dog when she wanted a bone! Alright, I give in. I can see you're dying to tell us how much you love trees. Why don't you tell us something about Białowieża? It'll keep our mind off the cold. You worked there, didn't you?"

"That's right."

"I've always wondered what's so special about it. I've never been there, but – I mean, it's just a forest, isn't it? They're all much of a muchness."

Zygmunt rubs his hands together in delight.

"No forest is *just* a forest, Felo. Each one possesses a set of unique characteristics, influenced by the species of trees that grow there, the geographical location, the quality of the soil, the plants, the animals that inhabit the area, the way it's managed..." Zygmunt pauses, trying to select the words which will best express what it is he desires to say.

"Give them here," says Tomasz. "You look ridiculous. Let me see what I can do."

Kozłowski hands over the broken spectacle frames, immediately feeling vulnerable as the world around him becomes blurry.

"The screw's gone," he explains, needlessly.

Tomasz tries to poke a piece of silver thread taken from his officer's insignia through the tiny hole where the screw should sit. A few interested observers gather around him, offering advice, itching to have a go themselves whilst, just ahead, Zygmunt discourses on the wonders of the Białowieża Forest.

"In medieval times, a forest was an area of land that was placed off limits by royal decree: it couldn't be cultivated or farmed because its primary purpose was for the king's pleasure, for hunting. But with the industrial revolution came a demand for vast quantities of timber, and a forest came to mean not a wilderness, but an area of trees grown specifically for commercial use."

"But what's wrong with that?" For the first time all day, Olgierd speaks without rancour. "What is the point of preserving something as a wilderness if it is of no use to man? Surely all you need to do is plant new trees to replace the ones you cut down?"

"Of course, Olgierd, that's right. We need timber. But a forest left to itself, without human intervention… That is something else entirely."

"Surely Białowieża is hardly untouched," says Młynarski. "It's been a royal forest for centuries. The Tsars used it as a kind of royal playground."

"Yes, but whereas a managed forest is to all intents and purposes a field of crops where the main concern is yield, in a forest that is used for hunting the trees and plants remain undisturbed, left to grow as nature wills."

As he continues to speak, the little group around Zygmunt expands, men shifting closer to him so that they no longer walk in rows but are bunched together. The guards do not appear to notice, or do not care. The world around them is stilled; the forest encompasses them. The tall conifers, grand and austere, stand like sentinels on either side of the path, towering above the sponge-like cushions of dark green moss. A red squirrel, carrying an oversized nut in its mouth, scuttles along a branch, sending a flurry of snowflakes cascading down onto Kozłowski's neck, where they melt, seeping into his shirt collar and making the red welts itch.

"Here," says Tomasz. "Try this."

Kozłowski places the glasses over his ears, grinning in delight as the forest comes into focus. He feels a strange peace within him, as if this scene has always been and will always be here, waiting for him.

Ralski leans forward. "You speak of the differences between a managed and a wild forest. What does Białowieża teach us, Zygmunt?"

Zygmunt nods. "To an eye accustomed to neat lines of spruce or fir, Białowieża looks unkempt, even neglected. But, once you begin to understand it, its true beauty reveals itself. A modern forest will contain only a handful of species, yet Białowieża boasts dozens of different types of tree: ash, birch, oak, spruce, linden, alder, willow. And it's not just trees: there are over a thousand different types of plant, many of which do not grow anywhere else in Poland. In spring, while the trees are still bare, the sunlight penetrates to the forest floor and you see carpets of flowers: wood anemones, dog violets, bird's-nest orchids, coral-root bittercress, the small cranberry. The forest is also home to hundreds of species of bird, as well as tree frogs, wild boar, deer, eagles, wolves, even moose. They all coexist, and are interdependent…"

So intent are they on Zygmunt's words that the prisoners do not notice as they pass through the camp gates, nor are they aware of the short walk from the gates back to their barracks, where Zygmunt seats himself at the small table in the middle of the room while his audience perch themselves on their bunks, listening in an attitude of attentive stillness to the words which flow from the tall, broad-shouldered forester. Zygmunt is not a poet, nor a philosopher. A few months ago, if you had asked him if he enjoyed his work, he would have shrugged and replied, "I like to be outdoors, it's infinitely preferable to sitting at a desk." Had you asked his secretary, Marysia, if her boss were capable of captivating an audience with his eloquence, she would have been puzzled. "Mr Kwarciński?" Cheerful, steady, solid Mr Kwarciński, who strides into her office every morning, rubbing his hands with a brisk "Brrr! It's a bit nippy out there today"? No, she would say that she had never heard him speak in such a way. Now, as he struggles to convey his fascination with the complex perfection of nature's plan, he finds the words tumbling from him, as Białowieża rears up before him, until he sees it as clearly as if he were actually there.

"You asked me what we have learned from Białowieża, Ralski: well, it teaches us how a forest would 'behave' without man. When a forest is managed, the trees are not permitted to grow old and die naturally. We cut them down in their prime, when they provide the best timber for our needs. Yet a tree does not end its existence when it ceases to grow: it has a long and rich second life providing a habitat and food for hundreds of different insects, bacteria, plants and animals: the larvae of rare butterflies, beetles and ants, lichen and moss. In autumn, there are mushrooms, so many different types that some do not even have Polish names. And the most common of them all, the majestic cep—"

"Please, don't torture me!" groans Młynarski. "What I wouldn't give for a plate of fresh mushrooms with soured cream…"

Zygmunt smiles. "My point is this: the cep needs dead wood in order to thrive. A wild forest is teeming with life, from the tiniest microbe to wolves and even bison…"

Olgierd yawns. "Sorry, old fellow: fascinating stuff, but I'm bushed!"

His words break the spell; the talk is over. The men stand and stretch, and a low murmur of conversation arises as they begin the task of removing their boots and hanging up their damp socks.

"…makes me think of childhood holidays in Austria…"

"…those nineteenth-century paintings of Russian forests – what was his name?…"

"…saw a bear once. Shame I didn't have my gun…"

"…derives from the Latin 'foris' outside, 'forestis silva', outside the wooded area…"

"… *la selva oscura*…"

"…at the end of the Great War there were no bison left at all. They had to import them, can you believe it…"

"…*Leszy*, guardian of the forest…"

"…always preferred a mountain landscape myself. Take the Tatry, for instance…"

"*...Borowy, laskowy, gajowy...*"

"...hiding in the forests to avoid conscription into the Russian army..."

"I remember," says Tomasz to Kozłowski, "on holiday one summer, my grandmother told us that, if a person gets lost in the forest, the Leszy will either set them on the right path towards home or he will lead them astray, depending on how well they have behaved. My sister Hanka burst into tears and refused to come on a picnic with us; when asked why, she confessed that she had picked some wildflowers the previous day and was worried that she might have offended the Leszy. My mother was annoyed with my grandmother for scaring her – she was only five or six years old at the time – but my grandmother told Hanka that the Leszy never harms children. It is only men he judges harshly."

Kozłowski remembers a book he had as a child. Its coloured frontispiece depicted an old man with a straggly beard and ivory-white skin. His eyes were bulging, he was as tall as the trees: this was the Leszy, the guardian of the forest. His mother used to read to him from the book, which was filled with stories of trolls and giants, magicians and princesses. He remembers the sense of loss he felt when she told him – as if it should be a source of pride – that he was now old enough to move out of the nursery and share a room with Ignacy, where he was expected to read alone whilst his brother studied. Often, in those days, he would drift from the bathroom, after brushing his teeth, to stand in the nursery doorway listening while his mother read to Gosia and Staś. There was a daily truce for bedtime stories: instead of arguing, the two of them would sit up in bed, one on either side of their mother, pressing close to her to look at the pictures, and to feel her warmth.

If the Soviets were expecting the white-handed officers to show themselves incapable of 'real' work, they must be surprised by the speed and efficiency with which the prisoners organise themselves. They must know, for they are documenting it meticulously, that in their camp they hold a most complete cross-section of professional society. Perhaps they assumed that, without any workers, the Polish ruling class might collapse in on itself, like a head with no limbs. For many of the men, however, it is work that saves them from despair: the routine of getting up early and working hard all day brings with it a prize, the ability to fall asleep as soon as their heads hit the straw, untroubled by the restless anxieties that eat away at those with more time on their hands. To sleep without dreaming, to lie on one's bunk without time to reflect, this is an enviable state. Those older or sickly men who are not required to work at all, or do not choose to do so, have nothing to shape their day or give it purpose; they dwell endlessly on the fate of their families, of whom they have heard nothing, and wait for the nocturnal call to follow little Kopyekin across the snow-covered yard to Lebedyev's mysterious domain.

13. Dirty water

A delegation of doctors, each representing one of the blocks, crowds into the corridor outside the office of the camp command, where Commandant Berezhkov and Dr Yegorov are confronted by Major Zaleski and Dr Levittoux.

"We have now had sixteen cases of typhoid fever, fifteen of amoebic dysentery," declares Dr Levittoux angrily. "I warned you that if hygiene is not improved you will find yourselves with an epidemic on your hands. Is that what you wish?"

Berezhkov, visibly disturbed by this news, addresses Dr Yegorov. "Is this true? Is there typhoid in the camp?"

"How am I supposed to know what diseases they bring with them?"

"But you have begun medical examinations? The prisoners have been examined?"

"Of course. No cases of typhoid or dysentery have thus far been reported to me by my own staff. I cannot answer for the competence of the Polish physicians."

Dr Levittoux's jaw tightens, but he says nothing.

One of the older doctors steps forward. "Excuse me." He clears his throat, stroking his matted beard with trembling hands. "Forgive me, but – ah - if you place a large number of people in a confined space with no washing facilities and inadequate food, disease will spread, and spread quickly. If there are sixteen cases of amoebic dysentery today, there will be fifty tomorrow."

"Well, we'll treat them, then, won't we?" snaps Yegorov. "In the Soviet Union we have first-class medical facilities and there is plenty of medicine for everybody."

"Indeed, I – ah – I have every respect for your medical facilities. However, even if you treat those who are suffering, without adequate hygiene you might as well be throwing your medicine away. I myself am conscious of— ," he stops momentarily, as if searching for the words, "certain – ah – symptoms with which I am all too familiar in patients. Spasms of the intestinal tract, nausea, elevated temperature…"

Kozłowski, present as the medical representative of blocks 16 and 17, where three men have recently fallen ill with dysentery, realises that what he interpreted initially as nervousness on the part of the professor is in reality the result of his attempts to conceal the fact that he is in severe pain.

"Water!" booms Major Zaleski. "It is vital that we have access to an uncontaminated water supply. I have inspected the former *banya* building," he continues, referring to a set of half-ruined buildings in which some prisoners were previously quartered. "And it is my opinion that, given the right materials, we can restore them to working order."

Berezkhov stares at Zaleski in astonishment. "You propose to rebuild the baths yourselves?"

"Sir," Zaleski throws back his shoulders, his broad face reddening, "you forget that you have in this camp some of the most skilled professional men in Poland. I have a team of engineers at the ready. If you will allow us, we will draw up full plans and costings."

Kirshin has emerged from his office and is observing the delegation with an air of interest.

"The main imperative for now," insists Major Levittoux, "is to prevent an epidemic. I cannot emphasise this enough: if hygiene is not improved immediately, your own men will be at risk."

"I decide what is and is not imperative in this camp, understand?"

Berezhkov swings round and marches back into the camp offices, Dr Yegorov scuttling behind him. Kirshin observes the crowd of officers a moment longer, before turning casually to follow them.

"I'm sorry, Dr Levittoux," says Major Zaleski. "I don't think they are listening."

It transpires, however, that Berezhkov and Kirshin were listening for one morning shortly after this meeting the prisoners are told that they are to be taken to the public baths in Starobelsk town.

"Prisoners will leave in groups of three hundred, one group each day, starting today. You will line up in rows of four." Immaculately dressed as usual in a blue overcoat, his belt fastened tightly around his waist, Stepanov caresses his cheeks while Major Zaleski translates.

Amidst the jubilation caused by the announcement, Dr Levittoux expresses surprise that their attempt to scare the camp authorities into action has actually worked. "Perhaps, after all, they will respond to our letter, too."

They march knee-deep in mud, flanked by teenage guards who shout at the men and poke them with their rifle butts. In the town, the women shelter under the eaves of their shabby houses, watching the passing prisoners with indifference. Dressed in identical padded trousers and the thick jackets known as *fufajki*, they remind Kozłowski of a row of penguins. The image amuses him and, as he smiles, he catches the gaze of a young girl – she cannot be more than seventeen – who stares back at him, as if fascinated by his good humour. Her fair hair falls in rats' tails around her narrow, bony face; her eyes, fringed with pale lashes, are the colour of dirty water.

"What are you staring at them for, you silly girl?" Her mother grabs her by her plait. "Come away!"

The march begins cheerfully enough, but as the driving rain continues unabated they gradually fall silent, exhausted by the effort of pulling their boots from the ever-deepening mud. In all likelihood, reflects Kozłowski, we will be as dirty when we return to the camp as when we left it.

For some time now a group of half-starved dogs which hang around the camp gates has been following the prisoners. As the distance from the camp increases so the dogs fall back, slinking off mournfully one by one. Eventually, only a single dog remains, a small black-and-white mongrel with large tufts of hair protruding from either side of his nose. The little dog keeps pace with the prisoners, trotting through puddles, his bright eyes fixed on a portly major who is marching next to the lawyer Prosiński.

Some of the officers whistle to the animal, calling "Here, boy!" and clicking their fingers, but the dog ignores them, his attention steadfastly focused on the object of his interest.

"How in heaven's name does he know?" exclaims Prosiński.

"You're not stupid, are you, boy?"

The little dog fixes the major with an expression of such comical devotion Prosiński bursts out laughing.

"Who is he?" whispers Kozłowski.

"You don't know? That's Maksymilian Łabędź. He's the best vet in Warsaw."

The *banya* is a big, single-storey building situated next to the river. When they arrive, the furnace is not yet lit and it is to be the first task of one group of prisoners to chop wood to stoke it, while others are sent to draw water from the river for the boilers. The wood is wet, the saws are blunt, the river banks so slippery they almost fall into the water as they attempt to get a purchase on the slope. The young guards stand over the officers, mocking their efforts.

"Not so grand now, eh, you soft sons-of-bitches? Let's see you do some real work for a change!"

After an hour or so the boilers are deemed sufficiently hot and the first group of officers is sent in to bathe. Some time later Kozłowski, Tomasz, Prosiński, Major Łabędź, Młynarski and about a dozen others, all filthy with mud and soaking wet, are called inside. The little mongrel waits patiently outside for Łabędź to return.

The first room is unheated, with a concrete floor covered with mud from the boots of the first group. Here three skinny guards wait, holding their rifles inexpertly. The director of the baths, the *banshchik*, orders the prisoners to undress and tie their clothes into bundles which the guards throw into a steaming cauldron before shoving the naked prisoners into an adjoining room, where another group of guards waits by a bench, each holding a hair trimmer.

A thin, spotty-faced boy beckons to Tomasz. "Sit."

"Hold on a moment," Tomasz backs away as he realises what is about to take place, "I'm not having my hair shaved."

"Our heads are full of lice, Tomasz," says Kozłowski. "It's not pleasant but it is necessary."

"I am not having my hair shaved off."

The guard grabs Tomasz and tries to push him down onto the bench. Tomasz struggles. He is stronger than the boy, who falls backwards onto the wet floor. One of the older guards grabs Tomasz, twisting his arm behind his back while the young boy clambers to his feet.

"Get down!" His spotty face red with fury, the boy brings his rifle butt down over Tomasz's back while his colleague, taller and stronger, kicks Tomasz's legs from under him, ramming his knee into his back while the first guard starts shaving. The boy wields his trimmer like a farmer shearing a wild sheep.

The *banshchik* appears in the doorway. "What's going on in here?"

"You can't do this," cries Tomasz, in Russian. "We're prisoners of war, not criminals!"

"No haircut, no bath."

Łabędź, the oldest in the group, tries to put a cheerful face on it. "It's true it's more hygienic like this, lads, isn't it, doctor?"

Kozłowski nods, although, as the blades tug at his scalp, he shares Tomasz's sense of shame.

"Besides," continues the vet, "it'll grow back again soon enough."

The blunt-edged trimmers yank the men's hair by their roots, making them yell in pain. The guards, confident now that they have the prisoners in their hands, mock them mercilessly, calling them a bunch of girls.

A line of women dressed in *fufajki* await the prisoners at the entrance to the bathing area, handing out tiny pieces of soap to each man. Łabędź, who has endured the haircut with equanimity, reacts in horror to this fresh humiliation, clasping his hands over his groin, which makes the women giggle.

"You'll have to reveal your crown jewels if you want your soap."

Młynarski leans across to the woman, addressing her in Russian. "Let me take it for him."

She shakes her head. "It's one each." Then, with a hasty glance towards the door, she thrusts the little piece of soap into his hand. "I don't know what all the fuss is about. It's only men as nature intended."

As he enters the bathing area a wave of heat hits Kozłowski. Their clothes have been dumped in a pile in the corner of the room, supposedly now free from lice but not noticeably cleaner. They are ordered to stand underneath the shower heads then, suddenly, deliciously, hot water begins to pour over them. He rubs vigorously at his skin, as if by slaking off the weeks of accumulated dirt and dislodging the wretched lice, which cling to his body with the tenacity of the condemned, he might rid himself of the memories of everything that has happened to them since their capture. The shower is soon over, however; the supply of water is shut off after only a few minutes, leaving the men shivering, some with lather still on their skins.

By the time they are dressed they are cold again. Outside, it continues to rain. The little dog jumps up and trots at Łabędź's heels all the way back to the camp. They march in silence through the village, now deserted, and Kozłowski thinks of the young girl who dared to stare at him.

When they reach the gate, the stray dogs try to follow the prisoners inside but the guards shoo them away. Somehow, the little black and white mongrel manages to slip past them, taking up residence under Major Łabędź's bed, where he remains for the duration of their stay in Starobelsk. The dog, whose bright black eyes gaze out inquisitively from behind broad tufts of fur, is soon given a name: Stalinek – little Stalin - which is then shortened to Linek.

14. Baudelaire

"Here you are, Zbyszek. Just sign here." Dr Levittoux places two boxes on the desk, sliding a sheet of paper across the table. "Any problems so far?"

"No, sir."

The medical representative of each block has been ordered to administer typhus vaccinations to all the prisoners. Kozłowski, having completed half of his assigned number, has returned to the clinic to collect the second half.

"Be careful not to waste any: I doubt Yegorov will authorise any extra vaccines."

"How are things in the clinic, Dr Levittoux, if you don't mind my asking?" He signs the paper, then hands it back to Levittoux, who places it in a grey folder which he adds to a pile on his desk. "Is Dr Yegorov a competent doctor, as you hoped?"

Levittoux fixes Kozłowski with a dry, amused gaze. "It is my impression, Zbyszek, that Dr Yegorov's sense of self-importance is in direct inverse proportion to his expertise as a doctor. Now, if you'll excuse me, I must hurry: Major Zaleski is trying to persuade Berezhkov to let him rebuild the camp baths. I've said I will lend him moral support, although I doubt it will do much good. Let me know how you get on with the vaccines, won't you?"

"Before you go, Doctor—"

Levittoux turns, his hand on the doorknob.

"— I was wondering if you'd heard anything about the letter."

"Not a peep, I'm afraid. *Serwus!*"

Kozłowski stands on the steps outside the clinic, watching Levittoux's purposeful figure disappear towards the offices of the camp command, his thoughts dwelling on Major Zaleski's dogged optimism. There are even rumours that he has placed a bet with Major Miller that he can persuade Berezhkov to allow him to rebuild the *banya* before Christmas. It has been nearly two months since their capture; Christmas, which had once seemed distant, is now a mere six or seven weeks away. Time is slipping past, yet not even the most incurable of optimists dares to put a date to the end to their incarceration. The truth is that nobody thinks about the future. The one focus of all their hopes and desires – the thing that Kozłowski wants, more than anything – is to have news of their families.

"I've been waving at you for ages, like a lunatic."

Tomasz stands before him, grinning. There is a fading bruise on his cheek, a souvenir from their outing to the baths.

"Sorry, I was miles away. What brings you here? You're not feeling unwell, are you? I wish you'd let me take a proper look at that."

"It's fine. Józef Czapski's ill. I've come to visit him. Come with me?"

"Alright, just quickly. I have to get these vaccines done before the end of the day."

They climb the stairs to the first floor, where a narrow corridor lined with undersized hospital beds leads to two small rooms, each with seven or eight beds pushed against the walls. Czapski is easy to find: his long legs extend over the end of the bed, his hair falling on the pillow like a red mane. Beside the bed, Młynarski and Ralski are seated on two ancient wooden chairs.

"How kind of you to come." Czapski's voice is a whisper, his lungs labouring audibly as he speaks.

"You look like a carved saint, lying here in splendour in these white sheets."

Czapski grins. "It is splendid indeed, Tomasz. Look: clean linen, a clean shirt. It's warm here, and light. And do you know the best thing? The blissful quiet!"

Kozłowski lingers in the doorway, reluctant to impose himself on this meeting between close friends. He envies the ease with which Tomasz talks with the artist, as if he has known him for years instead of weeks. It is a gift he has, this gift of comradeship, which Kozłowski knows he lacks. Kozłowski himself is in awe of Czapski, whose conversation, peppered as it is with allusions to poets, writers, philosophers and artists, only serves to underline his own ignorance; yet Czapski, unfailingly polite, always seems to assume that the young doctor will understand his references to Baudelaire, or Balzac, or Tolstoy. It is a courtesy that flatters and terrifies Kozłowski in equal measure, rendering him silent during the lively discussions that take place in the barracks when Czapski comes to visit.

"My neighbour," continues Czapski, indicating the bed next to him, which is occupied by a middle-aged officer, fast asleep, whom Kozłowski recognises with a jolt as Major Skarżyński, "is a little too garrulous for my taste. I lie here basking in the silence, and all he wants to do is talk! I feel guilty for even saying it: poor man, he's very unwell. His son was here in Starobelsk, you know. A young boy. They've sent him home, thank goodness. But the poor fellow cannot stop talking about him. It's driving me to distraction."

Czapski coughs again and lies back, exhausted.

"Are they giving you the medicines you need?" asks Ralski.

"I've heard the Russian doctor is a bit of a brute," adds Młynarski.

"Yegorov? I hardly see him. I've been looked after wonderfully well by our own doctors. Even Dr Vasilevna is perfectly kind, so long as Yegorov isn't around." Czapski pauses. His long fingers pluck anxiously at the sheets. "My only dread is leaving this bed. I hate the idea of quitting this quiet, this wonderful quiet!"

"Things will soon improve, Józef. Major Zaleski is working miracles. Soon we will have everything we need."

"You're right, Bronek. I should have more faith." Czapski closes his eyes, his head sinking back on the pillow, a smile lingering on his lips.

"Should we go?" whispers Ralski, after a while. "I think he's asleep,"

As Młynarski begins to rise from his seat, Czapski grips his hand. "Please. Not yet."

The three men sit in silence while Czapski rests. Kozłowski knows that he ought to go, that he must finish the vaccinations before the day is out. Yet he cannot bring himself to leave the little ward. Czapski is right: the room is blissfully peaceful. There has been no moment, since their arrival at Starobelsk, when he has not been surrounded by other people. Even at night men snore, or moan, or talk. What kind of torture can it be for an artist, accustomed to working in solitude, to be shut up all day and night with thousands of men chattering, debating, opining, complaining, worrying, hoping, reproaching, despairing?

"I have been trying to remember some lines of Baudelaire, Bronek. Do you remember?" With a great effort, Czapski begins to recite:

"Je suis comme le roi d'un pays pluvieux,
Riche, mais impuissant, jeune et pourtant très vieux,
Qui, de ses précepteurs méprisant les courbettes,
S'ennuie avec ses chiens comme avec d'autres bêtes..."

He is seized by a coughing fit so powerful it almost chokes him. Kozłowski is about to intervene when a nurse appears, squeezing through the narrow passageway between the beds.

"*Nu*, that's enough chat!" She pokes Młynarski in the ribs. "Look what you've done! Get out of here before I chase you out!"

Kozłowski waits on the veranda for Tomasz, who has slipped back upstairs to fetch his cap, left behind on Czapski's bed. The visit to Czapski has allowed Kozłowski to remove himself temporarily from his situation, as if, just for an hour or so, he found himself in a small country hospital where life goes on at the same gentle pace as it has done for decades, unaffected by the war. Perhaps there are such places, he reflects, right now, villages where they are spending their war in exactly the same way as they have spent every other day of their lives. A little less food, perhaps; disturbing articles in the morning newspaper; but their sun rises on the same scenes every day; untouched by bombs, untroubled by gunfire, the inhabitants of these little centres of calm carry on with their lives without fear of arrest, or capture, or execution.

He stares idly at the huge church, which squats like a giant beetle in the middle of the camp. It is always locked, and he has never seen anyone enter it. What is it that is so carefully hidden from view?

"I heard," Tomasz rejoins Kozłowski, and they begin to walk, "that the inside of that church is filled with grain. There's a truck that comes to fetch it at night, apparently, but it doesn't go to the locals: it is taken to Germany, to feed the troops."

"Where on earth did you hear that?"

"Zygmunt got it from that Ukrainian carpenter, Fomenko."

There are a handful of local workers employed in the camp. Few have any direct contact with the prisoners, but Zygmunt and Fomenko often work outside where, with less of a risk of their conversations being overheard, Zygmunt has gradually gained the Ukrainian's trust.

Kozłowski and Tomasz stroll slowly across the square, neither of them in a hurry to return to the cold claustrophobia of the barracks.

"Tomasz, you never told me how you know my sister."

Tomasz flushes, visibly taken aback. "I – I thought that perhaps you preferred not to discuss her with me—"

Kozłowski laughs, genuinely amused but also, somehow, ashamed. The truth is that, preoccupied as he has been with his own anxieties, it had never occurred to him that there was anything to discuss. The fact of Gosia's acquaintance with Tomasz had seemed unremarkable and, in the chaos of the past few weeks, he had forgotten the matter entirely. Now it dawns on Kozłowski that Tomasz's friendship with Gosia may be of more significance than he had at first assumed.

"It doesn't say much for my brotherly affection, does it? My only excuse is that old habits die hard: she's my younger sister, I've spent my entire life ignoring her. Have you known her long?"

"We met in Zakopane last spring. She's good friends with my sister

Hanka. They studied together. Hanka invited me to spend a few days with some friends and we—"

Tomasz breaks off as the camp gates open and a truck enters, carrying a load of timber. Two guards unfasten the tailgate.

"Hey, you!" One of the guards calls them over. "Get over here and start unloading."

Tomasz must help unload the planks, whilst Kozłowski tries to explain that he has been ordered to administer the typhoid vaccines.

"See? This is the order from Dr Yegorov. Look."

"Then why are you dawdling around here?" yells the guard. "Get on with it!"

The moment to speak of his sister is lost.

15. Patriots

"Gentlemen, Poland may have been defeated." Captain Ewert occupies the cramped space between the narrow rows of bunks in the Circus. "But this is not the end. Great Britain and France have gone to war to protect our sovereignty—"

"They've done precious little about it so far," calls a lieutenant from the back.

"You are right," replies Ewert, "but that does not mean they will never act. They, like Poland, were unprepared for the speed and ferocity of the German invasion. Even now, they are preparing their forces in readiness for a counter-attack. And then, my friends," Ewert looks around at his audience, his eyes gleaming with patriotic fervour, "then, they will march through Europe and they will smash the Nazis."

"But what about the Russians?"

"The Russians have no quarrel with Britain or with France. Stalin is an opportunist. When he sees that there is nothing to be gained from his alliance with Nazi Germany, he will withdraw, and then Poland will be free again!"

A cheer goes up at the end of this rousing speech.

The ostensible reason for the meeting is a discussion of the challenges presented by the necessity of digging sewage pipes to serve a camp of over 4,000 men, as well as the most effective method of draining the ditch that has been dug to serve as a communal latrine (nicknamed 'The Siegfried Line'). At the head of the meeting are three men: Lieutenant Kwolek, engineer and unofficial leader of the Circus; Ewert, an infantry captain; and Major Ludwik Domoń, also from the infantry. Those present at the meeting, like its leaders, are notable less for their engineering skills than for their fervent desire to rebel against their situation. Tomasz Chęciński and Feliks Daszyński have managed to squeeze themselves into a tiny space between two rows of scaffold, while Kozłowski and Zygmunt, their reluctant companions, are squashed at the back, craning to see over the heads of the twenty or so men before them.

It is Major Domoń's turn to address the men. "My friends, the primary duty of every Pole incarcerated in this camp is to resist. I urge you: do not speak Russian, for this is collusion. Do not obey the camp rules, as this will make their job more difficult. And do not go to work. Every small act of resistance on our part makes it harder for them to subjugate us."

"I have heard credible rumours," adds Kwolek, "that an international commission of the Red Cross will visit the camp soon to inspect the conditions under which we are being held. The more we can undermine Soviet efforts to tame us, the more of an effect it will have on the commission."

A ripple of excitement passes through the crowd. "When are they coming?"

"Is it the Americans? Or the British?"

"Will we be able to write to our families at last?"

Kozłowski, observing these excited exchanges, reflects that the most likely source for this particular rumour is Major Skarżyński. Discharged from the clinic, the old man has wasted no time in redoubling his efforts to make contact with the outside world, appearing daily at the camp offices bearing petitions to various foreign ambassadors, scrawled in pencil on the torn-out pages of his diary.

Ewert holds up his hand for silence. "I do not know the answer to your questions, but I am sure it will be soon. Meanwhile, my fervent wish is that none of us gives in to despair. I, for one, firmly believe that this is a trial sent to test our resolve. We have been subjugated before, many times, but our spirit of patriotism and our faith in a resurgent Poland have never been defeated. We shall prevail!"

Behind him, men are whispering:

"After dark, in here. Tomorrow night. Pass it on."

In a corner, Captain Kuczyński-Bej of the cavalry, his oval face youthful above a black goatee beard, confers quietly with Father Alexandrowicz.

The meeting concludes with the words of the poet Adam Mickiewicz, delivered by Major Domoń almost as a prayer:

"By the blood of all our soldiers fallen in the war for faith and liberty, deliver us, O Lord! By the wounds, tears and sufferings of all the prisoners, exiles and Polish pilgrims, deliver us, O Lord!"

The audience are so absorbed they do not notice the slight figure of *politruk* Kaganer of the Special Section standing by the door, staring idly at his shoes, listening. As the prisoners begin to file back to their barracks, Kaganer slips out unobserved.

The meeting, in itself, is nothing out of the ordinary: the prisoners have few books and almost no light in the evenings by which to read. There is no music, only the single loudspeaker pouring forth its endless torrent of propaganda. There are no newspapers, and no games. The prisoners have inevitably sought ways of keeping their minds busy and their souls from despair. For weeks the two dozen or so priests captured alongside the men have been conducting clandestine services in the barracks. Talks given by experts in various subjects have sprung up like mushrooms. In the first weeks, the subject uppermost in everybody's mind is the defeat of the Polish army. Attempting to make sense of what has happened to them, many officers debate the rights and wrongs of military policy during the September campaign. What singles out the little group of which Kwolek, Ewert and Domoń form the core is their sense of active purpose: these men see it as their patriotic duty to raise the morale of their fellow prisoners. For them, words are not sufficient: they desire action.

Kozłowski returns late to the barracks on November 11th. On his way from the water pump, where he stopped as always to wash the worst of the day's dirt from his hands and face, scrubbing under his fingernails until they are red, he came upon the dog Linek cowering under a pile of planks next to one of the half-built barracks, his front leg poking sideways at an unnatural angle. Despite his best attempts to convince Linek to come to him, the little mongrel refused to emerge from his hiding place and Kozłowski was obliged to fetch Major Łabędź. On hearing that little Linek was injured, the portly vet ran to the spot where the dog lay and threw himself onto his knees, heedless of the mud, to peer underneath the planks, calling softly to the terrified animal:

"Come, Linek, come to Maks, Lineczek, Linuś, my little doggie…"

The dog's ears pricked up at the sound of his master's voice; immediately he clambered to his feet and staggered towards the vet, licking his face and being rewarded by such kisses and caresses that Kozłowski felt embarrassed to witness so intimate a reunion. Łabędź gathered the dog up in his arms and, having examined the injured leg, pronounced the bone broken.

"Is there anything you can do?" asked Kozłowski.

"Do?" Łabędź appeared surprised by the question. "Of course there is. We will find a way to set your bone, won't we, Linuś?"

He ruffled the dog's ears and was rewarded with another devoted lick on his cheek.

"How do you think it happened?"

"Who knows?" Łabędź cast his gaze around the piles of wooden planks, the bricks, the shards of broken glass where old windows have been replaced with new. "Half the camp's a building site. There are many places where a curious dog might get into trouble, aren't there, Lineczek?"

With thanks to the good doctor, Łabędź hurried back to his barracks, the dog cradled in his arms.

The next time Kozłowski sees the dog he is limping cheerfully behind Łabędź, a homemade wooden splint fixed to his injured leg.

When Kozłowski finally returns to the bunkroom he finds it empty save for Ralski and the silent airman. Ralski, seated by the makeshift table fashioned from a plank purloined by Zygmunt from the carpentry workshop, is changing into his only pair of clean socks.

"It seems the least I can do, given the occasion." He glances up at Kozłowski with a wry smile.

It is impossible not to be conscious of the unnamed airman who lies, as always, with his scarred face turned to the wall. Many times Ralski has tried to convince the man to join the friendly group of officers whose comradeship might offer him solace in his suffering. Many times he has offered to fetch Father Adamski or one of the other priests, but the airman remains obdurately silent, indifferent to everything and everyone around him. Kozłowski has been permitted to change the dressings on his hands, but any suggestion that he might accompany the airman to the camp clinic to seek treatment for his face have been met with blank refusal. He appears to have no relatives in the camp; no visitors have come to seek him out; no friends have expressed concern on his behalf.

Ralski addresses the man's back. "I'm going over to the Circus. It's November 11th, you know. They've organised a celebration. Why don't you come?" He waits a few moments then, receiving no answer, shrugs. "Are you coming, Zbyszek? Tomasz and the others have already gone over."

Kozłowski likes Ralski and would happily spend an evening in his company, but the patriotic fervour of Domoń and his crowd does not inspire him. Rather, it depresses him, reminding him that the independence they are supposed to be celebrating is that of a country which has been obliterated from the map.

"What I would really like," he confesses with a smile, "is a long, cold beer and a game of cards."

Ralski laughs and says he understands, he understands. Kozłowski does not add that he has a horror of the Circus, that he cannot forget the first night he spent there: the incessant noise, the claustrophobic darkness, the men clambering up and down the scaffold like monkeys.

As soon Ralski is gone, the empty room begins to feel oppressive, the airman's presence as suffocating as smog. After twenty minutes, Kozłowski can stand it no longer: the company of his fellows, under whatever circumstances, must be preferable to endless, unanswerable speculation concerning his family's fate.

He is careful to stick to those paths that lie closest to the huts, far from the searchlight's penetrating beam, although the guards appear to take little interest in the prisoners' activities. Perhaps this is because they know there is nowhere for us to go, he reflects. We can hardly escape, so maybe they don't care what we do, so long as we stay quiet. It does seem odd, nevertheless, that the prisoners are so little scrutinised.

Reaching the Circus, Kozłowski makes his way through the seething mass of bodies towards the stage, which has been cleared for the evening. Upon it stands a small group of officers, among them Kwolek, Domoń and Ewert. Captain Kuczyński-Bej, positioned at the front of the stage, is reciting a poem from memory. Kozłowski spots Ralski, standing next to the engineer Zygmunt Mitera; behind them is Tomasz, listening with rapt attention.

Kuczyński's voice is deep and clear:

Mamo! Jak to już dawno, jak dawno się zdaje,
Gdym cię żegnał! Ta chwila jak we mgle mi staje
Przed okiem, zapatrzonem tam, ku naszej stronie!
Widzę twoje rozpacznie wyciągnięte dłonie,
Widzę ruch ten, gdy chciałaś, z bólu obłąkana,
Przed potworem dymiącym runąć na kolana,
I ten wieczór – i słońce gasnące szkarłatnie,
I jękiem rwie mi serce "Pamiętaj!" ostatnie!

A few metres away, on the other side of the platform, stands the red-haired poet Piwowar, staring at the church's domed ceiling with an expression of pained boredom. It is said that Piwowar has taken up residence underneath the stage in the cave-like space once reserved for hiding props. As the rapturous applause which greets the reading finally subsides, Piwowar leaps onto the stage, raising his hand for silence.

"Or-Ot is a fine poet, of course, and Siberia a fitting setting for a poem, but let us not be satisfied only with our good old favourites. Allow me, please, to share with you something a little more... *moderne.*" Piwowar pronounces this last word with ironic emphasis, taking from his pocket a tiny scrap of paper. "Fellow officers, I beg your indulgence for a modest few lines of my own, composed these last weeks in an attempt to make sense of all that has befallen us. If I express myself imperfectly, please forgive me." He closes his eyes and begins to recite in a high, lilting voice, as if in rapture:

Na polach rude płaty jesieni i krwi,
Piosenko omiń, piosenko zapomnij!
Pozostańmy w tych dniach zamiennych w gruzy
Kiedy dojrzewało serce
Kiedy w te dni
Tyle rosło miłości ogromnej...

A few prisoners protest; someone shouts: "Avant-garde rubbish!" They are hushed, however, by others. For the majority of the prisoners it matters not what is being read, it is sufficient that a reading is taking place and that it is in Polish. Piwowar's recital is greeted by muted applause. With a sardonic smile he bows, then disappears behind the prompter's box like a rabbit down a hole and does not re-emerge for the rest of the evening.

A short break follows this performance as Lieutenant Kwolek and his companions climb onto the stage carrying a wooden cross fashioned from odd pieces of wood, bound together with twine. Many of the cavalry officers have attached their spurs for this special occasion; their boots jangle as they mount the platform.

They lay the wood flat across two bunks, upon which a clean white sheet has been spread, then invite the crowd to move aside to allow Father Alexandrowicz to pass through. As the old priest says mass, the familiar verses spoken in a hesitant, wavering voice, a profound silence spreads across the rows of bunks. Right up at the top of the scaffold, where men perch like acrobats, the ritual words, not heard in this building for over twenty years, echo off the curved dome. Prayers said, the national anthem is sung.

Who could be proof against the longing that takes hold of the men this night? They are filled with an aching desire for home and family so powerful it brings tears to the eyes of those who would previously have been ashamed to weep.

Jeszcze Polska nie zginęła, kiedy my żyjemy, Co nam obca przemoc wzięła, szablą odbierzemy...

Where are their families now? What fate has befallen them? How far have the Germans advanced? What punishments are the Soviets meting out to those families in the East? The prisoners are so carried away that they do not trouble to modulate their voices but sing out with all their hearts:

Marsz, marsz Dąbrowski, z ziemi włoskiej do Polski...

Kozłowski can bear it no longer: tonight it seems that there is to be no escape from painful thoughts of home. Seized by an overwhelming desire to escape, he pushes his way back towards the door, finally emerging into the fresh air.

Outside, it is snowing. Kirshin, his hands in his pockets like a man out for a Sunday stroll, is standing outside the Circus listening to the sound of a thousand voices singing the Polish national anthem. He studies Kozłowski, his gaze, as always, measured and calm. To his shame, Kozłowski looks away, conscious only of the commissar's eyes on his back as he hurries to his block, slipping on the icy wooden walkway. For the first time since he arrived in Starobelsk, he is scared

16. A parade

Kozłowski is woken at dawn by guards running into the bunkroom:

"Work detail, up!"

There is no time for breakfast. Five hundred men are rounded up, along with Majors Zaleski and Miller and the entire planning group, and marched out of the camp at gunpoint. At first, it seems that they are being taken to work, but they pass the mill, continuing on beyond the town until, finally, a halt is called in the middle of an empty plain. Here, the prisoners are ordered to stand to attention and told that they must not speak or move. After several minutes, during which fear gives way to impatience, Major Zaleski steps forward to address one of the guards.

"Why are we being kept here when there is work to be done? May I respectfully request that we be allowed to return to the camp?"

The guard stares at Zaleski. Then he screams in fury, ramming his rifle butt into Zaleski's stomach.

"Salute me when you speak to me, you bourgeois scum!"

Major Miller is about to protest but Zaleski, doubled over in pain, grabs his arm to stop him.

At around midday the sky darkens and it begins to snow. Kozłowski shivers, his teeth chattering uncontrollably as his greatcoat grows damp and heavy; he shifts his feet, trying to dislodge the cold from his toes. Lunchtime comes and goes; the men have eaten nothing all day, yet they must remain at attention as the snow whirls about them, settling silently on their caps and shoulders. Kozłowski wishes only to know why they are being made to stand here so pointlessly. Ralski, however, looks around at the flat, empty countryside with an air of calm delight.

"I can smell winter," he whispers.

Curious to comprehend what it is that the botanist finds so fascinating in the dead landscape that surrounds them, Kozłowski tries to imagine it through Ralski's eyes: to their right, tall reeds the colour of straw stand in pools of steel-grey water; before them is the narrow, rutted track on which they arrived, a path that leads nowhere, lined on either side by stunted trees. On the ground lie patches of snow, flecked with rotting leaves. The reeds shiver in the icy wind. The trees reach their naked branches to the sky like skinny fingers. Soon, these movements will cease; the ground will freeze; the tree roots will lie dormant; small mammals will dig deep into the earth and curl up to sleep; only the crows will continue their search for food. The wind brings with it a light flurry of snowflakes which settle delicately on Kozłowski's face. He pushes out the tip of his tongue and feels the clean, metallic taste of snow.

When he was young, all the neighbourhood children would gather for snowball fights in the street outside the house in Wilno. He remembers one occasion when Staś directed a particularly hard shot at him. It landed directly in his face. He remembers the sensations exactly: the feeling of numbness, then heat, as if he were blushing, the taste of the snow mingled with blood where a stone, unseen inside the snowball, had split his lip. Ignacy, as the eldest, was supposed to be responsible for the younger ones. He grabbed Staś by the collar.

"Look what you've done, you idiot! Now we'll all be for it."

Kozłowski remembers watching them disappear into the house, exploring with his fingers the satisfying fatness of his swollen lip.

Suddenly, next to him, Lieutenant Prosiński is falling. Kozłowski struggles to catch him but Prosiński unconscious is heavy and he cannot hold him alone. Ralski tries to help but the guard screams at him to leave the man alone and it is left to Kozłowski to somehow get Prosiński's right arm around his neck and heave him upright. Major Zaleski protests that the Lieutenant needs medical attention and demands to know if the guard wants a prisoner's death on his conscience, but his words are ignored.

Finally, as dusk begins to fall, the *politruk* in charge looks at his watch and orders the guards to return to the camp.

Waiting at the gates is the red-cheeked young *politruk*, Kaganer, whom Kozłowski has noticed many times trotting at the heels of Commissar Kirshin. He sneers at the exhausted men as they stumble through the gates.

"Enjoy your parade, did you? I know how much you former officers of the former Polish army like to celebrate your country's 'independence' with a parade." He laughs heartily at his own joke.

Prosiński by this time is delirious with fever. Tomasz and Zygmunt take an arm each while Kozłowski runs ahead so that when they arrive at the clinic Dr Levittoux is waiting for them, along with Dr Vasilevna. She takes one look at the sick man and agrees at once with Levittoux that he must be taken immediately upstairs to the little ward where they treat the pulmonary patients. Dr Yegorov, thankfully, is not on duty.

Returning late from the clinic, Kozłowski finds the priest Adamski standing in front of a makeshift wooden cross hanging on a rusting nail on the wall between the tiers of bunks, a group of officers huddled behind him. Kozłowski does not participate in these improvised services as some of his friends do, but nor does he leave the room, as Hoffman and Szczypiorski do, instead lying on his bunk and listening to the familiar pattern of ritual words which he finds comforting, reminiscent as they are of his childhood, and of home. As Adamski begins to recite the Lord's Prayer, a sharp voice behind him cuts across the room:

"The service is to stop at once, on order of the camp commandant!"

Kopyekin stands in the doorway. Adamski pauses a moment, then, without looking back, he raises his hands, turns to the cross again and concludes the prayer. The little messenger turns and walks away.

Adamski ends the service with a blessing, takes his cross from the wall and, with every appearance of calm, prepares for bed. The men from the neighbouring barracks who have come in for the service file silently away. Those who remain climb into their bunks and lie down to sleep. Everybody gives the appearance of behaving exactly as they have done every Sunday since they arrived in the camp. And yet, nobody sleeps. Everyone knows that Kopyekin must return.

Some time later, just as he is drifting off to sleep, Kozłowski hears footsteps in the corridor. He peers over the edge of his bunk to see Stepanov in the doorway, his broad shoulders silhouetted against the bright corridor. With him is Kopyekin and the night guard, holding a rifle. Kopyekin marches into the room. This time, he knows exactly where he is going.

"You there, Adamski, get dressed and come with me. And bring your things." He pulls at Adamski's legs. "*Nu*, hurry up now."

The priest rises from his bunk obediently and stands in his underwear, barefoot on the muddy floor between the bunks. Every prisoner in the room is acutely conscious of the new command. Men who are called to interrogation are told, simply: "Get dressed and come with me". This new formula, "And bring your things", seems ominous. The priest dresses silently and places his meagre belongings neatly in his suitcase. Kozłowski notices that his hands are shaking. Nobody needs to be told that Adamski is being taken from the camp. Fear seizes the prisoners and they begin to say goodbye to the young country parson, their voices rising to a crescendo as he reaches the doorway.

"Lie down, all of you! Silence!" Stepanov pushes the priest so hard he stumbles. "Hurry up, Adamski, unless you want to propagate further your stupid bourgeois sermons…"

Adamski raises his right hand, making the sign of the cross to his terrified companions. "May God be with you! Blessed be Jesus Christ!" His round face, normally suffused with pink, is bloodless.

"Amen!" cries Tomasz, in tears.

The following morning, at breakfast, Kozłowski discovers that twelve of the army chaplains, including Fathers Alexandrowicz, Adamski and Suchicki, Rabbi Steinberg, Father Fedoronko of the Orthodox Church, Father Ilków of the Greek Catholic Church, and Superintendent Potocki of the Reform Church, have been taken from their barracks and removed from the camp, along with Captain Ewert, Lieutenant Kwolek, Major Domoń, Captain Kuczyński-Bej and several others who played a prominent role in organizing the events of November 11th.

A few nights later, they take the rest of the priests, along with Major Skarżyński. It now becomes clear why the camp authorities have so far done nothing to oppose the prisoners' acts of rebellion: like scientists waiting for a liquid to boil, they have been watching with curiosity to see which elements will rise to the surface in the froth of patriotic and religious fervour that has overcome the prisoners in the first weeks of their captivity. November 11th has provided them with the perfect opportunity to skim off those whose voices have been loudest and whose actions boldest.

17. Kirshin's show

"I can place Prosiński's name temporarily on the list of those not required to work. That should buy him a few days."

Dr Levittoux is seated in the little office where the records are kept, painstakingly filling in a requisition form. Kozłowski has come to ask if Prosiński, who has been in the clinic for several days, might be exempt from work a little longer.

"How is he?"

"He has a bronchial infection, not helped by standing in the freezing cold for three hours. I've got six new cases of men in various states of pulmonary collapse thanks to Kirshin's little outing. As if we didn't have enough to deal with." Kozłowski can feel the suppressed anger beneath Levittoux's calm manner. "But Prosiński's young and strong. He'll recover."

"I'll go up and see him."

"Don't. Yegorov's up there. Come by later once he's gone. By the way, there's a meeting," continues Levittoux, scribbling on the form as he speaks. "Kirshin's called all the block leaders and senior officers. If I'm not mistaken Prosiński is your block representative, is he not?"

"Yes."

"Why don't you attend instead, since you're here? Whatever it is Kirshin has to say, it's bound to be interesting." He looks up, fixing Kozłowski with his calm grey eyes.

221

"I'd – I'd have to ask the others, sir."

"If you feel you must. Tell them I ordered you to attend. It starts in half an hour." He looks up with the benign gaze of a teacher attempting to calm the nerves of an anxious student. "I'm sure they won't think you're trying to make yourself important, if that's what worries you."

"No, sir."

Major Zaleski, Major Miller and the other representatives wait in the clinic, conversing in low voices. The long line of patients has been dismissed, much to Dr Levittoux's irritation, in order to make way for the meeting, which is to take place in the only room outside of the camp offices large enough to accommodate so many people. A long table and several chairs occupy one end of the room, whilst the prisoners huddle at the other, as if proximity to one another will somehow protect them from whatever is about to unfold. Only Dr Levittoux takes a chair, balancing his folders on his knees as he tots up the number of patients needing treatment for this or that condition. Every single dose of medicine, every bandage, every plaster has to be requested personally from Dr Yegorov, in writing. Kozłowski hovers at the back, feeling vaguely out of place, as if he does not fully deserve to be present.

After a long delay, during which the waiting officers begin to grow restless, Commissar Kirshin finally appears, flanked by Petrov and Lebedyev. They seat themselves at the table facing the group of thirty or so Polish officers. Kozłowski observes Kirshin closely as the commissar casually unbuttons his leather jacket, makes himself comfortable, then places a single sheet of paper on the desk in front of him, smoothing it carefully before appearing to become deeply absorbed in its perusal. A cigarette is held loosely between his fingers, the smoke curling lazily up towards the ceiling. Kozłowski cannot help but admire the precision with which Kirshin enacts this little piece of theatre.

Unlike Kirshin, Petrov makes no pretence of being anything other than annoyed at having to attend, his glassy eyes roving restlessly around the room as he sucks fiercely on his cigarette. Lebedyev, on the other hand, appears entirely uninterested in proceedings: he sits with his legs outstretched before him, surveying the men with indifference through his tiny, piggy eyes. It is plain that this is Kirshin's show: the others are like saints in a triptych, one on either side of their master.

Behind the senior officers stands the red-faced *politruk* Kaganer, together with the young officer, Mitrov, his curly hair protruding from beneath his cap. Kaganer watches Kirshin avidly, as if he is taking note of every aspect of his boss's performance in order to reproduce it at some later date when he, too, will be the one upon whom all eyes are fixed. Mitrov, on the other hand, appears distracted, gazing absently out of the window. Noticing that Kozłowski is observing him, the young *politruk* smiles then looks down abruptly, as if remembering that smiling at prisoners is not permitted.

Kirshin allows the silence to continue for a few minutes longer; then, when his audience is fully primed, he clears his throat and begins his address:

"From today, this camp will be bound by strict regulations. The text of these regulations will be pinned onto the bulletin boards. Zaleski, you will immediately have them translated into Polish to avoid any misunderstandings. Is that clear?" Zaleski nods. Kirshin continues: "There will be no religious services, no prayers, no songs of any kind, neither religious, patriotic nor festive. All meetings, lectures and discussions are forbidden. It is forbidden to assemble on the camp grounds and to walk in groups of more than two. You may not keep a diary or make notes. You may not read books aloud."

On and on it goes, the list of forbidden things.

"No prisoner is allowed to leave their block after eight pm, except to go to the latrine, nor is anyone allowed to put out the lights at night. There is to be no observance of Sundays or other holidays of yours. All Soviet officers are to be saluted when passed in the camp grounds." Kirshin looks up. "Violation of any of the regulations listed will be met with the severest punishment. Is that understood?"

Lebedyev stares ahead, his face expressionless. It is impossible to tell if he is listening or thinking about what he is going to eat for dinner.

Petrov, on the other hand, squirms and twists his lips, mumbling as if in approval, all the time pulling viciously on the cardboard filter of his cigarette.

Kirshin continues, modulating his tone in preparation for the delivery of compensatory good news: "Radio loudspeakers will be installed in every block of the camp. Soviet newspapers will be distributed among you free of charge – *Pravda, Izvestia, Red Star* and others, as well as Polish-language newspapers."

There is a murmur of interest at this piece of information.

Kirshin smiles: "Yes, yes, *The Lwów Red Banner, The Wilno Red Banner* and *The Soviet Voice.* There will soon be a library, too, and a collection of appropriate games which prisoners may borrow – chess, draughts and dominoes."

Zaleski suddenly bursts out laughing. For the first time Lebedyev moves. He sits up straight and opens his little black eyes to stare at the insolent prisoner. Kirshin rises from his chair.

"That will do," he snaps. "This is a progressive country: we play games of intelligence and skill, not decadent capitalist games of chance. Card playing is not permitted anywhere in the Soviet Union and it will not be tolerated in this camp! You are dismissed!"

The officers disperse, heading back to the barracks to acquaint their comrades with the new regime.

Dr Levittoux, however, lingers, waiting until the other officers have gone before approaching Kirshin.

"Commissar, I was wondering if there has been any response to the letter submitted to you in October by the medical personnel."

Kozłowski admires Dr Levittoux's persistence. It has been many weeks since the request was made; most of the doctors in the camp have simply assumed that the letter was either placed straight in the bin or will never be dignified with a response. It is with some surprise, therefore, that he observes Petrov pulling from a folder a single sheet of paper which Kirshin hands to Dr Levittoux without a word. Levittoux, equally astonished, thanks Kirshin courteously and moves away to read the document.

Kozłowski joins him, along with Dr Kołodziejski, Dr Grüner and Dr Wolfram, a tall, striking-looking man who is responsible for the medical care of Major Zaleski and other members of the planning committee.

"What does it say?" asks Dr Wolfram.

Levittoux hands him the letter with a bitter smile. "See for yourself."

Dr Wolfram reads aloud, translating the brief text into Polish: "In response to your letter, we inform you that neither the Geneva Convention nor the Red Cross have any bearing on your situation." He looks up. "That's all there is."

"Who is it signed by?" asks Dr Kołodziejski.

Dr Wolfram examines the signature, under which is a typed title. "I've no idea who this person is or what these initials mean, but it was signed in Moscow."

"Well," Dr Levittoux takes the letter and folds it carefully in two. "At least they sent it to Moscow and someone answered it."

"My goodness, Henryk," exclaims Dr Grüner. "Your ability to find the positive in any given situation is truly admirable!"

Levittoux utters a rueful laugh. "Clutching at straws, Julian. Clutching at straws."

When Kozłowski relates to his bunkmates the list of new rules that are now to govern their existence there is a shocked silence. Ever since their arrival at Starobelsk there has been a constant flux in the number of prisoners, with new inmates arriving and the enlisted men leaving in groups large and small throughout October and into early November. Each prisoner has been moved several times, from the Circus to a barracks, from one barracks to another. Groups of friends have been formed and dissolved, reformed and dissolved again. Registration of prisoners has gone on and on for days; the medical examinations are only just complete. Everything around the prisoners has conspired to sustain an atmosphere of perpetual change . Now, for the first time, they are forced to accept the fact that Starobelsk is to be their home for the foreseeable future. The announcement of the incipient arrival of a library, a mobile shop, board games and a cinema projector might be cause for some celebration; yet it is this news, more than the long list of forbidden activities, which finally drives home the fact that they are alone: the enlisted men have all gone home; there is no news from the outside world; any form of open revolt will result in removal from the camp, who knows where? "Come with me and bring your things," said Kopyekin. The message could not be clearer: we have allowed you to have your fun; we have watched you let off steam and air your reactionary opinions; we have listened to your words of revolt. Now, it is time to settle down and accept your new role as prisoners of the NKVD.

18. Sovietish

"Gentlemen, I give you *The Interrogation*, a drama in a single act."

It is late. Fryderyk Hoffman stands before a group of close friends who cluster eagerly around his bunk. A performance has been promised, the first act of defiance to take place within their barracks since the imposition of the new regulations almost two weeks ago. Hoffman grabs a blanket, which he stuffs up his jacket to form an oversized stomach, then puffs out his cheeks, barking out his words in a thick Russian accent:

> **LEBEDYEV:** *So. Let me see now* (Hoffman pretends to scrutinise a document) *Your surname is Hoffman, your first name Fryderyk, your parents' names Gustaw and Anna, your rank is that of lieutenant, is that correct?*
> **PRISONER:** *Yes.* (aside, to the audience) *How does he know that?'"*

"You wrote it in your registration form, you idiot!" cries Zygmunt.

Hoffman winks and continues, miming in turn the giant Lebedyev and a comically terrified prisoner.

LEBEDYEV: *You are, of course, a member of the Polish intelligence service.*

There is a burst of laughter at this line.

PRISONER: *I most certainly am not.*

LEBEDYEV: *Then how do you explain all these stamps in your passport?*

PRISONER: *I travel frequently, both for my work and for pleasure.*

LEBEDYEV: *Admit it, you travel abroad as a government spy!*

PRISONER: *No! Really. It's mainly for fun.*

LEBEDYEV: *Fun? We do not have fun in the Soviet Union.*

PRISONER: *You can say that again.*

LEBEDYEV: *What – did – you - say?*

PRISONER: (cowers) *Nothing.*

LEBEDYEV: *Come now, why don't you tell us the truth? We know you were in the Soviet Union only a few years ago. Where were you, how long were you there and what was your aim? What Soviet citizens did you get to know?*

PRISONER: *I have never been to the Soviet Union.*

LEBEDYEV: *Why lie? We know everything anyway.*

PRISONER: *I have never been to the Soviet Union.*

LEBEDYEV: *So how is it that you speak fluent Russian?* (to the audience) *Ha! I have him now."*

There is another burst of laughter. Lieutenant Szczypiorski, unnoticed, slips from the room.

PRISONER: *I learnt Russian at school, and studied many works of Russian literature at university. I speak several languages...*

LEBEDYEV: *So you admit to being a spy!*

The men laughing so uproariously are bound together by a common experience which Kozłowski almost envies. As more and more of the officers in his barracks have been taken for interrogation, his curiosity has grown, as if they belong to a club from which he has been excluded. Unpleasant, even frightening, as the interrogations must be, he nevertheless feels a powerful desire to know what it is like to be taken from his bed at night and to stand before Lebedyev, or Mitrov, or one of the other interrogators. On more than one occasion he has been on the verge of asking Dr Levittoux about it, but a sense of reserve, or delicacy, has held him back: it seems indecent to pry when information has not been freely offered.

PRISONER: *Isn't it normal to speak several languages?*

LEBEDYEV: *No! Here in the Soviet Union we speak only Sovietish. We have plenty of words to describe what we wish to say. We have no need of your ugly, foreign terms.*

PRISONER: *But what about literature? Poetry? Art? Surely there must be writers whose work you enjoy who do not write in Sovietish?*

LEBEDYEV: *Why would I want to read anyone other than Soviet writers?*

PRISONER: *To expand your mind!*

Hoffman-as-Lebedyev stands up, waving his gun threateningly at the prisoner.

LEBEDYEV: *I would remind you that I am conducting this interrogation, not you! I will decide whose mind needs expanding. This stamp, here—*

He waves the prisoner's passport in his face.

LEBEDYEV: *—states that you were in Paris in 1938. What were you doing there?*

PRISONER: *I was attending a theatre performance. And visiting friends.*

LEBEDYEV: *Admit it: you were sent there to spy on behalf of the Polish government! Why else would you have been there?*

PRISONER: *I told you: to have fun.*

LEBEDYEV: *And I have told you*: (he whacks the passport on the desk repeatedly) *WE – DO – NOT – HAVE – FUN – in the Soviet Union –"*

At this moment, Kopyekin enters the bunkroom. "You – Hoffman. Come with me."

Silence falls as Kopyekin leads Hoffman out. The men turn away from each other, rolling over on their bunks to stare at the wall, or the ceiling, scratching themselves, closing their eyes as if to sleep. At least Kopyekin only said "Come with me," thinks Kozłowski. That means interrogation, not the other thing. Some while later, Szczypiorski slips back into the room and climbs onto his bunk.

The following morning, Hoffman returns, tight-lipped and pale. For the next few days he says little, spending every evening lying on his bunk, scribbling furiously around the margins of a copy of the *Wilno Red Banner*.

Tadeusz Biały is seated on a pile of timber outside the barracks, sketching something on the back page of his notebook with such intense concentration that it is a full three minutes before he glances up, starting in surprise to find Kozłowski watching him.

"What are you drawing?"

Biały holds the book out for him to see. "I should probably burn it."

The sketch depicts a small figure with large eyes fringed with long lashes, dressed in a ragged uniform and seated on a low chair of the kind used by children at school; his knees are almost level with his chin, his hands raised to his open mouth in a comic approximation of Edvard Munch's painting *The Scream*. Leaning over a desk is a giant of a man with tiny, black eyes set deep in a piggy face. He wears the cap of an NKVD officer and brandishes a revolver at the terrified prisoner.

Biały takes the notebook and scores through the drawing, obliterating it with quietly methodical precision.

"So how was it?"

They begin to walk, slowly, aimlessly, tracing, as always, a large circle around the outer edges of the camp.

"They seem to think that because I was a cartographer I had access to military secrets. As if I'm some kind of walking camera who needs only to be pointed in the right direction and I'll reproduce everything I've seen. I told them, I'm just an illustrator; I never had access to any sensitive material. Just because I can draw a map it doesn't mean I can actually read one..." He laughs bitterly. "If they only knew the truth. I can hardly even remember the names of the villages we passed through on our retreat..." He pauses, twisting the pencil between his fingers. "They threatened me. They said: 'You want your wife and daughter to be safe, don't you, Lieutenant? A pregnant woman needs extra care in times like these. Tell us what you know and we will make sure she is safe...' How do they know Teresa is pregnant?" His voice is anguished now. "How can I tell them what I don't know?"

Of all the inhabitants of their block, it is Feliks Daszyński who has been singled out for continued questioning throughout the month of November. The effect of these repeated interrogations is not to subdue him but, on the contrary, to feed his desire for escape to such an extent that it occupies his every waking moment. One evening, he gathers his friends around him.

"I have it. I have found my ticket out of here."

Młynarski, his closest companion, fixes him with an anxious gaze. "What is it, Felo?"

"You remember when King Amanullah of Afghanistan visited Warsaw in '28?"

"Yes, I was there. My father was in charge of the music. I remember they had to learn the Afghan national anthem."

"I was there, too. My father was part of the receiving party."

"I don't see what—"

"Listen! King Amanullah conferred upon my father an order which carried with it an Afghan princely title."

"Yes, mine received one too."

"Then you will be aware, Bronek, that the title brought with it lifelong privileges not only for the recipient but also for his descendants." Feliks surveys his bewildered friends in triumph. "I have written to the Afghan Ambassador in Moscow, begging to remind him that I am potentially an Afghan subject. I have asked for his help in releasing me from Soviet enslavement."

Zygmunt pales. "You used those words, 'Soviet enslavement'?"

"Can you think of another way of describing it?"

"But, Feliks," says Bronek, "those titles – everybody in the official receiving party received one. They were ceremonial. Please don't send this letter."

"Too late. I handed it to Berezhkov myself this morning. Why don't you write one too? The Soviets are dying to get in with the Afghans; they're sure to listen to the Ambassador. Imagine it, Bronek: we could be Afghan princes together, living in luxury in a palace in Kabul!"

The curved dome of the old church is silhouetted against a bright moon. Usually, if he has to come out at night to urinate, Kozłowski hurries back inside as quickly as possible, the cold eating away at his feet through the soles of his boots. Tonight, however, he lingers a moment, attracted by the hoot of an owl and the clarity of a sky in which the moon hangs, bright as silver, amidst the trillions of stars. This is the same sky as the sky of home, he tells himself. These same stars are visible to my parents, to my brothers, to my sister, my friends. He imagines his parents asleep in the big white house, the fruit trees silhouetted in the silent garden, the dog curled up on his cushion by the kitchen stove. He feels a longing almost as a physical pain, as if someone had grabbed his intestines and is twisting them. Ralski says that there are pygmy owls here, tiny creatures no bigger than a man's hand, and almost impossible to spot. He listens for the owl's call, hoping to spot the elusive bird, gazing up in fascination at the abundance above him: so many worlds, so many possibilities right here above his head! The owl hoots again, close by this time; he twists round in the hope of seeing it but instead spots Tomasz hurrying towards him, a blanket around his shoulders.

"Wait for me, will you?"

"Of course."

Kozłowski resumes his contemplation of the sky until, a few moments later, Tomasz joins him. They stand side by side looking up at the stars in silence, their breath forming clouds in the freezing air.

"It reminds me," says Tomasz, after a while, "of that moment when you first arrive in the mountains in winter. You've been on a train all afternoon, you have a good dinner, everybody's pleased to see one another, there's talk of tomorrow – Where are we going to ski? Has there been enough snowfall? Have you tried the new restaurant that's opened in town? Finally, everyone piles upstairs to bed with a promise to be up bright and early the next morning. Only then do you get a chance to step outside and breathe in the air, knowing that before you lie days of wonderful skiing and mountain hikes. Where are those friends now, Zbyszek? Can you imagine Zakopane under Nazi occupation?"

"That was where you met Gosia, wasn't it? In Zakopane?"

"You look like her sometimes, you know. Every so often – you have a particular look – sort of thoughtful and anxious; you frown and then you smile, as if you are uncertain how somebody will react."

"Do I? Really?"

"There, you're doing it right now!" Tomasz points to his face, where an anxious frown has been swiftly replaced by a nervous smile. "I'm sorry. It's meant as a compliment, you know. To look like Gosia."

At this moment, Kopyekin scuttles from the special section, followed by two guards. As he disappears around the corner, Kozłowski instantly realises where he is heading.

"Come along now, get dressed and come with me," Kopyekin is shaking Feliks' shoulder. For a moment, it seems that this is all he is going to say, then he adds: "And bring your things."

Kozłowski, standing with Tomasz in the doorway, out of breath, feels a flutter in his stomach.

Feliks takes his time to climb down from his bunk. "You see,

Bronek? I was right. My letter did produce results."

Smiling calmly, he places his few belongings into his bag. One by one, he takes leave of his friends, leaning down to whisper something to Młynarski, who squeezes his hand with an expression of such agony Feliks almost loses his self-control. Then, with a cry of "Long live King Amanullah!" he is gone.

19. *Chopin*

Kozłowski can just make out the faint melody of the piano above the heated debate between Olgierd, aggressively expounding on the superiority of the Polish nation, and Lieutenant Szczypiorski, who has recently become so incensed by Olgierd's constant needling that he has thrown caution to the wind and declared his communist sympathies. Round and round in circles they go, as if both men derive a perverse pleasure from repeating the same thing in the hope that, eventually, their opponent will tire, like a knight wielding a heavy sword, and concede defeat.

Since the departure of Feliks Daszyński each of his friends has sought refuge in behaviour that to others appears increasingly eccentric: Zygmunt spends every day outside, chopping wood without a break until dusk, whilst Olgierd has become increasingly vocal about his political beliefs, deliberately seeking out those who disagree with him; Ralski scribbles ceaselessly on the margins of old newspapers, writing, he says, a book about grass; Tomasz talks endlessly about escape, and his desire to fight, whilst Kozłowski has become so obsessed with his battle against the lice that his fellow prisoners are beginning to resent his nagging. Tempers fray, arguments flare up between comrades who normally live together peacefully. It is Młynarski, however, who suffers most acutely from the absence of his closest friend.

Loudspeakers have now been installed all over the camp, inside and outside the barracks, strung up in the highest corners of each room and on top of tall poles, safely out of reach of sabotage. They broadcast from early morning until late at night. Between the endless exhortations to the Soviet people to increase their productivity, there are news bulletins to which the prisoners listen avidly, desperate for some hint of the progress of the war; there are concerts, too, of classical music, played at an unpleasantly loud volume, the sound distorted – but it is music, nevertheless.

"Look at you, with your Red newspapers and your lectures! Why don't you move in with Commissar Kirshin while you're at it? You're a disgrace to our country, and to the oath we took on joining the Polish army!" Olgierd's face is red, his lip curled in an unpleasant sneer.

Szczypiorski is equally angry. "There's nothing wrong with wanting to find a different way of doing things, a way that gives every man a chance to make his mark in life, or do you think that snobs like you are the only people who have a right to rule?"

"So you think Stalin had the right idea invading Poland, is that it?"

"That's not what I said—"

"Well, what did you say, then?"

"Oh, leave the man alone, can't you, Szpakowski? I can't hear myself think." Hoffman looks up irritably. "He's entitled to his beliefs, even if you disagree with them."

Olgierd turns on Hoffman. "Well, you would support him, wouldn't you?"

Hoffman puts down his pen. "And what precisely do you wish to imply by that?"

"You know perfectly well what I mean."

"I must be very stupid, because I don't know, so you'll have to spell it out."

"Jews and Communism. Is that clear enough for you?"

Hoffman throws down his notebook, exasperated. "I'm a socialist, for heaven's sake. You might have noticed that the communists hate us even more than they hate fascists like you!"

"I am not a fascist. I'm a nationalist."

"Who hates Jews."

"Not at all." Olgierd draws himself up prissily. "My view is very simple: different groups of people have different beliefs and different ways of doing things, so it makes sense that each group should be able to govern itself."

"You make it sound so reasonable, Szpakowski, and yet what you are actually saying is that anyone not conforming to your narrow idea of Polishness – based on Polish ethnicity and the Catholic faith – does not have a place in Poland—"

"Don't Ukrainians want to live in an independent Ukraine? And Jews in Israel?"

"No. Zionists wants to live in Israel. Plenty of Jews are quite happy living in Poland and consider themselves to be Polish."

"But are they, Hoffman? That's all I'm asking: are they?"

Hoffman looks as if he will explode. Zygmunt, who cannot bear it when people argue, whispers: "It's not worth getting het up, Fred. Just ignore him."

Hoffman, however, is not listening. "So tell me, Szpakowski," he continues, standing up. He is much taller than Olgierd, his handsome shoulders broad and imposing. "A mongrel such as I, where do I fit in? Which part of me is to be allowed to live in your Poland? My father is half-German, my mother (as you so frequently remind me) is Jewish. Assuming that my Jewish half is to be sent to Israel and my German part must live in Germany – although, at the rate Hitler is going, that might after all involve remaining at home—"

"Shame on you! You see?" Olgierd turns to his fellow prisoners triumphantly. "A lack of patriotism. The mark of a Jew."

"It was a joke, Olgierd," mutters Zygmunt.

"Come on, Szpakowski, tell me" continues Hoffman, ignoring the insult, "my Polish quarter, where is it to live? And which part of me is it to be? Which section of my body qualifies as the most Polish? My face? Perhaps not: you might argue that my features are too Semitic. One of my legs, maybe? But which one? The left?" He points his leg daintily, like a ballet dancer. "Or perhaps my shapely *derrière*?" He pushes out his bottom. "Where would you have me live, Olgierd, in your pure Polish paradise?"

"I am simply saying that different cultural groups find it easier to organise themselves if they stick together."

"And I say that you should be careful what you wish for, because a Poland that consists only of people like you, Olgierd, may not be such a pretty place!"

"Shut up!" yells Młynarski, almost in tears. He is perched on the top bunk, his ear rammed against the speaker. "I can't hear!"

Kozłowski can bear it no longer. Grabbing his blanket, he pushes his way to the door, where Młynarski's boots are placed in readiness for anyone needing to make a quick exit to the Siegfried Line.

Outside, he reaches into his pocket for the tin in which he keeps the last remains of his tobacco. He has been saving it, rationing himself carefully, but tonight he feels an overwhelming urge to smoke. He rolls the crumbs into a strip of newspaper and lights the cigarette, drawing quickly on it before it can go out. Across the camp compound, standing under the loudspeaker next to the church, stands Józef Czapski, gazing at the ground in an attitude of profound thoughtfulness.

The news bulletins, broadcast every hour, consist generally of long enumerations of German victories, followed by an equally long list of British losses, rounded off by a stream of insults concerning the Poles. Nevertheless, within the mass of propaganda there usually resides a nugget of truth which the prisoners have become expert at extracting. This nugget is then shaped and interpreted according to the character and desires of the listener. They wait impatiently for these signals from the outside world, setting up a rota to ensure that no bulletin is missed. During the last week of November it has fallen to Czapski to cover the late evening shift. Every night, standing huddled in the freezing cold, he listens to reports on events on the western front, of which there are few, noting down any information which could be construed as news, ignoring the long reports from 'liberated' Polish territory, where it is said that rich Poles drink the blood of their impoverished people and starve them to death.

Although the news bulletin finished over twenty minutes ago, Czapski has not moved from his spot, despite the cold. He lingers, wrapped in thought, listening to the second movement of Chopin's Piano Concerto No.1 in E Minor, performed by the great Polish pianist, Artur Rubinstein. Joining him, Kozłowski is greeted with Czapski's habitual gentle smile and together they listen in silence to the final movement.

When the concert is over, Młynarski emerges from the bunkroom, hopping across the snow half in, half out of someone else's boots.

"There they are, you thief!" Młynarski trips on a lace as he points to his boots.

His cheeks, notes Kozłowski, are wet with tears. Czapski, tactfully silent, offers the remains of a thin cigarette. Czapski does not smoke but has a habit of accumulating cigarettes which he passes on to his friends. Młynarski accepts the cigarette gratefully, surreptitiously wiping his eyes with his shirt sleeve.

"I've noticed that, as a rule, they make no mention of the artist or the orchestra when they broadcast a foreign recording. Artur appears to be an exception."

"It was him, was it? I thought so. I wasn't concentrating when they announced the piece."

"Yes."

"Goodness."

"I felt as if I had been punched in the stomach."

"Yes. Goodness. Indeed."

Kozłowski listens to their conversation without interrupting, stamping his feet in a fruitless attempt to shake the cold from them and inhaling the weak, skinny cigarette. It is a bizarre chain of events, he reflects, that have led to a place and a point in time where Bronisław Młynarski hears his own brother-in-law playing Chopin on Soviet radio.

"The other thing I've noticed," continues Młynarski, "is that they broadcast Rachmaninov as a composer, but not as a soloist; Shostakovich yes, Stravinsky no. At least they give the names of the Soviet musicians: I've heard several friends play. It's good to know they're still alive. And working."

"I prefer the jazz broadcasts myself." Zygmunt joins them now, slapping his shoulders with crossed arms, his brisk manner concealing a series of sharp glances thrown in Młynarski's direction. "Just came to find out where you'd got to, Bronek. You alright?"

"If you call what they play jazz—"

"It'll do, whatever they call it. Less concentration required, less chance of falling into a dark mood. More importantly, a decent rhythm when you're chopping wood." He shivers. "I don't know about you, but I've no desire to gratify Berezhkov by freezing to death out here. Why don't we go back inside?"

"Have they finished arguing?"

"Oh, yes, quiet as mice in there now."

"By the way," says Czapski, as they are about to part. "I almost forgot: they announced on the news bulletin that Russia has invaded Finland."

20. *A conversation*

When they finally come for him, he thinks at first that someone has fallen ill. It is only little Kopyekin, however, prodding him with his bony fingers, telling him to come along now, come with me.

The room is small and painted green, with a single wooden desk behind which is seated a man whom Kozłowski does not recognise. He knows from the other prisoners that there are specialists sent regularly from Moscow to carry out the interrogations and that these are considered more skilled than the officers permanently stationed at Starobelsk.

The officer from Moscow has a long, intelligent face, his hair smoothed into a careful side parting. As Kozłowski enters, he shifts in his chair, folding his legs uncomfortably under the table.

"Do sit down, Doctor." The officer indicates the narrow wooden chair placed opposite the desk.

Kozłowski, startled by the Russian's use of his professional title, sits and watches as the officer leafs slowly through a grey folder that lies on the table in front of him. When he imagined his interrogation, for some reason it was always Mitrov seated at the desk opposite him, two young men with curly hair and glasses, like a perverted mirror image of one another, one round-cheeked, smooth-shaven, the other gaunt, with a patchy beard. What might his file say? The facts are fairly basic: his father is a lawyer, his mother a teacher, neither of them particularly eminent in their field, nor involved in politics. His family history is solidly middle class, no aristocrats hiding in the closet, just a long line of lawyers, doctors and teachers. Two brothers, a sister in Kraków. A passport entirely devoid of interesting or exotic stamps. A short medico-military record unblemished by acts of bravery or conspicuous gallantry.

As the man shows no sign of looking up, Kozłowski's attention begins to wander: on the wall directly above the officer's head are two bright light bulbs, presumably placed there with the intent of dazzling the prisoner. Next to them hang portraits of Stalin, Lenin and Marx, the all-seeing Trinity of the Soviet nations. Finally, the officer closes the folder, reaches behind him and switches off the lights, leaving the room illuminated only by the small side lamp on the desk.

"You'll have to forgive my Polish," he begins, with a pleasant smile. "I hope I don't make too many mistakes. I had the good fortune to visit your country when I was a medical student."

"You're a doctor?"

"Alas, I never qualified. Family circumstances forced me to cut short my studies and instead I had to find a more – ah – practical career. I'm so sorry, how rude of me." He leans forward, holding out a packet of cigarettes. "Would you care for a cigarette?"

"No, thank you."

"Very sensible. I wish I could kick the habit. It is so infernally addictive."

The officer leans back in his chair, blowing smoke softly up towards the ceiling.

"Where did you study?" Kozłowski cannot resist posing the question.

The officer appears pleased to be asked. "I spent six months in Lwów in 1914, studying at the medical faculty of the university. It was called the Franciszkański in those days, of course. Now I believe they call it the Jan Kazimierz. I was intending to make a career in neurology and hoped to stay on. However, the war intervened, I was called up; things changed, then it was too late. What can one do?" He gives an expansive shrug, drawing deeply on the cigarette. "We are all at the mercy of events that are greater than us."

Kozłowski tries to process the information he has just been offered. Have they chosen this man specifically because he has a medical background? They cannot possibly have interrogators whose skills match those of every man in the camp. A wave of exhaustion passes over him; he longs to allow himself to drift back into the comfort of sleep but he knows that he must not succumb. He fights to keep his mind clear as the officer continues recounting his story, delivered in fluent Polish, in pleasant, cultured tones.

"I spent the first two years of the last war as a medical officer attached to the Caucasus Army. I probably spent as much time bandaging horses as I did men." He laughs, tapping the ash from his cigarette into an ashtray. "It's hard, isn't it, the first time you are confronted with the kind of injuries that are inflicted on the battlefield. But I expect you were better prepared than I was..." He leaves the opening dangling tantalisingly before Kozłowski.

"I don't know about that. It's impossible to fully anticipate what you're going to encounter on the battlefield. We had very limited supplies, and it was extremely chaotic..."

Kozłowski is soon in the middle of a long conversation which feels as familiar and comfortable as a favourite armchair. In the weeks since his arrival at Starobelsk he has had no opportunity to speak of his medical experiences before his capture. There have been many discussions about the military campaign, conversations about friends and colleagues encountered or lost along the way, but nothing about what it was actually like to carry out the duties of a doctor in the field. Most of his closest friends in Starobelsk are not doctors, and the medical discussions he has had since his arrival here have all been concerned with the immediate needs of the prisoners in the camp.

"So many different obligations, some of them not remotely medical," he continues, unable to halt now that he has started. "Not just overseeing the division's dressing station, but trying to run a clinic for the civilian population as well…"

And here is his sympathetic interlocutor, nodding knowledgeably, discussing the technical advances in medicine from one war to the next, sharing his experiences of the effects of gas in the first war, asking Kozłowski about the best way to deal with a bone that has been shattered by a bomb blast. He even refers to the skills and talent of Dr Levittoux.

The conversation continues, fluent and caressing as warm water. For the first time, Kozłowski tells another person about the moment he found himself in a civilian hospital filled with patients but empty of medical staff, with only two women from the local village trying their best to look after everyone while the Germans advanced.

"I did what I could. I offered – I wanted – to stay, but they were scared that the presence of an officer in Polish uniform, and in possession of a horse, would attract unwelcome attention from the enemy. They asked me to leave. I felt that I was abandoning them."

He speaks of his wanderings at the head of a cavalcade of wounded civilians, trying to find a hospital which would take them in. The chaos on the roads, running out of petrol, the German bombardment pushing them ever farther east…

The Russian officer listens intently, writing nothing down. He offers up knowledge gleaned from the previous war, deferring with elegant humility to Kozłowski's more recent experiences before speaking of his own youthful dreams: his interest in neurology, a subject about which he appears to be remarkably well-informed. Then he enquires about the medical service in Poland, wanting to know if patients are expected to pay, and how hospital admissions are organised. Kozłowski expresses his frustration at the way in which the system of medical insurance penalises those who are without work, or whose employers do not pay their dues; he speaks of his dislike of those doctors who operate only a private 'cabinet' and mentions the difficulties experienced in poor rural areas, where access to a doctor can be severely limited.

The officer from Moscow explains that in the Soviet Union the state provides free medical treatment for everybody equally, regardless of their ability to pay, and that there are first-rate clinics all over the country, even in the remotest rural areas. There is a great deal of state investment in medical research as well, he adds. Is not Kozłowski struck by how much fairer and more democratic this system is for patients?

It is at this moment that Kozłowski realises how easily he has allowed himself to be led down a path chosen with consummate precision by his interrogator. The animated zeal which until this moment has enlivened his face disappears.

"I have no interest in politics," he replies, stiffly. His hand rises, involuntarily, to the side of his glasses, where he fiddles with the silver thread which holds it in place.

"Really? You seem so passionate about your profession."

"Fortunately, my profession has little to do with politics."

"Ah, but that's where you are wrong! Everything is connected to politics. Why, the very thing you were saying about the need to provide medical services to patients whatever their financial means, that is political."

"Well, I didn't mean it to be so."

"Yet you said that you wished for all men to be treated equally."

"As patients, yes. I'm hardly advocating revolution."

"But would you find it so hard to serve as a doctor under a political system that was dedicated to stamping out those inequalities of which you spoke so eloquently just now?"

Kozłowski does not recall having expressed himself in quite such terms. He said only that he does not personally agree with operating medical services on an exclusively financial basis. He remains silent.

"Come now, doctor, would you find it so hard to work here?"

Kozłowski shrugs. "I like my own country, thank you, whatever its faults."

"Wouldn't it be an even better place if some of those faults were ironed out?"

"Perhaps."

The officer smiles, pleased.

"But you could say that of any country," adds Kozłowski hastily. "I'm sure you would not claim that the Soviet Union is a perfect place."

The officer laughs. "Oh, no, indeed. But we're getting there. Slowly but surely, all of us together, working for the common good…"

At the end of the conversation – one could hardly call it an interrogation – the officer stands up and, with a genial smile, holds out his hand.

"It has been most agreeable talking to you, Doctor. I do hope we get the chance to meet again."

It seems churlish to refuse to shake his hand, so Kozłowski reaches out and feels the firm clasp of the other man's warm, dry fingers. The officer holds open the door. The interview is over. It has lasted three hours.

Kozłowski asks the guard if they can stop at the Siegfried Line. Thin white figures, huddled in blankets, dressed only in dirty underwear, shuffle along the path leading to the latrine. As he stands over the ditch watching his urine freeze into a little yellow mound, Kozłowski reflects uneasily on the interview. He had steeled himself to withstand an attack. Instead, he has been turned over and tickled like a trout. He is sure that he said nothing of which he should be ashamed. He spoke the truth, his truth as a doctor. There is nothing controversial in his opinions: they are common amongst many in his profession. And yet, he cannot help feeling as if in some way he has betrayed somebody, or something; his countrymen, or his country. The officer's friendly demeanour, the tone of the conversation, the way he thanked Kozłowski, the handshake at the end – everything leads to a shameful feeling that somehow he has colluded in whatever it was the officer wanted from him. He has participated in a friendly conversation with a member of the enemy's secret police.

When he returns to the bunkhouse Tomasz is waiting for him.

"How was it?"

Tomasz's friendly, sympathetic gaze somehow irritates Kozłowski.

"I don't know what you're staring at," he mutters. "You know perfectly well what it involves."

He rolls over on his bunk and stares at the wall. He has done nothing wrong, he tells himself. So why does he feel so angry and ashamed?

21. Everything and nothing

The prisoners have dispersed around the camp: they sit on their bunks, or outside in the cold, contemplating the little white postcards which Major Zaleski has purchased from the mobile shop on their behalf and distributed among them.

It was in the first week of December that Kirshin finally made the announcement. He did it in his habitual fashion, stressing how wonderfully benign the Soviet authorities are and how much care they take of their prisoners, before laying out the precise and narrow details of this latest act of generosity:

"You will be permitted to write home this month. You may write one letter only, which will be sent from Starobelsk at the end of this week. It will reach your homes in time for your annual winter holiday celebrations." He did not use the word Christmas.

A busy trade in paper and pencils soon establishes itself, with the prisoners taking it in turns to use a single pencil or pen. The difficulty then becomes for them to decide to whom they should address their single letter, and what they should say. That their correspondence will be read by the camp authorities is so obvious a fact that it does not need to be stated. Nevertheless, Major Zaleski gathers together the representatives of each of the blocks:

"Gentlemen, as you know, we are at last to be permitted contact with our families. Whilst this privilege is long overdue, I must ask you to warn your men to be discreet in what they say and to exercise the greatest caution about what they reveal. Do not think that by writing in a foreign language such as French or even Latin you will be safe. Indeed, your letter risks immediate destruction. I know this for a fact. Given the restrictions on the length of the letters, there will anyway be little room for us to indulge our imaginations. We must content ourselves with conveying the essential information to our families: that we are alive, we are healthy, we are prisoners. We will wish to be assured of the health and wellbeing of our loved ones. Aside from that, there is little else that we can say. Please, convey this information to your men."

The camp is overtaken by a strange mood as each man seeks to remove himself as far as possible from his colleagues in order to compose that impossible thing: a letter that conveys everything and nothing.

Kozłowski lies on his side, using a small piece of wood as a surface on which to write. He has acquired a small pencil stub, one of half a dozen currently being passed around the bunkroom.

He stares at the little white card before him. A memory of a summer holiday rises to the surface: his mother, seated at the breakfast table, staring in just this way at the empty white space on the back of a photograph of sunlit mountains (or was it lakes, or a castle?).

"There's never enough space to write anything interesting," she said fretfully.

To which his father, without looking up from the newspaper he was reading, replied:

"Why send them at all?"

"It's nice to get a postcard when someone is away."

"I don't see the point of them." Staś, lying on the ground playing with the dog, rolled over to address his parents. "What are they for, anyway? Are you trying to show off the fact that you're travelling to interesting places while some poor soul who's stuck in Warsaw is not?"

"Goodness! You're no help at all!"

Gosia reached over the breakfast table and took up the pen.

"All you have to do, Mama, is say: 'The weather is beautiful. The food is so-so. We have seen this, that or the other, and we're simply dying to tell you all about it on our return. Love and kisses, Maria, Artur, Ignacy, Zbyszek, Staś and Gosia.' There. Done." She slid the card back over to her mother.

"I'm not putting my name to that mindless drivel!" protested Staś, from the floor.

"You write something better, then, if you're so clever."

"I hope it's raining in Warsaw and that you're having a miserable time whilst we're sunning ourselves here in paradise. Sincerely, Staś.'"

"That's horrible!"

"At least it's honest."

The inevitable squabble that ensued between the two youngest members of the family effectively deflected their mother's attention from the task of finishing the postcard. Thus it was that the card was dispatched half-complete, without further reflection concerning the nature or quality of its contents, and marked with a small coffee stain where the tussle between the two siblings resulted in a spillage.

To which year does this memory belong? It is a familiar scene which could have taken place any summer, or every summer, and yet he has a vivid image of Gosia wearing a thin summer dress, posing with her hand cupped against her freshly-bobbed hair. How old could she have been then – fifteen? Sixteen?

"It's more practical like this," she explained to their mother. "And anyway, it's the fashion."

"Since when did you care about fashion?" asked Staś. "You're such a swot, I'm surprised you even know what's in fashion anyway."

"Leave her alone, Staś," said his mother. "I wish you two would stop arguing just for a moment."

The truth was that Staś, whose academic ability had until now been a source of easy familial pride, was bitterly jealous of the fact that his younger sister was beginning to catch up with him. As she was far harder-working than he, while his school reports were generally of the "Stanislas is a bright boy but needs to apply himself" variety, hers were beginning to read like a citation in support of the canonization of a saint.

"Maybe she's got a boyfriend. Have you got a boyfriend, Gosia? Does he wear glasses? He must be very short-sighted to like someone as ugly as you."

"That's enough, Staś!" His father brought his newspaper down onto the table with a thwack. "Don't speak like that to your sister."

"He's just jealous because I did better in chemistry than he did last year. And maths."

"I am not jealous!"

Staś, enraged, tried to grab Gosia's hair but she was too quick for him, dodging out of the way and, in the process, knocking over the coffee pot. Their mother placed her hands over her ears.

"Why do they call it a holiday?"

Kozłowski remembers watching the argument with a sense of pleasant detachment. Four years older than Gosia, three years older than Staś, as a university student he was in the agreeable position of having school grades far behind him and was thus able to regard his siblings' quarrels with the airy indifference of that most desirable of creatures: an adult. Their older brother Ignacy, meanwhile, who had already completed his degree and now worked in a bank in Wilno, regarded all three of his younger siblings with an air of patronising superiority. Heavily-built, his thin hair combed carefully across his head, at twenty-three he could easily pass for a man ten years older.

"For goodness sake, Staś!" He shook out his newspaper, open on the financial page, and pushed his spectacles up his nose. "I don't know why you get so upset. She's only a girl."

Staś raised his hands in the air like a victorious athlete, for he knew that his insensitive brother, in his desire to put an end to the argument, had inadvertently pressed the one button guaranteed to detonate his sister's rage.

Sure enough, she exploded: "What do you mean, *only* a girl?"

His mother was right: it is almost impossible to decide on the words with which to fill the small white box. There is so much he wishes to know about their life at home, about the Nazi occupation and the progress of the war, none of which they will be able to include in their reply, and there are so many questions his parents will want to ask him in return. First, then, the reassurances:

Dearest Mother and Father, I am well and relieved at last to have the chance to write to you. We were captured in September and since then have been in a camp in Starobelsk in Ukraine. Rest assured that my health is good and my spirits too. There is a clinic here which is run by Dr Levittoux. You remember him, of course. There are many doctors here, and I have the task of taking care of the men in my block. He stops. The banality of the words strikes him painfully, yet there is no way around it; he ploughs on: *Please write to me as often as you can. I cannot write much, so don't worry if you don't hear from me frequently. And please send me news of Ignacy, Gosia and Staś.* He debates whether to mention the fact that Staś was last seen trying to escape from Poland on a motorbike but decides that it is probably better to stick to generalities. *If possible, could you send me some warm linen? I know, Mama, that you will say I should have listened to you. You were right, as you always are, my dearest.*

He stops, overcome by a sudden longing for home. How much he would give to have his mother fussing over him now, to be able to respond with thoughtless irritation to her concern and then, having snapped at her, to hug her and tell her that he is sorry; how much he would like to see the patient affection in her eyes as she forgives him and irritates him again by asking him, for the fourth time, if he would like a cup of coffee. Before he was mobilised, his plan had been to move out of the family home at the earliest opportunity and find somewhere on his own. Prudence had forced him to wait until he had sufficient financial means to pay the rent. In July, he had applied for a more senior position at the hospital which would have permitted him to move out. Of course, the answer never came.

The men are busily putting the final touches to their cards before handing them in when Fryderyk Hoffman approaches Kozłowski.

"Zbyszek, could I have a word with you in private, please?"

Hoffman waits until they are safely out of earshot of the barracks before he speaks. "I have a rather delicate mission. It concerns Tomasz."

"Is he alright?"

"Oh, yes." Hoffman takes from his pocket a small rectangle of newspaper onto which he sprinkles tiny fragments of tobacco mixed with shreds of grass. "At least, I think he will be." Hoffman takes his time, rolling the cigarette paper carefully, apparently enjoying a private joke. "The fact is," he says, finally, "it appears that Tomasz is in love with your sister and is beside himself with anxiety about her. He knows that he ought to write to his parents, but of course what he really wants is to know is if she is alright. He's got himself into a state about it and can't find a way of broaching the subject with you. I found him pacing up and down by the perimeter wall like a lunatic and it all came spilling out." Hoffman cups his hands around the cigarette and lights it. He inhales deeply, contemplating Kozłowski with wry amusement.

"Goodness, is that all? Why on earth didn't he say something to me?"

"My impression is that he is unsure of your sister's feelings towards him and so does not feel – ah, how can I put it? – entitled to the status of boyfriend, or *beau*."

The urge to laugh is too strong: they both succumb.

"Oh dear! I feel guilty laughing. He takes it all so seriously—"

When Tomasz, on his way back to the barracks, spots his friends evidently enjoying a joke at his expense, he stiffens and, with a look that conveys both hurt and reproach, hurries past them without a word.

"Tomasz, wait— !"

Kozłowski finally catches up with him near the old church. Fixed on the noticeboards outside are colourful posters depicting young women in overalls driving tractors across fields of golden corn; alongside them, rows of rosy-cheeked pioneers salute cheerfully under a slogan which says, 'Today we celebrate the birthday of our father Stalin'.

"I'm glad you find me so amusing."

"Tomasz, don't be stupid. We weren't laughing at you."

"Weren't you?"

"No! Well, if we were, it wasn't meant unkindly. The truth is, it makes a wonderful change to be able to concern oneself with something so …" he searches for the word, "so agreeable."

"Agreeable."

"Yes. Look, Tomasz, if you're in love with my sister no one could be more delighted than me. But you could have said something, you know."

"I didn't feel I had the right."

"Just tell me what I can do to help. Anything."

"Really?"

"Of course. You're my friend. I'd do anything for you, you know that." To Kozłowski's embarrassment, Tomasz's eyes fill with tears. "No need to cry, old fellow. Just tell me what to do. You want to know if Gosia is alright, is that it?"

Tomasz nods.

"Well, that's easily resolved. Why don't I ask my parents? After all, they are in the German-occupied zone and should be able to contact Kraków. They could let Gosia know that there is a particular friend of hers here in the camp who would like to hear from her. Then – assuming she wants to – she can write to you and the next time we have the opportunity to correspond, you can pour your heart out to her as much as you like. What do you think? Will it serve?"

With his postcard duly amended to include a post scriptum, written in cramped pencil, conveying the information that his good friend Tomasz Chęciński is particularly eager to hear from Gosia, Kozłowski goes in search of the postman to hand in his missive before it is too late.

Having finally acknowledged to Kozłowski his feelings about Gosia, for several days Tomasz talks to him of little else. As they walk slowly along the perimeter of the camp, following the path that has been carved out of the snow, Kozłowski has the sensation of discovering a person for the first time, as if Gosia were a neighbour who had lived next door to him all his life and who is suddenly revealed to be a spy, or a famous scientist.

"She's so small – or perhaps she's not actually small but I'm tall so she seems small to me – but she's very strong. She's a fine mountaineer and, as Hanka said, she's rather serious, which is not to say she's dull; far from it, she's so intelligent—" Tomasz stops abruptly. "I'm sorry. I need hardly describe her to her own brother."

Kozłowski assures him that any compliment to Gosia will be taken as it is intended.

Tomasz continues, relating how, after their first encounter in Zakopane, it proved hard to meet. "I was so tied up with work in Warsaw, and she was in Kraków taking her final exams. There were just a few days in Warsaw in July when she came to visit your parents."

"I remember. I was on call at the hospital that week."

There was a family dinner during which Gosia told her parents that she had been offered a job as a junior laboratory assistant at the chemical institute in Kraków. If she achieved the right grades in her final exams she would start immediately. Kozłowski remembers with sudden clarity how happy Gosia had seemed; his mother had mentioned a friend who had come for dinner the previous night.

"Was that you? Did you come to my house for dinner?"

Tomasz confesses that it was indeed he, declaring that he spent a very pleasant evening at their house.

"Being grilled by my mother, I've no doubt."

Tomasz makes no reply to this, but describes in astonishing detail his parents' house, the garden, his impression of Gosia's father and mother.

"So kind and welcoming... your father... a really interesting conversation about Piłsudski..."

Kozłowski is only half-listening. He remembers, now, a summer morning at the breakfast table: seated in his dressing gown, his head burning from lack of sleep after a night at the hospital during which he had been woken three times, his attention had drifted in and out of a conversation between his mother and Gosia.

"…seems a very nice young man. He works in oil, you say? A lawyer of some sort?"

"…studied Political Science at Warsaw… keen to continue his studies…so many exciting ideas…"

He had stared out of the window at the garden, where his father was standing with a coffee cup in one hand and an apple, just pulled from the tree, in the other, lost in thought. The family dog, Tygrys, sat at his father's feet, tail wagging, evidently under the impression that the object in his master's hand was not an apple but a ball.

"…and is it a serious friendship, Gosia?"

"I never told her how I felt, Zbyszek," continues Tomasz, anguished. "We spent a week in Zakopane in August – a wonderful, magical week – but she was so excited because she had been offered the job at the Chemical Institute. I thought that if I started making declarations she would run a mile. Then I was called up and it was too late."

Tomasz falls silent, as if exhausted by the torrent of words. It is almost dusk; snow has begun to fall, drifting silently across the darkening sky.

Kozłowski, never comfortable with the discussion of intimate personal matters, searches for the right way to ask the next question.

"Tomasz, do you think – the way you feel – does Gosia …?"

"Reciprocate?" Tomasz shrugs, smiles, flushes, hesitates, bites his fingernails, shrugs again. "Perhaps. She gave me her photograph. But I wouldn't dare presume she feels anything more than friendship without some kind of concrete assurance from her."

Kozłowski cannot help reflecting that Tomasz was born into the wrong era: he should have been a knight in armour, not a soldier.

That night, with the first batch of letters now finally handed in, the prisoners, as they always do, sit down to talk.

"Who's going to read it, that's what I was thinking: Petrov? Stepanov? The idea that my most private thoughts will be read by that perfumed hulk—"

"I don't care. I wrote my darling and kisses and hugs and every affectionate term I could think of. Let them laugh if they want to."

"Are they allowed to send us packages?"

"I heard up to 2 kilos."

"I heard no parcels."

"I asked for some gloves."

"I said books."

"Do you think the post will be quicker from the Soviet-occupied zone or the German one?"

"Well, the Nazis are more efficient, that's for sure, but it all has to pass through Russian hands in the end, doesn't it?"

"When do you think we will hear back?"

"Hopefully before Christmas."

"I heard January."

"Now all we have to do is wait."

"Did you know," says Hoffman, *à propos* of nothing, "that the poet Piwowar got married only a month before the war broke out?"

Kozłowski lies awake, listening to the now-familiar symphony of snores and sighs, ignoring – as he has now learned to do – the incessant desire to scratch, and wonders what it would be like to read so many letters from so many men, searching them for signs of subversion, or secret codes.

My darling wife, Dearest Father, Mother, My sweet...

Are you well? How is your health? How fares my little boy? Is the dog safe?

Petrov cackling at the tender words, his feet up on the stove, his black pen swishing across the paper, crossing out place names, references to matters military. All those Polish names swirling around in his head, clumping together like weeds with their iskis and askis and oyskis...

Mitrov, head bent, reading intently.

A card with so many crossings-out you might wonder if the deleted words themselves form some kind of secret communication, evidence of a mind in turmoil.

When I last saw you/We parted so hastily/No news of home/My thoughts are with you always

Please write and give me news of yourselves and my sister.

I think of you all constantly.

I am well.

Your loving son.

22. The first post

Entering the newly-constructed kitchen, Kozłowski is met by the sight of Commissar Kirshin greedily stuffing into his mouth a piece of fried fish from a tray which Chef Antoni has prepared for the prisoners' lunch. Kirshin appears not the slightest bit embarrassed either by the arrival of Kozłowski or the queue of freezing prisoners waiting outside, mumbling only, "Nice fish. My compliments," before continuing his tour of the camp.

Kozłowski and Antoni are in mid-discussion concerning pasties and other delicacies for the prisoners' clandestine Christmas celebrations when the cry is heard outside.

"Post! The first post is here!"

Outside, the postman, an odd-looking prisoner dressed in an oversized overcoat, his hat tied over his head with a woollen scarf, is heading directly towards block number 16, a large black bag slung over his shoulder,

"No pushing, no shoving. Every man who has a letter will receive it." In the postman's hand is a bundle of letters which he unties, reading out the first name. "Ralski."

On the front of the card is a thick swastika and the postmark 'Reichsgau Posen', stamped in black ink.

"Szpakowski."

Olgierd holds out his hand, a slight, forced smile on his lips.

The postman continues reading the names. "Cierniawski, Jelonek, Bielecki." The first two men he names step forward, but at the third there is a silence. "Bielecki."

"Bielecki? Are you sure he's in this block?"

"It says here, clear as day, Flight Officer Bie—"

"Here."

There is a shocked silence, for nobody has ever heard the airman speak. The postman hesitates, eyeing with barely-concealed horror the stained bandages which cover the outstretched hand. With a curse, the airman jumps from his bunk, grabs the letter and disappears through the door.

There are only a few envelopes left in the pile.

"Młynarski."

"He's not here," says Prosiński. "I can take it for him."

The final letter is for Kozłowski.

"Don't be downhearted!" The postman surveys the dismayed faces of those men who have not received any mail. "There'll be plenty more soon, don't you worry."

As he slings his bag over his shoulder and sets off for the next block, whistling cheerfully, Kozłowski is struck by the impression that here is a prisoner who has found a job that he genuinely enjoys.

During the first period of letter-writing, the officers scattered round the camp in search of a quiet place where they might commit their private thoughts to paper; now, with the arrival of the first letters from home, the prisoners scatter again, each seeking a secluded spot where he might absorb whatever news fate has seen fit to bring him. They hold the envelopes in trembling hands, gazing down at handwriting familiar and postmarks unfamiliar, marks which, in themselves, are news, symbols of the worlds in which their families now live: names once beloved have been renamed and rendered strange, printed in black gothic or Cyrillic script: Krakau, Warschau, Posen, Vilnius, Lviv.

The letter from Kozłowski's mother is long, written in tiny, dense handwriting which takes up both sides of the paper:

December 12ᵗʰ 1939

My dearest Zbyszek,

You cannot imagine our relief at receiving a letter from you at last! These three months have been almost unbearable – your father and I have been beside ourselves with anxiety. Let me tell you the good things first: we are in good health; the house is intact; our neighbourhood escaped the worst of the bombing and, unlike many of our friends, we have been able to stay put. Dear Professor Wiśniewski and his wife are staying with us temporarily (their house was completely destroyed). Gosia is working in the laboratory in Kraków, which is now run by the Germans, although the Polish staff remain. At least she has a job and the means to support herself. She is living with my cousin Helena and her husband. I have passed on the message from her friend. Is he the young man she brought to see us in Warsaw? I liked him very much. Do you think it's serious? Of Staś we have no news at all. I have written to the Red Cross on his account, as I did on yours, my dearest. I am glad at least to know that one of you is safe. Now to the worst. I cannot put it off any longer, although I can hardly see the paper as I write. My dear Zbyszek, it pains me so much to have to tell you this: your brother Ignacy was killed by an incendiary bomb during the first week of the war. He died instantly and did not suffer, so I am told (perhaps they say that to every grieving mother). Elżbieta and the children remain in Wilno and are living with her parents. She is a strong young woman; she will survive this ordeal, I've no doubt. I just wish that they could be here with us. Your father, as you may imagine, is much affected by the loss of his eldest son. (Eldest? Only thirty years of age! Dear God in heaven! And here we are still alive!) He sends his warmest love to you and tells you to look after your health, and to do your best to remain in good spirits. I have sent you a package of linen. Let me know, if you can, if it reaches you. I pray for you every night.

    Mother

Ignacy, dead. Sensible, solid, sober Ignacy, his elder brother, life cut short. Ignacy, whose greatest ambition was to return home at the end of a day's work to be greeted by a kiss from his wife, the embrace of his children, and the sweet aroma of cooking. Ignacy, lifeless, blown to bits by a bomb. His children fatherless, his wife a widow. There is no word for parents who have lost a son, as there is no word for a brother who has lost a brother.

He last saw them in the garden of his brother's house in Wilno on the day Ignacy received his call-up papers. He recalls the afternoon with absolute clarity, a memory fixed in his mind from the last weeks before his world changed forever: Ignacy had been delayed in town and returned, wearing his brand-new uniform, to find his brother stretched out on a rug in the garden, with three-year old Olek seated on his legs pretending he was a motor car and six-year-old Magda feeding him cherries from a bowl.

"You look like a lord," said Ignacy drily, surveying the scene.

"How smart you look, Daddy!" cried Magda.

Olek clambered down from Kozłowski's knees, charging towards his father. "I want to try your hat!"

The eldest child, Zosia, said nothing, but gazed, enraptured, at the mirror-like shine of her father's leather boots.

"Where's Elżbieta?" Ignacy swooped Olek up with one arm, while taking Zosia's hand in his. Magda, meanwhile, resumed her position next to the bowl of cherries.

Kozłowski was about to say "Inside," but, as he opened his mouth, a cherry was popped between his lips so unexpectedly that it dropped to the back of his throat, lodging itself there.

"Now see what you've done, Magda! Poor Uncle Zbyszek, you've made him choke!"

Magda began to sob bitterly at her father's words of reproach, while Kozłowski, his eyes watering from the effort to expel the cherry, attempted to reassure her that he was fine. He was still coughing some moments later, trying to persuade the children that hitting him violently on the back was not going to help him now that the cherry had been dislodged, when Elżbieta came out into the garden, holding aloft a plate with a freshly-baked apple charlotte on it.

"Doesn't Papa look handsome?"

Elżbieta stopped, her face draining of colour. For a moment her eyes were filled with a fear bordering on panic, then she nodded briskly, fussing about the little wrought-iron table.

"Indeed he does, Zosia. Quite the hero. Be a darling," this she addressed to Zosia, who was now gazing up adoringly at her father's four-cornered cap, "and run inside to fetch a knife for the cake. I forgot it."

Zosia ran off, with Olek and Magdalena scampering behind her, leaving the three adults alone.

"Must they send you now?" whispered Elżbieta. "Zbyszek hasn't received his call-up papers yet, have you, Zbyszek?"

In vain did Ignacy seek to explain to his wife that each regiment was differently organised, that his brother lived in Warsaw, not Wilno. His orders had come and obey them he must, however much he would prefer to remain at home with his wife and children. He could not disobey his country just to please her, could he? A man had his duty to consider, after all.

So they had eaten the apple charlotte which Elżbieta said tasted of dust and, when the children had admired for the umpteenth time their father's new greatcoat and Elżbieta had addressed its shortcomings—

"It's so heavy, Ignacy dear. Surely you should be dressed in your summer uniform?"

"Summer will soon turn to winter, my dearest, and we have no idea how long the war will last."

—when the children had peered at their round, smiling faces reflected in his shiny boots; when Uncle Zbyszek had whirled them round in turn, Olek first because he was the youngest, then Magda, who giggled so much she gave herself the hiccups, then, finally, Zosia, protesting that at nine years old she was too old for such childish amusements, before finally succumbing with shrieks of delight as he swung her round and round; when supper had been served and the children sent to bed; when all of these things had been done, then Kozłowski took leave of his family a day sooner than planned because, despite her protestations that he must stay another night, despite the fact that it was a long journey back to Warsaw, young as he was and unmarried, Kozłowski could see that this last supper was as precious to Elżbieta as her children. She wanted to spend the evening alone with her Ignacy, her dull, dependable husband with his carefully combed hair and the little *pince nez* which he wore on his nose when reading the paper; she wanted to help him pack his bag, to remind him not to forget this, or that, to show her affection for him in a hundred pointless gestures, rolling his socks up neatly into a ball and ironing his handkerchiefs with determined force until they lay flat on the ironing board like communion wafers; she wanted to fuss over him and place the little medallion of the Virgin Mary around his neck as a talisman for his safe return. Zbyszek, young as he was, understood that Elżbieta needed to do all of these things for her husband because it was all that she could do. So he said goodbye to her in the doorway and she clasped her arms around his neck with uncharacteristic warmth, whispering, "Thank you, Zbyszek," before stepping back and calling out: "Good luck! Let us know when you get your papers!" She was less anxious about him going to war, she added, because he was a doctor, and doctors did not fight.

He had fallen asleep on the train back to Warsaw. It was the last time he had seen his brother, or his brother's wife.

In the other news, small consolations: his parents are well; Gosia is safe. And Staś? Perhaps he made it to France after all. Of course, the package of linen that is supposed to accompany his mother's letter has disappeared.

This day marks a profound shift in perception among those men who have received letters from home: the vacuum in which the prisoners have existed over the past three months is filled suddenly with a rush of words, thoughts and emotions. Until now, their isolation has been almost complete, the barrage of propaganda which blares perpetually from the loudspeakers their only source of information. This correspondence brings the war, and home, back into their existence. Those in receipt of news that their wives are safe, their children healthy, their parents unhurt, return swiftly to find their friends, clustering in animated groups to try to pull together the fragments of information they have gleaned in the hope of producing a coherent picture of the progress of the war.

"My wife and children are well, thank God!"

"Only minor damage to the apartment…"

"Six of them all in one small room, but at least they're in good health…"

And then, the extraordinary discovery that they are not alone in Soviet captivity.

"… says he is in Kozelsk camp, near Smolensk. Apparently there are several thousand Polish officers there, just like here."

"… my brother writes that our cousin, who is in the police, is in a place called Ostashkov, near Tver, along with thousands of border guards and police."

Others, less fortunate, retreat further into solitude as word comes of death, of imprisonment, of sickness, of loss.

At the end of the day in block number 16 the tally is as follows:

Ralski's wife informs him that she and their daughter have been forced to leave their apartment in Poznań. Their furniture and their books, including all of Ralski's work, the fruit of years of study, were thrown onto the street by German soldiers. Poznań is now part of the

German Reich, no place for Polish intellectuals. His wife has managed to make her way to Warsaw, hoping to find somewhere to live and a job of some sort.

Zygmunt has no news of home. He bears this with his customary stoicism and spends the evening sewing up a rip in his coat sleeve with tiny, meticulously-even rows of cross stitch.

Olgierd learns that his brother has been arrested and is in Pawiak prison in Warsaw. His sister, who works as a secretary for the Polish government, is safe in Paris. His parents are well, although his mother suffers from rheumatism.

Bronisław Młynarski, whose sisters are both in the US, discovers from a friend that the Warsaw Philharmonic has been disbanded and Polish Radio no longer permitted to broadcast.

Hoffman has no news of his family in Warsaw.

Tomasz has heard nothing from his family in Lwów.

Those without letters try to make the best of it, smiling politely as others pour out their relief to anyone who will listen. Biały, ignorant of the fate of his pregnant wife and young child in Wilno, ventures to observe that many of those with family in the Soviet zone of occupation have not had letters today, and expresses the conviction that their turn will soon come.

That night, the airman Bielecki does not return to the barracks. In the morning, his frozen body is discovered in the snow next to the Siegfried Line. Whether his death was an accident or an act of despair, nobody knows: the letter found in his pocket is left where it is, untouched; nobody wishes to know if it was the news contained within it that drove him to seek a final release from his suffering. It is easier to ascribe his death to simple bad luck.

23. *Christmas*

On Christmas Eve, the officers in blocks 16 and 17 gather around a tiny tree fashioned from wire by one of the prisoners. From its branches hang minute stars, carved from wood shavings by the same hand. It looks absurdly small and yet, to Kozłowski, it seems that he has never before seen anything so exquisite. Prosiński directs the evening's celebrations, calling in turn those men who have offered to recite a poem, or make a speech, or say a prayer. Tomasz gives a spirited rendition of Mickiewicz's *Arcymistrz*, after which one of the men from the adjoining room recites Norwid's *Fortepian Szopena*.

During the recitation Czapski appears, asking apologetically if he might be permitted to join their celebrations having witnessed, he explains, a scene during which one of his fellow prisoners, angry at a perceived slight, threw a bucket of soup over his bunkmate.

"The idea of spending my first Christmas in captivity shut up in that dreadful room is so utterly depressing that I decided to come in search of more cheerful company. Will you take in a poor refugee?"

His request is greeted with a chorus of protest.

"Don't be ridiculous, Józef!"

"As if you have to ask…"

Tiny, delicious pasties made by Chef Antoni are passed around, the celebrations culminating at midnight with a rendition of the carol *Bóg się rodzi*, after which each man solemnly turns to his neighbour and wishes him a Merry Christmas.

Later, Czapski slips away, a reluctant exile returning to his home among the sick, defeated captains. Watching the solitary figure cross the deserted yard, Kozłowski notes that there are no guards in sight tonight, although singing can clearly be heard coming from several of the barracks. Perhaps Kirshin and Berezhkov have decided that the celebration of their 'winter holiday' will lift the prisoners' morale. Perhaps it is a form of compensation, something to smooth over the disappearance of Major Zaleski from the camp the previous day, shortly after the triumphant opening of the newly-restored camp baths.

On Christmas Day itself, Major Miller is taken. Kopyekin disappears at the same time and is never seen again. The pair had recently formed an unlikely friendship, the fruit of Major Miller's assiduous efforts to charm the little messenger by means of flattery and cigarettes. It was Kopyekin who delivered to Miller the astonishing revelation that eight Polish generals are billeted in a house just a few hundred metres away from the camp gates. Miller's attempt to contact the generals doubtless added to the list of reasons for his departure. Kopyekin, meanwhile, is simply the latest in a series of camp workers who have been foolish enough to fraternise with the prisoners.

The departure of their leaders casts a shadow over the renewed hope that the opening of the new barracks and the arrival of the first letters from home have brought to the prisoners. The bitter consensus is that Zaleski and Miller have been judged to have served their purpose and been disposed of accordingly: they have rebuilt the camp more efficiently and to a far higher standard than the authorities could possibly have expected, and in the process they doubtless came to know far too much about the workings of the camp command for the comfort of those in charge. They had also, inevitably, grown close to Berezhkov and Kirshin, a state of affairs which could not be allowed to persist. It is testament to the effect of three months in captivity that the news is no longer greeted with outrage, or even surprise: every prisoner now understands that the price of daring to stand out from the mass of their fellows is to be cut down.

The completion of the buildings nevertheless marks a moment of change in camp life. Conditions become markedly easier as prisoners who were previously billeted in dirty, overcrowded barracks are assigned places in the huts. Młynarski, whom Zaleski had placed in charge of keeping a record of the prisoners interned in the camp, is moved to a new block, together with Zygmunt and the officers of the camp command, while the rest of their friends remain together in one of the new buildings reserved for Lieutenants. After enduring three months of misery in the Morgue, Józef Czapski is delighted beyond measure when he is finally allotted a place far away from those who have rendered his evenings so bitter and lonely.

The new blocks are more spacious than the old; they are bright, equipped with two tiers of bunks, shelves for kit and bread, brick stoves, and even small tables. More important still, they are clean. When Kozłowski lays his rucksack on his bunk he feels, despite everything, a surge of optimism. One battle, at least, has finally been won: in the new barracks there are no lice.

24. Why don't they beat us?

The days pass, the new year advances. Tomasz waits for news from his parents, but there is none, nor is there any word from Gosia. At first, he asks Kozłowski almost daily if he has heard anything from his sister then, after a while, he stops. Letters continue to arrive in the camp, none bearing Tomasz's name. He tries to hide his anxiety under a veneer of cheerfulness, giving away almost everything he owns, as if the impulse of generosity relieves him in some way, but he can barely conceal the energy that burns within him. With the construction of the barracks now complete there is less physical work to occupy those young men whose days were previously so active. Instead, they must focus their energies elsewhere: the clandestine talks which have long been a feature of camp life take on a more regular, organised character, often combined with long walks around the camp's perimeter; informal games of chess are organised into tournaments, one barracks competing against another, while groups dedicated to the acquisition of foreign languages spring up like mushrooms, amid much debate as to which language will offer the greatest advantage in a future of which none of the prisoners can guess the outcome. Should they learn German or Russian? English or French?

Bronisław Młynarski and a few other English-speaking officers walk together in the afternoons, trading anecdotes of their travels across America or the British Isles. Kozłowski sometimes joins them on their walks, hopeful of acquiring a few rudimentary English phrases. In truth, he is entirely dependent on Młynarski's translations, without which he understands not a word of what is being said.

"So what was it like?" asks Professor Rodoński of Captain Szumigalski, a civil servant from Warsaw whose lifelong passion is England and the English language. To this man the others always turn for corrections, for, although his accent is far from flawless, his knowledge of vocabulary and grammar is second to none. More than anything else, Szumigalski loves to talk about the holiday he spent in England in 1935, the single occasion on which he was able to visit the land of his beloved Shakespeare. Just as Szumigalski never tires of speaking of England, so Professor Rodoński is never bored of listening. Szumigalski beams, and prepares to discourse on his favourite subject.

"Green!" he declares. "It was so green!"

When one day Professor Rodoński produces a handsome two-volume set of the complete works of Shakespeare in a parallel text (purchased in exchange for a pair of woollen socks), the little group whiles away many agreeable hours comparing the precise meaning of the English text with its Polish translation.

So immersed are these two men in their favourite subject that they fail to observe the presence of *politruk* Kaganer, strolling with apparent nonchalance nearby. The others fall silent, or turn to speak in Polish of other things, banalities on the subject of the weather or the breakfast they have consumed that morning. Szumigalski and Rodoński, however, continue, oblivious.

"*All the world's a stage,*" cries Szumigalski, "*and all the men and women merely players. They have their exits and their entrances; And one man in his time plays many parts…*"

Kaganer scribbles in his little book.

Throughout January, the news bulletins report on little other than the Finnish campaign. The lack of Soviet breakthroughs, and the heavy losses inflicted by the Finns, are explained by considerable exaggeration of the effectiveness of the Mannerheim Line, a system of fortifications so devilishly effective – it is claimed – that even the might of the Soviet Army cannot penetrate it.

Fragments of news concerning other aspects of the war filter through from letters received from home: the allies remain paralysed, while the Nazis continue to sweep across Europe unchallenged. The propaganda bulletins have little cause to lie.

"Why don't they beat us or torture us?" Tomasz fidgets fretfully with a hand-carved wooden chess piece, flicking it round and round in his hand. "We're not made to dig in mines or break our backs making roads, as they do in Siberia. They don't starve us. Why not?"

"My dear Tomasz," says Ralski, "anyone would think you wanted to be beaten!"

Tomasz flushes. "But it's shameful, isn't it, to have so little to do?" His fingers grip the small knight on horseback. "Aren't you frustrated too? Wouldn't you rather be out there, fighting for your country?"

Hoffman, who is – as usual – absorbed in writing, looks up, amused. "You could try writing."

Tomasz shrugs. "I can't seem to settle."

Hoffman contemplates Tomasz, the expression in his eyes hard to read. Everybody knows that Tomasz Chęciński has not heard from his family because Tomasz hides nothing, not even his fears. Hoffman, on the other hand, says little about himself. His dry humour keeps his fellow prisoners at a distance, so that it never enters anyone's head to wonder whether he, too, endures the wait for news with agony. But he smiles: like many of Tomasz's older friends Hoffman's attitude towards him is that of an indulgent older brother.

"Why don't you get Bronek to teach you English?"

"No fear!" says Młynarski. "No offence, Tomasz, but you'd drive me to distraction."

It is Czapski who first suggests to Tomasz that he might give a lecture. At first hesitant, claiming that he is a poor public speaker, as well as too inexperienced to dare present his ideas in the presence of so many 'real' academics, nevertheless it takes hold of him, and before long he is to be found sitting on his bunk scribbling notes in the margins of the Soviet newspapers which are handed out at the library.

"A grand federation, stretching from Greece to Scandinavia: that is my vision of Poland's future."

An audience of around twenty men are packed together in the new barracks. Outside, snow stands two feet deep. A small stove – one of the new luxuries to which the prisoners have not yet become accustomed – keeps the room just above freezing but, nevertheless, the men are still wearing their greatcoats and caps, their breath hanging in the air like smoke.

"One great alliance across our continent, linking not just the smaller countries of eastern and central Europe, but those of the north and south as well." Tomasz's eyes are shining. He does not feel the cold. In his hand he clutches the copy of the *Lwów Red Banner* which contains his notes.

"It's a crazy idea." The drawling voice belongs to Lieutenant Otwinowski, who is leaning against one of the bunks, his hands in his pockets. "Besides, we've heard it all before. It's just another, bigger, even more impractical version of the Intermarium, and we all know how successful that idea was: every single country included in Piłsudski's plan is now under Soviet or Nazi rule."

"Except Finland!" someone calls out.

"Please, hear me out!" Good humoured, popular among his fellows, Tomasz surveys his audience with patient certitude. "We have to think beyond our present situation, and consider not just the political advantages of such an alliance – of which there are many – but the economic ones too. Think of the enormous resources that would be at our disposal: energy supplies, for a start; shipping – imagine the possibilities offered to Poland by an alliance that reaches as far as Scandinavia in the north and Greece in the south... access to the Baltic, the Aegean and the Mediterranean—"

"But, Lieutenant Chęciński," the economist Skwarzyński peers over tiny spectacles perched on the end of his nose, "even forgetting the political obstacles, which are too numerous to mention, you are talking about a dozen different countries, each with different legal and financial systems. How on earth would such a federation function in practice?"

"A joint federal government, of course! Each country would send elected representatives and together they would agree on the legal and economic framework."

This proposal is met with howls of derision. Otwinowski speaks up again:

"Are you seriously proposing that a group of a dozen or so individual countries would ever be able to agree about anything? They'd spent their whole time arguing about who was in charge, then half of them would gang up and accuse the other half of imperialist ambitions and the whole thing would collapse in the dust. It's insane!"

"I agree," says another. "And anyway, what country would willingly give up its sovereignty in favour of decisions taken by a bunch of foreigners a thousand miles away?

A small, dry-looking man, a professor of military history, intervenes:

"Actually, in favour of Lieutenant Chęciński's argument, it could be said that, if a country were offered a choice between forming a voluntary alliance in which all partners are of equal substance and that of being drawn into the orbit of a larger and more dominant neighbour – being *de facto* occupied - it would make considerable sense to sacrifice a certain degree of sovereignty in favour of added security and stability."

"My point exactly!" says Tomasz. "The only way in which smaller countries can hope to compete against larger, more aggressive ones, is to work together. Picture it! A bloc of countries cutting right across Europe could restrict Soviet access to western trade, as well as form an effective bulwark against future German aggression!"

"The reality of our future, Lieutenant," interjects another officer, "is that it is far more likely that after this war ends there will be only two countries controlling Europe: Germany and Soviet Russia."

There are protests at such defeatist talk. Sub-arguments develop about the likely outcome of the war. Tomasz struggles to be heard.

"Think! Think of all the different groups of people who were gathered under the umbrella of the Polish-Lithuanian Commonwealth. Think of the way the Austro-Hungarian Empire and, indeed, the Russian Empire encompassed many different people of varying ethnic and linguistic groups. Imagine, please – hear me out! Imagine if this system were to operate not under an all-powerful Emperor or Tsar, but as a group of equals, each member with equal powers, a true democracy—"

A red-cheeked major stands up. "I have never been to Greece, or Finland, or Yugoslavia for that matter, and I have no desire to do so. Poland is my home and Poland's borders are to me sufficient. Why do we need to look outside our own country, to be influenced by foreign ideas peddled by people whose habits and customs are incompatible with our own? No, gentlemen, I protest. This is without a doubt the biggest pile of poppycock I have ever heard in my entire life!" He pushes his way through the crowd towards the door. "As if we haven't got enough to worry about without crackpots amongst our own men peddling such downright unpatriotic ideas...."

Several men follow him out. Kozłowski, squeezed at the back of the room, observes that Tomasz's eyes are glistening. He feels pity for his friend, whose belief in his ideal is so fixed and so determined, whose character so passionate. There is a silence, then Skwarzyński speaks again, his measured tones carrying clearly across the room.

"There are without doubt some interesting points to debate here, in purely economic terms if nothing else." He clears his throat as the audience's attention focuses on him. As a well-known economist, his views carry weight. "It is mainly about economies of scale and a lifting of barriers to trade." He stops and looks around in case one of the red-capped *politruks* has sneaked into their meeting. "And when it comes to trade, we should indeed give serious consideration as to how best small countries can compete against bigger ones..."

Later, after the lecture is over, Kozłowski discovers Tomasz seated on a pallet, in tears.

"I'm an idiot, I know, to take it all so seriously."

"Come, there's still time for a stroll before it gets dark."

So they walk and they talk, with Tomasz expounding passionately on his ideas and Kozłowski listening patiently as they trace the same path as they always do, following the perimeter of the camp in the fast-fading afternoon light, past the little groups of prisoners discoursing on their favourite subjects.

"The real beauty of Piłsudski's plan was to split the retreating Russian armies into two by striking at right angles across its course..."

"...the influence of Dutch and Flemish architecture, exemplified by the work of Willem van den Blocke and his son Abraham, who designed the Golden Gate in the city of Gdańsk..."

"Copernicus's revolution in astronomy, which made a mockery of sense perception..."

They pass Skwarzyński, muffled in a thick scarf, explaining something to his habitual audience of two; there is Marcinkiewicz, the mathematician, a group of eager acolytes trailing in his wake; Major Soltan walks in silence with his nephew, Lieutenant Grocholski, a kind of meditation which they practise, without fail, every day; the old man Lipski, who has never once complained about the accident of fate that has landed him here, in a camp full of soldiers, is taking his daily stroll in the company of two officers whose conversation he finds entertaining; and there is Fryderyk Hoffman, conferring animatedly with his friends, the editors of the influential Jewish newspaper *Nasz Przegląd*, about an article written by one of their colleagues before the war.

"When I was a student," continues Tomasz, "I spent a great deal of my time examining the centuries of conflict which have bedevilled the European continent. I looked at the way in which the Russian and the Austro-Hungarian Empires fell apart after the end of the First World War, whilst other previously fragmented countries like Germany and Italy found unity in an idea of nationhood that has eventually led them down a path of fanatical belief. Then I saw what was going on in Poland and realised that it was the same struggle being played out in our own country, the endless argument between those who cling to a narrow notion of nationhood and those for whom it means something broader and altogether less well defined. My own family background is a case in point: my father fought in the Russian Imperial army, whilst my uncle was drafted into the German army and died at the Somme. My mother's roots are Lithuanian and Russian. Our family are Polish to our core, but what does that word mean? Why cannot these elements retain their individual identity, whilst also being part of a greater whole? Surely, Zbyszek," he turns to Kozłowski in earnest exhortation, "our best hope for the future must lie in strengthening our ties with our neighbours, not in turning away from them?"

25. A portrait

Outside the camp everything is frozen, all life buried deep beneath the soil, waiting for the annual miracle of resurrection.

Tadeusz Biały sits at a table, a piece of paper spread out before him. Perched awkwardly on a stool opposite him is Kozłowski.

"I've never sat for a portrait before. I don't know what to do with myself."

"Why don't you read something?"

"Alright." Kozłowski pulls from his rucksack his mother's latest letter.

Biały works in silence, his pencil moving swiftly across the paper with a soft, scratching sound. Soon Kozłowski forgets his self-consciousness, his attention absorbed by the concerns of his mother, who leaps from subject to subject – the difficulty in obtaining medicines for his father's lung condition, the shortages of this or that, the fate of their neighbours and their neighbours' children – before returning persistently to the three questions which preoccupy her most: the whereabouts of his youngest brother Staś, the absence of news from Gosia, and her anxieties concerning Ignacy's widow, Elżbieta, and their three children – *What are they living off? Are they still in the house or have they had to move? … I feel so helpless, my dear,"* she continues. *It seems the only thing left for me to do is to worry about everyone.* Soon, he will be able to reply to his mother's letter. He will tell her that he is convinced that Gosia's silence is merely the result of poor communications; as for Elżbieta, his guess is that her situation leaves her little time for correspondence. And Staś? If he is abroad he may not feel it safe to write home in case it causes trouble for his parents. And if he has been caught? *And you, my dearest Zbyszek, so far away. Why didn't you listen to me when I told you to take your winter underwear?*

It is a while before he realises that Biały is observing him with a wry smile.

"What?"

By way of reply, Biały hands the finished sketch to Kozłowski. Olgierd, curious, jumps down from his bunk to peer over his shoulder.

"That's very good! Do you take commissions, Biały? I've a fancy for one of these."

"My rates are reasonable. I take payment in pencils, paper or any other items you care to propose in exchange."

"Do you accept sweets?"

"That all depends what kind…"

While Biały and Olgierd discuss the terms of the proposed exchange, Kozłowski studies the portrait of a man. Biały's skill is not in doubt: he has conjured on the page a startlingly realistic likeness of somebody, but Kozłowski struggles to acknowledge that the young man with the gaunt face and hollow cheekbones in the drawing is really him. His spectacles are filthy, his uniform ragged, his beard patchy and uneven. What would his mother think if he were to send her this?

"You could at least have told me to comb my hair, Tadek!"

"Would you have preferred a Soviet-style portrait, against a background of corn sheaves, perhaps?" Biały strikes a mocking pose.

"I hadn't realised I look quite such a tramp."

"My poor friend. You're not offended, are you? What you need, Zbyszek, is a haircut." Biały rummages in his bag and brings out a pair of tiny, gold-plated nail scissors. "They're a little on the small side, I grant you, but we can try, although I'm not sure my skills as a barber are up to it."

"I can do it," offers Olgierd.

Kozłowski regards him with suspicion. "And your qualifications are?"

"I used to trim our dog's coat in the summer."

Biały beams. "The perfect man for the job!"

"Not so fast! Dog and human. The two are not comparable." Kozłowski pauses. "Come to think of it, do your worst."

Kozłowski is so delighted with his haircut that he allows Olgierd to trim his beard as well. By the time the job is done, half the bunkroom has gathered round to watch. Several officers request an appointment with Olgierd for a haircut, whilst others place orders for portraits. For the next few days, business is brisk: Biały draws with a feverish dedication, producing portraits of his fellow prisoners in exchange for supplies of paper, pencils and other necessary items purchased from the mobile shop. After the first few haircuts he reclaims his scissors, complaining that the constant use is blunting them. Olgierd, ever enterprising, manages to bribe one of the guards to give him another pair, but these are large, unwieldy, and unforgivingly blunt.

Some days later, Kozłowski sits a second time for his portrait, this time with his hair cut short and his beard trimmed. The next time the prisoners are permitted to write, Kozłowski sends his mother the second of Biały's drawings. The original he keeps in his knapsack as a future reminder.

When the postman finally calls out Tomasz's name he scrambles from his bunk to grab the letter, postmarked from Kraków. Without a word, he hurries from the room.

Hoffman adopts a girlish voice: "Darling, beautiful, handsome Tomeczku, the memory of your caresses makes me swoon …"

"Be careful what you say, Hoffman," says Zygmunt. "That's Kozłowski's sister you're talking about."

Hoffman shrugs. "Have I offended you, Kozłowski? Damn this!" He takes the ragged end of a newspaper cigarette, which refuses to burn, and throws it to the ground. "I'm sick of smoking grass!"

"So long as it's good news you may joke as much as you like. But the letter might be from his own sister, not mine."

"Have you seen any man in this camp move that fast for a letter from his sister?"

Kozłowski leaves a respectable interval of fifteen minutes – time enough for Tomasz to digest the contents of the letter and absorb any news, good or bad – before making an excuse and slipping outside.

Tomasz is in his usual spot, crouching against the perimeter wall, staring distractedly at the dark patch of earth where his boots have dislodged the snow.

"What's wrong, Tomasz? Is it from Gosia? Is she alright?"

"Read it. Go on, there's nothing in there to embarrass you or her. Please, go ahead."

The letter is in blue ink, the writing growing more cramped as she runs out of space.

January 3rd 1940

Dearest Tomasz,

I cannot tell you how relieved I was to hear from my mother that you are alive and that you and my brother are together. The thought that you and he are friends – well, I'm delighted, of course: it brings me great comfort. He is a good, dear man and you may always rely on him. I just hope he hasn't been telling you stories about what an irritating little sister I was when we were growing up! Please tell Zbyszek that I have written to him. The post is very unreliable: I discovered only recently that my last letter to my mother went missing. She explained that you are not permitted to write often, so if I do not hear from you I promise I will keep on writing. I do so hope that you are well.

Here, there is a blot in the ink, as if she has started to write something, then changed her mind.

> *Please, please don't worry about me, Tomek: I'm in good health; I have a job; we are warm and have enough to eat; most importantly, now that I know you are well I can sleep more easily.*

Kozłowski is about to chide Tomasz for scaring him unnecessarily: there is nothing here to torment you, he is about to say, when his eye skips to the next line. Gosia's handwriting seems to shrink, the letters shunted tightly up against each other.

> *The main concern at the moment, of course, is Hanka. I know that there are dozens of perfectly innocent reasons why I mightn't have heard from your sister, but you know how it is: one cannot help but worry. I've managed to establish that she arrived in Warsaw safely sometime in December, but since then there has been no news at all. None of our friends here in Kraków has heard anything. Please, if you do get the chance to write, let me know that she has reached Lwów safely and that your father is alright. I think about you all the time, dear Tomasz, and pray for your safe return. I will write again as soon as I can.*
>
> *Your Gosia.*
>
> *PS Enclosed in this letter is a small gift (I hope it is still there when you open it!). It is a trivial, stupid thing, I know, but it was all I could think of that would fit inside an envelope.*

As soon as Kozłowski reaches the end of the letter Tomasz snatches it back, staring at the cramped blue handwriting as if it will offer up an answer to his questions.

"What does she mean about Hanka? Why was she in Warsaw? She's supposed to be in Kraków. Why did she set out to Lwów? And why does Gosia talk about my father being alright? Has he been ill? Why is there no news from my parents?"

Kozłowski tries to reassure Tomasz with the usual platitudes uttered in these circumstances: I'm sure there's a perfectly logical reason for their silence/You know how unreliable the post is/You will surely hear from them soon... These optimistic scenarios, he reasons, are just as likely to be true as all the other possibilities that will be presenting themselves to Tomasz's imagination.

"What did she send you?" he asks, hoping to distract his friend.

Tomasz grins suddenly. "Look. You remember I gave you mine on the train?"

He pulls from his pocket a white linen square which he unfolds, handing it to Kozłowski with a shy smile. It is very small, only slightly larger than Tomasz's hand, and very plain, decorated in one corner with two initials in blue thread: *M.K.* The object is immediately familiar to Kozłowski: when they were children, each of the four siblings was given a set of seven white handkerchiefs by his grandmother, one for every day of the week, she said, so that they would never be without. She had embroidered them with their initials: M.K. for Małgorzata, Z.K. for him, I.K. and S.K for Ignacy and Staś. These handkerchiefs had accompanied the children to school, neatly folded in their pockets in the morning, crumpled and dirty by the afternoon. They had gradually diminished in number – ruined by use as makeshift bandages on cuts and grazes, left on the grass, or under a tree, or dropped on the floor of the school library – until the boys had outgrown theirs and only Gosia had continued using hers, although she had lost most of them over the years. He finds it unexpectedly moving, this little square of white cotton, this reminder of their easy, uncomplicated past life. He returns it to Tomasz, who places it carefully inside the top pocket of his tunic, his anxiety returning almost at once.

"How easy do you think it is to travel around the occupied zones? If Hanka wanted to go to Lwów, I'm guessing she had to go via Warsaw—"

"Your older brother is in Warsaw, isn't he?"

"Yes." Tomasz brightens. "Yes! Perhaps she went to stay with him first. How do people get from one zone to another? Are they allowed to travel?" Involuntarily, his fingers curl around the letter, threatening to crumple it. "Why are we so damned cut off here?"

For two nights after receiving Gosia's letter Tomasz does not sleep. In the daytime he paces around the camp's perimeter, not stopping to speak with his friends as he would normally do but striding on, absorbed in the dark impotence which has taken hold of his thoughts. On the third night, he is called to interrogation.

Kopyekin's replacement, a thin, grey-skinned youth, prods the prisoner with his rifle butt and gestures for Tomasz to get up, muttering his scripted words without conviction: "Get dressed and come with me". Tomasz slips obediently from his bed and stumbles from the room. Kozłowski follows them to the doorway, watching the tall, broad-shouldered figure loping across the courtyard.

Who will it be tonight? Lebedyev? The young one, Mitrov? A specialist from Moscow?

It is almost dawn when Tomasz returns to the barracks. He goes directly to Kozłowski's bunk and shakes him awake, gesturing silently towards the courtyard. They grab their blankets and slip outside.

Night is ceding gradually to day, the darkness steadily pushed back by a dull grey light which spreads slowly across the horizon, like paint seeping under a door.

"He knew all about Hanka."

"Who?"

They walk towards the kitchen, although it is too early for breakfast.

"Lebedyev. He knew all about her."

"Well, they will have read Gosia's letter, won't they?"

"He said she wasn't in Warsaw any more."

"He could have made that up."

"He seemed to know her, he said she was – what was the word he used? He said she was very 'spirited'."

"That doesn't prove anything. I suppose he threatened you."

"Of course. I said the usual things: that I refuse to compromise my principles, that my conscience is clear. Most of the interview was about my political theories – he'd got hold of something I'd written and tried to trick me into saying that my ideas are virtually communist anyway so why didn't I join them. Everything I said he twisted somehow until I hardly knew what I was saying. He told me that I am in the political vanguard, but what I seek to achieve can only be done by overthrowing the entire corrupt political system in Europe, which is run by unaccountable elites who serve only the interests of their own class." He laughs bitterly. "His words could have been taken from one of my own speeches."

"They probably were."

"'Join us, Chęciński,' he said. 'We need men like you. You could have an opportunity to make a real difference to the future of your country.' I felt physically sick. I told him that he had misunderstood me, that I was not for sale, and neither is my country. Then he threatened me: 'I do hope you won't have cause to regret your words. Women can be especially vulnerable in prison...' What if they arrest Hanka? Or have already arrested her?"

"Tomasz, they want to scare you into cooperating with them. They're not actually going to do anything about it, are they?"

"How do I know? Oh God, if only there were a letter from home, something that would tell me what is actually going on! I walked out of that interrogation and I felt shame, Zbyszek, pure shame, like a man who has set out in sunshine and has to walk home in wet clothes."

Yes, thinks Kozłowski, that is precisely what I felt too: shame, like a damp chill entering my bones. And yet Tomasz has the courage to admit his feelings, whereas I do not.

Over the next few days, Tomasz seems compelled to exhaust his body in an effort to stop up the flow of anxious thoughts which threaten to overwhelm his mind. He chops wood for the kitchens, shovels sewage at the Siegfried Line, fetches and carries, delighting his comrades by offering to take on tasks in their stead. He eats almost nothing, preferring to give away his food. It is Zygmunt Kwarciński who discovers him lying unconscious on the icy ground outside their barracks. He and Kozłowski carry him to the clinic, where he is immediately admitted by Dr Levittoux.

26. *What is lost*

Kozłowski is dozing on the ancient wooden chair when he is woken by the sound of Dr Yegorov's voice in the corridor, followed by Dr Levittoux's, neither of them visible through the half-open door. For a few moments their conversation is conducted in low voices. Soon, however, the voices begin to rise. First, Dr Levittoux, calm but insistent:

"I am telling you, Dr Yegorov, that this patient needs more acetaminophen if we are to stand any chance of bringing down his fever."

"And I am telling you, Levittoux," Yegorov's nasal voice carries clearly from the corridor. "That you have already exceeded the allotted quantity of acetaminophen for a single patient. If you consider him to be so gravely ill, he should be transferred to the town hospital."

"There is no need to send him to the hospital. He can remain here. He just needs more acetaminophen to bring his fever down."

"I reiterate, Levittoux: it is I who take the decisions here, not you, and I am telling you that this patient has already had too much."

A small movement in the corner of his eye catches Kozłowski's attention. Dr Vasilevna is standing in the doorway at the far end of the ward, apparently transfixed by the row in the corridor outside.

"So, Doctor, are you prepared to let a young man die because of a quota?"

"Do not ever speak to me like that again, Levittoux, or I will have you thrown out of this clinic for good, do you understand me?'

Vasilevna makes no sign of having seen Kozłowski, nor of having heard the argument, although the entire clinic has been privy to the row. Moving briskly among the other patients, she makes notes on the small clipboards that hang on the end of each bed. When she reaches Tomasz's bed she picks up the chart.

"Please," whispers Kozłowski. "Please, there must be something you can do to help."

Vasilevna steps back as if she has been scalded, her eyes darting around the ward; Dr Levittoux is now approaching Tomasz's bed and there is no escape. Vasilevna stares at the clipboard as if it contains something of unusual interest. When she looks up, she addresses Dr Levittoux in an expressionless tone.

"How is the young man progressing?"

"Not as well as I would like, Dr Vasilevna. He needs a higher dose of acetaminophen than I am able to administer here. If that were available, I feel sure his fever could be brought under control."

Levittoux holds Vasilevna's gaze so that it is quite clear what he means. Neither doctor acknowledges Kozłowski's presence. He watches them with open curiosity, struck by the expression on Levittoux's usually calm, good-humoured face: his eyes are dark, a muscle twitches in his jaw. Outside in the corridor, somebody has dropped something and Yegorov is berating the culprit for wasting precious supplies. Dr Vasilevna glances down at Tomasz. He looks absurdly young, his face pale and calm in sleep. With a gesture of helplessness, she hurries from the ward, her shoulders hunched as if she is trying to protect herself from a blow. Kozłowski watches her retreating figure with a feeling of sudden, overwhelming fury: why does she let that pig Yegorov push her around?

His anger sends him striding from the clinic so fast that he fails to take care as he steps onto the icy path. His leg slips from underneath him and he crashes to the ground, landing on his backside right in front of the mathematician Józef Marcinkiewicz who, surrounded by his usual circle of adoring acolytes, peers down at Kozłowski in astonishment.

"Oh, to hell with the lot of you!" he cries, pushing away Marcinkiewicz's outstretched hand.

Finding the barracks empty and his irritation undiminished, Kozłowski heads to the kitchens, where he spends the entire afternoon chopping logs until, eventually, his anger is overcome by exhaustion. He falls into bed soon after supper and wakes in the middle of the night with a crushing headache. He gets up and shuffles over to the Siegfried Line. Now wide awake, he wonders, momentarily, whether he should return to the clinic, but the sound of voices nearby attracts his attention. The lights are on in the kitchens, a warm, wheaty smell emanating from within. Curious, he pushes open the door and steps inside.

The new kitchens boast a range with several huge cauldrons in which the *kasza* destined for the men's breakfast and the soup for their lunch are prepared. The *kasza* requires six hours to cook and has to be stirred constantly, requiring volunteers, nicknamed 'gondoliers', to work through the night.

"What is lost in war beyond human lives? Not just the buildings reduced to rubble, nor the antique furniture handed down from our grandparents, nor the paintings on the walls, nor the grand piano or the precious violin, but the writing: the reams and reams of paper with our scribbled calculations, our records of experiments, our carefully constructed arguments typed up over months. The fruit of years of study and hard work, all gone."

Standing side by side at two enormous cauldrons, dressed in *fufajki* and overalls, are Edward Ralski and the engineer Zygmunt Mitera. Each holds a giant wooden stick with which he is stirring. Beside them, seated on an upturned log, is Józef Czapski, peeling potatoes. The single light which dangles above the cauldrons swings slightly in the cold breeze.

"And yet," continues Mitera, swirling the kasza with a practised twirl, "there is something liberating about discovering that one has nothing left to lose. When my brother died before the war he was so young, he had not had time to make an impact on the world. He wasn't married, he had no children, our own parents were long dead: he left no trace of his existence except in my memory and that of his friends. At the time, I thought that my work was going to be the one dependable aspect of my life. I clung to it, as a drowning man clings to a piece of driftwood. Then, in the space of a few seconds – *boom!* My apartment, all my books and all my work, reduced to nothing."

Ralski, lost in thought, stares down at the churning kasza while Mitera begins, absent-mindedly, to hum in a clear tenor voice. It is Czapski who notices Kozłowski standing awkwardly in the doorway.

"Come and join us," he says, indicating a stump next to him.

Czapski pulls the pail of potatoes over so that it stands between the two of them, while Mitera hands him a small paring knife. Czapski's hands are red from the freezing water in which the potatoes are soaking, but a smile hovers on his lips as he peels, his elbows resting on his knees.

The men work in silence for a while, Ralski and Czapski exchanging concerned glances as they observe Kozłowski's demeanour. It is common enough for a previously cheerful man to become suddenly withdrawn, even to fall into despair. Usually, it is the result of a letter from home.

"Why don't you tell us about America, Zygmunt?" says Czapski, brightly. "Lieutenant Mitera spent several years as a student in the States," he explains to Kozłowski. "I love to hear him talk about it. I've never been there, have you?"

Mitera smiles and twirls his baton and begins to speak, peppering his language with English phrases which Kozłowski has only heard in Hollywood films: *Sure thing. Howdy. You betcha!* He speaks of his American colleagues, of a Texan professor who gave lectures wearing a stetson hat, and a senior mathematics lecturer who played jazz piano at the parties they used to give at the faculty. He speaks of the informality of the American academics, how they greet each other with a *Hello, Jim* and a *Hi, Steve,* how casually they dress. He speaks of weekends spent with colleagues driving through the American landscape in their open-topped cars, its vastness wholly different to the bleak enormity of Russia, and describes a road trip he made with a young geologist from San Francisco who took him to see the Grand Canyon. Later, egged on by Czapski, Mitera entertains them with renditions of popular American jazz songs.

On through the night the conversation ranges, slipping effortlessly from art to mining, botany to poetry, history to geology and back again. There is no gossip, none of the seam of factionalism that runs through so much of the camp's conversation, no endless criticism of the authorities, nor the food, nor their fellow prisoners. There is only conversation, real conversation fuelled by a genuine desire to acquire knowledge for its own sake, and a profound respect for those with whom the conversation is shared. Kozłowski feels dwarfed by these men, ashamed of the anger which he has allowed to twist his thoughts, and of his ignorance. Gradually, as the conversation washes over him in gentle waves, a sense of calm overcomes him, cleansing and purifying him.

He is woken by Czapski, the artist's long face gazing down into his, eyes alight with amusement.

"What happened?"

It is dawn. Mitera and Ralski are gone. Two other kitchen workers are now stirring the kasza. The kitchen is bustling with movement and the morning queue for breakfast has already begun to form.

"You fell asleep, my friend."

Kozłowski looks down in surprise to find the potato bucket in front of him, the paring knife on the ground. "I fell asleep sitting down? Like this?"

"We were very impressed. I said that perhaps it's a trick acquired by doctors when they're on call. Ralski said it's because you're young."

"I'm sorry." Kozłowski stands up, stretching. His back aches, his knees crack painfully. "Where are the others?"

"Mitera's gone to get some sleep. Ralski's gone over to the clinic to find out how Tomasz is doing. I'm on my way there now if you'd like to accompany me."

"I – I think I'll take a walk first, if that's alright. I'll be along in a while."

"Are you sure?"

"Yes. Thanks. I need some fresh air."

Kozłowski hurries away, the memory of his anger the previous night returning with unforgiving clarity, along with a jumble of other feelings which he cannot yet name. Concealed beneath them all, squatting invisible like a toad, is grief for his brother Ignacy's death.

He had thought that he had accepted Ignacy's death as a fact of his new life: awful and tragic but, as one death among thousands, hardly worthy of any 'special' kind of mourning. We are at war, he told himself, and in war men die every day. We must accept their deaths and get on with our lives as best we can, no longer those we chose for ourselves but those which have been forced upon us by circumstances. So why is it that grief should choose this precise moment to make itself known to him?

He does not know it yet, because he is young, that it is in the nature of grief to sneak up on you when you are least prepared, to grab you by the throat and threaten to suffocate you. He does not see that the anger he feels towards Yegorov is the same anger that Ignacy always roused in him by insisting, in his dry, superior way, that he knew better than his younger brother. He does not understand that his anxiety about Tomasz – his desire, his one desire above all things, that his friend should not die – has provided a stage on which his grief for his brother can finally parade. He knows none of these things, only that a great storm is brewing inside him and that he does not want any witnesses to the moment when it finally bursts forth.

He makes his way as fast as he can to the far edge of the camp and sits down by the wall, where he begins to sob, one heaving breath after another, on and on until eventually, after several minutes, the storm subsides. Feeling curiously peaceful, he sits for a while with his eyes closed, ignoring his freezing backside perched on a flat stone, feeling the weak winter sun on his face.

A cold, wet sensation on his fingers makes him open his eyes to find a dog licking his hand with an expression of industrious concentration.

"Which one are you, eh?" He fondles the dog's ears. "I can't remember all the names they've given you mutts. Is it Linek? Churchill? Foch?" The dog wags his tail. "Foch, are you?"

"Dr Kozłowski!"

He gets up hastily, hoping that Dr Levittoux will not notice his reddened eyes.

"I bumped into Czapski. He said that I might find you out here. Shall we take a walk? I could do with some fresh air: I've been at the clinic all night. Hello, little doggie." He bends down to pat the dog.

"How is Tomasz?"

"You'll be pleased to hear that Lieutenant Chęciński's fever is much abated, thank heavens. He has turned a corner, I hope."

"Well, that is wonderful news, sir." A wave of relief passes through Kozłowski, and his soul lightens.

They stroll on for a while in silence, the dog trotting after them. As they walk, it becomes obvious to Kozłowski that Dr Levittoux has come in search of him out of concern – perhaps voiced to him by Czapski – and is grateful for his tactful silence. Glancing sideways, he notices that Levittoux's face looks drawn, with dark shadows under his eyes.

He blurts the words out without thinking. "How do you manage it, sir?"

"Manage what?"

"Not to punch Yegorov's block off."

Levittoux smiles. "Oh, he's no different from a dozen irritating bureaucrats I've encountered over the years. Every workplace boasts a man who can drive you to distraction if you let him. The trick is not to let him, because you're never going to change him." He shrugs. "If we were in Poland I'd simply look for a new job. Or amuse myself by disobeying him. But what can we do?"

They continue walking in silence, Levittoux taking deep breaths as if he wants to clear his lungs of all the stale air that has accumulated within him in the stifling little clinic.

"I heard a rumour that they might be moving us."

"Really? Where?"

Kozłowski explains that Tadeusz Biały was taken for interrogation recently. "They're always very interested in him because he was employed as a military cartographer: they seem to think he had access to privileged information. He told me that at the end of the interview he said something like 'All I want is to see my home again' and Lebedyev replied, 'You may see it sooner than you think'."

"Have you discussed this with anyone else?"

"It seemed better not to. I just wondered, since you're in daily contact with the Russians, whether you had heard anything."

Levittoux frowns. "I haven't."

"It's probably meaningless."

"It probably is, but it's intriguing nevertheless."

They approach the main square in front of the church where Kirshin is standing, as usual, on the steps in front of the special section, arms clasped behind his back.

"I'd better go," says Levittoux. "I'd like to get something to eat before I have to get back. Thank you for trusting me, Zbyszek. I will try to find out if there is any truth in what Biały was told."

Kozłowski makes his way slowly back to the barracks, Foch trotting cheerfully behind him. When he crosses in front of the main gates, the Alsatian dogs which are chained up at the entrance begin to bark and pull at their chains. Foch shrinks; cowering, the little mongrel slinks behind Kozłowski's legs, lowering its muzzle to the ground in a pose of such abject submissiveness that Kozłowski almost laughs: even the dogs here are kept in line by fear.

"There you are! Not you, Kozłowski," Młynarski pats Kozłowski on the shoulder with a good-humoured smile. "This one." He bends down to caress the dog. "Naughty little Foch, we've been worried about you."

"Is he yours?"

Młynarski laughs. "Hardly. He's taken up residence in our barracks, under my bunk. But he's an odd one, this little doggie. Very curious indeed."

"The thing about Foch," explains Zygmunt over breakfast, taken out of habit standing outside in the cold, although there are now tables inside the barracks, "is that he only ever appears in the camp during the week. Every weekend, without fail, he disappears."

Kozłowski looks down in surprise at the little dog, who is panting steadily, his hopeful gaze shifting from one man to the next in expectation of scraps.

"Don't look at me like that." Młynarski addresses the mongrel with a wave of his spoon. "There's scarcely enough for us humans without having to feed you too."

"You say that every day, Bronek," says Zygmunt, "and yet you always feed him."

"I can't resist him. It's his ears." Młynarski indicates the arrangement of Foch's ears, one pointing straight up, the other bent and ragged. "He tore the right one on the barbed wire. Major Łabędź sewed it up with some thread and has been cleaning it religiously every day. I'd swear Foch's cleaner than we are. Aren't you, boy?"

Kozłowski contemplates the dog curiously. "Where do you think he goes at the weekends?"

"We reckon he has an owner who's away during the week," says Zygmunt.

"We've tried sending messages," adds Młynarski, "but we've not had a reply."

"Messages?"

"Just information about ourselves and questions – What is life like on the outside? What is happening in the war? What do you think of the Germans? That sort of thing. We tie them round his neck. He has long hair so nobody can see."

"Have you had any answers?"

Zygmunt bends down to ruffle the dog's ears. "Not a peep. We won't give up, though, will we, Foch? We'll keep trying."

27. An angel

"I thought I saw an angel sitting by my bedside last night."

"Zygmunt was here. Does he qualify?"

Tomasz smiles. "It wasn't him."

Kozłowski explains that his friends have been taking it in turns to keep watch over him. "Only when Yegorov is not around, of course, and that crusty little nurse, the fat one. She always shoos us away. The others don't seem to mind."

"How long have I been ill?"

Kozłowski replies that Tomasz has spent a total of two weeks in the clinic. He does not tell him that they feared for his life.

"I had such dreams. Awful nightmares: my father dead, my mother hauled off on the back of a cart, my sister being interrogated by that pig Lebedyev, Gosia in the hands of the Gestapo..."

Fragments of his last interrogation had swum in and out of the dreams, he said. Lebedyev perched on top of a piano, like a circus ringmaster with a whip. *Always back to the same old patriotic tune! Like a barrel organ and a set of performing monkeys!*

He does not know that he tossed in his bed, moaning, clutching at the sheets, sometimes sitting up with his eyes wide open, terrifying the other patients until one of them, an ageing captain, asked for Tomasz to be removed to another ward. The fat little nurse laughed scornfully: "*Nu*, where do you think we should put him? On the veranda? There's no space as it is. You'll have to put up with his screaming just like the rest of us have to put up with your snoring."

"Last night it was different. No bad dreams, just peace—"

Kozłowski interrupts him. "Let me go and find Levittoux. He has worked so hard to make you better."

"No, wait." Tomasz frowns. "There was someone here. She was sitting right where you are now. She was reading."

Tomasz describes how, when he finally emerged from his fever, he lay still, scarcely daring to believe that he was alive; how he slowly took in the sounds of the ward around him, counting them off, one by one, in an effort to ascertain their reality: the steady breathing of the other patients; the snoring captain; the buzz from the electric light in the corridor which flickered on and off all night. "Then I opened my eyes and looked over at the window. Snow was falling steadily; thick, dense flakes of white drifting down through the air, like stars, illuminated by the searchlights. I made a mental tour of the camp…" of the barracks where his comrades were sleeping; the path leading to the Siegfried Line, marked with the little mounds of frozen yellow snow; the kitchens, where Chef Antoni performs his daily miracles; the blind white eyes of the special section windows. "Lebedyev was there again and I thought I was back in the nightmares. But then I saw her." A small prick of pain in his left arm, followed by a swift rustling movement. Her head was bent, she was reading something, he could not see what, but he had the impression that she was holding a torch to illuminate the page. She was dark-haired, her hair pulled back in a chignon, and she was dressed in white. "My first thought was that it was my mother. Then I thought that perhaps it was Gosia." As his mind drifted in and out of consciousness, hazy still with fever and dreams, he became convinced that there was something about her that was not quite mortal. "I decided that whoever she was, she was here to help me. And suddenly I knew that everything was going to be alright."

"Then what happened?"

"When she saw that I was awake she leaned over me and placed her hand on my forehead. I remember how cool and dry it felt. I looked up and found in her eyes an expression of tender happiness as astonishing as it was brief, but when I smiled back at her she disappeared. I was left staring at the empty chair, wondering if I had dreamed her presence after all. Is it the fever, do you think? Was I hallucinating?"

Kozłowski walks through the little wards in search of Dr Levittoux, eventually finding him tending to one of the kitchen gondoliers who has scalded his leg. The burn has become infected and Levittoux is carefully pricking the pus-filled bubbles with a needle, mopping them dry before applying a greasy ointment to the skin.

"Tomasz is awake."

Levittoux nods, returning his attention to the patient's leg. Kozłowski lingers, his mind preoccupied with Tomasz's words.

The patient's voice interrupts his thoughts. "You know it's rude to stare."

"Sorry. I was miles away."

"Well, stay miles away," continues the patient. "I'm in enough pain as it is without you staring at me like a great booby."

Levittoux glances up in amusement. "I'll be with you in a few minutes, Dr Kozłowski."

"And he's a doctor too!" cries the patient. "Surely you've seen it all before, or are you a doctor of philosophy? There's enough of them here, philosophizing all day long instead of doing something useful."

"I'll wait in the corridor."

Levittoux nods again, intent on winding a bandage around the patient's leg.

"Jesus Mary, doctor, that hurts!"

Despite Yegorov's order that patients be ejected as soon as they are able to feed themselves, for the next few days Tomasz is permitted to stay on the ward, entertained by a constant stream of visitors, including his chess opponents, who arrive bearing the hand-carved chess set contained within a mess tin, and a chessboard borrowed from the library, which they balance on Tomasz's knees. When the fat nurse comes on the ward she shoos them away but, like the stray dogs, they creep back in, until the other patients complain that there is too much noise and they are banished. Then, only Czapski remains, reading to Tomasz from a dog-eared copy of Balzac's *La Femme de Trente Ans* or reciting from memory the verses of Baudelaire, eyes closed in concentration bordering on rapture.

As his physical strength returns, so Tomasz's mind once again grows preoccupied with the fate of his family. When he begins declaring to his visitors how shameful it is to remain so idle Kozłowski grows concerned that his obsessive desire to occupy his body in the hope of pacifying his mind will again play havoc with his health. Dr Levittoux argues energetically with Yegorov to allow the lieutenant to stay longer in bed, despite the complaints of the elderly captain – supported by the fat little nurse - that if the young man is well enough to receive so many rowdy guests he is well enough to leave the clinic. It is Czapski (kind, thoughtful Czapski!) who has the idea of bringing Tomasz paper and pencil, encouraging him to turn his mind once more to his political ideas. After hours spent staring blankly at the scraps of paper scattered on his knees, suddenly, the words begin to flow. The other patients watch in astonishment as Tomasz writes frantically, filling page after tiny page, scribbling down his half-formed plan for the grand federation of states which so many of his fellow officers find absurd.

"Are you going to the clinic?"

"I am, as a matter of fact."

"Will you take this in for me? Save my legs."

The postman hands Kozłowski a letter with a Lwów postmark. "It's for young Chęciński. Should cheer him up." He leans in conspiratorially, his breath warm and stale. "The lady doctor, Vasilevna, she received a letter today." The odd-looking man has taken a liking to the young doctor, who always listens politely to his anecdotes and who once found him a dressing for a cut on his finger which threatened to become infected. "It's her son who writes to her. He's in the army. Stationed in Wilno, you know. Been very ill – got blood poisoning from a cut and nearly died."

"How do you know all this?" Kozłowski gazes at the postman's oval face. Under the thick scarf which holds his cap in place he is entirely bald, giving him the air of an inquisitive parrot.

The postman taps his nose. "What you don't know can't hurt you. Got to go. Thanks for the favour. *Serwus!*"

Tomasz is sitting up in bed writing when Kozłowski enters. Seeing the letter in his friend's hand, a series of emotions - hope, delight, anxiety, fear - cross his face in swift succession. With an excuse about an errand downstairs, Kozłowski withdraws to allow Tomasz privacy to read the letter.

He is halfway down the stairs when he hears a cry from the ward, followed by Tomasz himself, wearing only a long white shirt, the bed sheet trailing behind him.

"She's safe!" He holds the letter out as if to demonstrate the truth of this statement. "Hanka is safe! My father is well. My mother writes that they are all together in Lwów. No harm has come to them. God be praised! Oh, thank you." He embraces Kozłowski, enfolding him in a tight, bear-like hug. "Thank you for being the bearer of such wonderful news." He strides back into the ward, where the other patients are staring at the tall young lieutenant. "They're all safe!"

No man in that room can begrudge Tomasz his moment of joy: during their time in Starobelsk each prisoner has suffered the same suspense to a greater or lesser degree. Sometimes a letter brings relief, sometimes a different kind of certainty. Even the ill-tempered captain contents himself with saying only: "Well, well. No need to get so overexcited about it. You'll knock something over."

"What's all the fuss about?" Yegorov marches into the ward, Dr Vasilevna hurrying behind him. "Why is this patient out of bed?"

Kozłowski is about to explain but Tomasz, in his joy oblivious to Yegorov's fury, takes the doctor's hand, shaking it enthusiastically. "Thank you, dear doctor. To think I was ready to die—" Ignoring Yegorov's astonished face, Tomasz turns to Vasilevna. "And you, dear Dr Vasilevna. It was you, wasn't it, who kept such careful vigil by my bed at night. I see that now—" Tomasz does not see the expression of terror in Vasilevna's eyes, nor the look of furious enquiry which Yegorov shoots at her as Tomasz continues. "It was your prayers that saved me, I know it – I felt it even in my fever, that you were willing me to survive…"

Dr Levittoux enters the ward. With a swift glance he takes in Yegorov's twitching jaw and Vasilevna's shrinking terror. He grabs Tomasz by the shoulders, tutting loudly.

"Dear me, Lieutenant Chęciński, what are you doing out of bed so soon?"

He and Kozłowski steer Tomasz, who is taller than both of them, back towards his bed.

Vasilevna, flushing a deep scarlet, hurries from the ward.

"This man is obviously well enough to be discharged." Yegorov addresses Levittoux with barely-concealed dislike.

"Yes, I agree," says Tomasz. "I should like that very much."

"With the greatest respect," says Dr Levittoux, "Lieutenant Chęciński is still far from well."

Fortunately for Tomasz, his body chooses this moment to confirm Dr Levittoux's diagnosis by causing him to pass out. They just manage to catch him as he slides to the floor.

"Jesus Mary!" sighs the captain as Kozłowski and Dr Levittoux drag Tomasz back to his bed. "Will he never leave us in peace?"

It is only later, when he has had time to reflect, that Kozłowski remembers to pose the question that has been puzzling him.

"Was it her, Dr Levittoux? Did Dr Vasilevna give Tomasz the extra medicine he needed?"

"What do you think, Zbyszek?"

"I – I don't know, sir. I'd like to think she did."

Finally, Tomasz is well enough to leave the ward. Leaning on Kozłowski's shoulder as he makes his way down the clinic steps, he is filled with exuberant energy, talking ceaselessly about the future.

"After the war, Zbyszek, I'm going to introduce you to my sister. You'll like her, I know you will. We'll go walking together in the mountains, you and Hanka, Gosia and me. I'll show you my favourite place in Zakopane. Imagine the fun we'll have!"

"I can't imagine what your sister would see in someone like me."

"The same as I do, Zbyszek: a steady, watchful, wonderful fellow."

For some reason, Kozłowski feels wounded by this description of himself.

"Steady and watchful? You make me sound like a spy! A boring spy!"

"Don't be offended, Zbyszek. You're not offended are you? Goodness," exclaims Tomasz, as Kozłowski refuses to meet his gaze, "there's no pleasing some people. I said wonderful, too."

28. *Kaganer gives a talk*

The little hut assigned for the prisoners' 'political education' is lined with several shelves of books, mainly political works in the Russian language. Laid out neatly on a table are copies of Russian and Polish-language newspapers. The wooden floor is covered with a fraying red carpet. In the corner, propped up next to a small stove, leans a pair of black galoshes. Next to them is a chair and a desk. On the desk is a neatly ordered pile of books and a grey folder. The door to the room where the films are projected is ajar, the whirring sound of the projector audible beneath the loud music which accompanies the film. Outside, it is raining, the first real rain of the new year.

Kozłowski surveys the contents of the small glass cabinet before him: dusty photocopied newspaper articles entitled "The USSR - Land of Victorious Socialism" and "The Third Stalinist Five-year Plan", as well as a display of books and documents relating to "The Life and Work of Joseph Vissarionovich Stalin". Pride has always kept him away from this place, as if the act of entering it would somehow render him complicit in the camp authorities' endless quest to 're-educate' their prisoners. Today, however, perhaps because of the rain, which is making him feel melancholy, or out of boredom, for there is nothing much to do, he has decided to come and watch a film. He does not much care what it is: it is sufficient that the room is dark and that there are images in black and white up on the screen. Today is February 10th 1940, his twenty-seventh birthday.

He stands for a while, water dripping from his shoulders onto the carpet, listening to the rain outside and the music in the next room, his eyes on the empty chair and the grey folder laid neatly upon the desk. A sudden impulse makes Kozłowski step forward to lift the cover of the folder.

...a request was made for a transformer to be sent which would convert the electric current from 220V to 110V, along with a Pathenor electric dynamo generator to facilitate mobile screenings of films - to

include, this month, the titles The Great Citizen, The Parade of Youth, The Lone White Sail...

The sound of a door opening and closing, followed by footsteps along the corridor, alerts him to the return of the librarian. He places the folder back on the desk and arranges himself hastily in an attitude of casual interest before the bookshelves.

The young *politruk* dries his hands on the back of his trousers before seating himself behind the desk and pulling a small rubber stamp from the drawer.

"If you want to borrow a book you'd better be quick. I'm about to close up."

"I just came to watch the film."

The *politruk* looks at him with a faint, puzzled smile. "So go in if you're going to. It's nearly the end."

He slips in at the back, shuffling along the row until he finds an empty chair squeezed in between two men who shift aside without taking their eyes from the screen, where – to the sound of soaring music – a small blond boy is leaning from a boat, waving at someone unseen. Once his eyes have become accustomed to the darkness, Kozłowski looks around him. The room is crowded. A few of the men he recognises as belonging to the small coterie of communist sympathisers; Lieutenant Szczypiorski sits among them, his boyish profile silhouetted against the bright screen. The others in the audience he does not recognise: a small band of high-spirited second lieutenants who keep up a running commentary on the film; a man with a notebook who has the air of a professional critic. One or two others sit alone, heads averted, gazing into the darkness with an air of distraction, as if they are not fully present.

The film ends and the blinds rise with a clatter, revealing *politruk* Kaganer busily winding the cord around a metal peg.

"There will now be a short talk," declares Kaganer, as the men push back their chairs. He indicates to the projectionist that the door should be closed to prevent the audience from leaving. "The subject of today's discussion is 'The fraternal alliance of the peoples of the USSR – the great family of Soviet peoples'". There is a groan from the young lieutenants. Kaganer, ignoring them, glances around the room with the air of a teacher about to impart great wisdom to a group of ignorant but grateful students. He orders the projectionist to stoke the stove "so that the prisoners may listen in comfort." While the projectionist kneels down to open the little door and shove in some extra logs, Kaganer contemplates his audience with a broad smile. "You see?" his gaze seems to say. "You see how well we take care of you?"

They sit in the crowded little room, steam rising from their jackets. Kozłowski gazes dispassionately at the red-faced *politruk* who delivers his lecture in a didactic monotone which, together with the warmth emanating from the ceramic stove, is already sending several members of the audience off to sleep.

Outside, the rain continues to pour down remorselessly, driving black holes into the snow. Inside, the air is fetid with the odour of stale breath and damp socks. It is extraordinary, he reflects, how quickly we have become accustomed to the conditions in which we live. Over the past few months, he has deliberately shut from his mind all thoughts of his former existence: he does not allow himself to dream of taking a hot shower, or changing into freshly laundered clothes, or drinking a morning coffee. These simple, everyday acts he had always considered not as luxuries but as a right, the kind of activities that any civilised human being should expect to enjoy as part of his daily life. Under present circumstances such thoughts are clearly laughable, so he does not indulge them. And yet... sometimes a memory will surface unexpectedly: a thunderstorm in Warsaw last year, one of those odd, astonishing storms which sometimes burst in early summer after a bout of intense heat. In a matter of minutes the entire length of Krakowskie Przedmieście had cleared, shoppers and office-workers dashing for cover under the shop awnings, the women shivering in their colourful cotton dresses, the white shirts of the men sticking to their backs. He remembers vividly the sense of excitement he felt at the sheer power of nature as the rainwater battered down on the canvas above their heads, and the sight of the pale, goosebumped skin on the arms of a young woman who stood watching, mesmerised, as the rainwater rushed along the gutter, swirling down into the drain.

Gradually, he becomes aware of a steady dripping sound on the floor next to him. The roof is leaking. Major Zaleski would never have allowed that to go unnoticed, he would have been in Berezhkov's office immediately, insisting that it be repaired. Where is Zaleski now? And Major Miller? Where do they take the men who are pulled from sleep at night and told to 'Come with me and bring your things'?

There is a thud outside the window as a chunk of snow slides off the roof and lands on the ground. Spring is declaring war on winter; the elements are engaged in their yearly battle. Persephone must soon return from Hades. Hope will come again. The officers in front of him are whispering.

"Have you heard? They're moving us…"

"They say we're being sent home…"

Kozłowski emerges from the political talk to find the prisoners being mustered outside the church, the loudspeakers temporarily silenced. He pushes his way through the crowd to join his friends, who are clustered near the back.

Hoffman greets him with raised eyebrows. "Been fraternizing with the Reds?"

Olgierd swings round in surprise. The disapproval in his gaze irks Kozłowski.

"Don't be stupid," he replies, irritably. "I've just been watching a film. There's precious all else to do. What's going on here?"

"Kirshin is about to make an announcement, apparently."

There is a loud squawk as Petrov switches on the megaphone. He flinches, his elbows flapping as he struggles not to drop it.

"He looks like a heron that's picked up a snake," remarks Hoffman.

Kirshin takes the megaphone from Petrov, raising it to his lips.

"Prisoners! I wish to share with you a very important piece of news: the Soviet Army has broken through the Mannerheim Line. Finland's defeat is now assured. In recognition of the importance of the event, and as a token of our generosity towards you, an extra ration of bread will be added to your evening meal."

The loudspeakers immediately begin to blare out music, the din drowning out the prisoners' less-than-charitable reflections on the nature of Kirshin's munificence.

The fact that Kirshin himself has taken the trouble to repeat the news of the Soviet victory over Finland, broadcast on the loudspeakers earlier that day, suggests a variety of different interpretations, depending on the cast of the character of the individual concerned:

"The fact that Kirshin is telling us himself means it must be true."

"The fact that Kirshin is telling us himself means it's all lies."

"The Mannerheim Line is a pretty major fortification. If they've got through that, Finland is done for."

As the Commissar doubtless intended, the prisoners return to their barracks despondent. Keen to capitalise on this, he orders an increase in the number of political talks for the following day.

29. Rumours

"Guess what?" The postman has a look of sly excitement on his face. "I've been told to hand out the entire postbag at the end of the month." When Kozłowski only stares at him blankly, the postman sighs. "Dear oh dear, don't you see? Normally, I'm only supposed to give out a few letters every few days, but I've been told to hand them all out at once. Now do you get it? Don't tell anyone else, mind. That's classified information I'm giving you." He taps the side of his nose and, with a cheerful wink, walks off whistling.

"I called you several times from the veranda. You were miles away." Kozłowski looks up to see Dr Levittoux descending the clinic steps. "Walk with me? I'm just heading over to see how young Chęciński is getting along."

Although Tomasz was discharged from the clinic a fortnight ago, he is under strict instructions from Dr Levittoux to rest as much as possible. They walk slowly across the wooden walkways that cover the softening ground.

"Do you have something on your mind, Zbyszek? Forgive me if I'm prying, but you seem unsettled."

Kozłowski recounts what the postman has just told him. "I was wondering what on earth it might mean."

"I think it means that the rumours you heard are true: Dr Kołodziejski overheard Yegorov giving instructions to Dr Vasilevna to assess which of the patients are well enough to travel. He also told me that Captain Czapski had a postcard from his sister saying that she and several other women from the Red Cross, including Dr Kołodziejski's wife, are taking it in turns to wait at the train stations on the line demarcating the Russian and German zones of occupation. They've been waiting there with hundreds of packages for us because they've been told that we will either be returning to Poland or passing through there on our way towards German camps."

"But where are they going to take us?"

"I wish I knew."

They find Tomasz hanging by his hands from the beam of the barracks door, pulling himself up and down energetically.

"When I recommended rest, Chęciński, this is not quite what I had in mind."

"I'm getting back in shape, Doctor." Tomasz grins, his face gleaming with sweat.

"You need to take it easy."

"I've never felt better. Honestly. Fit as a flea!" He drops to the ground. "Besides." His voice drops to a whisper. "I need to get in shape for the journey. You know they're moving us out?"

"We were just talking about it."

"Well, it's true. I heard Kirshin himself discussing it with Berezhkov. I was coming out of the kitchen – Kirshin was there, doing one of his inspection rounds; funny how he always shows up on baking day.

299

Anyway, he stopped to chat to Chef Antoni, as he always does – 'How are the pasties, chef?' 'Never better, Commissar, would you care to taste one?' – the usual routine. Then Berezhkov comes up and says something to Kirshin, who nods, says thank you very much to the chef and off they go. As they were walking away, I distinctly heard Kirshin say to Berezhkov, 'You know, I'll miss those pasties when they're gone.'"

"Might he have meant, when the pasties have all been eaten?"

"No, because Berezhkov replied, 'Perhaps the Germans will send us some in the post.'" Tomasz looks triumphantly from Dr Levittoux to Kozłowski. "You see?"

"But what does it actually mean?"

"Well, isn't it obvious? They're sending us home! We'll probably end up in a German POW camp."

"Would that be any better than being here?"

"It's got to be better: it's in Poland!"

"But what about prisoners who come from eastern Poland, like you, Tomasz? Where will you be sent? To another Soviet camp?"

"I don't know and I don't care. Don't you see?" He seizes Kozłowski by the arm. "It's movement. It's change."

"But why?"

"Goodness me, does it matter? Maybe they need this camp for something else. Perhaps there are Finnish prisoners who need to be accommodated somewhere." Tomasz studies Kozłowski's uncertain face. "Surely the least we can do, Zbyszek, after so many months of isolation, is enjoy the possibility of hope?"

Kozłowski says nothing. He does not wish to articulate the thought that is running through his mind: what if it is not better than here? What if we are to be sent not to Poland but to Siberia, to a real labour camp?

As the weather gradually grows warmer and the days longer, Ralski has become obsessed with spending as much time as possible outdoors. Every day he visits the same spots in the camp, looking under the trees and alongside the walls for signs of spring, collecting specimens and seeds in his tin. Every evening he reports back to his friends on what he has seen: a few more green shoots here, a couple of insects there, two birds, buds on the branches…

"Sh! Listen!"

Kozłowski cocks his head as Ralski seeks and then finds what he is looking for.

"See? On that branch, there." In the branches of the poplar sits a blackbird, its yellow beak wide open in song. "Isn't that glorious? And look, here—" Ralski crouches down and gently pushes away the remnants of the snow to reveal tiny shoots of fresh grass. "How can one not feel hope?"

The camp authorities appear to be in a mood of expectation as cars are dispatched to and from the train station, depositing a stream of high-ranking NKVD officers outside the camp offices, to be ushered inside by Kirshin and Berezhkov, who hover attentively. The bustle, and the sight of the camp gates opening and closing as more and more cars arrive, transmit to the prisoners the certainty that something important is afoot. They, like their captors, begin to move with an air of greater purpose; clusters of officers gather together, deep in speculation; gossip travels like electricity, carrying rumours that grow ever more fantastic.

Tomasz, now fully recovered, seems if anything to have more energy than before. Unable to concentrate on any single thing for more than a few minutes, one moment he is scribbling away at his notes, telling everyone that he has almost completed the final chapter of his book, the next he is jogging around the camp's perimeter, or chopping wood. To his bunkmates he declares simply that it is the imminent arrival of spring that is behind this surge in energy.

"I am like a tree." He stretches himself to his full height, raising his hands in the air. "I feel my sap rising. Like the ancient woodland gods, I am preparing to tear up my roots and walk!"

To his close friends, Tomasz is more direct. "I am not going to miss the opportunity again: this time I will escape. I'll get to France somehow and I'll fight. That's why it's so important that I'm in good shape, don't you see?" With a grin he breaks into a run, waving back at them. "I'll catch up with you!"

It is now his daily habit to run instead of walk along the perimeter of the camp, lapping any of his friends who happen to be outside – past Czapski and Ralski, whose frequent halts to inspect the changes on the ground slow their progress; past Zygmunt and Młynarski, side by side, heads bowed in concentration as Młynarski attempts to teach Zygmunt some basic phrases in English; past Major Łabędź, throwing sticks for the irrepressibly cheerful Linek. Tomasz's energy is infectious; it makes his friends smile and their spirits rise, but none of them makes any comment on his plans.

The dog Foch has been absent from the camp for longer than usual. His habit so far has been to spend five days in the camp, followed by two days away, presumably at home with his master. Despite Zygmunt and Młynarski's tireless attempts to make contact with his owner, the little messages attached to the dog's neck have to date received no response. One morning in March, however, Foch appears in the camp after an absence of ten days, filthy and hungry, his coat marked with dried blood. Around his neck is a tiny bag made of cigarette paper, with an inscription in small, distinct Russian characters:

> *Dear Friends. According to rumours you will soon be leaving Starobelsk. People are also saying that you might go home. Whether this is true we don't know. We hate the Germans as much as you do. May God protect you.*

At the end of March, an officer from the camp's special section, a nondescript fellow whom nobody has ever noticed before, is sent to Moscow. He sits like a general, alone in the back of the big black car that is to take him to the station. When he returns the following day he carries a buff envelope which he takes directly to the offices of the camp command.

"What d'you make of this, then?" Zygmunt, accompanied by Młynarski, shows his friends a paper they have found lying on the floor in their room. "We think one of the guards must have dropped it."

Olgierd, Kozłowski, Biały and Tomasz cluster round him to study the crumpled piece of paper: on it is a typed list of place names, written in Russian.

"It looks like some kind of itinerary," says Tomasz.

Zygmunt turns triumphantly to Młynarski. "You see!"

"I didn't say I disagreed—"

"What sort of an itinerary? May I- ?" Biały leans forward to scrutinise the place names. "I wish we had a map."

"It's heading south, whatever it is." Olgierd runs his finger down the list. "Look: Kharkov, Poldava – This one – see – Bendery – This leads to the Rumanian border—"

"They're going to hand us over to the allies!" declares Tomasz. "They're going to send us to France, to fight!"

Two nights later, the prisoners of block number 16 are woken by one of the night guards, who pokes his head through the door, shining his torch in the men's faces.

"Does anyone here speak Greek or Rumanian?"

Nobody replies, either because nobody possesses the required skills or because they have learned that if there is something the NKVD need to know, they usually know it before they ask. The guard does not insist but shrugs and closes the door, plunging the room back into darkness. Immediately, the men begin to whisper among themselves. The question can only mean one thing: a journey south, towards allied territory.

"The chance to fight has come at last," says Tomasz to Kozłowski. "Then, at the end of the war, if by God's grace I survive it, I will return to Poland and ask your sister to marry me."

Over the next week, the anticipation grows until it envelops even the least excitable members of the camp. Commissar Kirshin stands on the steps outside the church, stubbing out cigarette after cigarette until a little mountain of cardboard is formed beside him.

30. *Parrot hour*

Finally, on April 5th 1940, the representatives of each barracks are ordered to present themselves in the offices of the camp authorities, where they are issued with a list of names of 195 men who are to pack up their things and wait in the central square in front of the old church building, whence they will be sent home – *damoj* – that very day. The prisoners will be evacuated towards central points, explains Berezhkov, then sent on to Poland to their place of birth, whether it is under German or Russian occupation.

The camp erupts in excitement. In block number 16 a crowd gathers around Prosiński, listening avidly as he reads out the list of fifteen names on which, to his astonishment and delight, he finds his own. He smiles in disbelief as his friends slap him on the back and call him a lucky dog. Then, with a final glance at the state of his beard in the tiny fragment of mirror nailed to the end of his bunk, he picks up his bag and bids his friends farewell.

The chosen men wait in the spring sunshine, their meagre belongings clutched in their arms, chattering excitedly while their comrades hover as near as they dare, calling out messages for those back home.

"Say hello to my family... you've got the address, haven't you?"

"Don't forget the letter!"

"Make sure to give Jasia my best!"

All chatter ceases abruptly as the camp gates swing open to reveal a group of eight men, escorted by two guards, whom the prisoners immediately recognise as the generals whose proximity was discovered by Major Miller just before Christmas: General Billewicz, General Haller, General Kowalewski, General Orlik-Łukowski, General Plisowski, General Sikorski, General Skierski, General Skuratowicz. They march past their men, medals glinting in the sun. As one, the prisoners salute their long-absent leaders.

"They must be doing it by rank," whispers a young lieutenant as, one by one, the generals disappear into the church building.

"Then how do you explain those?" His companion points to a captain and a major who are amongst the chosen men.

"Yes," interjects another. "They chose six from our hut – we're all majors – but there are several captains from block 20 so it can't be by rank."

"Maybe it's by surname?"

"Might it be according to your politics, or your social rank?"

The names, however, appear to have been chosen entirely at random: they present no pattern that the prisoners can discern.

"Perhaps they have a parrot in there who picks the names from a hat." The poet Piwowar, dark-eyed, his red hair tangled, has emerged from the Circus for the first time in weeks.

Over the next few days and weeks more men are called. The nondescript officer travels backwards and forwards to Moscow, alone in the back of the black car, returning always with a large buff envelope which he takes directly to the camp offices. Still no pattern emerges in the choosing of men, and the moment at which the names are read out is consequently nicknamed "parrot hour". Some of the more daring prisoners eavesdrop outside the office where the lists are given out. As soon as the first names are called, they race off to share the news with their bunkmates before the guards emerge to find the lucky men. Cavalry officers who have not worn their spurs since November 11th fix them onto newly-polished boots, lending an air of parade-ground grandeur to the occasion as they march out of the gates.

For the men who remain, normal routine no longer applies. They gather by the gates, the crowd of those-who-have-not-been-chosen, watching their comrades head joyfully towards home. Kirshin stands on the steps of the central church to wave them goodbye.

"You are leaving," he says, "for a place where I would like to go myself."

One afternoon in mid-April, Kozłowski walks over to the clinic in the hope of speaking to Dr Levittoux. The wards are almost empty now: of the Polish doctors only a very few remain; any patients too unwell to travel were transferred to the town hospital at the end of March, accompanied by Dr Yegorov, who did not even trouble himself to say goodbye to the colleagues who had worked so tirelessly with him for the past six months. After searching in vain up and down the deserted corridors, Kozłowski finds Yegorov's office door open. Inside is Dr Vasilevna, seated at Yegorov's heavy wooden desk. When she looks up at him he sees that her grey eyes, usually so inscrutable behind her heavy glasses, are red with tears.

"Whatever is the matter, Dr Vasilevna?"

"Our dear, good Dr Levittoux has gone!"

How could he have missed Levittoux's departure? He recalls, then, that the previous day he had not gone to the gates because there was a big send-off for one of the prisoners in his block and he had been caught up in the celebrations.

"But why are you crying, Dr Vasilevna? Surely it is better that he is going home?"

The look that Vasilevna gives Kozłowski is filled with such bitter despair that he recoils in surprise. She says nothing, however, but rises from the desk and hurries from the room. It is the last time he sees her: when he comes to say goodbye, she is already gone.

Edward Ralski has almost filled the tin box with seeds and other shreds of nature which he has salvaged over the months of their captivity. He kneels on the ground, busily taking samples from the grasses which in recent weeks have pushed their way up through the earth and now grow in profusion around the gravestones.

"New life, Zbyszek." He sits back onto his heels, shading his eyes against the bright sunlight. "It happens every year and yet it never fails to enchant me."

"They've called your name."

Ralski stands up, slipping the little tin into his pocket. "I know." He falls silent, gazing at the vivid green of the new grass. "Perhaps on our way home I will finally be able to observe the Steppe grasses in the full glory of their spring growth. I should like that above all things."

Zygmunt Kwarciński and Olgierd Szpakowski are called together, an unexpected bonus for them, a double loss for Młynarski. They memorise the names and addresses of each other's families and make a pact that as soon as they reach anywhere where a letter or telegram might be sent, each of them is to contact the other's family at once with the news that they are all safe.

When Major Łabędź is called, little Linek chases after him, yapping furiously. Łabędź caresses the dog, smoothing down his ears and his moustache, and instructs the dog firmly to sit and wait. This Linek does, in obedience to his master, although his whole body twitches with the desire to run after him. His tail wagging uncertainly, his backside half raised from the ground, he waits in anticipation of the moment when Łabędź will turn around and tell him that he might follow him. That evening, Kozłowski finds the dog still waiting in the same position. The following day Linek, too, is gone.

It is late April when Tomasz Chęciński is called. He has somehow managed to exchange his uniform for a ragged civilian coat and a battered cap which he wears back to front on his head.

"I'm going to jump from the train. I'll make my way to Istanbul, and then somehow I'll get to France. I'll fight. Perhaps I'll die, but at least I'll die fighting instead of vegetating behind a barbed-wire fence." He reaches under his bunk and pulls from a hiding place beneath the boards a sheaf of papers, covered in tiny, scrawling handwriting. These he hands to Czapski. "I'd like you to have these, Józef. My notes for the book."

"Wouldn't you prefer to keep them with you?"

"I don't want to risk losing them. Anyway," he adds with a grin, "I know what I believe. Feel free to pass them around once you've read them. I'm always on the lookout for converts."

Czapski slides the papers carefully into his pocket. "You should have been a missionary, Tomasz."

Tomasz clasps Czapski closely to him, whispering a parting message into his ear. When Czapski draws back, he has tears in his eyes. He turns away hurriedly.

"Take these letters and post them for me, will you, in case I don't get the chance?" Tomasz holds out two envelopes, one addressed to his parents in Lwów, the other to Gosia in Kraków. "If you see Gosia before I do, tell her how much I love her, won't you? You won't be embarrassed to say so, will you, Zbyszek? I know what a diffident fellow you are. Tell her I have her handkerchief. I've hidden it inside my wallet, in the lining, here." He taps the side of his boots. "They won't find it there." He enfolds Kozłowski in a tight embrace. "Goodbye, my dearest friend. Until we will meet again." With a last, long, affectionate look at his friends Tomasz strides out into the bright morning sunshine. To those he has left behind, it is as if the colour has suddenly drained from the room.

IV
The art of forgetting

w pęknięciach ciszy
cierpliwie się plenię
czekam aż padną mury
i powrócą na ziemię

wtedy okryję
twarze i imiona

Patiently I spread
in the cracks of silence
I wait for the walls to fall
and return to earth

then I will cover
names and faces

(Tadeusz Różewicz, *Grass*)

1. Milestones

For several nights after the hearings Kozłowski cannot sleep. Margaret finds him at dawn, seated in the rocking chair in the nursery, cradling Kate.

"Whatever is the matter, Zbyszek?" she asks, again.

Again, he tells her that it is nothing.

The wall that separates him from the past must be painstakingly repaired, the gap where it has been breached stopped up. Without oxygen it cannot thrive, he reasons. Without light it cannot be seen. Therefore, the discipline is not just not to speak of it; it is not even to think of it. He practises as a gymnast practises, assiduously and with complete commitment, until the act of forgetting becomes so entrenched it is almost second nature.

The years pass, marked by the ordinary milestones of an ordinary life: the children grow up and go to school; Margaret works part-time as a GP whilst Kozłowski, after two years at University College Hospital as a general surgeon, undertakes specialist training at Moorfields Eye Hospital, leading to a post as registrar, then consultant. He develops an interest in cataract and begins to research new methods of treating the condition. He works with dedication, joining committees and boards, lecturing and teaching. A workaholic, his colleagues call him, jokingly. Only rarely does the past break through the fabric of his peaceful existence to jut out, awkward and painful, like a needle.

One Saturday morning, in the spring of 1956, when the Iron Curtain has lifted just sufficiently to permit the resumption of communications between Poland and the West, Kozłowski receives a letter from his mother informing him that during the eight-year silence his father has died.

He takes the letter, with his coffee, to the little room which Margaret calls his study, and, closing the door behind him, sits down at his desk to read it again.

As you know he had been ill for many years. Well, finally it was too much for him. At least he outlived you-know-who. I missed you then, Zbyszek. I was sorry you could not be there to see him in his final days.

He allows himself for a moment to imagine what it would be like to make that final visit to his father, to see once again the street in Józefów, the white metal balustrade set atop the long brick wall; the houses surrounded by lush gardens dotted with apple and cherry trees. The knock on the front door, the movement in the window upstairs revealing, briefly, a face, a curtain gripped anxiously in a hand; then, a few moments later, hurried footsteps. She would be smaller than when he last saw her. Her hair, which had been streaked with grey when he left, would be white.

He imagines his father lying on a daybed by the window, an ivory chessman, his cheeks sunken, his white hair and beard wispy.

"Dad?" Kozłowski speaks softly, then louder. "Dad!"

His father's hand in his, bony and cold. When Kozłowski kisses him on the cheek, it is like kissing paper.

"Dad?"

He is pulled reluctantly from the scene his imagination has supplied, poor recompense for the absence of its counterpart in reality, to find his six-year-old son in the doorway, a toy train in his hand.

"It's broken, Dad. Can you fix it, please?"

"Not now, Tom," he snaps. "Don't nag, for heaven's sake."

Immediately he regrets his words as his son recoils then turns, disconsolate, to wander from the room. He hears Margaret explaining to Tom that Dad is upset because he has had bad news.

Why can he not find a way to express the tenderness he feels for his children? Faced with the enormity of their love for him, why does he respond as if he has been stung? Margaret sees it, although she never speaks of it, instead compensating by being doubly loving, taking her little ones in her arms and smothering them with kisses. This decent, diffident man, their father – so hard-working, so diligent, so scrupulously polite to his colleagues at work and to the teachers at parents' evenings which he always, unfailingly, attends; this man who shows up uncomplainingly to dinner parties and games of weekend tennis, who scrutinises his children's homework and helps them with their maths, who glues Airfix models and digs a pond in the garden so that his daughter can keep frogs – remains nevertheless at one remove from them, as if a small but vital part of him is absent, or distant, an unassailable citadel in a hidden corner of his soul that his wife had thought – had hoped – to have vanquished.

Later, Margaret finds him pacing around the perimeter of the park as he always does when he is preoccupied, following the wall which encircles it, his hands thrust in his pockets, the dog, on the lead, trying to keep up.

"You'll pull his head off if you're not careful."

He leans down to pat the little mongrel, who pants at him happily.

"Poor Scruff. I'm sorry."

He tweaks the dog's long moustache.

Margaret is seated on the bed, moving the stethoscope across her daughter's back as she instructs her to breathe in and breathe out again. Kate, in vest and pyjama bottoms, gazes patiently up at her father, who stands in the doorway observing his wife and child. Margaret listens, head bent in concentration. When she collected Kate from nursery today they said she had been complaining of a temperature and a sore throat.

"I had a child in the surgery today, Zbyszek, with rickets. Rickets! Can you believe it? In this day and age. A poor, wizened thing he was. The mother drinks, Dr Barratt says. Right, my love," She pulls the stethoscope from her ears. "Stick out your tongue and say 'Ah'."

"Ah," says Kate obligingly as Margaret presses down on her tongue with a wooden spatula and shines a torch down her throat. Kozłowski smiles encouragingly at Kate, who smiles back at him from behind the torch.

"We used to see it a lot," he says. "Malnutrition, vitamin deficiencies. I remember a young man who thought he had gone permanently blind."

Margaret looks up, interested, the torch still directed down her daughter's throat.

"From malnutrition?"

"Once they fed him up his sight returned."

"Mummy!" the words come out indistinctly as Kate tries to speak with the spatula in her mouth.

"Sorry, love." Margaret extinguishes the torch and searches in her doctor's bag, bringing out a small cardboard packet. "Right, into bed. Penicillin for you, my girl. Some nasty white spots on those tonsils."

Tom, in his pyjamas, materialises next to Kozłowski.

"Can I have a go with the stethoscope?"

Margaret hands Kate a pill and holds the glass of water while she swallows it.

"Not now, Tommy. We don't want you catching it as well."

"Does Kate get to stay at home?"

"What are we today? Wednesday. Yes, you'd better stay in bed a couple of days. No good you passing it around to everyone. I'll call them in the morning. Thank goodness tomorrow is my day off."

Kate grins at Tom, clutching her doll and wriggling down under the covers.

"'Snot fair."

Tom wanders off, leaving Kozłowski to watch as Margaret tucks Kate up in bed, giving her a kiss on the forehead, a quick stroke of her reddened cheeks.

"You'll be fine. I'll get you some orange squash to drink, alright?"

They sit in the kitchen drinking tea, Kozłowski watching Margaret as she bustles around preparing Tom's packed lunch for the following day. She keeps looking at him, as if she is expecting him to say something. He remains silent, however, his eyes following her around the kitchen.

"Zbyszek, you never say what is going on in your head."

He is puzzled by this comment, unsure whence it has arisen. "I'm sorry."

314

"That's what you always say!"

"I wasn't really thinking about anything in particular."

"Well, give me a try." She slices some cheese for the sandwiches. "Go on."

"Um. I was thinking about stethoscopes, actually."

"Stethoscopes."

"It's like a part of a doctor's uniform, but I don't use one any more because I've no need to check my patient's lungs. Watching you with Kate made me miss it, somehow. I used to like the feel of it round my neck. Like a tie."

She utters a short laugh. "Strange. But I know what you mean. Go on." She starts slicing up a tomato, placing the pieces on top of the cheese.

"And malnutrition. I was thinking about children with malnutrition, and the long-term consequences to their bodies. How those years of deprivation still affect them in later life. It made me think about my nephew and niece."

"And?"

"And nothing." He shrugs, takes a gulp of his tea. "Why?"

"Oh, I don't know. I was wondering, how you are feeling about it all. For example, did your mother say anything about your father's funeral? How is she bearing up, did she say?"

He stares at her uncomprehendingly.

Suddenly, Margaret puts down the knife and leans on the kitchen table.

"What is it, Margaret?" He stands up, alarmed, realising that she is crying. "What's wrong?"

She takes a deep breath, wipes her eyes briskly, slaps the two pieces of bread together and wraps them. "It's nothing."

He remains beside her, waiting for her to explain.

"Oh, for goodness sake! Don't keep looking at me like that."

"I will keep looking at you like that until you tell me what is wrong. Is it Kate? Are you worried about her?"

"Heaven's above! No, Zbyszek, it's not Kate. Kate is perfectly fine. It's you!"

"Me."

"Yes, you. Zbyszek, it's been a week since your father died and you haven't said a word about it. Not a single word!"

He continues staring at her in bewilderment.

"Sometimes, it's like living with a – a…" she searches for the word, "a sphinx. Yes! It's like living with a sphinx."

He blinks, trying to comprehend what it is about him that could possibly resemble the mythical creature. Something in his expression must have amused Margaret, because the humour returns to her eyes.

"Yes," she says, affectionately, kissing him on the cheek. "A sphinx is what you are: a bloody great mystery."

He follows her upstairs, watching her as she brushes her teeth.

"I'm sorry if I upset you, Margaret."

She sighs. "I know."

His mother now writes regularly from Poland, cheerful letters wanting news of the children and his charming wife and his own career. He sends her photographs and drawings made for her by Kate and Tom; in return she sends greetings cards with pictures of fir trees and holly, baby chicks with eggs: *Wesołych Świąt*. Happy Easter. Best wishes on your name day. She dies, at the age of 78, in 1963.

One Christmas, planning their annual visit to Scotland to visit Margaret's parents, she suggests that, instead of travelling by car as they usually do, they should take the overnight sleeper train to Edinburgh.

"It will be so much more relaxing. And fun for the children. They can have their own compartment, next to ours."

Kozłowski agrees without giving the matter much thought, and so it is that they find themselves, together with their luggage and three large bags filled with Christmas presents, toasting the holidays with whisky from a flask over a picnic meal of Scotch eggs and sandwiches.

After climbing up and down on their bunks for nearly an hour the children finally fall asleep and Margaret slips back into their compartment to find her husband contemplating the double bunks with an odd, uncertain air.

"Do they not have these in Poland?"

"Of course they do."

"Well, I'm exhausted," she declares, yawning. "Do you mind if I sleep at the bottom? Just in case one of the children needs me in the night."

He wakes to find that the train has stopped. Rolling over to push aside the blind, he sees that it is already dawn and that the train has come to a halt in the middle of the countryside. It is snowing heavily, thick flakes falling onto a flat landscape of fields and dry stone walls. Margaret stirs, poking her head out of the blind.

"Oh, how lovely! It's snowing!"

"I wonder why we've stopped."

"Probably a signal."

They wait a while, gazing out at the snow in silence. Eventually, Kozłowski realises that Margaret has fallen back to sleep. Why has the train not moved?

He jumps down from the bunk and slips his feet into his shoes, grabbing his dressing gown before quietly sliding the bolt on the door and venturing out into the corridor. Another passenger is smoking by the window, elbows leant idly against the frame.

"Do you know why we've stopped?"

"Snow on the track, apparently."

"Isn't it normal to have snow on the track in Scotland?"

"We're not in Scotland yet, mate."

"Where are we?"

"Just outside Newcastle."

"Is that far from Edinburgh?"

The man laughs. "A fair bit."

Kozłowski goes in search of the guard. Finding him standing at the open carriage door engaged in conversation with a track worker in an orange jacket, he asks, "Excuse me, are we going to be held up long?"

"Hard to say," replies the guard. "What d'you reckon?" he addresses the track worker, who glances appraisingly up and down the track.

"They've got several inches of snow to dig out at Morpeth. Reckon it'll be even worse up at Berwick. Wouldn't really like to hazard a guess how long it'll take to clear."

"But what are you going to do?" Kozłowski addresses the guard with a sense of irrational but growing panic. "We can't sit here all day."

"Don't worry, we'll get moving again soon enough. Why don't you go back to sleep? Or have a cup of tea?"

"I don't want a cup of tea," says Kozłowski, his voice rising. "I want the train to move."

"Calm down, sir. There's really no need to get in a state. We'll soon get the train moving again."

"I am not in a state."

The sound of her husband shouting brings Margaret from the cabin then, after he has explained that really it is unacceptable that a train should be brought to a halt for a few inches of snow, and the man in the corridor has chipped in with his opinion that some people would do well to calm themselves down, Tom appears at the door.

"Why is Dad shouting?"

Margaret tells him to go back to sleep, but Tom declares that he is no longer sleepy, his attention riveted by the sight of his father pacing restlessly up and down the corridor in his dressing gown.

"Please, if the train is not going to move then can you let me off?"

Kozłowski's evident distress prevents the guard from losing his temper entirely. Instead, he addresses the agitated passenger calmly but firmly, as he has been trained to do. "I'm sorry, sir. Passengers are only allowed to disembark at the station."

"Zbyszek, darling, why don't you come back inside?" Margaret's eyes dart up and down the corridor as more people emerge from their cabins to see what the rumpus is about. Another guard appears, conferring in whispers with the first guard.

"Could you not please make an exception?" insists Zbyszek. "You see, I am not feeling very well, I must get off this train at once."

"I'm sorry, sir. I don't see how I—"

"Zbyszek, please—"

"Why is Daddy so upset?"

"Go back to bed, Kate, please!"

"Please – just – let – me – off – this – train!" His breath is coming in short gasps, his heart is hammering in his ears, his chest is tight.

"Zbyszek, please—"

"Tell the man to calm down, for God's sake, before he wakes the entire train."

They are staring at him as men stare at a hunted animal that has been wounded and will not die.

The episode is never mentioned, either by Kozłowski or by Margaret or even by the children, who have been instructed by Margaret not to question their father on the subject.

"But what was wrong with him? Why was he so afraid?"

"He was feeling ill, that's all. It happens to people sometimes."

The next time they go to Scotland to visit her parents, they take the car.

One Sunday in 1971 Kozłowski is outside in the garden, digging a trench for a pond, his head pleasantly empty of thought, when a persistent, repetitive sound gradually enters his consciousness. Laying down the spade, he walks indoors and picks up the phone.

"Hello?"

There is a slight pause, then a woman's voice, "Dr Kozłowski?"

"Yes."

Another pause. There is a washing sound, the white noise of a long-distance telephone line. The woman replies, in Polish: "I don't know if you will remember me: my name is Felicja Rynkowska."

At first he does not understand what she has said, so she repeats it, this time in American-accented English. Now it dawns on him.

"Felicja? From Meshed?"

She explains that she is calling him from Michigan, where she now lives. She is a doctor, by the way, she says, but that is not why she is calling.

"It's about my father. It's taken me a long while to find out what

319

happened to him. I knew that he was captured by the Soviets in 1939, but I've only recently managed to establish that he was taken to a camp called Starobelsk. Elżbieta told me that you were in that camp, Dr Kozłowski."

The words seem to come to him from the end of a long, narrow tunnel.

"Yes. I was."

"Did you know him? Lieutenant Rynkowski."

He scans his memory for the name but there is nothing. Not even an echo.

"I'm sorry, Felicja. There were thousands of us there."

"Oh well." She sounds unconcerned. "I guess it was always a long shot."

"I'm sorry," he says, again.

"What for? I went hiking with Zosia last year, Dr Kozłowski. In the Catskills. Have you ever been to the Catskills? It's very picturesque."

After a brief and disconcerting conversation, Felicja thanks him for his time and apologises for disturbing him, adding that she is a pathologist now and that she always thinks fondly of him, grateful for the encouragement he gave her to pursue her career in medicine.

"I looked after Zosia like you told me to, Dr Kozłowski. She and I are still good friends."

He has to think for some time before he remembers what it is that she is referring to.

The children finish school and leave for university. After graduation and their first jobs in London hospitals, Tom travels to Adelaide, where he takes up a post as a junior registrar, meeting and marrying a fellow Brit; Kate chooses Edinburgh to begin her clinical career, then travels to Ottawa on a six-month placement which soon becomes permanent. In 1979, the first grandchild is born. When Kozłowski and Margaret are invited to fly out to visit the new family at first he resists, attempting vainly to articulate that desire to stay put that grows stronger with every passing year. He tries to explain to Margaret that the journeys he made during the war left him unable to relish upheaval, or change, only to fear it.

"I know you think me selfish, but can't they come and stay here instead?"

Eventually, however, she prevails and he accompanies her, a reluctant traveller to her adventurer.

In 1980, strikes erupt in Polish shipyards. Kozłowski's students turn up at the hospital wearing Solidarity badges; they collect money on the steps outside, chanting *Solidarnosh, Solidarnosh*. Kozłowski pays little attention to events in the land of his birth, preoccupied as he is by the business of his retirement. Finally, at the age of 68, he acknowledges the truth of what his colleagues, and Margaret, have been saying to him for several years: that it is time to cede his place to a younger man. And so, in December 1981, a party is given to see him off. His colleagues raise their glasses and thank him for his invaluable service over nearly thirty years, presenting him with a set of golf clubs as a retirement gift, although he does not play golf.

On December 11th 1981, a snowstorm hits the south of England, paralysing roads and railways. Two days later, martial law is declared in Poland. Grainy footage on the BBC shows General Jaruzelski reading to the nation from a prepared sheet. Behind him, the flag of Poland. The journalist makes his report via telex, speaking of a military presence on the streets of every major city, of strict censorship and a curfew. Angry crowds shouting obscenities at the soldiers are met with riot shields and truncheons.

"Now for other news," continues the newsreader. "Heavy snow continues to cause travel chaos across the south of England..."

Margaret is suggesting that he eat his supper whilst it is still warm, but Kozłowski remains seated, gazing abstractedly at the images of cars trapped in drifts of snow. She puts the supper away and sits down next to him.

"You never talk about Poland."

He looks at her blankly, as if not seeing her, then picks up his tray to take it into the kitchen.

"How long is this damned snow going to last?"

2. A doctor and his patient

Margaret is even busier during her retirement than she was during her working life, approaching it as an opportunity to do all the things she wanted to do while the children were growing up: she plays tennis with a group of local friends; she gardens; she goes to art galleries and museums, the theatre, the cinema; she travels as much as they can afford: to France and Italy, and further afield, to Canada and Australia to see their children. Sometimes, when she can persuade him to do so, Kozłowski accompanies her, otherwise she goes with friends, on organised tours of the kind advertised in the pages of The Times, to look at paintings in the Uffizi or chateaux in the South of France. For Kozłowski, retirement is simply an extension of his working life, the only difference being that, instead of being paid to go to work every day, he gives his time for free, sitting on committees devoted to the scrutiny and assessment of research, editing learned journals, chairing charities which fund initiatives to bring cataract treatment to developing countries. When Margaret asks him whether he would not like to spend more time having fun, Kozłowski's initial response is to laugh.

"We – do – not – have – fun – in – the – Soviet Union!" Then, seeing that Margaret is staring at him in bewilderment, he adds, mildly, almost apologetically: "I like to work."

The routine of getting up early and working hard all day brings with it a prize, you see (he does not say): the ability to fall asleep as soon as one's head hits the pillow, untroubled by the restless anxieties that eat away at those with more time on their hands. To sleep without dreaming, to lie on one's bed without time to reflect, this is an enviable state.

One afternoon, seated in the garden of a rented cottage in the village of Orford, where they have come to spend a quiet week on the Suffolk coast, Kozłowski looks up from the book he is reading and sees that Margaret has fallen asleep in her deckchair. He calls her name, thinking that perhaps she is just enjoying the sunshine on her face, but she does not reply, and the sag of her jaw tells him that she really is sleeping. He looks at her carefully, as a doctor rather than as a husband: there are deep shadows under her eyes, her complexion is sallow; she has, he notices, lost weight. Her handkerchief has fallen onto the grass. He picks up the little linen square - a gift from him one Christmas which she especially treasures, her initials embroidered on it in red, MK, by Kate - and places it, carefully, without disturbing her, on her lap.

For almost a year she holds the sickness at bay, cheating it by carrying on as if it has no business interfering with her busy life. Margaret wants to squeeze as much as possible out of what remains, and her joy at visiting her young grandchildren outweighs the exhaustion that overtakes her as soon as they return home to London.

The moment comes, though, when Margaret is too ill to travel. Then, the families come to them. It is a long way to bring young children, halfway across the globe, and money is tight, but Margaret is the lodestone to which they are all drawn. She sits up on the sofa draped in blankets, watching the toddlers play on the living room carpet, oblivious to their mother crying in the kitchen or their father sitting solemnly with their grandfather, a baby dandled on his knee, discussing the number of months left before it will all be too late. This is the visit where they leave in tears, asking their father to keep them informed of every slightest deterioration in their mother's condition, promising to come back as soon as he needs them, asking him, telling him:

"Are you sure you'll be alright? You will phone us, won't you, as soon as things get worse?"

With meticulous care he lays out her medicines, reading each label and noting the bottle's contents. He brings her sandwiches which she scarcely touches and orange juice to slake her thirst. He accompanies her to the hospital for treatment until she reaches a stage when there is no treatment. Then he stays at home with her, ironing her handkerchiefs into neat little piles which he places in the chest of drawers, just in case she needs them;

trudging out each day to do the shopping, helped by a small army of Margaret's friends who bring dishes of home-made shepherd's pie and apple crumble and sit with Margaret for hours on end, knitting or reading to her, making her endless cups of tea which she does not drink. At night they leave him alone, and he carries his wife upstairs to bed. She weighs almost nothing in his arms.

Every evening, he brings the television into the kitchen so that he can eat his supper while watching the news, less a source of information than of therapeutic relaxation, a wave of words and pictures which calms his mind after dinner each day. So when, in June 1989, he turns on the television to see Warsaw on the news, and an announcement concerning free elections in Poland, he does not at first register the changes that are afoot. It is only as events in Eastern Europe begin to dominate the bulletins that he starts to focus on what the newsreader is actually saying. He is becoming somewhat deaf, so he has to turn up the volume in order to be sure he understands. His next-door neighbours knock on the door to ask him to turn the television down but Kozłowski, being hard of hearing, does not answer.

Still he cannot grasp it. For weeks, he expects to see pictures of tanks on the streets of Warsaw. Instead, the euphoria continues.

He goes out to the newsagents and buys every single paper he can find, in case the television is not reporting the matter with sufficient accuracy. He cuts out articles, sticking them carefully into a scrap book. The rest of the newspapers he discards, leaving them in piles on the floor of his study, out of his way.

In the evenings, after the news bulletins are over, he reads. Alone in the almost-silent house he finds refuge, as he has always done, in the pursuit of research, in the study of his profession. And yet, one night, as he listens to a broadcast on the World Service about the formation of a coalition government in Poland, he allows himself to think, for the first time in many years, about his sister, and about the war.

Day by day Margaret becomes a little less present. Her friends tactfully step back, leaving Kozłowski to attend to her needs.

He calls the children to tell them that it will be any day now. His son is only able to negotiate a week off work so he has to ask his father how long he thinks it will be. Kozłowski says three, maybe four days, it is hard to tell. Nobody speaks of the expense; time enough to think of that when the moment comes.

On television, in the evening bulletins, young men and women sit astride the Berlin Wall, jubilant, holding hands. In Poland, free and fair elections, the real thing this time. One by one they fall; the communists unseated, at last.

He drives back and forth to the airport, picking up first one, then the second child. On the way home in the car they ask him: How is she? Is she in pain? Am I too late?

The day comes when they must dress themselves in black, pulling out the carefully-folded suits and shirts which they have had to think ahead to pack, Kozłowski rooting in the back of the cupboard for the black trousers which he never wears, folding a handkerchief into his top pocket. The journey to the church in a black hearse, staring out at the rest of the world going about its business, stuck at a traffic light, catching the eye of a person waiting in the car next to them, who looks away, embarrassed to stare at grief. The church, the impersonal friendliness of the ushers, the service given by the protestant priest, the rituals familiar and yet unfamiliar... *Our Father... Thanks be to God... On earth as it is in heaven... Amen.*

Kozłowski sits at the front of the church, flanked by his children and their partners, a display of family solidarity. He stares at the coffin and thinks about the body that lies inside it. Soon they will carry it away to burn it, and later he will receive a jar containing her ashes. And then? Standing there in line with his children, his head begins to swim and the years suddenly elide.

"Are you quite alright, Doctor?" Dr Cochran's voice seems to arrive suddenly in his head, without passing through his ears.

"Are you alright, Dad?" His daughter's face, concerned, peering into his.

You look rather unwell, if you don't mind my saying.

"Just a little faint that's all."

He is grateful for the ritual of the church service: it gives them a pattern to follow, a form with which to express their grief. He shakes hands with the priest and thanks him for the service, then stations himself outside the church door to greet the guests as they pass. *Thank you for coming; so sorry for your loss; such a wonderful woman; we shall miss her. Please don't forget, food and drink at ours, you must come.*

His children leave to go back to their lives and their jobs on the other side of the world. At the airport, his daughter tells her father to look after himself and remember to eat; perhaps, she suggests, he could get someone in to look after the house. His son shakes his hand and tells him to take care. "Come and see us soon, eh?" His voice has already taken on the Australian inflection. Kozłowski duly promises that he will do all of these things: he will eat and take care of himself and he will come to visit, just as soon as he has recovered from the shocking expense of the funeral. His daughter-in-law hugs him and cries, while his son-in-law shakes his hand and tells him to stay well. And that is that. He returns home, and he is alone. It is 1989 and he is 76 years old.

3. Unfinished business

It happens very gradually, the falling off of those around him: at first, Margaret's friends telephone to ask him how he is getting along; they stop by, sometimes, with gifts of cake, lasagne, home-made soup. After a while, the visits become rarer; eventually they come to a halt. For a while after Margaret's death Kozłowski's own colleagues and friends keep at a distance, not wishing to intrude. When he fails to turn up to various committee meetings, they make allowances for a grieving widower. Slowly, the absence of contact becomes a habit on both sides. They rarely call him; he never calls back. The desire in him to stay put, which he suppressed for Margaret's sake, now finds no obstacles to its fulfilment; it grows steadily more powerful, until eventually it dictates his existence. His children telephone him regularly from their homes abroad, at agreed hours in order to accommodate the difference in time. He asks them diligently about their lives and takes an interest in what they have to say, but he does not possess Margaret's social ease and, without her presence, the glue that has kept their family together begins to unstick. His children, absorbed in their busy lives, do not call so often as they once did and, since he rarely remembers to call them, contact becomes rarer. When, at Christmas, Kate asks him to come and stay with them in Canada he makes an excuse, citing tiredness, old age and lack of funds. His son explains that it will be difficult for them to come to England this year – money is tight and work – *Well Dad, you know what it's like* – and now there are three children to consider. Kozłowski hastens to reassure him that he understands and that Tom is not to worry: he will be fine on his own.

Slowly, his solitude becomes a habit so entrenched, his interactions with the outside world so infrequent, that eventually everybody takes it for granted. Neighbours remark:

"You never see anybody go in or out of that place."

On April 13th 1990, President Gorbachev of the Soviet Union makes a public admission of Soviet guilt for the murder of fourteen and a half thousand Polish prisoners of war in the three camps of Kozelsk, Starobelsk and Ostashkov in April-May 1940. Responsibility for this Stalinist crime, he states, lies directly with Lavrenty Beria and Vsevolod Merkulov. The NKVD dispatch lists of the prisoners are handed over to the Polish leader, General Jaruzelski.

There it is, finally, the ending that has for so long eluded him. He reads and rereads the article in Gazeta Wyborcza, delivered via the POSK in Hammersmith. The prisoners of Kozelsk were murdered in Katyń Forest, those of Ostashkov in Tver, and those of Starobelsk at the NKVD offices in Kharkov, their bodies buried in the sixth quadrant of the wooded park nearby.

They had not, after all, been taken very far away. They had not drowned in the icy waters of the Barents Sea; they did not lie buried in the snow of Kolyma or Nova Zemlya.

A flood of information - newspaper articles, television programmes, documentaries, books - follows hotfoot on the official revelations. As the boot that has held down a nation's memories is finally lifted, the history of the Second World War is suddenly made fresh, and terrible events that happened many years ago resurface with a violence that nobody in the West can hope to comprehend. The skeletons of western Europe are clean-picked and sanitised; you can look upon them squarely and they will no longer give you nightmares. The unfinished business of the war in the East now rears up from the grave, the rotting flesh still hanging from the bodies of the dead.

It arrives in the post, a blue airmail envelope with a commemorative stamp marking the fiftieth anniversary of the Katyń massacre, a ragged red triangle on a black background.

> *Dear Zbyszek,*
> *I expect you will be surprised to hear from me after all these years. I managed to get your address from the British*

Embassy, would you believe it? I hope this letter finds you in good health and that you have had a happy life. Gustaw (my husband) passed away last year, but I am fortunate in having my wonderful grandchildren to occupy me. Three of them, all in their teens. They are my greatest joy, their future my greatest concern. Things are changing so fast here.

The reason I am writing, as I am sure you can guess, concerns Tomasz. I recently received a death certificate for him, dated April 1940, with his place of death given as Kharkov, Ukraine. I thought you would want to know. We have waited long enough, haven't we? Now we can finally lay him to rest. I wasn't sure how much of this news is considered worth reporting in the West. Here there is talk of little else. It is overwhelming, at times. Perhaps you also know that they are sending out a team of experts to conduct exhumations in Kharkov and Tver, and I believe they are returning to Katyń, too. After they have completed the exhumations, they are hoping to make a proper cemetery and a memorial. I am looking forward to the day when I will be able to visit my brother's grave. Perhaps we will meet there?

With all my best wishes to you and your family,
Hanka

"We would like you to give a talk, Dr Kozłowski."

The young woman perches on the chair in his study, in a place recently vacated by the cat, the cushion of which is probably (he reflects) – undoubtedly – covered in cat hairs. He should warn her, but there is nowhere else to sit.

"There are so few of you left who can speak first hand about what it was like. It would be undergraduates, mainly, plus a few postgrads. A recording would be kept in our archive for researchers to use."

He blinks, an old man with unruly white hair, fiddling with the edge of his oval glasses, the lenses of which are smudged with fingerprints. He is seated behind a desk piled with papers, books and post-it note reminders, a cigarette balanced between two fingers, stained yellow with nicotine. His hands tremble slightly now, and the ash grows long until he taps it, finally, into the overflowing ashtray.

"What it was like?"

"What was it like, Stratford?" asks Professor Rodoński.

Szumigalski beams, and prepares himself to discourse on his favourite subject.

"Green! It was so green!"

But I don't have Czapski's skill with words, he tries to tell her, or Młynarski's flair for storytelling. She insists that it is not skill that is required, simply the act of remembering. I am no expert on the politics of the situation, he counters. This, too, is brushed aside.

"It is not the politics that interest me, Dr Kozłowski. With everything that is happening in Poland now the political aspect is not going to be forgotten. What is important is for young people to be able to hear the voice of someone who was actually there."

She makes it sound so simple, but the reality is that the act of remembering, as she calls it, is not such an effortless thing. You have to understand, he wants to say, once I start remembering, I cannot stop. They will rise, and they will overwhelm me.

"I know it's a lot to ask, Dr Kozłowski, but don't you see how terribly important it is that the memory of these men is not lost?"

Something about her earnest passion makes him unwilling to dismiss her completely, so he promises to give the matter some thought. She brightens, reaching across the table to touch his arm.

"Thank you."

Once she has gone he sits a while at his desk, reflecting on what she has asked. His eyes wander idly along the crowded bookcase, alighting on a clutch of slim volumes squeezed at the end of the shelf. Czapski's two books, Młynarski's memoir, all unread; the report of the Madden commission, sent to him by the government-in-exile, never opened. He extracts a volume from its place, releasing as he opens it a small cloud of dust, which makes him sneeze.

Flicking through it to the index, he is astonished to find there, along with the testimony of General Anders, Bór-Komorowski, Felsztyn, Wołkowicki, Kot, a reference to a witness who wished to remain anonymous, a Mr G – himself. Carefully, he passes without looking at them the pages where his own words are recorded, alighting upon the deposition of a Dr Wodziński from Kraków, which he begins to read.

> *The following day they took us to the scene of the crime. The terrain consisted of a number of small hills along which were marshes covered with grass. Along the top of the hills, woodland paths branched off from the main road through the woods, running from the main road in the direction of the Dnieper River to an NKVD dacha nearby. There were both deciduous and coniferous trees in the woods. The older pine trees, measuring up to 20 metres in height and 25 centimetres in diameter at the foot, were found on the biggest mound. In the wetter parts, the trees were silver birch and alder. To the south of the mound, in the direction of the Dnieper River, the trees were all spruce, all less than twenty years old, planted deliberately. In the region of the biggest mound, some 300 metres from the main road, were the graves. A Red Cross flag flew from a wooden structure. Although it was the end of April, it was chilly in the hollows of the ground and snow still lay in the woods.*

What was it Olgierd's sister had said? Something about the trees telling the truth? He flicks through another volume, alighting on a page at random.

> *If one digs up a small conifer one can tell by the condition of the root shoots how many years have elapsed since they were torn or cut in the process of transplantation. It follows that in 1943 a forester should have been in no doubt as to*

*whether the small trees in question had been transplanted in
the late spring of 1940 or the autumn of 1941.*

Is this what they will be doing in Kharkov now? Sending out a team
of experts to dig up the remains of his friends? He remembers the
photograph of the general, only three years dead: the squashed
features, the remnants of hair. What will be left of them now, after
fifty years?

A photograph in the newspaper catches his attention: a group of men
and women are gathered around a table, on which lie a number of small
objects. The woman is small, with a pointed chin and close-cropped
hair which must be grey or white; a pair of large earrings, of the type
one buys on holiday in India or Thailand, dangle from her ears.
Underneath the photograph is a list of names. He counts carefully from
left to right until he matches the face with the name: Dr Felicja
Rynkowska, Professor of Forensic Archaeology, Michigan State
University, Ann Arbor, volunteer at the Kharkov exhumation.

> *"What's that?"*
> *Felicja holds out the notebook, in which she has
> painstakingly drawn a picture of the skull, complete with
> annotations.*
> *"I had a friend once," he says, sitting down cross-legged
> next to her. "His name was Tadeusz. He found a skull in the
> earth and drew it, just as you have done."*
> *"Was he a pathologist? I am very interested in pathology."*
> *"No, he was an illustrator."*
> *"Whose skull was it?"*
> *"I've no idea. I'm leaving, Felicja. I have to join the army
> in Iraq."*
> *She nods, intent on correcting something in her drawing.*

Is that her? After all these years?

Here she is again, the young woman, seated, this time, on the edge of the chair, wise to the cat.

"I was just wondering if you had had time to consider my proposition. About the talk. I was thinking – if it would be easier for you, I could interview you here."

She pulls from her bag a small black device which she places on the table.

"Dr Kozłowski, of the 395 men who survived the Katyń massacre, there are only a handful still alive and you are the only one in the UK, as far as I know."

He blinks at her, this living rarity, this rare bird. "But everything is known now," he replies, indicating the pile of newspapers on his desk. "What is it that you need from me?"

"As I've said before, it is not the circumstances of their deaths that concern me, Dr Kozłowski. What I am interested in are the lives the prisoners led in the camp."

She is persistent, he will say that for her. She asks him again to think about it, leaving him her telephone number, scribbled on a little business card.

In an interview printed in the newspaper Dr Rynkowska relates that a total of fifteen mass Polish graves have been discovered, of which eight are 'wet'. The 'wet' graves are 3 meters deep, with water coming up as high as 75cm; the remains can only be reached by transferring out several hundred buckets of a greasy substance arising from the decomposition of the soft parts of corpses. In some of the 'dry' graves, corpses are preserved in their entirety, with hands, legs, toes, nails and faces intact. They lie in disorder as if thrown from vehicles, some with hands tied behind their backs by a rope having two characteristic knots, or by barbed wire. Sometimes complete bodies are found, but only where the large drills, the so-called 'meat grinders', had not passed over. During the 1970s here, as in other cemeteries in the Soviet Union, gigantic industrial machines destroyed the traces of Soviet crimes. In some graves in Kharkov 60-70% of the skulls had been crushed.

FR: Perhaps it would have been better if the bodies had remained hidden for a few hundred years.
IV: Why would that be?
FR: In that case, this would not have been an exhumation but an archaeological dig.
IV: Is that so very different?
FR: Oh yes. Far less upsetting for everyone involved.

There is a picture of a row of trays containing a variety of objects – buttons, buckles, medallions, rings. The technical team clean the objects and if they can identify the owner they offer them to the families. The rest will go to a museum. They are already planning a museum, but its existence is far in the future. Now, the main discussion is about creating a suitable memorial in each of the three sites.

He reads on through the night, compelled to fill in the gaps in his knowledge as if he were attempting to resolve a giant jigsaw puzzle, until the first birds begin to sing outside and a grey light dissolves the darkness. All the while the clock ticks on the shelf, marking time running out.

Zbyszek, what about Tomasz?

She is sitting on the window sill, kicking her legs like a bored child. He ignores her, stretching out his right leg in front of him and watching it as it hangs there, not quite straight. Without realising it, he has grown slow in recent years. He prods his thigh and discovers it to be skinny and wasted. Where have his muscles gone? His legs are painful, his back is bent; he finds breathing very hard. Nowadays they say that smoking is bad for you. All those years as a doctor, smoking over twenty a day. Apparently, it has done his lungs no good at all.

You can't remember, can you? You've forgotten them.

Of course I can! There is just such a lot of information to absorb about the circumstances of their death.

You heard what she said. She doesn't want the 'circumstances of their death'. She wants their lives and you can't tell her anything because you've buried them so deep you can't find them anymore.

That's not true!

Then what's stopping you?

I'm tired, that's all.

He pulls himself up from his seat and shuffles upstairs to lie down on his son's old bed, where he falls into a light, restless sleep.

At the edge of the 6th quadrant in Piatykhatky Park stands a woman. She is small and spare, with short white hair, dressed in the kind of trousers worn by hikers, a neat rucksack on her back. She stands at the edge of the forest, watching the exhumation.

Before her are dozens of holes, some of them several metres deep, each occupied by a small team of volunteers battling against the slippery, stinking mud. It has rained overnight, leaving the paths waterlogged and the holes like sinking ships, filling with liquid. Bones protrude messily from the earth, signals of earlier excavations. The rain has settled now to a steady drizzle, coating everything in a layer of squalid dampness. The rain is prelude to the snow which will surely follow in the next few weeks, when the ground will harden and their work will become impossible. She steps back under the canopy of the trees, taking shelter from the rain, and he becomes conscious of a deep silence surrounding her. The single backward step which she has taken to avoid the rain has removed her from the familiar noise of the outside world - the dull clanging of spades, the squelch of mud, the calls of one colleague to another – and brought her into the silence of the forest. He can hear it: the faint creaking of the trees, a distant crack of dry wood, the steady drip of rain from an overhanging branch. A scene that has always been there, waiting for him. Is it Felicja, standing watching them working in the graves?

There is another figure, slight and slender, with dark hair worn in a bob, a too-thin summer dress whipped by the wind, her arms clasped around her body to keep warm. Over her shoulders, an oversized man's coat.

Please, Zbyszek.

"Do you remember any of the medical staff, Dr Kozłowski?"

"Of course I do. There was Dr Levittoux..." he hesitates. "Dr Wolfram looked after Zaleski's feet."

There is a pond at the bottom of the garden, long forgotten, covered in weeds. When the pondweed is cleared and the water refreshed, the sediment is violently disturbed. The sand mingles with the water to create a muddy cloud that rises, swirling, to the surface, billowing out like a liquid whirlwind.

He is sitting in his armchair, his mind resting on a blank piece of paper that lies on the table before him, when he becomes conscious of a strange sensation, or the lack of it, in the right side of his face, like a spark of emptiness. When he tries to raise his right arm to touch his cheek, he finds that it does not respond.

I can't do it, Gosia.
You must, before it's too late.

He leans down to open the bottom drawer of his desk where, underneath a pile of old papers, is a grey folder inside which lie the remnants of his past: his old military ID, his alien registration card, his Polish civilian passport; letters from his mother, Gosia, and Hanka written during the war.

In the folder he finds, to his astonishment, a portrait, drawn in pencil on a rough piece of paper, of a bespectacled young man with gaunt cheeks and a stubbly beard whom he does not, initially, recognise as himself. Then, a sheaf of notes scribbled on cigarette papers and old Russian newspapers.

hundreds of different insects, bacteria, plants and animals: larvae of rare butterflies, beetles and ants, lichen and moss...

The search for documents, ID tags, letters, Polish money, military insignia, valuables, religious items, eagles from caps, military buttons. It is his insides which are being excavated by those giant diggers, his skull lying on the dissecting table, and Felicja is peering over her glasses to inspect him. Hmmm, you see the bullet entered here, in the nape of the neck, about the height of the third vertebra of the neck. Kupry's speciality.

In spring, while the trees are still bare, the sunlight penetrates to the forest floor and you see carpets of flowers: wood anemones, dog violets, bird's-nest orchids, coral-root bittercress, the small cranberry. The forest is also home to hundreds of species of bird, as well as tree frogs, wild boar, deer, eagles, wolves, even moose. They all coexist, and are interdependent...

Now he is standing in one of the wet graves, his rubber boots disappearing into the slimy mud. Next to him, grim and silent, Gosia is working loose a long bone which has become sandwiched between two lumps of solidified clay. This is a strange kind of archaeology, he thinks. Felicja stands at the edge of the grave, watching them.

"Well done!" she cries, clapping her hands. "Good work!"

How can this canvas painted with death be part of the same story as their lives?

No, gentlemen, I protest. This is without a doubt the biggest pile of poppycock I have ever heard in my entire life!

In the late summer sunshine the wooden walls of the room where they keep the skulls give out a pleasant, warm aroma. Through the dirty windows shafts of sunlight illuminate the yellow skulls: their teeth, the dark cavities where their eyes would have been. There is something very beautiful about a skull of any sort. Birds skulls, they are such delicate things; like egg shells, tiny, some of them.

in late spring it grows long, silver-grey spikelets which resemble feathers – hence its name ...

The row of trays contain a variety of objects – buttons, buckles, medallions, rings. Anyone who handles the objects has to wear white cotton gloves.

Yet a tree does not end its existence when it ceases to grow

A pair of delicate ladies scissors, once plated in gold, now tarnished.

"Odd, don't you think?"

"Perhaps his wife packed them for him. Or perhaps they had some sentimental value for him."

Lieutenant Biały, I can confidently state that you are still alive!

A young man films the exhumation. They have found someone who was involved in the killings and now they are interviewing him: half deaf, nearly blind, an old man with a guilty conscience. *Kupry's speciality.*

Here is a corner of a book. It has survived because it was inside a bag. All that remains is a section of the front binding, a corner on which a fragment of a page has stuck. With a magnifying glass it is possible to see the faint imprint of the words *Dzieła dramatyczne Williama Sh -.*

On the other side of the room are trays containing tiny shreds of green serge, threads of silver from the insignia of rank, larger chunks still identifiable as leather boots. Here are pieces of a suitcase, turned back to reveal, underneath, the faintest outline of a pencil sketch.

When the diggers move on, there remains behind a fragment of cloth, underneath which lies a small metal tin, the top of which has been knocked off. Inside the tin, a paper envelope; within the envelope, now exposed to sunlight and to the moisture of the rain which falls in the evenings as the air cools, tiny seeds of grass which begin to sprout, unnoticed, their little roots curling into a bed of soil and rotted wool.

"Isn't that glorious? And look, here—" Ralski crouches down and gently pushes away the remnants of the snow to reveal tiny shoots of fresh grass. "How can one not feel hope?"

A technician makes a surprising discovery: hidden between the two layers of leather which form the outer and inner sections of a boot are fragments of paper, and a piece of material later identified as linen. The body on which the boots were found had initially been wrongly classified as a Ukrainian civilian. It was only the Polish military boots and the letter which enabled them to identify the wearer as one of the prisoners of Starobelsk. A few lines of the letter are legible.

brings me great comfort. As I am sure you have discovered, he is a good, dear man and you may always

The linen, identified as a fragment of a handkerchief, bears the initials MK.

IV: What conclusion would you draw from such a discovery, Dr Rynkowska?

FR: I would imagine the letter and the handkerchief were of some particular personal significance to the officer, and for this reason he chose to hide them in case they were taken off him during a search.

IV: And the civilian clothing?

FR: Who knows? Perhaps his uniform had been damaged.

"Were you badly treated in Starobelsk? Physically, I mean?"

"Oh no. They never beat us or tortured us, as they did in Gulag camps, or at the Lubyanka." He falls silent. Overhead, a plane heads slowly for Heathrow. "He talked to me about medicine. I felt as if he knew me."

"Who, Dr Kozłowski?"

"Was it something I said? Is that why? Did he think I was on his side?"

"Who, Dr Kozłowski?"

It is too late, Gosia, It can't be done. When I try to recall their faces now I see only their deaths.

You know the remedy for that, don't you, Zbyszek? Read it, please, before it's too late.

But it's for you.

Please, Zbyszek. Read it. For me.

In the grey folder where he keeps those few reminders of the past is a letter, unread, the single record of a love affair. He takes it from the manila envelope in which he placed it, for protection, many years ago. His sister's name and her old Kraków address are written in Tomasz's spidery hand. The envelope is sealed.

He opens the cream flap and pulls the letter from inside. His hands are stiff and he almost drops it as, carefully, he unfolds the single, faded page and begins to read.

> *My dearest, darling Gosia,*
>
> *Do you remember when we first met in the mountains near Zakopane? That walk we took with Hanka and the others? We were so absorbed in talking that we fell behind, do you remember? We climbed up and up for almost two hours, until we were walking along the top of a ridge; ahead of us was a descent into a valley; on either side were those beautiful mountains. Do you remember, Gosia? I see it as clearly as if I were there today. The others were up ahead, waiting for us as we came down from the ridge, and you said we'd better catch*

up, but I waved at them to carry on. I just wanted to spend more time alone with you. You knew that, of course, didn't you?

Do you remember how I took your hand and asked you to listen to the silence? We stood with our eyes closed and felt the grand roar of nature dinning in our ears. Then I kissed you for the first time and held your face in my hands. You asked me why I was staring at you and I said that I was trying to remember every detail of your face so that when they called me up I would be able to picture you. You said, "I could just give you a photograph." I replied thank you very much but I prefer the real thing. We held hands and walked on until we reached the bottom of the valley. Do you remember all of this, Gosia? I have held it in my mind every day since our capture. It is the memory which, above all others, sustains me in moments of despair.

They took your photograph from me, but that image of your face is as clear and fresh to me now as the mountain stream where we stopped for the picnic.

By the time we reached the bottom of the valley we were both hot. I lay down on the grass to rest and you – mischievous girl! - you crept to the stream and dipped your handkerchief into the water, then you dropped it onto my face and sat down next to Hanka. I yelled – it was so cold! - but when I looked around to find the culprit, you looked right back at me, as innocent as a child. I have that handkerchief with me now.

If I don't make it back, Gosia, then I want you to know that I love you with all my heart and desire only your happiness. I dream often of the mountains, of the pure air and that vast expanse of nature stretching out before me. If it is not granted to me to survive this war, you must go walking, often, in memory of me. Will you do that? I cannot tell you how much I long, after these months of confinement, to be free to walk, without stopping, exactly where I like.

Take care, my darling.
Your loving
Tomasz

Between the moment when the envelope slips from his hand and he bends down to pick it up he sees it all, as he falls, the picture which has eluded him for so long. The mass of fragments, sharp shards from the shattered whole, he finally sees them in their entirety.

As he falls from his chair towards the floor, where he encounters, with a thud, the hard wood that lies beneath the swirling carpet, they come tumbling from the recesses where he has hidden them over the years. They come back to him, now, in all their brilliance, so young and so alive.

Standing by a railway track in the freezing mud, waiting for a train which will take them to an unknown destination.

He sees it with brilliant precision, as if it were happening right now.

A mass of soldiers waiting by the rails, thousands of enlisted men taken prisoner in Poland's eastern provinces. The column of officers marching past them until, finally, they are ordered to halt and told that they are to be loaded onto a train that night. The *politruks* move amongst them, shining torches in their faces, taking down their names and rank.

The roll call goes on and on, the officers shivering in the cold. Kozłowski shivers, his coat soaked through from the driving rain. He has not seen Edek since the ambush. Is he dead? Wounded? He strains to find a familiar figure amongst the thousands of men.

"Feliks! My goodness! How wonderful to see you alive!"

A group of lieutenants cluster around a brown leather suitcase, on top of which a man is seated, asleep, his shoulders covered by an enormous sheepskin rug. The officer named Feliks greets the group with delight, friends lost and now found. They exchange anecdotes about their war with an air of lighthearted unconcern, seemingly oblivious to the misery of their surroundings.

"…encountered him just outside Lublin looking for all the world as if he were setting out on a picnic. '*Mon cher ami*,' he said. 'Why don't you join us? We're heading for my estate. I'm told the cellar is still intact…'"

"That restaurant on Nowy Świat where we met last month, bombed to smithereens…"

"…carrying furs and a silver candelabra. I said to her, 'My dear, are these the most useful things you could think of bringing?'…"'

Kozłowski thrusts his hands deep into his pockets, staring at his boots as they gradually sink deeper into the grey mud. A young blond-haired lieutenant glances over at him enviously. His own summer boots are soaked through.

A rumbling noise signals the arrival of a train of empty box-cars. It looms out of the darkness, rattling on endlessly until, finally, it comes to a halt and the prisoners are ordered to get inside. They clamber on board, spreading mud everywhere, an outbreak of false jollity covering the sense of shock that seizes them as they enter the dark carriage.

"I do beg your pardon, are those your legs?"

"They're not tree trunks, that's for sure!"

"After you, I insist!"

Each man seeks a space for himself, forming a line along the wagon's edges, their legs spread out before them. The last to climb in must squeeze themselves into the middle, back braced against back, legs intertwined.

The guard pulls the door across the wagon and bolts it shut, leaving a small gap about four inches wide, flashes of torchlight penetrating an otherwise total blackness.

The train begins to move; the jokes cease; the prisoners gradually fall silent. Kozłowski, squeezed in the far corner of the carriage, his back pressed uncomfortably against the metal wall, checks the luminous dial on his watch. It is 3am on September 26th 1939. It is nearly a week since their capture, not even a month since the beginning of the war. He closes his eyes, squeezing them shut, as if by doing this he might keep the fear that is rising in his throat at bay.

V

An ending

Tacy mi nagle przyszli, jakich chciałam.
Śnili się, ale jakby ze snów wyzwoleni,
posłuszni tylko sobie i niczemu już.

They suddenly came back, exactly as I wanted,
In a dream, but somehow freed from dreams,
Obeying just themselves and nothing else.

(Wisława Szymborska, *Memory Finally)*

1. The lost city of the past

They have moved him somewhere, he is not sure where. When he opens his eyes he sees above him a cream-coloured ceiling with an unfamiliar light. The bed he lies in is uncomfortable, the sheets sliding off a mattress which is covered in a layer of plastic, or is it rubber? His head is hot, supported by thin, synthetic pillows. He is vaguely aware that he no longer moves from this place. There are no trips to the bathroom, nor to the kitchen to make cups of tea and eat food from a tin.

He tries to remember his last days at home. He has a memory of something falling onto the floor, of bending down to pick it up, then of lurching forward, unbalanced, his head hitting the floor with a hard thud. He remembers that he was not able to move his limbs, that he felt no urgent desire to move them: lying on the floor felt somehow appropriate, as if this was where he was meant to be. A warm, damp sensation between his legs, then a foul odour; the cat sniffing at his face, whiskers tickling his cheek. After that, time lost its order, the chronological arrangement of things dissolved, the accepted pattern of this, then that. He had no notion of day or night, only of an infinite space within his head where the past stretched out, brightly illuminated, like a prize ready for him to collect. He swam amongst his memories with the ease of a walrus who has thrown off the burden of gravity to rediscover his true element. Here, underwater, he found an entire world, still intact: the great, lost city of his past.

When they found him he stared at them in outrage, although they did not seem to see his fury. Why have you come to interrupt me, he wanted to know, although his mouth would not open. Why have you stripped me naked so that I am cold? Why are you taking me away from my home? They ignored him, talking above his head as if he were already dead.

Now this place, with the cream ceiling and the broad lampshade made of white plastic. Outside, somebody calling: *Nurse. Nurse. Nurse.*

347

Over and over again, as if that is all they have ever said. *Nurse. Nurse. Nurse.*

He has a strange sensation that there has been a visitor; a hand clasping his, eyes gazing down into his. What is the word people use? Beings you bring into the world, little things which squall and scream then grow up and go away, what are they called? It was one of them.

"Dad? Dad?"

He is dimly aware of voices, faces crowding above him, blotting out the light. A cold object on his chest. He knows what that is. He used one. Only they were made of wood, not metal.

The light is switched off. Finally, he is alone. He wants to return to his memories, to find his way back down to that deep, bright, shining place in order to reach the end.

Kozłowski stands in a clearing in a forest. It is late spring. The sound of birdsong echoes among the trees. Above him, a brilliant blue sky. He is waiting for something, or someone, he is not sure precisely what, or whom, but he is content to stand in this pleasant spot, his eyes taking in the tiny flowers which carpet the forest floor, his face feeling the gentle warmth of the sun, his bare feet touching the black soil under the fresh, spring grass.

There is just one thing left to do. Now that he has the proof he always said he needed – the order given, the exact description of what occurred – he must picture it. He cannot remember it because he was not there, because he went on and they did not. In order to reach the end he must – he *must* – imagine it.

2. Their ending

The prisoners emerge from the carriages of the *stolypinka*, blinking and stretching. The journey from Starobelsk to Kharkov has taken just less than a day. A short journey, in Russian terms.

They are loaded onto trucks which, finally, after a long delay, set off towards the centre of Kharkov. This is puzzling; they have been expecting a long train journey, not another trip by road, into the city. Tadeusz Biały sits opposite Tomasz, watching him with the same silent question in his eyes: why are they taking us into Kharkov? Olgierd is regaling the other officers with a stream of jokes which keeps most of them laughing long enough to forget the bewildering brutality of the guards, the sudden change in direction, the unexpectedness of their journey.

"Take a break, can't you?" grumbles a major. "It's clear enough they're not sending us home. It's labour camps, I'm telling you. I've always said you can never trust the Russians. Haven't I always said that?" His plaintive voice rises above the sound of the engine. "We're heading north, I tell you. It's Siberia for us."

"So why are we stopping here?"

"Yes, why are we going to the centre of town?"

"Maybe there's no connection between Kharkov South and North," says Olgierd, "so they're putting us here overnight."

Tadeusz Biały sits quietly, gazing intently at the floor. Zygmunt is beside him, powerful, reassuring, as calm and flexible as the trees in the forest. They push him, he bends but he does not break. Not like me: I am scared now. I don't like this situation; there is something about it that doesn't feel right. He feels a hand on his arm and looks up. It is Zygmunt, smiling at him.

"Talking to yourself is the first sign of madness, you know."

In the truck behind them, Ralski is squeezed next to a wheezing captain with a bristling moustache which tickles his ear. Ralski forces his mind to focus its attention inside himself. He shuts out, as he has done so many times before, the noise of the engine, the chatter of the men's voices, the complaints, the arguments, the expressions of optimism and hope. He concentrates his whole being on trying to conjure before him the image of his home, the view of the garden afforded by his study where he has spent so many hours of his life, his wife seated next to him, both of them writing, the clock ticking peacefully, his little daughter playing outside, intent on the progress of a ladybird upon a blade of grass. Their daughter, the future scientist. He blocks from his mind the images conjured by his wife's first and only letter, of German soldiers throwing his family out onto the pavement, his papers and his books piled high in the snow. He tries to block this memory, but he cannot.

Tomasz focuses only on the moment in the near future when the opportunity to escape will surely present itself. He will not allow himself to be disheartened. We are in transit, he tells himself. There will be other chances. He will not spend the rest of the war in a prison camp. He will find his way to France, where he will fight, and after the war is ended he will return to Poland and marry Gosia. The vet Łabędź, next to him, is sweating. He takes out a handkerchief and wipes his forehead, glancing up at Tomasz with a faint smile:

"So many men together in such a small space!" He frets about his little dog. "Who will look after Linek now?"

The trucks pull up outside NKVD headquarters on ul. Dzierżińskiego 13. It is late now, and the street is deserted. The officers are led into the building, where they are searched. Their luggage and Russian money are taken from them, as well as their coats and belts. Ralski struggles with the guard as his collecting tin is taken from his pocket.

"Don't worry," says a senior officer, a tall, swarthy man with heavy-lidded eyes. "Your things will be given back to you later. *Da, da.* Everything will be returned to you, of course."

Mollified, Ralski allows himself to be taken to a cell. Inspection, that's what this is, just like at Starobelsk.

The men are locked in, crammed together like cattle, to wait. After a few minutes, a name is called. One of the officers is pulled from the cell.

"Where are you taking me?" asks Major Łabędź, suddenly fearful.

The other men wait for the answer in silence.

"Do not worry," comes the reassuring voice of the heavy-lidded man. "You are being taken for interrogation."

"Again?" Olgierd steps forward angrily. "You've already interrogated us a hundred times. There's nothing more for you to find out." A few men murmur their agreement, but the large officer, unperturbed, simply nods.

"Do not worry. You are being transferred, that is all."

This calms the men somewhat: transferred where, they would like to know. At Starobelsk, Kirshin said they were going home. *Damoj.*

At ten-minute intervals two guards appear and take one officer. After two hours, Olgierd is called. "See you on the other side," he says to Zygmunt, with a wink. As they march him off, Zygmunt feels an odd sensation, as if his stomach is fluttering down into a pit.

Olgierd is taken to the end of a long corridor which leads to a courtyard. Here, two more NKVD guards are waiting. They grab his arms and, before he can resist, his hands are tied. This is the first time since their capture that he has been bound.

"There's no need for that! I'm an officer of the Polish army, do you understand?"

One of the guards pushes open the door while the other marches Olgierd out across the courtyard towards another building. The courtyard is dark, save for the light emerging from the door on the other side, where a senior NKVD officer waits. The air smells damp and cool. A covered civilian truck is parked by the door, the tarpaulin at the back pulled down. A man with a cleaning bucket and mop leans idly against the wall, smoking a cigarette. He watches Olgierd with indifference as the Polish officer is led inside.

Forty minutes later, Zygmunt is called. He is taken along the same corridor as Olgierd and out into the same courtyard. The same scene meets his eyes, except that the man with the bucket is emptying it, sloshing it down a gutter in the far corner before refilling it with water and detergent. He returns, carrying the heavy bucket in one hand, just as Zygmunt passes him. Their eyes meet for a second before the door closes behind Zygmunt and the cleaner resumes his position next to the truck. He lights another cigarette and waits.

Zygmunt is taken along a narrow corridor, then down a stairway to a basement. Another corridor leads to a door, in front of which stands another guard. The guard opens the door and Zygmunt is ushered inside.

Ralski has been practising his habitual technique of focusing his mind on memories of his home, his wife, his garden; he tries to remember the titles of all the books that used to line the shelves in his study; he goes through the names of all the professors who taught him at university and all the students whom he has taught in turn. He remembers the day when he first met his wife and the day his daughter was born. Through these memories he manages to pass down to a place deep within himself which is where he finds God waiting for him. He has to travel very, very far to reach it, for it is a place of such stillness and tranquillity that, like a pond, the slightest disturbance sends ripples over it and other, more pressing thoughts rise to overcome it.

He does not hear his name the first time it is called. Tomasz rouses him with a gentle pat on the shoulder.

"It's your turn." They embrace. When Tomasz steps back to look at him, he exclaims, in surprise. "Goodness, I can see right through into your soul!"

"I do hope Czapski is alright," says Ralski, suddenly.

As they cross the courtyard Ralski stops for a moment to inhale the damp air which smells of spring. The guards, perplexed by this peculiar action, do not hinder him but wait as he gazes up at the sky. The night is overcast. There is no moon and there are no stars. The senior officer waiting at the door calls to the guards, a short whistle that brings them to their senses.

"*Nu*, hurry up now. No dawdling."

Ralski smiles politely at the officer who is holding open the door for him. This is the head of the NKVD, Kharkov Oblast, Pyotr Safonov. "Thank you."

He is led down the stairs and into the basement, along the corridor and into a small, windowless room. There is a strangely muggy feel to it, as if all sound inside it has been bottled up. Behind the desk sit two men.

When Tomasz Chęciński's name is called he jumps up and pushes his way to the front of the cell. He is a popular figure, and his departure is like that of a gladiator going off to fight in the arena: in his odd civilian coat, now beltless, with the hat worn back-to-front, he has the air of a resistance fighter. All he needs is a gun slung over his shoulder and a belt of ammunition across his chest. He is led across the courtyard, past the truck, down the stairs, along the narrow corridor and into the room.

One of the men seated behind the desk is a prosecutor, the other is Timofei Fedorovich Kupry, Commandant of the NKVD in the Kharkov Oblast.

"Name?" asks the prosecutor.

Tomasz gives his name.

"Date of birth?"

He gives his date of birth.

"Place of birth?"

He gives his place of birth.

"You may go."

Is that all? thinks Tomasz. As he turns to go, he catches a glimpse of the two guards who are standing right behind him.

He does not see Timofei Fedorovich Kupry get swiftly and silently to his feet, bringing from under the desk a 7.62 calibre pistol which he brings expertly to Chęciński's head, aiming precisely upwards from a point beneath the occipital bone. The bullet surges through Tomasz's brain and emerges just between the nose and hairline. Death is instantaneous. There is almost no blood. This is a method perfected by the Cheka long ago. It is swift and efficient, and leaves few traces.

Tomasz's coat is swiftly pulled over his head and his body dragged out of the basement, up the stairs, out of the door and into the courtyard where the truck is waiting, the tarpaulin pulled up in readiness. The two guards, aided by two more who are positioned inside the truck, haul the body onto the pile already lying there. Tomasz Chęciński's body is thrown onto that of Edward Ralski, who lies close to Olgierd Szpakowski, Zygmunt Kwarciński, Major Łabędź and twenty five others whose names have already been called that night. The guards pull the tarpaulin back down over the back of the truck. The cleaner checks carefully around the truck for blood stains. Finding none, he steps back to take up his position against the wall. Another officer has checked the corridors and stairs for blood: he nods to Pyotr Safonov, who gives the signal to the two guards that they may go and fetch the next candidate.

In the basement, the gun is reloaded, the bullet casing from the previous shot is placed carefully in a drawer, the smell of cordite wafted away.

When the truck is full, it is driven to a forest which lies around 10 kilometres from Kharkov, to an area known as Piatykhatky which has been used as a burial ground by the NKVD since 1939. Here, graves have been dug on either side of a track covered with black cinders. The truck stops, the two guards pull up the tarpaulin, and the bodies are pulled out and thrown, one on top of the other, into the mass graves. Here, already, lie Dr Levittoux, the lawyer Prosiński, the writer Hoffman, the poet Piwowar, Tadeusz Biały, Major Zaleski, Major Miller, Józef Marcinkiewicz, Zygmunt Mitera; the snobbish cavalry officer Otwinowski, Dr Wolfram, Dr Grüner, Dr Kołodziejski... They are all here, present and correct. Lime is sprinkled on each layer to aid the decomposition of the bodies. For several nights this continues, until the operation is done.

For fifty years they lie here, undiscovered, except by local school children who, playing on the black cinder paths between the trees, find metal objects lying on the ground: military insignia, buttons decorated with eagles. The children trade their mysterious booty with their schoolmates, exchanging them for sweets, or marbles.

Kozłowski will never know why his story has gone on to arrive at its natural end, his flesh sagging, muscles wasted, in this bright room with the plastic lampshade, while theirs did not. He knows only that now, at last, he can see his friends again, as young and vital as they were when they left Starobelsk, and that they are waiting for him here in the forest: Ralski, Zygmunt, Biały, Levittoux, Olgierd - all of them. Tomasz Chęciński strides towards him, arms open in greeting, the peasant's hat perched on his blond head.

Here you are at last, you devil. What took you so long?

ACKNOWLEDGMENTS

I would not have been able to write this book without the valuable support of two organisations: the Harold Hyam Wingate Foundation awarded me a Wingate Scholarship which enabled me to begin researching the 1940 Katyń Massacre, whilst a Royal Literary Fund Fellowship allowed me to write and complete the book. I would especially like to thank Steve Cook and David Swinburne at the Royal Literary Fund for offering me a unique opportunity to combine my writing, film-making and teaching lives. Anna Seifert-Speck and Mark Holborn very kindly read early drafts of the manuscript, Magda Koziej corrected my Polish, and Larissa Kouznetsova answered my Russian questions. Rosemary Hunt generously lent me many books which I have yet to return; I will always be grateful to her for giving me such an excellent grounding in the Polish language. My thanks go to my agent Louise Greenberg for championing the book so steadfastly, and to my editor and publisher Robert Peett for his consistent support and encouragement in working on the text. And to Alex and Hal, as always, for putting up with me so patiently.

Although this is a work of fiction it is closely based on historical events and many of the characters who appear in the scenes which take place in Starobelsk and Griazovets are based on real people. I am deeply indebted to the many historians and scholars who have written about Katyń, and to those survivors whose reports of their experiences provided inspiration for this work.